SKYLARK

S.M. Carrière

Renaissance

Diverse Canadian Voices

RenaissanceBookPress.com

Cover image and divider by S. M. Carrière; design by Nathan Fréchette. Interior design and typesetting by Éric Desmarais. Edited by Cait Gordon, Meaghan Côté, Myryam Ladouceur and Ev Cimesa.

Legal deposit, Library and Archives Canada, October 2018.

Paperback ISBN: 978-1-987963-39-7
Ebook ISBN: 978-1-987963-43-4

Renaissance Press
http://renaissancebookpress.com
info@renaissancebookpress.com

This book is for all the kind-hearted misfits out there.

It doesn't matter if your light is broken.

Shine.

It can change the world.

PROLOGUE

In the year 2360, a colossal shift in human consciousness occurred. We learnt that we were not as special as we thought. Life did exist elsewhere, and it came as a shock when that life crashed into us. In the summer of that year, an envoy of five ships appeared in our skies. We were afraid. And so, before even learning their purpose, we unleashed our human hell upon them.

The first ever United Council convened. It consisted of one representative from each of the five regions of the world: Australasia, the Americas, Europe, Eurasia and Africa. The Council was tasked with confronting the threat from outer space. They created the USC, or the United Space Corps—a combined, earth-wide military force specifically trained to combat extra-terrestrial threats to the planet. For the first time in history, humanity was united. This union, while a step forward for mankind, was marred by the same thirst for violence that had pitted humanity against itself for millennia. The only difference now was that we knew of and despised beings other than our own kind.

In that first strike against the five ships hovering in our atmosphere, one alien ship crashed to the ground, destroying almost all of Edmonton, Canada.

Unsurprisingly, the invaders retaliated. It was true they were smaller in number, but they proved fierce and skilled opponents. Despite human military forces outnumbering them some twenty to one, the invaders captured and defended a large swath of territory stretching from the eastern edge of British Columbia to the Quebec border. The four remaining ships touched down at evenly-spaced distances across this territory. They did not continue their campaign against us. Rather, they dug in to defend their newly won lands. Humanity assailed them from air, land, and sea, but their defences could not be breeched. The losses were unimaginable.

The war ended in a stalemate.

As part of the cease-fire agreement, the lands the invaders had already won remained in their control. No further demands were made on the part of the invaders. The Canadians living in those territories were removed. Many went to live in other parts of Canada, but a large number of Canadians were displaced into the United States of America, living in large refugee camps in Detroit and New Jersey. This evacuation became known as the Canadian Diaspora.

Human-controlled areas were fenced off, protected by heavily armed turrets placed at regular intervals.

Almost every human religion took up the cause, calling the invaders *Daemon*. The name stuck. Though a cease-fired had been declared, so much anger and hate existed that we hovered in limbo, ever ready to take up arms again.

Life, even some forty years after the war, was tense.

Humanity, devastated and constantly under threat, lived under a never-ending martial state, controlled entirely by the United Council. Food was heavily rationed. Hunger and crime were rampant.

The alternative was worse.

Beyond the fences along the borders of British Columbia lived the daemon. Past this divide, all that could be seen were the empty streets of what used to be a thriving city—except at night, when the diseased came out. They shuffled along, made mindless and savage by the effects of radiation poisoning caused by the continual failures of our aging nuclear power plants and the shocking fallout of the weapons used against the daemon. Those who were ill and could not afford anything but the poorly-maintained and desperately overburdened state healthcare were often cast out by their caretakers, who could not afford to keep them while they waited for the attention of medical staff. They were left to die slowly beyond the fence, creating a buffer of disease between humanity and the daemon.

Of the daemon inhabitants we knew almost nothing. In keeping with the cease-fire agreement, they were rarely seen near the turreted fences. The empty desolation between their settlements and ours housed only death. Every so often, one of the ill, shuffling husks that was once a person attempted to storm the fence giving hints as to their growing intelligence.

Life was difficult, but, as life does, it endured.

- *Introduction*. **Renegade: The Formation of the First Intergalactic Alliance. Admiral Scott Pierce, ASC. Penny Whistle Publishing. 2452.**

1

Gabriella was horribly lost and she knew it. She had seen a white rabbit. Rabbits were such a rare sight. She had become excited and followed the creature in a merry chase, not caring that she had crossed through the chain link fence before losing sight of it. The hole in the fence was barely noticeable. Gabriella saw it only because the rabbit had used it. She was only just small enough to squeeze through.

Now it was coming on dark and Gabriella found herself in a deserted city. Houses that were once tall and stately crumbled around her. Abandoned cars, most now burnt-out shells, sat on the cracked, empty roads; silent, eerie sentinels to the deepening night.

Worse still, though only eight and a half, Gabriella knew of the horrors that waited in the dark beyond the fences of civilization. She had learnt all about them in school. Once she realized where she was, she ran frantically back through the winding, deserted streets trying to find the fence.

It was nowhere in sight.

Exhausted and afraid, Gabriella sat down in the middle of the road, tears streaming down her face, making small tracks through the dust that had settled there. She clutched her perfectly coiffed doll close to her chest.

With the sun starting to fade, the shadows had begun to stir. The horrors that lurked in them shuffled back and forth, waiting for their chance to emerge safe from the sunlight that burnt their flaking skin.

Terrified, Gabriella sat, unable to move, and stared with wide eyes as the first of the horrors shuffled from its hiding place in the shadows of an abandoned house. It turned its head and became rigid as it met Gabriella's horrified gaze. Screaming, Gabriella scrambled to her feet, turned and ran. An eight-year-old, however, could not match the speed of one of these diseased once-humans.

The creature shrieked and gave chase. In just five strides, it caught Gabriella by her hair. Squealing in pain and abject terror, Gabriella struggled as the creature dragged her to the ground, hissing and spitting at her defiance.

More horrors joined the hunt as the sun's light vanished from the streets. One grabbed her leg. Still shrieking, Gabriella struggled hard, slipping from their grasps twice. Each escape proved short-lived.

One, stronger than the others, caught her at the hip. With both hands it lifted her from the ground by the thigh. Hanging like the doll she still grasped in her hand, Gabriella tried to kick herself free, to no avail.

The hungry horror opened its mouth, revealing a row of shattered green teeth. Gabriella squeezed her eyes shut, expecting those terrible teeth to rip through her leg at any moment. Instead, she tumbled to the ground.

It took her a moment to realize that, despite landing hard on her forearm, she remained largely unharmed. She looked around. The horrors were distracted momentarily, their blank eyes matching their stupid expressions.

Gabriella looked behind her.

A raven-haired woman fought Gabriella's attacker with glowing short blades that somehow extended from her forearms. Seeing an opportunity, Gabriella started to crawl.

A mistake.

The movement caught the attention of one of the slack-jawed horrors. It lunged at Gabriella. The girl shrieked as the creature tackled her to the ground. It stood, lifting her by her hair. Gabriella kicked the thing full in the chest and heard the crack of its brittle ribs, but it barely paused as it lifted her to take a bite from her cheek.

Again Gabriella fell to the ground before any harm could be done. She looked up to find a glowing purple blade protruding from the creature's chest. It spasmed as the blade withdrew. Then, with a swift purple flick, the horror's head fell to the ground and rolled into the gutter. The raven-haired woman bent and picked Gabriella up at the waist.

"Hold on," she breathed in the girl's ear. Then they were running, fleeing away from the safety of the fence as everywhere the shuffling monsters closed in.

With the irradiated horrors now streaming from the houses into the darkening streets, the woman changed her tack. Her run turned into a swift and deadly dance, spinning around one horror here, beheading another one there, on and on. The jerking and spinning nauseated and disorientated Gabriella until she felt certain she would be ill.

After almost an hour of ducking and dodging, twirling and sidestepping, the crowd of horrors thinned. Then they were free, running headlong down an empty street. The horrors did not follow. Gabriella glanced back. They stood as if hindered by an invisible wire, howling after what might have been a good meal but not daring to take a single step further.

The running woman slowed, then stopped. Breathing hard, she set Gabriella down on a burnt-out car.

"Are you all right?" she asked, her English oddly accented.

Gabriella pulled her doll close to her and nodded.

"Did they bite you?"

Gabriella shook her head and smiled shyly. The woman smiled back, her violet eyes crinkling pleasantly at the corners.

"You're beautiful," Gabriella whispered. Then she burst into tears and reached for the woman. The woman immediately picked her up and held her close.

"There, there," she soothed. "It's all right. They're gone. They can't hurt you now."

Gabriella nodded but continued to bawl, pulling the woman as close to her as possible and trembling.

"What's your name?" the woman asked, when Gabriella calmed a little.

"Gabriella," the girl answered, hiccupping between sobbed syllables.

"A beautiful name. And how old are you, Gabriella?" the woman murmured. Still holding Gabriella close, she started walking.

"Eight and one half."

"Truly?"

"Uh-huh."

"Well, you are very brave for only eight and one half. I bet you're tired."

"Uh-huh."

"Lucky for you, it just so happens that I live not too far away from here. There will be some warm supper and a hot shower. There is only one bed, but we can share it, all right?"

"Uh-huh."

"All right," the woman said.

By the time the pair reached their destination, night had fully descended. Fishing keys from her pocket, the woman unlocked the front door of the building and stepped in. Unlocking another door, she slipped inside what was, in fact, a fairly spacious single bedroom apartment. The woman set Gabriella on the couch and went back to the door to lock it and take off her shoes.

She muttered something and all around the room candles jumped to life. Gabriella looked around her in wonder.

"I'm sorry about the candles. I can get no electricity from here."

"How did you do that? Are you magical?"

The woman laughed softly. "Magical? Perhaps. There is a light that surrounds everything and everyone. I know how to bend my own light with my mind to make the candlewicks catch. Perhaps one day I will show you how."

Gabriella simply stared at the woman, her eyes as large as platters. "You think I could do that?"

"Of course you could. I can see your light. It is very strong."

After a short pause in which Gabriella tried to understand just what the woman meant, she asked, "Why do you live here?"

"Because it is my home," the woman answered with a shrug. She walked to Gabriella, knelt down and began to methodically check her over for injuries.

"That's going to be a nasty bruise," she noted of Gabriella's forearm with a smile. "Other than that, you've just a scraped-up knee and a bruise on your thigh. Looks like you're going to be all right after all." The woman smiled up at Gabriella, who smiled back shyly over the top of her doll's now considerably messier hair.

"And who is this?" the woman asked.

"Sherrie."

"Sherrie?"

"Uh-huh."

"Another beautiful name!"

Gabriella giggled.

"Well, I think you ought to have a bath and clean yourself up before dinner, yes?"

Gabriella nodded and the woman stood, extending her hand to her. The girl took it and hopped down from the couch. She walked a short way down the hall to the first door on the left. The woman opened it to reveal a small bathroom with a bathtub at the far end.

"We may not have electricity," the woman said with a smile, "but we do have plumbing, and I can heat the water."

"With your light?"

"Yes, with my light. Come on, I'll show you how it works."

Before long, Gabriella sat happily in the bath, soaping herself down and playing with the bubbles. Meanwhile in the small kitchen, the woman pulled out some pre-frozen soup from a freezer-turned-ice-box and placed it in a pot. Sighing, she added a small amount of water, then opened the front of an old-fashioned wood stove. She refilled the wood and blew the embers into a small fire.

Satisfied it would stay lit, she shut the door and walked to her room. She had injuries to look after.

Lieutenant Bennejin "Skylark" Skye stared blankly at the wall of the transport he shared with the newly formed United Space Corps Strategic Division Team 6. Bored did not cover precisely how he felt. Earth patrols were rarely a treat.

Pulled from the streets at eight, he had seen more excitement in his first eight years than the twenty that followed. Still, it was required of the United Space Corps to do tours back on the home world, and it was nice to step out of the recycled air of a spacecraft occasionally.

"Bored, Lieutenant?" Unit Commander Brody asked, a smirk twisting his grey moustachioed lips.

"I love my job, sir," Lieutenant Skye replied absently.

To most, Commander Brody came off as an arrogant, jumped-up

street kid with a bullying streak wider than the Bering Strait. They never understood his particular brand of humour. It was street humour.

Lieutenant Skye did. Perhaps for that reason, he and Commander Brody looked out for each other. In a world filled with privileged snots who bought their commands, Skye and Brody were some of the few who earned it.

Unit Commander Brody grinned. The transport stopped in Docking Bay 96 at the USC Vancouver Headquarters with a resigned whine. The team stood. The door slid open and the sudden noise of a bay bustling with personnel filled the transporter. Following Commander Brody, Lieutenant Skye and the rest of Team 6 marched wearily from the transporter towards the barracks.

"Commander! Commander!" an administrative lieutenant called, chasing Commander Brody. The team halted behind the commander, who waited patiently for the man to reach their position.

"Sorry, sir," he said. "Rest will have to wait. You and your team are expected in room 501 for a briefing."

"We've just done a tour, Lieutenant," Commander Brody said.

The lieutenant shrugged, then marched away. Rolling his eyes, the commander trooped his team to the elevators.

"Man, I just want a shower," Lieutenant Binks said.

"You'll get it, Lieutenant," Brody said. "After."

Binks grunted. "Yes, sir."

Five floors whipped by at incredible speed, stopping with a stomach-dropping jolt.

"Gods, I wish they'd fix that," Brody grumbled. He stepped from the elevator and led his team to room 501. Not bothering to knock, he entered, saluted, then paused in surprise at the sight of a paler than usual British Ambassador.

"Gentlemen," Captain Michaels greeted. "I know you've had a long night. Please take a seat."

The team virtually collapsed into their chairs, exchanging glances with one another and stealing peeks at the ambassador.

"This is Ambassador Clegg, as I'm sure you're aware," Captain Michaels said.

"Am I to assume special ops, sir?" Brody asked.

"Almost," the captain said. "With a great deal more at stake."

"Oh?"

"Ambassador Clegg's daughter has gone missing. We fear she may be beyond the fence."

"She's dead, then," Brody said a matter-of-factly. The ambassador winced.

"We don't know that," Captain Michaels said.

"Yes," Brody said, "we do. Nothing living survives out there. If the corpses didn't get her, then the daemon sure as hell did. There's no way she's alive."

Captain Michaels scowled at Commander Brody and indicated the ambassador, who now looked close to tears.

"Of course," Brody quickly amended, "miracles happen."

Captain Michaels rolled his eyes and cleared his throat. "I understand that yourself and one of your team members are both street orphans. Am I correct?"

"Yes," Commander Brody said guardedly. It was a touchy subject for both himself and his lieutenant. Prejudices against the desperate and destitute of the ghettos often kept either of them from promotion.

"Is it true that part of your initiation into the street gangs is you had to survive one night beyond the fence?"

Brody shook his head, but Lieutenant Skye answered, "Yes, sir."

Commander Brody turned to his lieutenant in surprise. "Did you?"

"Yes," Skye answered. He looked down at his fingernails, then balled his hands into fists to hide their tremble.

"What the hell? I heard about that, but no one I know ever did!" Brody stared at Skylark with wide eyes. "What gang made that a requirement?"

"Gang is perhaps a strong word," the lieutenant said. "More like a hungry rabble of kids trying to be tough. There were five of us," he said. "Only two made it back."

"So," the ambassador said quietly, "it is possible."

"For an eight-year-old who survived on the street, yes. For a girl who has never been anywhere without a nurse? It's a different story."

"Lieutenant!" the captain barked.

Lieutenant Skye looked at him a moment, then turned back to the ambassador. "Sir," he finished.

The ambassador smiled slightly. "It's all right, Lieutenant. I'm aware of the chances of… of my daughter's survival. But I have to do something."

"So if I'm getting this right, you want us to go beyond the fence and look for your daughter?" Commander Brody asked.

"Or… or her body," Clegg replied, unable to keep the tremor of grief from his voice.

"Right, off we go again, I suppose."

"Not at night," Lieutenant Skye said. "You'd need the entire Corps to take those bastards on at night. They're not nearly as active during the day."

"Why not?"

"Radiation has made their skin sensitive to light. The sun can burn them to ash."

"I've heard the same from the turret guards," Lieutenant Binks added, only to be silenced by the glare of both his commander and the captain.

"The fuck happened out there, Lieutenant?" Commander Brody demanded.

Lieutenant Skye shrugged. "I was late getting back in. They chased me as the sun came up. Two couldn't find shelter in time. I watched them burn from safely behind the fence."

"So, you are uniquely qualified then, Lieutenant," Captain Michaels said.

Skye frowned. "I wouldn't say that I was, Captain," he said.

"You know more than the rest of us. That puts you in command."

Skye looked up sharply. "Sir?"

"Your command, Lieutenant. I expect you and your team out there the moment the sun comes up, got it?"

Glancing uncertainly at his commander, Skye nodded. "Sir, yes, sir."

"Commander Brody?"

"Sir?"

"Your assistance has been requested to help quell a gang in Sector Y346. You are to report to Commander Garson at dawn tomorrow."

"Yes, sir."

"Good. Dismissed."

The team stood and saluted as both the captain and the ambassador left the room.

"We're all dead," Binks said.

"Poor bastard," Skye said, his eyes on the haggard figure of the ambassador as he slunk away.

"All right. Shower and bed folks," Commander Brody said. He looked across and grinned. "By your leave, Lieutenant."

Skye raised one eyebrow and curled his lip at his commander in distaste. Brody walked away wearing a grin that was closer to a sneer.

"Man, sometimes I hate that guy," Lieutenant Binks said.

"Don't take him too seriously, Binky," Skye answered. "You lot do what you want, I'll see you in the mess at 0500 sharp."

"Sir, yes, sir," Binks said with a sharp salute.

"Stop it," Skye said, walking away. Binks laughed and the squad disbanded for the evening.

Sleep did not come easily to Lieutenant Skye that night. A past he had buried long ago invaded his rest. Memories he had supressed kept him tossing and turning, his jerky reactions yanking him violently out of his half-sleep, leaving him slick with sweat and fighting back tears.

That night beyond the fence was the single most terrible night in his life. It had left him a trembling leaf for three days before the military police picked him up and took him to base. So tense had his underfed body been that the MPs did not change his crouched position despite lifting him. He rose in the air, hunched over his knees like some bizarre human boulder. He sat like that in the truck the entire way to base, until he fainted from hunger. It took a week after his eyes opened again to get him to acknowledge anyone at all.

He did not want to go back.

When sleep finally did find him, it arrived in short bursts and each time ended with Skye almost falling out of his bed as he fought the mutants behind the fence in his dreams.

"You look like hell," Binks said when Skye arrived at the mess. "Sir."

"Shut up," Skye answered. He rubbed his eyes. "Everyone ready?"

"Yes, sir," the five squad members replied. They eyed him suspiciously.

"Guys, I'm fine."

Binks grinned but said nothing. They marched quietly to the transporter dock.

"I'm not sure about this," Corporal Green, the only female member of the team, whispered to Binks in a broad Australian accent.

Binks looked over at her. "You got a problem with Skylark, you got a problem with me," he replied.

Ahead, Lieutenant Skye smiled. USC Strategic Team 6 might be a new formation, but he and Lieutenant Binks went back a long way together—all the way to basic training. As long as Binks was on his team, he was sure someone would always have his back. Their transporter at Platform 89 was nowhere in sight.

"Yo, did they leave without us?" Binks asked.

"Late getting in," a docking administrator said, checking the schedule that flashed on the podium at the edge of the dock. "They radioed in just a few minutes ago."

"We got to get us more transport pilots," Binks grumbled.

"They're doing what they can," Lieutenant Skye said. He squinted down the length of the dock. "Final weapons check."

The team set to work, checking over their weapons and ensuring everything was in working order. Lieutenant Binks was not the only one to see Skylark's hands shake, but he was the only one to address it. He and Bennejin had gone through both basic and senior training together, as well as flight school and infiltrator training. Though Binks came from a wealthy family from northern Vancouver, he and Bennejin had managed to work past their vast differences.

"Nervous, Skylark?" he asked conversationally.

Lieutenant Skye nodded, knowing full well he wouldn't be able to lie to Binks.

"I've been there before, Binky. I don't want to go back."

"Well, they're allergic to sunlight, right? And we'll be there during the day, right?"

"There is less than twelve hours of sunlight, fewer than that, even, because the buildings provide shelter from direct sun. Long shadows are just as dangerous as nightfall. And we have no idea where the girl is. It's a lot of area to cover."

"You're full of good thoughts."

"We're going to be there past nightfall, Binky," Skylark said. "You best be prepared."

"What happened out there? When you were little?"

Not for the first time, Skylark refused to talk about it. He simply shook his head.

"Transport's coming," the docking administrator said.

Skye and Binks looked up. The transport came hurdling down the docking channel.

"She's going to crash," Binks said.

Skylark said nothing. He watched the speeding transport with a frown and pursed lips.

"Seriously," Binks said. "She's going to crash."

The transport braked so hard sparks leapt from the rails in the channel. The team stepped back from the edge of the channel, wincing. They expected the transporter to smash against the buffer at the end of it. No such crash occurred. The side door of the transporter opened and the pilot stood by the door control, a maniacal grin painted on his heart-shaped face.

"Good morning!" he said, a slight Scottish accent creeping through his good cheer. "It's going to be a beautiful day!"

USC Team 6 stared incredulously at the man. The docking administrator shook his head and keyed in the time of arrival.

"All aboard!" The pilot left the door and returned to his seat.

"You heard him," Skylark said. He and Binks entered the transport last, exchanging a glance before so doing.

"Damn caffeine runners," Binks muttered darkly. The left side of Skylark's lips turned up in a lop-sided smile.

"Alrighty? Everyone in?" the pilot asked over the speakers.

"All in," Skylark answered.

"Excellent!"

The door of the transport slowly lowered, then locked with a whining hiss.

"All right, boys," the pilot said.

"Fuck you," Corporal Green muttered. She rubbed her shaved head and shot a look at her commander. Skylark laughed softly.

"This old girl is the safest transporter in the USC fleet, and I'm the best damned pilot you'll ever meet," the pilot's voice said over the communications link.

"I call bullshit," Binks said.

"We'll have you to the fence in a little under an hour."

Skylark looked up at the ceiling of the transporter. It was a two-hour journey to the fence.

"Right," Binks said. "They stick us with the crazy pilot."

"Of course they did," Skylark answered. "Weren't expecting special treatment, were you?"

Binks shrugged. "Just something better than rock bottom would be nice."

Skylark smiled. "This isn't rock bottom," he said. "Trust me."

Binks looked over at his friend. "What are you thinking 'bout?"

"That poor girl," Skylark said. "And the chewed-up bones we're going to find."

There were a thousand more questions Binks wanted to ask, but he knew better. Despite the lieutenant's blue-eyed charm and good humour, something lurked beneath—something profoundly sinister. Binks didn't want to bring all that to the surface. Years of observation told him that Lieutenant Bennejin Skye wasn't all that far from the edge. Perhaps that was why women flocked to him. Good looks only got one so far, but add something slightly dangerous, and you've got a potent sexual cocktail.

"You remember that hot Latina pilot you were banging in flight school?" he asked instead.

That brought the desired reaction from Skylark. The lieutenant grinned.

"What was her name?" Binks asked.

"Jen."

"Man, that girl had a butt on her. Never forgave you for getting her."

Skylark snorted. "And you had Miriam. How could you be jealous?"

"Oh yeah! That was her name!"

"You guys are disgusting," Corporal Green said.

"Easy, Honey Badger," Binks said with a smile. "Just reminiscing about beautiful women."

Corporal Green glared at Lieutenant Binks, then turned her back on him.

"Jen was gorgeous," Skylark said. "Crazy, though."

"The pretty ones always are," Binks agreed.

"Pigs," Green grumbled to herself.

The team settled into easy silence. Skylark looked them over. A recent formation, Team 6 had yet to settle into a rhythm. Newest to the group was Jacqueline Green, a tough carrot-top with a shaved head, an Australian accent and a temper. Everyone had taken to calling her Jack. Never having attended flight school, she had not been awarded a call sign, but she had been the top graduate of infiltration training last year. She had never seen a fight though, and her inexperience was telling.

Aside from Binks and Skylark, Corporal Matt "Doorman" Shae and his brother Corporal Frank "Spike" Shae made up the rest of the team. The twins were indistinguishable from one another and Commander Brody had stopped bothering to try. Skylark had not yet quit trying, but he often got it wrong. The twins were also excellent soldiers. Though they lacked infiltration training, they were able to pick up the necessary manoeuvres very quickly and worked exceptionally well together.

Spike looked over at his new commander and nodded. Skylark nodded back, then returned his attention to the ceiling of the transporter. The engine grumbled in an alarming fashion, but the pilot seemed unconcerned and so Lieutenant Skye tried his best to ignore it. Instead, he concentrated on using a technique one of the USC psychologists suggested he try. He focussed on his breathing and attempted to empty his mind. In so doing, he could slow his heart and put his worries away, enabling him to face battle evenly and without emotion.

Anyone who had fought with him considered his strange, mechanical control of emotion inhuman, but not one complained. They knew you needed to be something other than human to fight and return to the fight. There was no one better to have at your side than a dry-eyed, calm soldier. No one had ever seen Lieutenant Skye so much as flinch in combat.

"We're here, boys!" the pilot said. "Hold on tight!"

No sooner had he spoken than the transporter lurched, throwing Spike and Jack from their seats.

"Jesus Christ!" Doorman said, pulling his brother up.

"Sorry!" the pilot said, sounding anything but. The lights in the transporter flickered and it lurched twice more.

"The fuck?" Binky demanded.

"Hey," Skylark barked into the communication device near his seat. "Who taught you to fly?"

"Your mother," the pilot answered.

"Fucking transport pilots," Binky said.

One final lurch, a great deal of squealing and the transport stopped. The door popped open.

"Welcome to the fence, boys," the pilot said.

"All out," Skylark ordered. The team jumped from the transport to the dock with great haste.

"You're welcome," the pilot said as the door closed.

Like a shot, the transport fled the docking station. Skylark watched it go, shook his head and turned back to the station. Though small, it was well structured and very well defended, looking more like a prison than a docking station. The fence, a barb-wired monstrosity, stretched from beyond the turreted compound far into the distance on either side. All around the compound sat the slums, a ghetto of starving children, cracked-out mothers, missing fathers—a festering pustule of violence, famine, and disease. It was once Bennejin Skye's home. It looked alien to him now, but the sounds and smells dragged unpleasant memories to the fore. Skylark scowled as he fought them back.

"Commander," a docking administrator greeted. He reached his hand out to Lieutenant Skye.

"Lieutenant, actually," Skylark said, taking the man's hand.

"Ah, yes. Sorry. Follow me, if you please."

Signalling his group, Skylark followed the administrator into the compound.

"Have you located where the girl might have gotten through?" he asked the administrator.

"We believe so. There is a small hole just north of the compound. It doesn't look large enough to fit anyone through, but it's the only thing close enough."

"Is that how you got through?" Binks asked.

"No," Skylark answered. "We climbed."

Binks looked up at the looming fence. "Christ."

The docking administrator shot Skye and Binks an inquiring look, then continued. "The guards have refused to open the gate until the sun hits the fence," he said apologetically.

"They're smart," Skylark answered.

"We were expecting you much later," the administrator said.

Skylark smirked. "We were expecting to arrive a lot later."

"Sent you with H-Man, I suppose."

"Don't know. Is he a crazy Scot with little regard for transporter capabilities?"

"Sounds like him."

Skylark grinned.

"I can offer some coffee and a small meal while we wait on the sun."

"That sounds like a good idea."

"This way, then." The administrator took a sharp turn and Skylark and his team followed. They emerged from one of the tunnels leading to and from the docking station into a large room busy with civilian police, military police, and compound staff at breakfast.

"Is that sausage I smell?" Binks asked, his eyes growing large as he breathed in the scent.

"Stand down, Binky," Skylark said softly.

"Find a seat, gentlemen. I'll come for you when the guards are ready to open the gate."

"Thank you, Administrator...?"

"Anders. Sorry. I should have introduced myself earlier."

"We'll live."

"I have to get back to work. Make yourselves at home."

"Thank you."

Lieutenant Skye led his squad to an empty table and sat down. Not long after, staff brought cups of coffee and plates. Binks barely waited for the plates to be placed on the table before he snatched his up and stood.

"What?" he demanded when Skye turned to him in surprise. "I'm hungry!" Binks turned to join the queue for food. The rest of the squad followed. Skye contented himself with the hot coffee. It was good coffee, real coffee, not the freeze-dried shit they served in space.

"Well if it isn't the Space Corps," an MP said.

Lieutenant Skye opened his eyes and looked up.

The military policeman stood at Skylark's table, his arms folded across his chest, an unpleasant, smug smirk on his face. Skylark stood.

"How are the namby-pamby space cadets these days?"

Binks turned back to the table to see the stand-off between his commander and the MP. He looked down at his plate.

"Shit," he hissed. He put the plate down on the bench and turned to the woman behind him. "Yo, hold my place." He left the line and headed for the table.

"You're speaking to an infiltrator," Skylark answered, tapping the small round pin beneath the star with wings that marked his training as a space fighter pilot. "You sure you want to start something?"

"Lieutenant," Binky said, drawing the attention of both men. "Is there a problem?" Tall and muscular, Binky was an intimidating presence.

Skylark felt the other members of his team gather around him. He looked the MP over with disdain. "No," he said finally. "I don't think there will be."

"Frangella!" a senior MP barked from the middle of the mess hall.

The MP in front of Skylark jumped and snapped to attention as his senior officer approached.

"Are we having a problem, Frangella?" the man demanded irritably.

"No, sir," the MP replied. "Just a chat, sir."

"Well take your chatter where it's wanted."

"Yes, sir." Frangella marched smartly away, but not before throwing daggers at Skylark with his eyes.

The senior MP sighed. He turned to Skylark and extended his hand. "Major Frank Hallow."

Skylark took the man's hand. "Lieutenant Skye. We're here on a retrieval mission, sir."

"I heard. The British ambassador's daughter. Very sad. What I want to know is how the hell she got out of the damned compound."

"Kids can be surprisingly inventive, sir."

The major snorted. He narrowed his eyes at Skylark. "Wait. Dark hair, blue eyes... Skye...? Bennejin Skye?"

Skylark blinked in surprise. "Yes, sir."

"Damn, boy! You got big!"

"Sorry, sir?"

The major grinned. "You will not remember me, son. I'm the one who pulled you off the street twenty years ago. Now you're Space Corps? And an infiltrator. You've done well."

Skylark smiled slightly, not expecting the sudden warmth coming from Major Hallow. "I had help. Would you like to join us for breakfast, Major?"

"Yes, actually. It's not very often we see a success coming from the streets around here."

Skylark and Major Hallow sat, the major accepting a steaming cup of coffee from a nervous cadet. The rest of Skylark's team departed, hoping to retrieve their places in the food line.

"So, you made it through," the major said. His brown eyes twinkled. "You're a tough little nut."

"Seems so, sir."

"Enough with the 'sir.' I get that from the bootlickers all the time. Call me Frank."

Skylark observed the man in front of him briefly, his eyes giving nothing away in their searching gaze.

"All right, Frank."

"Thought about you a lot after the psychs took you away. Underfed and shaking like a leaf in that little ball you made yourself. Didn't think you'd make it, to be honest. Lots of street orphans don't."

"A lot don't have a reason to."

"And what was your reason?"

Skylark shrugged. "No idea. I'll find out, I suppose."

"Ah, a philosopher!"

Skylark smirked. "Sure."

Frank laughed and leant back in his chair, grinning. "So, tell me about yourself, son."

"There isn't all that much to tell."

"Hell there isn't. You know, I was going to go for the Space Corps when I signed up for service."

"Why didn't you?"

"I kept finding kids in the street that needed food and shelter. Had to stick around and help. And I didn't pass the test."

Skylark smiled.

"Wouldn't have it any other way," Frank said.

"Do you see many kids come through?"

"Less and less. Rising birth mortality rates, fewer kids being born, fewer making the first few months, fewer surviving the street. It's hell out there."

"Always was," Skylark said quietly. He took a sip of coffee and let the aroma fill his senses for a moment.

"Good, eh?"

"Very."

"Do you get the real stuff in space?"

"Nope," Skylark said, shaking his head. "Freeze-dried shit."

"Then I'm glad I didn't pass that test."

Skylark laughed.

"Uh," Binks said from behind his lieutenant.

"At ease," the major said, waving his hand dismissively.

"This is Lieutenant Binks, Binky," Skylark said.

Binks nodded at the major. "Sir." He sat down.

"Lieutenant."

Conscious of the ranked MP in front of him, Binks was heroically well-mannered while eating his breakfast. Skylark watched him a moment, smiling his lop-sided smile.

"I should get back to work," the major said, standing.

Skylark and Binks stood immediately, Binky's mouth half full. They saluted. The major offered a sloppy one in return. He then extended his hand to Skylark.

"It was very good to meet you, Lieutenant Skye. Again."

"And you, Major Hallow," Skylark said, taking the man's hand and shaking it firmly. "And thank you. For everything."

"You know, I can retire happy now," Frank said, grinning. "There's not a lot of thanks you get for hauling starving children into the back of a truck. I'm glad to know I helped even one get out."

"I'm glad to be out."

"Good luck out there, Lieutenant. Keep safe."

"Yes, sir."

The major walked away and both men sat down again.

"You not eating?" Binks asked, as he stuffed his face with scrambled eggs.

Skylark shook his head. "Not hungry."

Before Binks could admonish his friend, this being the second day without food for Skye, the rest of the team arrived and sat.

"What's with the major?" Jack asked, before remembering that Skylark was now her commander. "Sir."

"Someone I owe, is all," Skylark answered.

"Cryptic," Jack said, pouring ketchup onto her eggs.

They ate quickly, knowing their hour would soon be up. Sure enough, the docking administrator approached before Binks was even halfway through his meal. "The guards are ready now."

"Thank you," Skylark said. He stood, his team following suit.

"Leave the plates, the cadets will clear that up."

"As you like." Skylark turned to Binks, who was still shovelling food into his mouth, though he stood. Lieutenant Skye scowled at him.

"I'm hungry!" Binks said.

Shaking his head, Skylark moved off, leaving Binks no choice but to put down his fork and leave the table.

They followed the docking administrator through the facility, moving up several flights of stairs before they stepped out into the central courtyard of the compound. It was a surprisingly beautiful space set against the starkness of the rest of the compound. A treed park stood to one side with a paved area and benches. In the centre stood a statue dedicated to Brigadier-General Russell, who died heroically in the war against the daemon. Blooming flowers surrounded the base.

They passed beneath its shadow before coming to the gate. The gate looked much like the rest of the fence. Twenty feet tall and covered in barbed wire, it made a crude sight after the beautiful courtyard.

"All right, gentlemen," the administrator said.

"For fuck's sake," Corporal Green muttered.

"Maybe he can't tell you're a girl because you're wearing Space Corps armour," Doorman said helpfully.

"Which has fucking breasts," Green pointed out.

"And they're lovely," Doorman answered. Jack punched him on his armoured shoulder. He and his brother laughed.

"You may approach the gates. They will open only wide enough to let you pass, and only when you are three feet from it. Good luck, gentlemen."

Skylark turned to the administrator and shook his hand. "Thank you. See you soon. I hope." He put on his helmet, lowered the visor, prompting his team to do the same, and walked up to the gate.

"We travel north to the hole, and start our search from there," he said as the gates creaked open.

"Yes, sir," his team answered in unison.

Together, they walked through into no man's land.

2

"Ambassador," Captain Michaels greeted as the Brit walked through the door. "You look terrible. Would you like a scotch?"

The ambassador shook his head. "Thank you. I appreciate you letting me wait with you."

"It saves me a phone call and, having children myself, I know this must be horrendously difficult. I wouldn't want to be alone."

"This Lieutenant Skye... He's really the best choice?"

"He's clever. Very clever. And he's been there before. Best of all, most of his team, including himself, are infiltrators."

"What is that, exactly? USC terminology has always confused me."

"They're trained for special missions, Ambassador. Specifically, for entering hostile areas unnoticed for precision strikes and assassinations. They're also our deadliest hand-to-hand and short weapon specialists."

"Ah. I see. It just seems..."

"Ambassador?"

"I mean, I appreciate everything you're doing. But if what they say of that place is true, then surely it's suicide."

"If there is anyone who can get your daughter, Ambassador, it's a team of infiltrators. And if not," the captain said with a shrug, "no one is really going to miss a street kid."

"Looks like the spot," Lieutenant Skye said through his communicator. He crouched down by the hole and pulled at a thread stuck to the broken fence while his team covered him, scanning their surrounds for any sign of movement. He stood and held it up. "She was wearing pink. That should help us identify the remains." He turned and looked down the abandoned street. "All right, pairs." He pointed at Doorman and Spike. "Binky, Jack, on me. We travel east. Keep in sight, and whatever you do, stay away from the windows and doors. We sweep the streets first." He flipped open a compartment in his left vambrace and began typing into the console hidden there. "Sending rendezvous coordinates. If you don't find anything we meet there. Then we begin a building sweep."

"Yes, sir," Binky answered.

The team moved into formation. Skylark signalled them forward and they split up, beginning their search of the streets.

"This place gives me the willies," Binks said as he covered Skylark's flank.

"You and me both," Skylark answered.

"You two mind toning down the chatter?" Jack hissed. "You're freaking me out."

"Christ, this place is a maze," Doorman's voice said over the comm. Or was it Spike's? Skylark could not tell.

Their search lasted a long time without sign of the girl. Skylark watched the shadows stretch with growing unease as he made his way to the rendezvous point. They arrived to find Spike and Doorman waiting for them.

"Anything?" he asked. Both men shook their heads.

"Fuck," was Skylark's only response.

"See that?" Binks asked.

Skylark turned to spot something shuffling in the shadows. "Son of a bitch. It's them. Weapons ready."

"It's not that late!" Jack said.

"No. They must be hungry."

"What are they?" Jack whispered.

"Muties. Most of them sick as dogs. Radiation poisoning. Mostly."

"Fucking great. Radio-active mutants," Binks growled.

"That's why you're wearing your armour, Binky. All right, pull back. We'll have to get to the rooftops."

"Why?"

"Because they're not as good at climbing as they are at running, Binky. Now pull back."

The group of five withdrew, keeping their eyes and weapons trained on the broiling shadows that hovered at the door of one large building, waiting for the shade to grant them access to their quarry.

"They're everywhere," Spike said.

Skylark glanced over his shoulder to see that Spike had stopped. He turned, letting Jack and Binks cover him.

"Spike?" he asked.

Spike nodded his helmeted head toward another building. The shadows moved just beyond the door. They moved behind every door. And every window.

"The fuck?" Doorman asked. "Why are there so many? I thought they were sick!"

"Damned if I know," Skylark answered. "Perhaps they're breeding."

"Well, great. Just great."

"Contact!" Jack called, before firing a double tap. Something shrieked.

"Back to the fence," Skylark said.

"Can't," Spike said.

Skylark looked at him, then beyond him. Hordes of mutants shuffled in the shadows, turning them from purple-grey to black. They were mindless, drooling humanoids riddled with odd, oozing growths.

"Who would want to breed with that?" Binky asked.

"Take it where you can get it, I suppose," Skylark answered. "Stay in the sun. Move as a group."

The team shuffled back.

"You do know that the shadows are pushing us deeper, don't you?" Spike noted.

"Yes," Skylark answered. "We don't have a choice. The first available sunlit pipe and we climb. Now keep moving."

Their steps were dogged by the mutants. They kept to the shadows, flitting from building to building with an agility no one would have thought possible.

"They're faster than I remember," Skylark noted sourly.

"Fuck!" Jack said, firing another double tap. The bullets hit nothing but wall.

"Shoot at what you can hit. If we're going to be here all night, we'll need to conserve ammo."

"Yes, sir," Jack said.

"Keep moving."

"I don't like this," Binky said.

"No one does, Binky," Spike replied.

"Hold," Skylark whispered.

"Sir?" Doorman asked.

"Cover me," Skylark said.

Doorman and Spike dropped to their knees, Jack and Binky remained standing. Skylark ran forward and picked something up from the ground. It was a scrap of pink satin. He stared down at it a moment before turning his eyes to the ground. There were signs of disturbed gravel as might happen in a struggle, but no signs of a body being dragged, and certainly no blood.

"Sir!" Spike yelled a split second before Skylark was tackled to the ground and into the shadows of the nearby building. In the roll to the door, Skylark dropped his gun. Grunting, he kicked off the mutant that had taken him down. It staggered back into the light where his team cut it down. He never saw it fall. Grasping talons from the doorway caught hold of his armour and pulled him into the building.

"Skye!" Binks yelled.

"Hold your position," Skylark barked over the comm.

He fought the attackers off and managed to get to his feet. Completely surrounded by hungry mutants, Lieutenant Skye felt his chest tighten.

"Sir!" Binky's voice said over the comm.

Outside, the sound of gunfire filled the air as inside, Skylark forced himself to relax into the fight. If he was going out, he'd go out fighting. Grasping, clawed hands flashed out at him. Skye reacted instinctively, his training taking over. His only conscious thought was to get to the door, then to his gun. Instinct and training proved an effective combination. In a desperate move, he dived for the door, taking its remaining guard with him.

They landed hard in the dirt. Keeping a firm grip on the mutant, Skylark rolled over into the sun and kicked the creature off him. It shrieked as the sun began to sizzle its skin. Skylark retrieved his weapon and the satin scrap and ran to his team's position.

"Welcome back, sir," Spike said.

"Move!" Skylark barked.

The team broke cover and ran, careful to keep as much in the sun as possible, shooting their way clear when sunlight wasn't available. They gathered behind a burnt-out car and turned, their guns ready.

"What the fuck?" Binks asked.

Skylark frowned. The entire city of mutants had stopped, standing in an undulating line as if held back by an invisible barrier. He turned his attention to the sky. Twilight. There should be nothing stopping them from advancing in a single devastating line. Then Skylark noticed it, a strange painted symbol on a window nearby. They were in daemon territory.

"Fuck. Fuck, fuck, fuck, fuck, fucking fuck!"

Spike turned to Skylark. "Sir?"

Skylark pointed at the symbol. "Daemon territory."

"What the hell did you break formation for, anyway?" Binky asked.

Skylark held out his hand to reveal the scrap of pink satin.

"The girl's?" Jack asked.

"I think so."

"They got her, then."

"No. There were signs of a struggle, but not a single drop of blood."

"Hey," Binks said. He reached out and lifted a single, tiny white court shoe from the ground.

"A doll's shoe?" Spike asked.

Skylark took it. "According to the briefing file, she always carried a doll. She never went without it."

"So, what? She fought her way past the muties?"

"Or the daemon did."

"What would they want with an eight-year-old child?" Jack asked.

"Not sure. Not sure I want to find out." The lieutenant turned his attention back to the frustrated horde standing in a line. He touched a button on his chest plate.

"This is Lieutenant Skye, come in."

Static answered.

"Hello? Anyone there?"

More static.

"Well, fuck," Skylark said. "We're in dead air."

"Maybe they didn't think there'd be anyone needing reception out here?" Binky suggested.

Skylark grunted and turned his attention back to the groaning line of mutants. "I think we're safe from the muties for now, but that means we're facing worse. Keep your eyes out. Stick to the shadows. Night vision on."

Everyone pressed the switch on their helmets.

"All right, let's move."

On the tall, flat rooftops of daemon-controlled territory, a single sentinel crouched. He observed the human intruders with mild curiosity. They were either extremely stupid, or extremely brave. It amounted to the same thing. They would be extremely dead before long.

Major Hallow stood at the window of his office in the compound and stared out over the wastes that now housed the half-human mutants that had been expelled from the ghettos. Turret Three had reported gunfire and Frank himself had seen the flashes of light in the distance.

That had been half an hour ago. He picked up his radio.

"Anything, Tower Three?" he asked.

"Negative, Major. It's just black out there."

Frank threw the radio on his desk in disgust. He picked up a glass of brandy and fell into his office chair. He opened his desk drawer and pulled out a file. Opening it, he pulled out a slip he had written for himself detailing the names, weights, and ages of the children pulled from the street twenty years ago.

Many of the names were crossed off.

Frank picked up his pen and scanned the sheet for a name. Finding it, his pen hovered over it a moment.

Bennejin Skye, 8 y.o., 47 in, 38.3lbs.

The hand holding the pen shook and Frank threw the pen away in disgust.

"What a waste," he said, downing his brandy in a single shot.

The unit moved slowly through the streets. This section appeared much neater. Though grass and stunted shrubs grew in the cracks, much of the paving of the road remained intact. The buildings, though abandoned, did not appear near to collapse.

"What are we looking for, exactly?" Binks asked.

"Another shoe," Skylark snapped irritably.

"Yes, sir."

"Sorry."

"Accepted."

They moved quietly through much of the night, seeing nothing.

"Sir," Doorman said. "Is it just me, or does that look like an apartment with its lights on, down the street?"

Skylark looked carefully. Though the curtains were drawn, the small slips of a golden glow that shone through and around the curtains belied the presence of light.

"The fuck?" Binks breathed. "Daemon?"

"I don't know. I didn't think they lived in apartments. It's worth investigating. Spike, Doorman?"

"Good as done, sir," Spike said.

The twins moved off swiftly to commence their sweep. The rest moved down on the opposite side of the street until they were before the lit window.

"All clear on our end, Skylark," Spike said over the comm.

"Good. Return." Skylark adjusted his visor and pressed another button. The helmet's inbuilt heat sensor immediately buzzed to life. Skylark scowled.

"Sir?" Binky asked.

Skylark said nothing as he saw the heat figures move. One, average height and quite probably female, bent over and gave something to a much smaller figure.

"Not possible," Skylark said.

"Sir?" Binky asked again.

"Heat scan indicates two inhabitants. One is a woman, one a child."

"Human?"

"Not certain. Might be."

Seeing Spike and Doorman peek around the corner, Skylark signalled them, then crossed the road quickly. He tried the handle of the apartment building and found it unlocked. He slipped inside, took position and waited for his team to follow.

Slowly, they crept up the stairs to the second floor. Light shone from the crack beneath the door. It was bright and golden, and wavered ever so slightly.

Skylark removed his helmet and pressed his ear to the door. A young, high voice hummed happily.

"Gabriella?" a deeper, richer, but feminine voice called.

"Yes?"

"Did you brush your teeth?"

A pause. "Yes."

"Are you lying?" The female sounded amused.

"Yes," the younger voice replied.

"Come on. Brush your teeth. It's bedtime."

A petulant sigh. "Come on, Sherrie. Time to brush your teeth."

A soft thud, and the lights flickered, then light footsteps vanished to somewhere deeper in the apartment.

Skylark pulled back. "The child's name is Gabriella," he whispered.

"Isn't that...?" Binks whispered in return.

"The name of the ambassador's daughter. Yes."

The team stood in stunned silence a moment. Footsteps, heavier than a child's, moved to the door. Skylark stepped cautiously back and readied his weapon. The door didn't open. Instead, the deadbolt clicked. The footsteps moved away, then the light went out.

Skylark waited half an hour before he pulled out his electronic lock pick. He carefully inserted the device into the deadbolt and clicked it to life. He moved painfully slowly, hoping the sound of the bolt unlocking would not echo in the quiet apartment. The snail-like pace ensured the noise was muffled. It still sounded too loud for Skylark. He winced as it clicked.

Pausing again, he waited to see if there was a reaction to the sound. Silence answered him. After a few moments of waiting, he slowly pushed the door open. The sounds of a shower started. He moved swiftly into the room and to the only opening in the wall, which revealed a kitchen and a hall. The rest of the team followed. Despite their armour and boots, USC Strategic Team 6 moved silently.

The room cleared, Skylark moved to the hall. He walked quietly down until he came to the bathroom. The door was ajar. Steam billowed out of the room, moistening Skylark's face. The same flickering golden light that had once come from under the apartment door lit the steam. Skylark pushed the door open wider and stepped inside.

"I was not expecting visitors," the rich feminine voice said.

The golden light, Skylark noticed, came from a candle that sat on a ledge inside the shower stall. He lifted his gun and aimed at the shadow behind the curtain.

"I should have been quieter," he said softly.

"It's not your noise that gave you away. It's your smell."

"My smell?"

"Yes. Steel and oil and something else entirely unfamiliar."

Skylark's heart sank slightly. "Not human, then," he said.

"You sound disappointed."

"Where's the girl?"

"Gabriella is probably in the bedroom hiding under the bed. I told her to if ever something happened."

"Binky."

"I'm on it, Skylark," Binks answered. He walked quickly down the hall and peered into the bedroom. It looked deserted. He dropped to his knees and peeked under the bed. The large, terrified eyes of a little girl stared back.

"Affirmative, sir. She's here." Binky rose to his feet. A glowing blue blade pressed against his throat. His startled gaze followed it to a dark-skinned arm, and he followed that arm to the glowing blue eyes of an angry daemon. He reached for his gun, but the daemon pushed the blade against his throat harder and shook his head.

"Get out of the shower," Skylark said.

"You didn't say 'please.'"

"Out."

The woman behind the curtain sighed. "Be a gentleman and hand me my towel, would you?"

Skylark glanced briefly at the red towel hanging on the back of the door behind him. Even reaching for it would put him in a vulnerable position. "Not a chance."

"Fine," the woman said.

The water stopped abruptly and she slowly reached for the curtain. The porcelain blue skin of her fingers surprised Skylark. Daemon were dark-skinned. However, she did possess the black fingernails typical of the aliens.

Ever so slowly, she pulled back the shower curtain.

Lieutenant Skye's lips parted in surprise at the naked beauty presented to him. Raven black hair hung straight and dripping over impossibly pale skin, pale skin that covered a shapely but strong form. Large, wide set eyes, a brilliant purple hue, bore into his blue ones. Full, naturally red lips pursed as she regarded the intruder in her home. Her gaze slipped past Skylark.

"You're late," she said.

Skylark turned to see who she was talking to and was met with a glowing blue blade at his throat and the burning blue eyes of a daemon trained on him. The daemon reached for the towel hanging on the door and tossed it to the woman.

"Cover up," he growled.

The woman smiled and wrapped the towel around her dripping body.

"Your weapon," the daemon demanded, extending his spare hand to take the gun.

Skylark hesitated.

"No heroics," the alien growled. He grabbed the gun from Skylark and handed it off to an unseen accomplice.

The woman said something incomprehensible. The daemon raised its brows at her but nodded. He grabbed Skylark by his armoured shoulder and dragged him into the living room, where newly lit candles now spread their warm light. His teammates knelt on the floor, their helmets removed and their arms bound behind their backs.

Four daemon stood, their glowing blades touching the back of his teammates' necks. A hot flash of anger flushed through Skye, making his body rigid, but he knew there was nothing he could do. Skylark joined his team, forced to his knees. The pressure of a blade tip pressed against the base of his skull and his hands were bound.

"Don't move," his captor said.

"I'm sorry," Skylark whispered to his team. No one answered.

The door to the apartment opened and another daemon walked in. This one wore a bizarre crown of gold. Two flattened semi-circles rested on his head across his brow. They did not meet, leaving a gap of an inch and a half at the front and back of his head. Two golden bands were wrapped tightly around his muscular forearms.

He nodded to the others and straightened as the pale woman entered the room, now fully dressed. She smiled at the new daemon and they embraced.

"Paba," she said.

The daemon smiled and kissed the woman's brow. He turned to Skylark and his team. "Who is your chief?" he demanded.

No one answered.

"Who is your chief?" he demanded again.

"I am," Skylark said, looking up. He did not bother to disguise his anger and did not fear to meet the daemon's gaze. The daemon stepped forward and delivered a powerful backhand on Skylark's cheek. Skylark grunted and fell heavily on his side.

"Paba!" the woman said. She reached out and grasped the daemon's arm. He shook her off and said something to her in his language, pointing at Skylark. The woman said nothing, but folded her arms and pursed her lips in distaste. The daemon turned back to Skylark's captor and barked orders. The subordinate daemon grasped Skylark's armour at the neck and hauled him back onto his knees. Skylark closed his eyes to steady his swimming vision. It only made him nauseous, so he opened his eyes again.

"You all right, man?" Binks asked.

Skylark grunted.

"You come into my daughter's house!" the crowned daemon growled. "What would you hope to achieve?"

Skylark could not conceal his surprise. He glanced at the pale woman briefly. "Your daughter?"

The daemon took a single step forward and lifted the lieutenant clear from the ground. "I will kill you, little man-creature," he snarled.

"Paba," the woman said again, sounding exasperated.

The daemon ignored her. He shook Skylark. "Why have you come?"

"Your daughter has something that doesn't belong to her," Skylark said steadily. "We want it back."

Without letting Skylark go, the daemon turned to his daughter with a frown. She spoke to him in their odd language, using gentle tones. After she finished her brief explanation, the daemon tossed Skylark aside. He fell heavily on one knee and then backwards. He groaned in pain. Skylark's captor once again hauled him up into a kneeling position.

The crowned daemon and his daughter conversed quietly. His voice seemed agitated and angry. She remained soothing and gentle. At length, they seemed to reach an agreement and the woman left the room. The crowned daemon turned back and glared at Skylark, his eyes pulsing electric blue.

Eventually the woman returned, holding Gabriella's hand. The girl gasped when she saw the seven-foot tall aliens around the room and hid behind the woman's leg.

The woman spoke, forcefully this time, and the daemon sentinels retracted their blades immediately, earning a flicker of annoyance from the crowned daemon.

"It's all right," the woman said to Gabriella. "No one is going to hurt you. I won't let them."

Seemingly assured, Gabriella let herself be led to the crowned daemon. The woman bent down and picked her up.

"Gabriella, this is my father," she said to the girl. The girl smiled shyly.

Blinking in surprise, the crowned daemon smiled a little in return. "Hello, Gabriella," he said, all anger suddenly gone from his voice.

"Hello," Gabriella said. Then she buried her face in her doll's hair and giggled nervously.

"And this is?" the daemon asked, touching the doll's face.

"Sherrie," Gabriella said.

"Sherrie," the daemon replied. "She's pretty."

"Uh-huh."

The gentleness of the daemon when faced with the tiny human girl disarmed Skylark. He watched, not believing his eyes.

"My daughter tells me you got lost beyond the fence."

"Uh-huh."

"How did that happen?"

"I was chasing a rabbit."

"A rabbit?"

"Uh-huh."

The daemon cocked his head at his daughter. She said something to him and understanding flooded his features. "Ah! I see. Did you catch it?"

"Nuh-uh." Gabriella shook her head.

"Perhaps next time you'll be more careful."

"I will."

"Good."

The woman turned to Skylark's team. "Stand," she commanded. Warily, they did. Skylark was last, his battered body protesting.

"Gabriella," the woman said. "These men were sent here to look for you."

"Hi," Gabriella said shyly, hiding her face in her doll's hair.

Despite their current circumstance, Skylark could not help but smile. "Hello," he said. "Your father is worried about you."

"Your father thinks you're dead," Binks grumbled quietly. Skylark elbowed him swiftly.

"Uh-huh," Gabriella answered.

"Are you all right?"

"Uh-huh." Gabriella yawned.

"That's enough excitement for one evening," the woman said. She set Gabriella back on the ground. "Go to bed. I'll be there in a moment."

Gabriella tottered off without another word. The woman turned back to Skylark. She cocked her head and left the room briefly. She headed to the kitchen, opened the ice-box and pulled out a pre-made ice pack. On her return, she pressed the pack against Skylark's swelling cheek.

"You took a great risk coming here," she noted.

Skylark used his ample pauldron to take the pack from her and press it against his cheek.

"Orders," he said. Then, "Thank you."

"I would say 'you're welcome' but I fear it would give you the wrong impression."

Skylark smiled at that, wincing as he did so. "We don't want to be here either."

"How did she get past your ugly fence?"

"There was a hole. It's not very big. But then, neither is she."

"You cannot take her back now. It is dark and your hungry dying are everywhere. We will wait for the sun."

"Seems appropriate."

Binks leant in towards his friend. "You don't actually think that they're just going to let us go, do you?" he whispered.

"If my father had his way, you would all be dead already," the woman answered him. "But, I promised the child I'd take her home."

"Why?" Skylark asked.

The woman simply shrugged. She turned to her father and spoke. She went on her tippy-toes and kissed the daemon on the cheek before retiring to bed. The daemon watched her go before turning his attention back to the captives.

"There is couch," he said waving to the furniture behind them.

The squad turned and, Jack leading the way, went to the couch to sit. With their bulky armour, there was only room for three. Binks took the floor, leaning his back against one of the armrests of the couch. Skylark elected to stand, leaning his back against the wall. Keeping the ice on his cheek, he turned his gaze upward.

Silence fell. A cat poked its head into the living room from the hall. Deciding it didn't much like the look of the people in the room, it turned and trotted to the bedroom instead.

The crowned daemon watched it with a bemused expression, then rolled his eyes and shook his head. After a long pause, he left his position and went to the bedroom. Through the haze of his fatigue, Skylark noted his exit, then closed his eyes. The crowned daemon shook him awake. Skylark frowned at him. It was still dark out, and Team 6 snored fitfully.

"Come," the daemon said.

Confused, Lieutenant Skye followed the daemon to the bedroom. The daemon stood aside and Skylark stepped in. He froze. The woman lay asleep. Beside her head, resting its little head on her shoulder was the cat. Further down, Gabriella slept, her arm resting across the woman's stomach, her little hand still clutching her doll.

"Why are you showing me this?" Skylark asked in a whisper.

"I have seen you. You are not like the others," the daemon answered. "Time to go."

Letting Skylark lead, the daemon walked him back to the living room. There, Skylark leant against the wall and turned his attention to the ceiling, trying to empty his mind. Instead, it was filled with recent memories of a very naked alien standing dripping wet in her shower.

The other members of the team, it seemed, had no issue falling asleep. Binky's head rested on Jack's knee. Her head had fallen forward. Spike and Doorman rested on one another.

Skylark remained against the wall, staring up at the ceiling.

Regular checks convinced Skylark that the aliens did not sleep. They stood, still as stone, guarding their captives, but were moved to action any time Skylark shifted his weight. The crowned daemon especially watched him, his anger dissipated now and replaced by intense curiosity. Twice in the night, Skylark found the courage to meet his gaze directly. Far from being embarrassed about his staring, the daemon's curiosity only seemed to intensify.

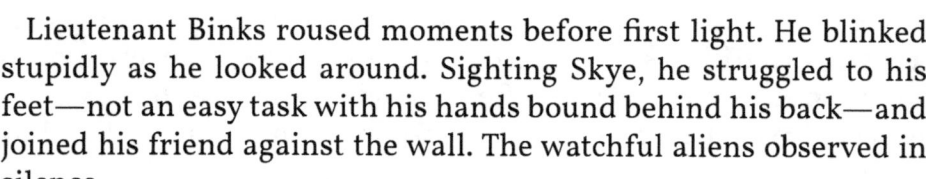

Lieutenant Binks roused moments before first light. He blinked stupidly as he looked around. Sighting Skye, he struggled to his feet—not an easy task with his hands bound behind his back—and joined his friend against the wall. The watchful aliens observed in silence.

"You sleep at all, Skylark?" he asked.

Skylark shook his head.

"That's three nights running, man. You must be cracking."

"Probably," Skylark replied.

Binks grinned. "Sleeping sitting up sucks dick," he said.

Skylark laughed softly.

The light broke over the horizon and the others started to stir. Jack was the next to wake. She stretched, stood, sat, and stretched again.

"I'm about ready to cut my own hands off," she muttered.

"Good morning, Corporal," Skylark said.

"Sir," she greeted. "You sleep well?"

"No," Binky replied for him. "Sick bastard didn't sleep at all."

Jack looked at him. "Again?"

Skylark shrugged.

Movement in the hall indicated that either Gabriella or the woman was awake. It turned out to be the woman. She noted her father with a small smile and spoke quickly to him. He grunted and replied gruffly. Her smile broadened. She strode over to him and planted a kiss on his cheek. Yawning, she walked casually to the coffee table where Skylark had let fall the now very warm ice pack. She observed him a moment.

"It will be a little while before Gabriella wakes up. Do you want more ice?"

"No, thank you," Skylark answered.

"The bruise suits him," Binks said, flashing a cheeky smile. From his corner of the room, the woman's father growled and Binky's smile vanished. The woman turned to her father.

"Tea?" she asked sweetly.

The daemon grunted and the woman walked to the kitchen, where a very hungry cat joined her. It mewed pathetically as she prepared the wood stove and the kettle. At length, she pulled out some meat scraps from the fridge and put them into the cat's bowl. The cat set to with gusto.

"Silly thing," she said affectionately. She gave the cat a couple of pats, then returned to the living room to await the kettle. While she and her father conversed quietly in their language, Skylark and Binky observed. There were plenty of smiles and a few quiet laughs. Conversation rarely turned to serious matters, and when it did, the woman would frown and shake her head. Whatever it was her father suggested, she was not keen on it.

As they talked, the sun shone its golden light into the living room, warming it. Skylark turned his face to the window and closed his eyes, enjoying the rays a moment.

Sunrises were one of the few things he missed about Earth.

At length, Gabriella walked from the room, her doll hanging limply from one tiny hand, rubbing her eyes. The woman immediately went to her.

"Good morning," she greeted, kissing Gabriella's flaxen crown. Gabriella whimpered in return and held her arms up. The woman smiled and lifted Gabriella into a tight embrace.

"What would you like for breakfast?"

Gabriella grumbled something incomprehensible.

"Speak up, dear," the woman said. "I don't speak mumble."

Binks turned to Skylark. "You know what's weird about that?" he said quietly. "It's so fucking normal. You'd think she was her mother."

"Is it?" Skylark asked. He would kill to have known that kind of normal.

"Yo, man. Sorry. You're so chill I sometimes forget you were an orphan."

Skylark shrugged. "No problem."

But it was a problem and Binks knew it was not mere curiosity that painted the lieutenant's features. It was the strain of containing a queer jealousy, if a grown man could possibly be jealous of a thoroughly lost and frightened little girl. The kettle began to whistle.

"Toast and jam it is," the woman declared. She turned and went to the kitchen, Gabriella still hanging off her front. After a moment, she returned with two cups of tea. She placed them both on the lamp stand near where her father sat, went back to the kitchen, and returned with a plate and Gabriella in tow. She set the plate on the coffee table.

"Eat up," she said.

Gabriella sat down and started to play with the jam-laden toast on her plate before she took a bite. The woman sat with her father and retrieved her tea. They conversed again, the woman keeping an eye on the girl as they talked.

When Gabriella finished her meal, the woman ushered her to the bathroom to wash her face and brush her teeth. They returned some time later, fully dressed and ready to begin.

"It is not far to the border," the woman said in her accented English. "From there you must cross corpse territory on your own. We will go no further."

"Sounds doable," Skylark said. "Now if you could cut our bonds and give us back our weapons—"

"When we get there," the crowned daemon said. He stood, stretched and walked to the door.

The woman turned to Gabriella and knelt down to look her in the eye. "This is it. You have everything?"

"Uh-huh," Gabriella said gravely.

"All right, then," the woman said. She stood and took Gabriella's hand. Straightening herself, she walked from the apartment, the door held open by her father.

Two daemon followed, then Skylark's team, then the remaining daemon. They assembled outside the building before walking on. Gabriella tired quickly, and the woman picked her up without thinking as the girl began to stumble. Their pace quickened after that.

The woman walked at the head of the group, accompanied by one of the daemon, who occasionally made faces at Gabriella and set her giggling. The pair seemed on very friendly terms. Skylark watched them, unaware that he now walked beside the crowned daemon, who watched him for a while.

"They grew up together," he said at last, drawing Skylark's attention. The lieutenant frowned up at him.

"My daughter and the majan. His mother has great hopes for them, but I fear he does not like women in that way."

Skylark blinked. "He's gay?"

"Gay? That is your word for a man who loves men? Perhaps. He has not said as much, but I suspect it is so."

"You seem pretty okay with that."

The crowned daemon shrugged. "Some men like women, some men prefer other men. Some men are not interested in either." The daemon shrugged again. "It is of little consequence in the end."

Skylark smiled and turned his attention back to the majan and the woman.

"Your English is quite refined," he noted at length. "Where did you learn it?"

"Her mother," the daemon replied, nodding at his daughter.

"Where did she learn it?"

"She spoke it," the daemon said, smiling slightly.

Skylark stopped in his tracks. "Wait. Her mother was *human*?"

"Yes."

Skylark opened his mouth to ask more questions, realized he would be stepping over his bounds and clamped his mouth shut again.

"We met in the days of the war," the daemon offered, watching Skylark carefully. "She was young then and a nurse. I had been separated from my clan and, in the fight, I was shot three times. Here." He tapped the left side of his chest. "After a while, I could not breathe. The world started going dark and I fell into a door. I managed to drag myself into a corner and there hid from your human soldiers. She and her family were fleeing. She tripped over my legs. When she realized I was hurt... I will never forget."

"What?" Skylark asked.

"She stopped running. She knelt at my side and treated me. She made it so I would live longer, giving my clan a chance to find me. When I thanked her, I think she understood. She touched my cheek, then ran away. I can remember that clearer than any day since." The daemon looked at his daughter and smiled sadly. "She has her mother's face; the shape. I remember at the time thinking I had never seen anything so delicate in my life. It is a strange dichotomy you humans possess—to revel in destruction yet be so frail."

Skylark could not help his grin. "How did you end up with a daughter?"

"The usual way," the daemon answered, grinning broadly. His smile faltered a little. "I was Sentinel when I saw her again. It was three years after the... how do you humans call it? The ceasefire. I had been sent to relieve the Sentinel of the sun. Some moments into the twilight I saw her, scratched and bleeding, and wandering as if in a daze. There were fewer of them then, your hungry dead, and they were more cautious or perhaps not as clever. They followed behind, perhaps hoping she would fall of her own accord. She looked close to it. I recognized her immediately. I did something I am not proud of. I abandoned my post to pull her from danger. She collapsed in my arms. The rest, as you say..."

"Is history," Skylark murmured. He looked over at the woman again. She was now playing pony with Gabriella, who shrieked happily when her ride pretended to buck. The majan laughed in delight and offered to relieve the woman. She turned Gabriella over to him, and he placed her on his broad shoulders. Now the pony, he played the part to his fullest.

"It is odd, I think, to see your enemy being themselves," the daemon at Skylark's side said. "You realize that there is very little that separates you after all."

"Why did you attack?" Skylark asked suddenly.

"We came. It was you who attacked. We were in need of a home; tired, and haggard, and would have welcomed talks. But those missiles were ill-mannered and I was not in the mood for treating with brutes, so we fought back. We won our home. Thankfully, I suppose, given your natures, we have been left alone."

Skylark scowled but said nothing.

"I imagine you were taught something different."

Skylark nodded.

"Well, perhaps the truth is somewhere in between."

The lieutenant walked in contemplative silence. His companion joined that silence and it surprised Skylark how comfortable it was. He was convinced that had they met as something other than enemies, he'd have liked this crowned daemon.

It took three hours to arrive at the burnt-out car where the doll's shoe was found. Gabriella's giggling ceased and she stared out at the dead city filled with dying mutants, her face serious. She leant from the majan's shoulders and reached out to the woman, who took her and hugged her close.

Skylark's bonds fell away. He let his arms drop, then stretched the ache from them. Noticing his team similarly freed, he walked forward to where the woman stood.

"We should get moving," he said.

The woman glanced at him and nodded. "All right, sweetie," she said to Gabriella. "It's time." She tried to lift the girl from her, but Gabriella held on tighter. "Oh sweetheart," the woman said with a sigh. "You want to go back to your father, don't you?"

Gabriella nodded, her head buried in the woman's hair.

"Then you have to let go. The men are ready to leave."

"Come with me," Gabriella pleaded.

"I can't. Your father would not like that."

Gabriella burst into tears.

"Hush," the woman soothed. "It'll be all right. Just think how happy your father will be to see you."

The girl nodded but continued to cry. She allowed herself to be pried from the woman's chest and went willingly into Skylark's arms but did not stop crying.

The crowned daemon signalled his men and they produced the team's weapons and helms. They suited up immediately. Binks helped Skylark, as the sobbing girl occupied both the lieutenant's arms.

The woman stepped backwards, biting her lip, and her father walked forward to meet her. He placed a comforting hand on her back.

Skylark turned to them. "It appears we owe you much," he said. He extended his armoured hand.

"Perhaps you will remember the kindness," the crowned daemon said. Despite the armour, Skylark's hand felt small in the powerful grip of the daemon.

"Thank you. What do I call you?"

"I am the tehoros, All-King."

"Then thank you, Tehoros. I am Lieutenant Skye."

They shook hands firmly.

"You will be able to alert your friends now, Lieutenant Skye."

"It's dead air."

"Because we wanted it so."

Uncertain, Skylark shifted Gabriella's weight and pressed the button on his chest plate.

"This is Lieutenant Skye, do you copy?"

"I'm sorry, say again?" came the response over the comm. The team exchanged glances.

"This is Lieutenant Skye, USC Strategic Team 6. To whom am I speaking?"

"Lieutenant Skye, this is Gate Compound 19—"

"Give me that!" said another voice. "Lieutenant Bennejin Skye?"

"Yes."

"How the fuck...? Never mind. This is Major Frank Hallow at Gate Compound 19. What is your status?"

"It's good to hear your voice, sir. We're in good nick, all things considered. We have the girl."

"I'll have a body retrieval team at the gate. What's your ETA?"

"Negative on that, sir. She's alive."

There was a pause.

"Say again, Lieutenant."

"The girl is alive, sir."

"What? How?"

"Long story. We're about two hours out. We're running the gauntlet and would probably need some cover fire as we approach the gate. These bastards are hungry and bold as hell."

"You have it, Lieutenant. See you in two."

"Yes, sir." Skylark addressed his team. "Right, this is the plan. We run like hell. Stick to the sun and shoot our way through when there is no sun. Doorman, Spike, you're on point for the first leg. We clear?"

"A two-hour run in full sun wearing armour," Doorman said. "Great."

"Pussy," his brother teased.

"Are we clear?" Skylark asked again.

"Yes, sir," his team answered in unison.

"Good. Let's move."

Doorman and Spike took off, ran the first block, then knelt, their guns at the ready. Skylark turned back to the tehoros and his daughter and saluted. Then he turned back.

"Be brave," he whispered to Gabriella. The girl nodded and stifled her tears. "Atta girl." And then he was running, flanked by Jack and Binky.

They moved through the desolate city and for the first hour saw little trouble. Hour two saw action. It was little enough at first, a curious head at a window, the shifting of shadows that told the team they were being watched. But the shadows had begun to lengthen and there was sufficient cover for the hungry mutants to begin to track them.

"Look alive," Spike said, firing at one bold mutant that tried to sprint to the shadow of a car. It fell onto the ground and immediately started smoking.

Gabriella whimpered.

"It's all right," Skylark told her. "That's one less monster that will be coming for us."

Gabriella nodded and hugged Skylark as close as she could. She squeezed her eyes shut. Skylark put his hand on her back and hugged her closer. "Almost home," he said.

Half an hour later, he wished he had not spoken. They were pinned down at a crossroad that had buildings so artfully placed, they provided shade on all sides.

"Reloading!" Binks bellowed. Jack took his position.

"Aren't you glad you aren't running?" Spike yelled over the gunfire.

"Shut up," Doorman answered.

"There," Skylark said, pointing at the thinnest section of the mutant horde. "We rush it firing and hope to hell we make it through."

"Sounds like fun," Binks said.

Skylark holstered his rifle and unholstered his pistol. He picked up Gabriella, whom he had placed on the ground, to take part in the firefight. She clung to his leg until he reached down for her.

"You're doing great," he told her. "Not long now. Ready?"

Gabriella whimpered.

"Hold on tight." Then to his team, "On three. Ready? Three!"

Firing carefully as he ran, Skylark led the charge until Binks caught up and took over point. Doorman and Jack took flank and Spike brought up the rear. They punched through the mass of mutants and sprinted into the sun. Spike ended up dragging one on his back. It held on for a long time before giving up and falling to the ground. A moment later, it burst into flames.

"Vampire fucking zombies," Spike yelled as he ran.

The team sprinted, not bothering to try and hold formation, save for keeping Gabriella safe. They were aware that their speed was matched and often surpassed by the mutants who dogged their steps. Fortunately, the shadows were not yet encroaching on this particular road.

"I see the gate!" Binky said.

"I see them, sir!" an army sergeant said. He stood with Major Hallow in the south gate turret. He handed the major his binoculars and pointed. "There."

Major Hallow looked. All five members of the team were running like hell up a street and one of them held a little girl.

"I'll be damned," the major breathed. He checked their immediate surrounds. Black flashes of the mutants on the move surrounded the team.

"Have the turrets concentrate their fire at the first crossroad in their direct path," he ordered.

"Yes, sir." The sergeant spoke into his radio and Major Hallow did the same.

"Lieutenant Skye, this is Major Hallow. Come in."

"A little busy, Major."

"I can see that. We're clearing a path for you. I need you to stop."

"Affirmative." Skylark stopped running and signalled his troops to do the same. Jack fell to her knees.

"Up," Skylark said. "Get on your feet, Jack. There'll be time for that later."

"Yes, sir," Jack said between gasping breaths. She struggled to her feet as the turrets started firing at the buildings at the crossroad immediately before them. There, the shadows of the buildings almost touched. The mutants waiting in ambush shrieked and scattered.

"Run through on my mark, Lieutenant."

"Yes, sir." He relayed the orders to his team. "Go, go, go!" he yelled the minute the turrets stopped firing.

They sprinted again, passing through the crossroads unhindered. They proceeded this way for the twelve remaining blocks before they reached the cleared tract of land between the beginning of the city and the fence. Relief brought fresh strength to their legs. Doorman taking point, Binky and Spike flanking, and Jack bringing up the rear, they raced for home.

One desperate mutant hiding in the rubble grabbed at Jack's ankle as she passed the final building and yanked back. Jack screamed as she fell, her gun flung from her grasp.

Skylark turned as she was dragged back into the city. "Jack!" he screamed. He tossed Gabriella to Binky. "Go!"

"Skye!" Binky yelled.

"I said go, damn it!" And then Skylark was gone, sprinting back into the city, pausing only long enough to retrieve Jack's weapon.

Swearing, Binky turned and sprinted the last distance to the safety of the compound behind the fence. He stopped and turned, letting a now wailing Gabriella slide down to the ground.

"Daddy!" she screamed. She ran forward to her father who, newly arrived, ran for the gate. Binky barely noticed. He stared at the seemingly empty city.

Skylark had re-entered the city largely unnoticed. The mutants had someone else to occupy their time. He followed the drag marks to the third building down the street. Jack's helmet, its visor destroyed, sat on the first step. From somewhere inside, Jack screamed.

"Jack!" Skylark yelled. He entered the building, finding Jack in the middle of a vicious fight with the mutants. She bled heavily from her scalp.

"Jack, down!"

Reacting immediately, she dropped to the ground and Skylark fired her gun at the gathered mutants, scattering them long enough for him to reach her. He shoved her gun in her hands, lifted her by her shoulder and unshouldered his own rifle.

"Head up, soldier," he said. "Fire at will."

Though dazed, Jack somehow found herself responding. She lifted her head, pulled the trigger and held it, spraying bullets into bodies of mutants. Together, they cleared a path outside.

Half-carrying her, Skylark guided her at a sprint back towards the gate.

Binky stared, unheeding of the medical staff and MPs that had flooded the compound. He brushed off any attempts for anyone to guide him to Medical, as did Doorman and Spike. They stood together and stared at the street down which Jack and Skylark had disappeared.

"There!" Spike yelled.

True enough, Skylark and Jack were running. Jack's helmet was missing, her head covered in blood and lolling drunkenly. Still, her legs pumped as she propelled herself forward.

"Open the gate!" Binky yelled. "Open the damn gate!"

The gate opened and he sprinted to his commander. Doorman and Spike ran out to either side of the opening and shouldered their rifles, picking off any mutants desperate enough to brave the sun in the hopes they could catch the corporal and the lieutenant. Binky slid to a stop as he reached the pair. He took Jack by the shoulder and helped Skylark drag her to safety.

Once all inside, Jack and Skylark both fell to their hands and knees, breathing hard. The gate creaked shut.

Jack immediately threw up. Noticing, Skylark struggled to his feet and went to her.

"I'm sorry, sir," she said through her heaving.

Skylark knelt by her side and removed his helmet. Sweat trickled in rivulets down his face and neck. "Nothing to be sorry for. You did good, Jack. You did good."

A flurry of limbs crashed into the lieutenant. It took him a moment to realize that Gabriella had escaped her weeping father again. He smiled slightly and hugged her, then pulled back.

"You did good, too," he said.

Gabriella smiled her shy smile, burying it in her doll's hair.

"Oh, before I forget." Skylark reached into an armoured pouch and pulled out the doll's shoe Binky had found.

"Her shoe!" Gabriella squeaked in delight. She took it and immediately placed it on the doll's foot. "Thank you."

Skylark nodded and looked up at her father, who had chased his daughter. The ambassador offered his hand.

"Yes," he said. "Thank you."

Skylark took the offered hand, but could not find the strength to stand, or speak. The ambassador collected his daughter and immediately escaped the chaos that was the compound courtyard.

Skylark watched them go a moment before closing his eyes and bowing his head. The medics had converged on Jack and were helping her onto a gurney. Binky put his hand on his friend's shoulder.

"Come on," he said, hauling Skylark to his feet.

Skylark grunted. His vision swam a moment, then everything fell away.

Binky caught him as he reeled backwards. "Medic!" he yelled.

Two medics swiftly arrived and checked Skylark over briefly before a gurney was called. With Binky's help, they lifted Skylark on and wheeled him away.

Binky turned and found Major Hallow waiting. He saluted.

"None of that," the major said. "The lieutenant?"

"I don't know, sir. He just passed out. He's been running on nothing but coffee and guts for three days now, sir."

"You and what remains of your team are to report to Medical immediately. Anders will show you the way."

The docking administrator appeared from behind the major.

"Yes, sir."

Before long the entire team had been stripped, bathed, checked for radiation and bites, then sent to the ward for a good meal and lots of rest. Jack and Skylark were moved to a separate clinic where they could be more carefully observed. They lay side by side in a sealed room, unconscious.

That was how Binky found them when he visited. Jack had an IV and a blood bag, and Skylark also had an IV stuck into his arm. Binky shook his head.

"How are they?" he asked one of the medics as she did her rounds.

"Stable. Neither of them have been bitten, which is good. Corporal Green has lost a lot of blood and Lieutenant Skye is suffering from extreme fatigue and dehydration. I'll bet he hasn't eaten anything in a couple of days either."

"No. He hasn't."

"Well, he should. The man doesn't have enough fat on him to support his mass for long."

"Yeah, well, he might if you say 'please,'" Binky said. "He sure as hell doesn't listen to me." He dragged a chair to the side of Skylark's bed and sat down.

The medic smiled, made notes and moved to check on Jack. Before long the room was empty save for Binky. He pulled out a ratty magazine and started flipping through the pictures.

Skylark stirred and his eyes fluttered open. "Hey," he murmured.

Binky dropped the magazine and stood. "You stupid son of a bitch!"

Skylark smiled. "Jack?"

"Unconscious, but it looks good."

Nodding, Skylark closed his eyes and let himself slip into sleep again.

"He took a big risk," Major Hallow said from the door. "Going after her like that."

"Yeah," Binky said. "That's Skye, though."

"Is it now?"

"Yes, sir. I remember first day of hostilities during basic. I couldn't keep up. He damn near carried me the whole way."

Major Hallow moved into the room to stand beside Binky.

"Man," Binky continued. "My dad fought tooth and nail to get his kids into good schools and I go and sign up to the USC instead. The first thing I do when I get there is make friends with some punk white kid from the ghetto. My mother was not impressed."

"Your family is affluent, then?"

"Yeah. Well enough."

"Why did you sign up?"

Binky shrugged. "School's not for everyone and I didn't want to be under my parent's thumb all my life."

"I see. So, the USC?"

"Sure, why not? And if I die, they get a hefty bonus so..."

Major Hallow smiled. He looked down at Skylark.

"You tell your lieutenant I want him in my office the minute he's allowed out of bed."

"Yes, sir."

Ignoring the salute, Major Hallow left the room. Binky picked up his magazine and sat back down.

4

Three firm knocks at his office door brought Major Hallow's attention away from his paperwork.

"Enter."

The door opened and Lieutenant Skye walked in. The major stood, smiling broadly. He walked out past his desk and extended his hand. Skylark took it with a smile.

"You wanted to see me, sir?"

"For God's sake, Skye. It's Frank. Sit."

Skylark obediently sat down. Major Hallow returned to his seat. "I've kept tabs on you, you know," he said.

Skylark raised his brows. "Sir?"

"Every kid I pulled off the street, every kid I signed in, I've kept tabs on. Oh, I don't send letters or anything like that. I just like to know what they're up to." Frank pulled open the drawer that contained the lists. He pulled out the file and flicked through the pages. Pulling one out, he handed it to Skylark, who took it and scanned the sheet. He looked up when he got to his name.

"Every time I got word of an imprisonment, or a death, or an MIA notice, I'd cross a name off."

"They're all crossed off."

"Except for you. The unlikeliest one of them all."

Skylark frowned at the major.

"When we pulled you from the street, you were so malnourished you were nothing more than skin stretched over bone. You were shaking and sick and wouldn't uncurl yourself from that damned ball until you finally fainted. I thought you were dead the moment they wheeled you into Medical."

"I don't remember."

"I know. Your psychologist said you had repressed memories, and that you wouldn't ever speak of them except in the most basic terms. Terms like 'My mother didn't want me' or 'I spent a night beyond the fence.' No details. You never did tell him about your mother or what happened that night beyond the fence."

"I thought this stuff was supposed to be secret. Client-patient relations or something."

"It is. I have clearance."

Skylark smiled slightly. He put the paper carefully down on the desk. "Is that why you asked me here? To talk about my mother?"

"No," Frank said, smiling. "Though I am curious." He peered at Skylark, who looked unimpressed, before breaking into a wide smile again. "I've seen your file."

"Obviously."

"Your aptitude results are off the chart. You excelled in infiltrator training and graduated the second highest in your class at flight school. I want you to realize just how exceptional that is for someone like yourself."

Skylark scowled.

"Chronically underfed children usually have developmental challenges to overcome, as well as social ones, Lieutenant. Not enough nutrition for the brain causes all sorts of problems ranging from intellectual disabilities and learning difficulties to all manner of personality disorders. That the worst I've seen written about you is 'deeply repressed,' is remarkable and I'm calling you exceptional."

"Thank you," Skylark murmured looking down at the table.

The major pulled the paper towards himself. "Twice now I've put a pen beside your name, ready to cross it off. Once, when you were eight years old, and then again a week ago during your retrieval mission. I'm not going to do it again. You keep your head down, stay out of trouble and I'll do whatever I can in my limited capacity to help you out." The major extended his hand to Skylark. The lieutenant stood and took it and they shook firmly.

"I'm proud of you, son," Frank said.

"Thank you, sir," Skylark murmured again.

"Dismissed."

Skylark saluted smartly and walked quickly from the major's

office. His chest felt like it was expanding and compressing at the same time and breathing was difficult. No one had ever told him they were proud. Walking without awareness, he made his way back to Medical and sat on the end of his bed. He sat in silence for a long time.

"Hey," Binky said, popping his head around the corner, jerking Skylark back into himself. Skylark looked up with a frown.

"You all right?" Binky asked. "You look pale."

"I'm fine," the lieutenant replied.

"Transporter's on its way. We're about ready to go."

"Thank you." Skylark stood and followed Binky to the dock where Anders met them.

"Please tell me it's not the crazy mo-fo from last time," Binks said.

"Does anyone even say mo-fo anymore?" Anders asked as he keyed information on the touchscreen podium at the end of the dock. A horrific screech filled the air as the hovering transport alighted the rails of the docking channel alerted everyone that Binky's worst fear was realized.

"Damn," he said.

Skylark smiled, not bothering to speak as the pilot slammed on the brakes, stopping just shy of the buffer at the end of the channel. The door popped open and the pilot grinned from the door.

"Never thought I'd see you lot again!"

"Yeah," Binky said. "We were hoping the same."

Laughing, the pilot returned to his seat. USC Team 6, resigned, boarded the transport. Skylark waited for everyone else to board before he stepped on. He glanced back and saw Major Hallow standing with Anders. The major nodded and Skylark smiled before vanishing into the transporter. It lurched away.

"That boy is going places," the major said to Anders with a smile.

"Yes, sir," Anders said. Who was he to argue?

Chief Petty Officer Grant stared at the screen of Way Station S8-09. An engineer by training, he'd been called down to check on some anomalies in the machinery. Stationed in space less than a month, he was homesick and irritable.

Part of a complex web of targeted wormhole generators, this way station was the outermost post. Located beyond the outer worlds of the galaxy, it was set up to serve as a jumping port to other galaxies, though no stations yet existed beyond this point.

Despite having all the possible luxuries one might expect in space, Grant hated it. He was always cold. He missed the golden warmth of Earth's sun. Now he stood at the door of the server storage room, staring at the screen that announced with a loud buzz and a red light that his swipe card was malfunctioning. He swiped again, and again the console buzzed and flashed red.

"You cannot be serious," he said. He pressed the comm. link button on the console. "Vic, you there?"

"Yes indeedy," came the voice at the other end. "What can I do for you?"

"The damn door won't open. Again. Can you override the console from there?"

"No problem."

The console buzzed again, this time flashing green. The automatic doors slid open with a barely audible hiss. The lights in the room were down. Swearing, he stepped through the doors and pulled out his flashlight. It took a moment of blinking light and slapping the head of the flashlight against his palm before he got the thing working. He froze. The machines were all covered with something firm, and slightly wet. He walked up to one of the machines and prodded the substance with his finger.

"The fuck?"

An odd clicking sound behind him made Grant turn. The light hit something enormous and shiny with twelve multi-facetted eyes. Its dripping pincers clicked open.

Chief Petty Officer Grant screamed.

5

"To the commander!" Lieutenant-Commander Binks said, raising his shot of tequila high.

It had been four years since the retrieval mission in daemon territory. USC Team 6 had become well known for their extremely successful, if slightly renegade, missions around the galaxy. With a ninety-seven per-cent success rate and no team fatalities to date, brass were fighting amongst themselves over whose missions got the team.

Around the group of five USC officers, dancers writhed in time with, or sometimes not, the pounding club music.

Newly made Commander Skye raised his shot glass. "To the best fucking team in the USC!"

"Boo-yah!" the team answered and everyone drank their shot.

"Hey handsome," a slender blonde in a tight red dress said to Skylark as she walked past the table. She flashed him her most winning smile before walking slowly to the bar. Skylark turned to watch her exaggerated hip movement.

"For fuck's sake, Skye," Jack said. "Don't keep her waiting!"

Pushed by everyone on his team, Skylark stumbled after the woman. He met her at the bar, sliding comfortably by her side.

"Lucky bastard," Spike said, signalling the waitress.

"Lucky bitch," Jack replied, grinning.

"You think we'll see them married?" Doorman asked.

Jack and Binky scoffed.

"Married?" Binky said. "Are you out of your mind? Can you see that man married?"

The team turned to observe Skylark. He noticed and turned his back.

"Sub-Lieutenant Miranda Rast," he said. "Fancy meeting you here."

"I'm here with friends, big boy," she replied saucily. "Don't flatter yourself."

"Shame," he said, pulling away.

"Hey," Rast said. "Let me buy you a drink. You know, to congratulate you on your promotion."

"Are you trying to get me drunk, Rast?"

The woman laughed. "You should be so lucky." She turned to the barman. "Two sunset shots, please."

"Yes, ma'am," the barman said, serving up the shots and taking the money with remarkable speed.

Miranda handed one to Skylark who accepted it graciously.

"Congratulations, Skylark," she said. They downed their drink and she took his hand. "Come dance." She led him to the floor. Skylark pulled her close, but she pulled away again.

"You haven't said anything about my dress," she said, pouting girlishly. "Do you like it?"

"Very much," Skylark answered, pulling her in again.

"Yeah? You think I look good?"

"Always."

They stood in the middle of the dance floor and, like many other USC officers on shore leave on that same dance floor, did less dancing than was appropriate.

"Miranda again, huh?" Binky said, grinning as he handed Skylark a plate of food. "Why don't you just marry her and get it over with?"

"Shut up," Skylark said, wincing under the fluorescent lights of the USC Vancouver Headquarters mess. Binky laughed. Jack joined their table soon after, taking care to make as much noise as possible.

"Really?" Skylark asked her. She simply grinned and slammed the ketchup bottle onto the table.

"Fuck you," Skylark muttered and Binky laughed again.

"Man, white folk just can't handle their drink," he said.

"Fuck you," Jack said as she started to slam eggs into her mouth.

"Your fork is not a shovel," Spike said, sitting down.

"Like you can talk," Doorman said, taking the other seat. Doorman had gotten a small tattoo on his cheek three years ago, something Skylark appreciated very much. He hated mixing them up.

Spike shoved Doorman, who shoved back.

"Hey! Hey!" Skylark said. "If you spill my coffee, I'll kick your asses!"

The shoving stopped.

From the railing of the upper floor where the flag officers ate, Vice Admiral Hunt and Commodore West watched them.

"That's Team 6?" the vice admiral asked.

"Yes, sir."

"They appear... unorthodox."

The commodore smiled. "That is a polite way to put it. They're on the fringe, that's for sure. Commander Skye allows a certain level of... levity from his team, but I've never seen a unit work more effectively in the field."

The vice admiral grunted. "Have them brought to the war room when breakfast is over."

"Yes, sir."

"Skye," Commander Wheeler said.

Skylark stood and extended his hand to the exhausted-looking commander. "Wheeler. I heard about Franz. I'm sorry."

Commander Wheeler nodded. "We all are. He was a good soldier."

"He was."

"I've been sent by Commodore West. He wants you and your team to meet with Vice Admiral Hunt in the war room at 0800 sharp."

"We just got shore leave," Spike muttered. Skylark silenced him with a glare.

"We'll be there."

"I'll tell him."

Skylark nodded and Wheeler marched away.

"Poor bastard," Skylark muttered.

"Franz was the one he was banging, right?" Doorman asked his brother. Spike shrugged.

"Some respect, Doorman," Skylark said. He sat back down. "Best get breakfast down. You've got a little under forty minutes."

It surprised no one that Jack finished first. She leapt from the table, stowed away her dishes and ran.

"What's her rush?" Binky asked.

"Some of us like to bathe, Binky," Skylark said with a small smile. "Speaking of..." He stood, stretched and gathered his plate. "War room. 0750. Don't be late."

"Yes, sir," the rest of Team 6 answered.

Shaking his head, Skylark made his way to the showers. He was showered, dressed and in the war room by 0745. Jack had arrived some minutes before.

"That was quick," Skylark said.

"Contrary to popular belief, most men take far longer in the showers than women do."

"Noted." Commander Skye seated himself beside her.

Jack smiled.

The other three arrived and took their seats. At 0805, Skylark checked his watch. At 0815, he growled.

The vice admiral arrived at 0820 and Team 6 stood to attention.

"At ease," Vice Admiral Hunt said. In perfect unison, the team relaxed their stances.

"Sit," Hunt said, a slight frown on his face.

"Problem, sir?" Skylark asked once he was seated.

"To be perfectly honest, Commander, I am surprised by your, granted, short display of discipline. Observing you in the mess this morning gave me the impression you are a little lax in that department."

"I let my team speak their minds, sir. That doesn't mean they don't know respect."

The vice admiral grunted. He handed the team members black file folders.

"We received a distress beacon from Way Station S8-09 early this morning at 0230. You'll find the transcript in the file."

Skylark opened the file and flipped through the pages. He pulled out a sheet with the heading *Transcript*.

He read the single word printed upon it and looked up. "Indiscernible."

"That's right." The vice admiral passed a hand over the round black device in the centre of the table. It immediately projected a holographic menu. "Here's the actual recording."

The room fell silent as the recording played. It sounded like nothing more than static with two feedbacks—a buzzing and a high pitched mechanical whine.

"This is it after our sound engineers managed to unscramble it."

The static fell away and was replaced by buzzing and clicking, punctuated by screams.

"Jesus," Jack said.

"We know we're not alone out there, Commander," Vice Admiral Hunt said. "The war with the daemon proved that."

"You think this is another alien attack?"

"I'm in the dark. No ships were detected, or the military stationed there would be entrenched in a space fight. From the information we gleaned from the station before all contact was cut, not a single fighter was deployed. The warning systems were not activated. If anything, this is likely an inside job. Way Station S8-09 is a long way from home. Space dementia is not uncommon."

"No," Skylark said. "It's not."

"The Council has asked the USC to deploy teams to investigate. I'm sending three and I want you and your team to lead."

"Which teams, sir?"

"6, 12, and 87."

Skylark looked up sharply. "You're sending Commander Wheeler's team?"

"Problem, Commander?"

"He just lost a member of his team, sir."

"He's been replaced as of this morning."

"Sir—"

"You may permit your inferiors to speak freely, Commander, but I will remind you that I do not."

Skylark gritted his teeth. "Yes, sir."

"Good. There is no time to delay. I want all teams deployed no later than 1500. Dismissed." Not waiting for Team 6 to stand to attention, the vice admiral left.

"Bastard," Jack said.

"He's brass," Skylark said. "They're born that way. That's why they become brass. Take your files. Let's go."

At 1409, Commander Skye and Team 6 stood on Docking Platform 90 waiting to be transported to the space station for transfer on the USC interstellar ship *Magellan*. Team 87 arrived not long after.

"Commander," Skylark greeted, taking Wheeler's armoured arm warmly.

"Skye," Wheeler answered. He looked drawn. He stood aside. "This is Sub-Lieutenant Rast," he said, introducing his newest team member. "Our new team member."

Skylark reached out his hand. "Yes. We've met," he said, sounding less than thrilled.

"No way," Binky said. He had to turn away to hide his laughter.

"Hawkward," Spike said quietly in an unnaturally high tone. Jack elbowed him but could not hide her smile.

"Welcome to USC Strategic, Sub-Lieutenant," Skylark said, shaking her hand.

"Happy to be here, sir."

Binky had to move away. Skylark watched him walk to their packs, his face impassive, but the steel in his blue eyes indicated he was unimpressed with his friend. Wheeler frowned, but before he could ask, Commander Framboise and Team 12 arrived.

"Commanders!" he greeted in his loud, French accent.

"Framboise," Skylark said. They shook hands. "Looks like we're in for something new," he said, grinning.

"Let's hope. Standard rescues are getting boring."

Commander Framboise laughed, and a speeding transport practically fell through the port in the roof.

"What? Again?" Binky said, rolling his eyes.

"Gentlemen!" the Scottish-accented pilot greeted once the door opened. "As soon as I heard it was infamous Team 6, I *had* to take the job!"

"Is that standard issue, Christie?" Skylark asked, nodding towards the pilot's kilt.

"I won't tell if you won't," Officer Christie said, grinning. He left the door and returned to the controls.

"Graduated to space transport, Christie?" Jack asked as she clambered aboard.

"More than that, Jackie-O."

"Should we be worried?" Binks asked.

"Don't know. Everyone in?"

"Team 6 in," Skylark said.

"Team 12 in," Framboise said.

"Team 87 in," Wheeler said as he clambered aboard.

"All right," Christie said. "Buckle up!"

Binky strapped himself tightly to his chair, earning strange looks from members of the other teams. "Oh, you'll want to buckle in. Trust me."

"Up, up and away!" Christie exclaimed. The transporter jerked upwards and shuddered, jerked up again, then lost power and dropped.

"Oopsie," Christie said gleefully.

"I'm convinced he's having us on," Binky said.

Skylark grinned. The power returned and the transporter shot upwards.

"We're clear. You can unbuckle if you like," Officer Christie said.

"Hell no!" Binky replied.

The chuckle that echoed through the comm. sounded sinister.

"You know this guy?" Wheeler asked Skylark, pointing at the cabin.

"A little," Skylark answered, smiling. "We've had him on a few of our Earth missions. He's a little eccentric."

"Yeah. I noticed."

The teams settled in for the two-hour journey to the space station. Jack hummed quietly, her eyes closed.

"What song is that?" Skylark asked her.

She smiled and, without opening her eyes, said, "A song my mother used to sing."

"It's pretty."

Jack opened one eye and spied on her commander. He stared blankly ahead, as he always did when parents were mentioned.

"Hey," she said. She gave him a light punch on his shoulder and a smile. He smiled in return, leant back in his seat and turned his eyes to the transporter's ceiling. Jack closed her eyes again and silence settled over the group.

Their arrival on the station was remarkably smooth.

"You're losing your touch, Christie." Skylark said as he disembarked.

"The station's docking bay is more expensive than a docking channel," Christie answered. Skylark laughed.

"Commander Skye," a female docking administrator said, running to him. "I'm Docking Administrator Bergquist. Pleasure to meet you, sir."

"The pleasure's mine. How can I help you?" He reached into the hold.

"You can leave your bags, sir. We'll make sure they get to the *Magellan*."

Skylark straightened. "All right."

"Sir, Captain Gergiev, captain of the *Magellan* would like a word with you."

"Lead the way, Docking Administrator Bergquist." Team 6 started moving forward. The administrator stopped them.

"Just Commander Skye," she said.

The team exchanged looks.

"Stand down," Skylark said. He nodded at the administrator and she turned away. He followed her through the busy docking bay.

"What's this about, Administrator?" Skylark asked as the pair marched sharply through the throng.

"I can't say, sir."

Skylark fell silent until he spied a large ship docked by way of a boarding bridge at one of the windows.

"Is that her?"

"The *Magellan*? Yes, sir. That's her."

"She's massive."

"The latest in the fleet, sir. Primarily a research vessel, she's fully equipped for combat and can travel faster and steadier through the generated wormholes than any ship in the world. Or out of it, as the case may be."

Skylark grunted.

"We're here, sir." Docking Administrator Bergquist stopped so abruptly Skylark almost ploughed straight into her. She motioned to a door left ajar and immediately left. Skylark walked forward and raised a fist to knock.

"Come in, Commander Skye," a gruff voice said from inside before the commander had a chance to.

Surprised, Skylark stepped inside the office. A grey-haired man stood at the window, staring out into space. He turned when Skylark entered.

"Ah, the Wonder Boy. I've heard a lot about you, Commander."

"Most of it good, I hope."

"Depends whose telling it," the captain replied. "You're wearing your armour."

"Yes, sir. It's easier to wear than carry."

"Sit."

Skylark did. Captain Gergiev looked him over critically. "I read your report on your excursion into daemon territory four years ago. I'm calling you on it."

Skylark frowned up at the captain. "Pardon?"

"I fought those fuckers in the damned war. There's no way in hell they'd ever have let you go."

"Are you—?"

"I've read all about your career, Commander. You and your team are little more than mavericks who happen to have remarkable luck. You're undisciplined, and you lack the proper respect for authority. Whatever it is Frank Hallow sees in you, whatever bullshit you fed him about what happened beyond that fence, I'm not buying, you understand?"

Commander Skye stood slowly. "I'm sorry you had to fight them, Captain," he said coldly. "They're massive bastards and one backhand was enough to put my lights out for a second, but it might have all been avoided if we didn't fire missiles at them in the first place."

"Who the hell told you that?"

"Their tehoros. It means All-King in their language, by the way. Think of me and my methods what you like, but I will not sit here and be called a liar, sir." He leant forward. "And there will be trouble if you think you can bully me."

"I am the captain of the *Magellan*, Commander."

"And you are well out of line."

"Then we are going to have a problem."

"No, sir. You do your job, I'll do mine and we leave each other alone."

Captain Gergiev narrowed his eyes at the commander before squaring his shoulders. "Dismissed, Commander."

Skylark saluted and stormed from the room. Captain Gergiev smiled. He picked up the phone.

"You were right, Frank. He's a hard man to rattle. No, no, there won't be trouble. Well, depending how he acts. Well, I like to know how men act under pressure. Oh, I think he'll do fine on my ship."

Skylark had no idea where he was going, but that didn't stop him from storming there.

"Skylark!" he heard Binky yell. He stopped, but did not turn.

Binky jogged to his spot. "We're all aboard, Comman—woah. You all right? You look fit to kill."

Skylark clenched his jaw.

"Let me guess, captain's a brass-hole."

A sudden laugh escaped Skylark. "Brass-hole?"

"Like that? Thought it up just now. Anyway, I was sent to bring you onto the *Magellan*. She'll be debarking soon."

Skylark nodded. "Lead the way, Binky."

Knowing better than to talk when Skylark was in a bad mood, Binky simply led the way to the bridge and thence onto the ship.

"Quarters are this way. We're sharing a room. 12 and 87 are down the hall on the right and left respectively. There's actually room for fifty teams, but we're the only three on this trip."

Binky led him to the quarters. The doors slid open to reveal a spacious room with three bunks and one double bed.

"Commander gets the bed," Binky said when Skylark noticed his gear sitting at the end of the bed.

"Thanks," he said gruffly.

"Pecking order, Commander," Jack said from the top of the third bunk. "That's why it was invented. And you can take off your armour now. We won't need it for a week."

"Unless some crazy new alien comes out of the black to smack us down," Spike said from the top of the second bunk.

In the bunk beneath him, Doorman grunted a laugh from between the pages of a book. It was unclear if his brother's comment amused him, or if he had just read a particularly funny passage.

Sighing, Skylark went to the bed and began to remove his armour.

"Here," Binky said. He passed his hand over a small red panel beside the bed. The wall opened up to reveal an armour mannequin. It slid forward smoothly. "They've thought of everything."

"Impressive," Skylark admitted. He arranged his armour on the mannequin and passed his hand over the red panel. The mannequin retracted into the wall and it closed. He smiled.

"Binky played with his for half an hour," Jack said.

"Shut up," Binky said.

"I don't doubt it," Skylark said. He sat on his bed and, grabbing one of his bags, pulled out his standard issue boots. He laced them on quickly then took a moment to simply sit.

"Ladies and Gentlemen," a voice crackled over the comm. "This is Lieutenant Hayden. Please stand by for the inaugural greeting from the captain."

A slight pause.

"Good day crew and passengers aboard the *Magellan*. This is Captain Gergiev. I'd like to extend my warmest welcome to our new members on this, our second journey into space, primarily the civilian scientists of the United Council and USC Strategic Teams 6, 12, and 87."

"Fuck you," Skylark muttered under his breath.

"Everyone is on board and we're right on schedule. We will begin flight check momentarily. I expect to be commencing flight in ten minutes. Dinner will be served at 1800 sharp. Thank you."

"I wonder what the food here is like," Jack said. "It's got to be better than the last time we were out in the black."

"Of course it's going to be. They've got civilians on board, Union Scientists, in fact, and they'll go crying to the Council if they don't like anything," Spike said.

Skylark grunted, checking his watch. "Anyone got a map of this ship? I want to check out their training facilities."

"I do," Binky said. "I'll come with." He grabbed his jacket and followed Commander Skye from the quarters.

"What's eating him now?" Spike asked as the door closed behind them.

"You can be such an arsehole, Spike," Jack said. She leant back in her bunk and put her hands behind her head.

"Whatever," Spike muttered.

"Hey," Binky said, pointing at the holographic schematic of the ship he held before him. "A shooting range, free-train gym, weights room, and damn, a salt water pool. What is this, a holiday house?"

Skylark glanced at the schematic. "That's a sizeable gym."

"Yeah. Looks like they were expecting at least fifty using the heavy bags."

"Perhaps when she's full capacity."

"Maybe. I heard they're building a tonne more like her. It's going to be the standard transport ship of the USC fleet, apparently."

"Where the hell did they get the money to pay for that?"

"Taxes, dumbass."

Skylark smirked but said nothing. After a moment, he said, "Looks like a joint venture. I see every colour of uniform."

"Yeah, but United outranks everyone."

"Only in combat situations and only if the commanding officer is deemed unable to lead."

"That's what I said. Left here."

Skylark turned the corner.

"So, you gonna tell me what made you so mad earlier?"

"I don't like the captain."

"Why?"

"He's a brass-hole."

Binky grinned. They walked along in silence through white corridors milling with crewmembers running frantically to and fro as they prepared for travel.

"Ladies and Gentlemen, we are now flying. It will take us two hours to reach our first Way Station. Welcome to space."

"I didn't feel anything," Binky said.

Skylark looked as surprised as Binky felt. "Smooth," the commander said at last.

"Very. Right, the free-train gym should be the second door on the right."

Skylark opened the door and stepped out onto the metal balcony that overlooked the enormous free-train area.

A row of twenty heavy bags hung along a wall. A mesh storage locker revealed focus mitts, kicking paddles and shields, as well as sparring equipment. On the opposite side of the room, a rope obstacle course had been set up, filling a third of the room. Surrounding the course were rock-climbing walls, with a bouldering section. As of the moment, the gym was empty, making it seem massive.

"Nice!" Binky said. He descended the stairs into the space. "It's huge!" he yelled up at Skylark.

Not long after, Skylark joined him. "I'd have killed to have this gym during infiltration training."

"Right, so the lockers and showers are downstairs. The pool and weight room are sub basement. Check 'em out?"

"Absolutely."

They descended the stairs into the locker room.

"Nice," Binky said, pointing to a sign. "Unisex."

The pool and weight room proved equally impressive. The pool was the length of an Olympic pool but had six lanes instead of eight and the weight room had almost every piece of equipment one could possibly need to keep their bodies strong in the vacuum of space.

Skylark and Binky inspected them.

"Skye?"

"Yes?"

"It's 1738."

"Right. Dinner. Let's go." They ascended to the balcony again. Before they left, Skylark looked over the gym once more. He nodded in mute approval.

The mess hall was full by the time Skylark and Binky arrived at 1756. Jack waved her arm in the air the moment she saw them. She sat with the rest of Team 6. Teams 12 and 87 occupied the tables on either side. It was a small patch of concentrated navy blue in a sea of many different uniforms.

Binky and Skylark took their places at the table.

"So," Spike said. "Like what you saw?"

"Yes," Skylark answered.

"The showers are unisex," Binky said, grinning. He sat heavily in his chair.

"Oh goodie," Jack said, rolling her eyes. She and Skylark exchange a quick smile before the new recruits in the crew came out carrying trays filled with plates.

"I smell garlic mash," Doorman said, an appreciative smile lighting his face.

Skylark looked around as the privates began serving everyone as quickly as possible. Team 87 was missing its commander.

"Hey, Rast," Skylark said, leaning back in his chair and touching her arm.

"Yes?" Rast replied.

"Where's Wheeler?"

She shrugged. "He said he'd be here."

Skylark nodded and turned back to his table, frowning. The teams had been served and were well into their meal when Skylark caught the sub-lieutenant's attention again. "Do you know where he would be?" he asked.

"The quarters still, maybe," she said. Skylark didn't let her finish. He stood and approached one of the servers.

Captain Gergiev watched with interest as Commander Skye spoke quickly to one of the servers, accepted a second plate of food, then proceeded out of the mess. He took a deep drink of his wine.

6

Commander Wheeler sat on his bed. He absent-mindedly played with a ring he wore on his dog tag chain as he stared down at a photo of Franz and himself taken on a recent holiday in Mexico. They were tanned and smiling, sharing a massive margarita in the shade of a straw umbrella.

"You need to eat, John," Skylark said from the doorway.

Commander Wheeler placed the photograph face down on the bed and drew himself up, fighting the tears that continually threatened.

"I wasn't hungry," he said.

Skylark walked into the room and placed the plate of food he carried on the bedside table. "Bullshit."

Noticing the photo frame, he picked it up and turned it over. He slowly sat down on the bed as he stared down at it. Commander Wheeler turned away.

"When was this taken?"

"Two months ago," Commander Wheeler said. "We had shore leave and decided to spend it away from fucking soggy Vancouver."

Skylark smirked. "Understandable."

Wheeler reached up and played with the ring again. Skylark watched him a while. "You were married."

"Two months ago," Wheeler whispered.

"Mexico?"

Wheeler nodded. "He had planned the whole thing. Our first morning we went for a walk on the beach at dawn and then he just knelt, right there in the waves and pulled out the rings... I, I had no idea he... anyway. We decided we didn't want to wait. We found somewhere that still sold marriage licenses to gays for cheap and we got married. I have never been that happy, Ben. Never. And now he's gone." Unable to continue, Wheeler broke down. He covered his face and wept. "It was my command, Ben. I killed him."

Skylark placed a comforting hand on Commander Wheeler's shoulder. "No you didn't. The fucker that pulled the trigger killed him."

Incapable of speech, Wheeler simply sobbed.

"Your team know?"

Wheeler nodded. "They threw us a surprise engagement when we got back from the beach." The memory brought a sad smile to Commander Wheeler's face. "We all got wasted that night."

Skylark smiled.

Glancing up at Skye, Wheeler asked, "How long have you known?"

Commander Skye shrugged. "A while. Not about the marriage, though. That's news."

"Yeah well, neither of us wanted to be kicked out of the USC. Gays were doing well and then the war happened, and suddenly we're public enemy number fucking one all over again."

Skylark nodded.

"You're awfully cool about this," Wheeler said.

"I met a man once. Well, a daemon actually. And he told me 'Some men like women, some like men, and some men like neither.' That is the way of it and getting angry about it will change nothing. It's not anyone's fucking business who anyone else loves."

Wheeler blinked and smiled through his tears.

"Listen, I'm taking my team to the training facility at 0530 tomorrow. You lot should join us."

"I think we might," Wheeler said. Skylark stood and so did Wheeler.

"Eat and rest up. I'll see you and your team at 0530."

"Until tomorrow, then."

Skylark patted Commander Wheeler on the shoulder as he passed.

"Ben," Wheeler said when Commander Skye arrived at the door. "Thank you."

Skylark nodded, then left the commander to his meal.

The mess had largely emptied by the time Skylark returned to his table. He was waylaid by Corporal Hank, a member of Team 87.

"You spoke with Wheeler, Commander?" he asked.

Skylark nodded. "He's grieving, Hank. It'll take a while, but he'll come 'round."

"Thank you, sir." Hank took Skylark's hand. "He's a good commander."

"Yes. He is."

Hank smiled, gathered his plate, and left the mess. Skylark returned to his seat.

"Your food is cold," Binky said.

"Noted."

"He all right?"

Skylark smiled as he ate his cold meal. "Not yet. But he will be. Team 87 will be joining us for training tomorrow morning."

"We have training tomorrow morning?" Jack asked.

"Yes. 0530."

Jack groaned.

"Suck it up, princess," Skylark said. "We're a week out and I don't want you losing your edge."

"Awww, you think I have an edge!" Jack said. "That's the most romantic thing I've ever heard."

"Go on with you," Skylark said, waving his hand and smiling.

Jack grinned at him but didn't move. It was then that Skylark noted no one had turned in their plates yet, despite the fact they were clearly finished their meals.

"What's going on?" Skylark asked.

"We're waiting on you, Commander," Spike said.

"Since when?"

"Since Captain Brass-hole over there keeps looking at our table. Binky said you had a run-in with him."

"Ah," Skylark said. He took another bite of his meal. It was nowhere near as tasty cold.

"Want to tell us about it?" Jack asked, putting on her best act of one of Skylark's many overly attentive female suitors. She rubbed her hand on his arm. "Big boy."

Skylark narrowed his eyes at her. "That's fucking creepy coming from you, you know that?"

Jack grinned. "But seriously, what happened?"

"He called me a liar. Said my report about our run-in with the daemon wasn't accurate. We would never have made it out alive if we'd actually met a daemon."

"What?" Doorman said. He looked over at the captain. "What a prick!"

"Everyone can stop glaring at him any time now," Skylark said. The team immediately turned back to the table.

"Hurry up and eat, Skye," Jack said. "We've a game of craekers to finish."

"Still? I thought you finished that up during leave."

"We've started another one," Binky said.

"When?"

"Just now."

Skylark rolled his eyes. He finished his plate, then stood. His team immediately followed suit. They gathered their plates and left the mess in a pack. Not one of them looked back.

The rest of the evening was spent at leisure. Team 6 played craekers, a card game with an insane point system that ensured it lasted for days on end, save Commander Skye. He studied the black folder Vice Admiral Hunt had given him from his bed.

"Ladies and gentlemen, this is Captain Gergiev. Please be advised all military decks have a strict lights-out policy. Lights will dim at 2230 and turn off at 2300. Military personnel are to be in bed before lights-out. Thank you."

Without looking at it, Doorman lifted one fist to the speaker and raised his middle finger. The lights dimmed.

Sighing, Commander Skye put away his folder. "You heard him. Bed. Now."

Grumbling, Binky put the cards and scoring sheet away and everyone retired to their respective bunks.

"Night, Commander," Jack said, her grin audible.

"Goodnight, Jack," Skylark answered.

"Night, Commander," Binky, Spike, and Doorman mocked in falsetto voices. Jack giggled.

"Goodnight, girls," Skylark replied.

"Boo-yah," Jack said.

Half an hour later, the lights went out.

"Those USC Strategic teams give me the creeps," Canadian Air Force Colonel Jacques Paquette admitted to Captain Gergiev over a friendly game of rummy.

"They're meant to," British Army Colonel Sandersen replied. "They're trained to be creepy. They're all cracked."

USC Captain Gergiev grunted. "With what those boys go through every mission, we'd all have cracked too." He played his turn. "I tell you, Jacques, they're a tough bunch of men and women."

"Heard you gave Wonder Boy a shakedown," Sandersen said.

"I tested the waters a bit."

"And?"

"What Frank said is true. He's a hard man to intimidate, doesn't much care for rank, either."

"All right, so what did you do to the rest of his team?"

"Pardon?"

"I saw the way they looked at you at dinner tonight. What did you do to piss them off?"

"I gave their commander a shakedown," Gergiev said, smiling.

Skylark woke sharply at 0400. He tossed and turned in bed a while before giving up on the prospect of sleep. He reached under his bed and pulled out his training bag. Sliding on his trousers and boots, he headed from the quarters to the pool complex. The pool was empty. Had anyone else been up, Skylark would have been surprised. Glad no one else was around, he slipped out of his clothes and into his swimming briefs. In a matter of minutes, his lean, muscular frame was gliding smoothly through the water.

It felt good to be moving, even if it was at a time when he was supposed to be sleeping. He swam for forty minutes before slipping out of the water. He dried and changed and waited for his team. They arrived right on time, dressed and ready for training.

"This place is huge!" Jack said as she descended into the free-training gym.

"This place is awesome!" Spike said.

Commander Wheeler appeared. "Holy shit," he said.

Skylark grinned. "Welcome to heaven, Team 87," he said. Wheeler led his team down the stairs. Not one looked nearly as awake as he did.

"Commander Skye," Wheeler greeted.

"Commander Wheeler," Skylark answered.

"All right team," Wheeler said. "Commander Skye is your commander for the morning. You will prove your worth and if I hear one word of complaint, that princess will be polishing boots for the remainder of the journey."

Skylark grinned. "Against that wall in a line," he said. Both teams immediately sprung to action. "Warm up run, back and forth. You must touch the wall each length. No cheating. That means you, Spike."

Spike grinned.

"Go."

The teams started running, with Wheeler and Skye setting the pace. Skye had not given them a time limit and everyone knew that pushing too hard too soon could spell disaster. Matching pace with the commander was the safest way to ensure they didn't gas out early.

Fully aware of the strategy, Skylark toyed with the teams. Some lengths he slowed to a crawl. Others he sprinted.

When Jack swore at him under her breath, he laughed.

With only an hour available to him, Skylark kept his drills simple and focussed on cardiovascular work. By the end of the hour, members of both teams collapsed to the ground, soaked in sweat and breathing hard.

"Good enough for now," Skylark said, gasping for air. "Hit the showers."

Groaning, the teams did as they were told, vanishing to the showers below. Skylark clapped Wheeler on the shoulder and joined them. Wheeler followed, smiling.

The teams arrived together for breakfast, seating themselves in a mixed fashion this time. There was plenty of laughter as the teams ate.

"Listen, Ben," Wheeler said. "That was a lot of fun. Thanks for the invite."

"We'll be there every morning, Commander."

"Seriously?" Spike asked.

Skylark ignored him. "You're welcome to join us."

"Sounds good."

Binky turned to his commander. "And what time did you get up, sir? I didn't even hear you."

"0400," Skylark said.

Binky scowled. "The fuck you up so early?"

"I didn't plan it, Binky."

Binky grunted.

After breakfast, the teams were free to go wherever they wished. Commander Skye returned to the quarters to review the files once more. The rest of the team decided to do some exploring. They returned after lunch, concerned when they did not see their commander in the mess.

Jack entered first to find Skylark fast asleep on the bed, the black file open on his lap. Smiling to herself, she took up the folder, closed it and slid it in a drawer under the bed. Skylark stirred.

"Hey," Jack said softly.

"Hey," Skylark murmured.

"You missed lunch."

"Uh-huh." Barely awake, Skylark shifted his weight. Jack went to his feet and removed his boots.

"Thank you," he slurred.

"Yeah, well, I owe you." Jack covered her commander with a blanket and left the room.

"He in there?" Binky asked, jogging up.

"He's sleeping," Jack said.

Binky peered in through the window on the door. "Huh. That's what you get for going for a swim at 0400."

"Come on, let's get out of here."

"Yeah. Hang on. Gotta get the cards."

"If you wake him, I'll kill you."

Binky grinned. He pressed his finger to his lips and entered the room. Very quietly, he retrieved his cards, then snuck back out. "Man, he must be tired. He usually wakes up when anyone enters his room."

"Come on," Jack said. "I've got three arses to kick."

"In your dreams, girl."

7

The week wore on in much the same fashion, though Skylark was not caught napping again. The ship's passing through the way stations and into the artificially created streams were barely felt.

Shortly after lunch on the fifth day of travel, Skylark was summoned to the bridge. He arrived to find it a spacious white room with three tiers, each containing six stations where crewmembers were hard at work.

"Preparing to leave the stream, Captain," one said.

"On my command, Officer Wang," Gergiev answered. He stood in front of the captain's chair, watching the artificial slipstream zip past the ship.

"Yes, sir."

"Count me down, Officer."

"Destination in three... two... one."

"Now."

Officer Wang, one of six pilots working pulled slowly back on his control. The glass screen, which covered half the domed ceiling and the front wall, went from the furiously zipping white tunnel to black, dotted with distant stars and galaxies. Skylark did not feel the deceleration.

Sitting right in the centre of the screen was Way Station S8-08. It spun slowly, an effect of its launch some thirteen years ago.

"Beautiful, isn't it, Commander?' Captain Gergiev asked, staring up into distant space.

"Yes, sir," Commander Skye answered.

Gergiev turned to find Skylark at attention by the elevator.

"At ease."

Skylark relaxed.

"Welcome to the bridge of the *Magellan*. What do you think?"

"She's a beautiful ship, sir."

"Yes she is. My daughter designed her, did you know that?"

"No, sir."

Gergiev grunted and took his seat, a plush swivel chair on the top tier. He motioned for Skylark to approach. Skylark did.

"This is the last way station before we hit our target. It'll take us 29 hours to reach it. Station S8-09 has not responded to any of our hails since commencement of this mission. Your teams are ready?"

"As ready as we can be, sir."

"That will have to do, I suppose."

Gergiev observed the flash of irritation that crossed Commander Skye's features and smiled slightly.

"I understand you know Major Frank Hallow, Commander Skye."

"Knowing might be too strong a way to put it, sir. I've met him."

"How did you find him?"

"I liked him," Skylark answered guardedly.

"We were friends in school, did you know that?"

"No, sir."

"We applied to the USC together. I passed, he didn't. He went into the military police instead and was sent to the compound at Gate 19. He speaks highly of you."

Skylark did not reply.

"Did you know he turned down two promotions so he could keep hauling kids into the back of his truck like some demented child-catcher?"

"He's a good man, sir."

"The man's a bleeding heart. He could have been colonel by now."

"Rank is not an indication of a man's worth," Skylark said coldly. "Sir."

"Your misplaced loyalty is intriguing, Commander."

The ever so slight bunching at Commander Skye's shoulders told the captain that he had struck a nerve.

"Loyalty is earned, Captain Gergiev," Commander Skye said, his voice still frosty. "And is therefore never misplaced."

The captain observed the commander with a small smile, before nodding. "If Frank had men like you under his command, instead of those snivelling boot-lickers, he'd probably have made colonel despite his idiocy," he noted.

Taken aback by the entirely unexpected and out of character compliment, Skylark raised an eyebrow.

"I have been instructed by the Council to inform you they will be sending a team of scientists aboard with you on your mission."

"That's inadvisable," Skylark said. "They're civilians."

The captain shrugged. "It's not my place to question the Council, Commander."

Skylark nodded. "Then I request the teams sweep the station first, to assess risk and minimalize potential fatalities. The civilians should remain behind until given the all-clear."

"That is a reasonable request," the captain said. "I will take it under consideration. Dismissed, Commander."

Skylark stood to attention, saluted and left the bridge. He was waylaid on his journey to his quarters by Sub-Lieutenant Rast. She grabbed him and dragged him into a tight, barely lit service hall.

"Well, finally," she said.

"Rast. What are you doing?"

"I'm taking some downtime, sir," Rast answered smiling up at Skylark. She placed her hands on his chest, feeling the muscle beneath his shirt.

"This is hardly appropriate."

"Fun though," she pushed him back, manipulating him until his back was pressed against the wall. She let her hand slide down his front until it reached his belt. His hand snapped around her wrist and he pushed her back against the other wall.

"Not appropriate," he said firmly.

"Oh, come on, Skye," Rast said. "I get into Strategic and suddenly you don't want me anymore?"

Skylark met her eye. His mind and body wanted two very different things at the moment. He drew a slow breath in, taking time for him to compose himself.

"Something like that," he replied.

Rast raised her brows in surprise, then smiled. She shifted her hips, making sure she brushed against him. "Bullshit," she said. She stood on her toes and kissed him.

Skylark responded without thought, wrapping his arm around

Rast's waist and pulling her in close for a hard kiss. It took some time for him to remember that he was supposed to be letting her down. She was now a member of Team 87. It was hands off from here on in.

He pulled back with a grunt. "Miranda, no."

Rast plunged her hand down the front of his trousers. "That's not what this says," she said.

Skylark grabbed her arm and pushed her back.

"You are dismissed, Sub-Lieutenant," he said.

"Seriously, Skye?"

"Dismissed."

Sub-Lieutenant Rast stepped back and crossed her arms in front of her chest. She looked Skylark over critically. "Fine. You know what? Fuck you, sir. I can do better." With that she spun on her heel and marched from the service hall.

Skylark turned and rested against the wall, leaning his weight on his forearms as he struggled to come to grips with the heat in his trousers, which was now painful.

"You can stop eavesdropping now, Jack," he said.

Jack appeared around the corner and leant one shoulder against the service hall wall. She crossed her arms and smirked. "Need a moment there, Commander?"

"I'll be fine," Skylark said. Trying to prove his point, he straightened. It lasted a fraction of a second. Wincing, Skylark resumed his position.

"Want help? I can get one of the recruits here to help you out. There's a cute brunette who's been spying on our early morning training sessions. I'm sure she'd be glad to help. This is a service hall after all."

"Fuck you," Skylark said, laughing.

Jack grinned. "Ice water, then?"

"That might be an idea."

Jack stepped in and wrinkled her nose. "Does it really hurt all that much?"

"More like discomfort. A lot of discomfort. Painful discomfort."

"Huh. Boys are weird."

Again, Skylark laughed. "Not nearly as tough as we pretend," he said.

Jack went to his side and leant her back against the wall. "I didn't like her anyway," she said with a sniff. "Hot as hell, but spoilt. Bet no one's ever turned her down before."

Skylark tried to recall if he had ever turned her down before today. "You might be right," he grudgingly admitted.

"I am right. Petite, blonde, beautiful. Girls like that have never had to fight for anything, let alone a guy's attention."

"She's not that pretty."

Jack raised her eyebrows.

"I mean she is, and then she starts talking."

Laughing, Jack punched Skylark's shoulder. "You are terrible!"

Skylark laughed.

"Feeling better?"

He shook his head. "Not really."

"Can you walk?"

"Not really."

"I'm impressed with you, you know that?"

Skylark spun himself around and rested his back against the wall. He slid his hands behind his back. "Why?"

"A week not entrenched in hostile territory, and you haven't fucked a single person. Then along comes blonde bombshell and you turn her down, even though it does... whatever the hell this is."

"Yeah. I'm almost regretting that."

"So what's up? You sick or something?"

Skylark grinned. "No. Just trying to keep my mind on the mission. None of us can afford distractions."

"Can I ask you a personal question, Commander?"

"Sure."

"You're not weird about screwing people who aren't really all that into you, are you?"

Skylark glanced at Jack. "Not especial—"

"Good." Jack reached behind the commander and pulled down a handle. The door Skylark was leaning on opened and he stumbled backwards into a small room lit in red, with machinery whirring noisily.

"Jack, what the f—"

Jack grabbed Skylark by his shirt and pushed him against the back wall and kissed him hard.

"Shut the fuck up, Skylark," she said.

Stunned, it took Skylark a moment to realize that Jack had undone his belt. He grabbed her wrist. "Stop."

"Look," Jack said matter-of-factly. "I'm your friend, and you're in pain. So I'm doing what a friend should do."

"Jack—"

"I'm not looking for a wedding ring, you dumb fuck," Jack said. She slowly unzipped his trousers. Skylark's control was fading.

"You're my team," he croaked. "This is wrong."

"You're obvious. It's not. Besides," Jack said. "I've always been curious."

"Curious?"

"Yeah," Jack said, kissing Skylark again. "What keeps hot girls like Miranda coming back when you're such an arsehole?"

Skylark broke. He grabbed Jack at the waist and pushed her into one of the machines. She pushed back, trapping Skylark's ankle so he fell onto his back. What followed was rough, with Jack pushing back as hard as Skylark gave.

The silence that followed surprised Skylark by being extremely comfortable.

"So," Jack said at last, smiling. "That's what a week without fucking does to you. No wonder you're such a horn dog."

Skylark laughed. "Yeah, I guess so."

Jack got up and went to collect her clothes. She tossed Skylark's to him as she found them. Skylark sat up and caught them but didn't rise from the floor. He watched Jack with a frown.

Jack straightened when she noticed. "You start acting all weird about this, I will kick your arse," she said.

Skylark smiled slightly, but said nothing. He watched her as she dressed.

"For fuck's sake, Skye. What is it?"

"Pardon?"

"You clearly want to ask me a question. Shoot."

"It's just… I thought, please don't take this the wrong way. I thought you were…"

"Gay?"

"Yeah."

"I am."

"Oh."

"That's right." Jack grinned. "Not every woman thinks your perfectly sculpted stomach is all that wonderful."

Skylark stood and slowly dressed, still scowling.

"Look, as far as I'm concerned, nothing happened. It wasn't anything special. I mean it was fun but it didn't mean anything. All right?"

Skylark looked at her.

"All right?"

"All right," he said. "I think."

"You think? Don't get weird on me, sir."

"This is new territory for me, Jack."

"You've fucked hundreds of women, Skylark."

"Yeah, but I actually care about you. Just—"

"Just not that way. I get it. Look, nothing happened. Nothing's changed. Now get dressed. Binky's looking for you." Jack opened the door, peered around to ensure the coast was clear, then left. She looked back and shot Skylark a wink, then vanished.

Skylark leant against the cold metal wall of the small room and stared up at the ceiling. He sighed.

"Shit."

That evening, the mess hall served as an impromptu war room for the three teams. Skylark quickly explained the Council's request, his counter request, and two versions of a plan depending on what the captain decided to do. They all poured over a holographic schematic of Way Station S8-09 and devised a movement plan that made the most sense to them. Teams 87 and 12 let their commanders discuss the plan. Team 6, as they were infamous for, were much more involved.

When the general plan was agreed upon, Teams 87 and 12 left, leaving Team 6 to coordinate the specifics of their particular role in the plan. The discussion broke down several times, twice into arguments and three times into a long string of jokes and jibes.

Captain Gergiev and Colonel Sandersen watched from the second floor of the mess.

"He runs his team like a goddamn circus," Colonel Sandersen noted.

"And they're still the best team the USC has ever produced. That should tell us all something."

"Frank's gotten to you, hasn't he?"

Captain Gergiev smiled and shook his head. "I had a chat with Wonder Boy last night," he said. "I hate to admit it, Colonel, but I actually like him."

Colonel Sandersen snorted.

"Though," Gergiev said, "he could use the occasional beat down."

"I've watched them train a bit," Sandersen noted.

"I hear they've taken to training in the mornings."

"Do you remember when we could run all day and not give a damn?"

"I never could," Gergiev said, smiling. "That's why I became a captain."

At first, Skylark had been deeply concerned about Jack. But she had been very much herself, neither expecting nor even hoping for preferential treatment. She did not display any body language that might suggest a deeper attachment to Skylark. There was no flirting, no meaningful looks, not even any bawdy jokes. It put Skylark at ease—about their tryst, at least.

So, there could be no excuse for his current sleeplessness. He lay on his bed and stared up at the ceiling, purging his mind of distracting thoughts. What he achieved was very near sleep. If complete awareness of every breath of every team member who shared the quarters with him, and the acute sensation of the movement of the ship despite her smooth flight could be considered sleep, then Skylark slept extremely well.

It didn't matter that his eyes did not close, or that his shoulders did not relax. What mattered was that when the quarter's lights flickered on at 0230, he was prepared for the mission.

Skylark left his bed immediately and dressed. He already had most of his armour on by the time Binky rolled out of bed. Binky observed his friend with bleary eyes.

"Let me guess," he said. "Didn't sleep a wink."

Skylark shook his head, secured his gauntlet and went to the twins' bunk. He kicked it. Hard.

"Up," he said when Doorman's eyes opened. "Now."

"Yes, sir," Doorman murmured. He punched the bottom of the top bunk to rouse his brother, then rolled out of bed.

"Breakfast in ten," Skylark said. "Look lively."

Jack was the first of the team to be dressed. She fought with her pauldron straps for a few minutes before Skylark walked over and helped her.

"Here, let me."

"What kind of soldier can't put on her own armour?" Jack muttered.

Skylark smiled his lopsided smile as he adjusted the straps. "One with really short arms," he said.

She punched his armoured shoulder. "Shut up."

Skylark turned to his team. "Ready?"

"Yes, sir!" they answered in unison.

"Shoulder your weapons. Let's go."

The team filed out of the room, joined moments later by the fully armed and armoured members of teams 87 and 12. The night crew scampered out of the way as the teams moved through the halls.

"This is Captain Gergiev. Prepare for arrival. Commanders Skye, Wheeler and Framboise, report to the bridge immediately."

"Damn," Framboise said. "I was actually looking forward to breakfast."

"I'll see you in the bay," Skylark told his team. He and the other two commanders broke off from their teams, arriving at the bridge a few moments later. Their salute was dismissed by the captain who ushered them silently to his side.

"Long-range scans indicate life support systems are still fully functional," he said. "But there's no signs of life. Bio mass scans have come back unintelligible. It's not even a scrambled message. Engineers are insisting there is nothing wrong with the equipment."

"So, what you're telling us is that you have no idea what's going on," Skye said.

"That about sums it up, Commander," the captain answered. His back to the commanders, he made sure he sounded stern, but a smile hovered at the edges of his lips.

"Approaching exit, Captain," one of the six pilots on the bottom tier said.

"Count me down, Lieutenant," the captain said.

"Arrival in three... two... one."

"Now."

One pilot pulled slowly on one leaver while another pushed one button, waited several seconds then pushed another four rapidly and in deliberate sequence. The wormhole disintegrated around the ship and the *Magellan* floated gently. Way Station S8-09 hung in space before the screen, only now it looked like a misshapen lump of brown stone.

"What the fuck?" one of the crew on the bridge whispered. All eyes turned on the captain.

"What the hell is that?" he said.

Commander Skye walked forward and frowned at the mass. "It's not rust. It's not red enough for that."

"It's kind of shiny," Wheeler noted. "Could it be organic?"

"What are you thinking?" Framboise said. "A giant space turd happened to impact the station?"

Skye smirked. "We'll be keeping our helmets on for this one, life support or no," he said.

"Sir," an engineer said. "Primary scans indicate that the substance is primarily dust."

"That is a glob of sticky space dust?" Captain Gergiev demanded.

"Yes, sir."

"What made it sticky, I wonder?" Wheeler mused. He turned to Framboise. "If you say space jizz, I'm going to hit you."

Commander Framboise grinned and remained silent. Skylark laughed softly.

"Signal the docking tunnel," Captain Gergiev said. "Let's see if it responds to an override."

"Aye, Aye, Captain," an engineer on the third tier said. He looked down at his console and started touching the screen rapidly.

"Nope. Nope. Nope. Nope," he muttered to himself as he tried various methods of getting the docking tunnel to extend. "Got it!" he exclaimed.

Everyone watched as the tunnel pushed against the brown material. It stretched like skin, before ripping as the tunnel punched through. A small, vaguely square patch of the material floated away from the docking tunnel. Skylark watched it as it disappeared into space.

"Sir," a communications engineer said. "I'm getting a signal now."

"Patch it through, Petty Officer."

"Yes, sir."

A screech of static, followed by a muttered apology from the engineer, and then a robotic voice echoed from the comm.

"—assistance. This is Way Station Nine, Sector Eight. I repeat, this is Way Station S8-09. Mayday. Mayday. We require immediate assistance. This is Way Station Nine, Sector Eight. I repeat, this is Way Station S8-09. Mayday. Mayday. We require immediate assistance. This is—"

"Turn it off, Petty Officer," Gergiev said.

"Yes, sir."

"The automatic system," Skylark said.

"Can we hail them, Petty Officer?" Gergiev asked.

"If we're receiving an outbound signal, they ought to receive an inbound one, sir."

"Try it. Perhaps that skin is keeping our scanners from finding signs of life."

"Yes, sir. Hailing now."

The comm. beeped twice. Everyone waited. No response. The communications engineer tried again. No response.

Captain Gergiev turned to Skylark.

"In light of..." he waved his hand vaguely at the screen and continued, "that, I agree that you and the rest of Strategic clear the station before the civilians are permitted on board. They and the Council will be informed of my decision immediately. You will join your teams in the docking bay."

"Yes, sir."

"Dismissed."

The commanders saluted and left in silence. On the elevator ride down, Framboise cleared his throat.

"I'm thinking that rescue missions mightn't be that bad after all," he noted.

Skylark grinned. "We'll see."

"You see that thing?" Binky asked by way of greeting when Skylark found his team in the docking bay. He pointed up through the glass wall at the brown blob floating beyond. "The fuck is it?"

"That," Skylark said, "is the station."

"We're actually going in?" Doorman asked.

"Yes. Nothing's changed."

"Fantastic."

"Nothing's changed, Doorman. Look out for each other, keep your eyes peeled, stick to the plan."

"In that order, sir?" Spike asked.

Skylark smiled. "In that order, Spike."

"Gentlemen!" a familiar voice boomed across the bay. Everyone turned to see Christie marching towards them in a flight suit.

"Jesus fucking Christ," Binky said.

"Sorry to keep you waiting. We've been given the green light by the gracious captain, so how's about we load up, eh?"

"Lead the way, Christie," Skylark said.

"Yes, sir." Humming a Scottish tune, Officer Christie walked the teams to a long ship that looked a little like a pig's skull in shape.

"That's new," Skylark noted.

"Welcome to the USC Strategic *One*," Christie said. "The first long-haul fighter in all of space travel history."

"She's a bit big to be a fighter," Skylark noted as the docking administrator keyed in the code to bring down the access ramp.

"Maybe," Christie said. "But she flies like a dream, houses five single person fighters in her belly, and quarters enough for a team of five, an engineer, and a medic with space for refugees, a fully functioning kitchen, and, best of all, pilot's quarters."

Skylark whistled.

"Yep," Christie said. "I understand that they've gone into full production. Every team is to be getting one."

"No way," Binky said. He turned to Skylark and grinned. "Your very own ship, Captain."

"Stop that," Skylark said. He'd be lying if he said the idea didn't intrigue him, though.

"You're cleared to board, Commander," the docking administrator said.

"Whee!" Christie said, running up the ramp.

"He's not actually going to be our pilot for this, is he?" Binky asked the administrator. The woman simply smiled and returned to her console. Binky sighed and turned, realized that everyone had boarded, and ran.

"Sorry," he said to Skylark when he caught up.

"She's cute," Skylark replied. He slapped Binky's shoulder and walked into the ship as the ramp lifted. Grinning, Binky followed.

"Right," Christie said. "Those are the personal fighters." He indicated the space-ready jets that sat on either side of the metal walkway Team 6 now traversed. "Medical is straight down that way." He pointed to a door flanked by spiral stairs directly in front of them. Christie started up the stairs. "Second floor, living quarters and common room, kitchen, and refugees' quarters. Make yourselves at home. Third floor is all mine, baby."

Christie started up the single spiral staircase that led to the cockpit. Skylark followed him up. The cockpit and pilot's quarters were combined. A door directly behind the pilot's chair opened into what amounted to a very small studio apartment.

"Perfect," Christie said, smiling.

"Not bad," Skylark agreed.

"Won't be needing it this mission though. She's just a transport today. But one day, one day I will fly one of these babies, and I will live in her like a proper man should."

Skylark smirked.

Christie turned to him. "You see the commander's quarters yet?"

"Commanders get their own?"

"Everyone gets their own. The refugees get little sleeping cubbies, like that really weird hotel in Tokyo. Crew get larger rooms. But the commander, he gets the best digs. Come on, I'll show you."

"USC Strategic *One*," a voice said over the comm. "You are cleared for take-off."

Christie looked back at the dash and pursed his lips.

"Another time, perhaps," Skylark said.

"Aye, all right." Christie left the pilot's quarters and sat in his seat. He wiggled his fingers in delight very briefly before pressing the comm. button.

"This is Officer Christie. Commencing pre-flight." He flicked a few switches, changed his mind and flicked them back, changed his mind again and then turned his attention to the touch screen dash. He manipulated a few images around. The engine whirred to life.

"Flying's changed since I went to school," Skylark noted.

"Don't worry. The personal fighters run on older technology."

"Good."

"Officer Christie again," Christie said into the comm. "All good.""

"You're looking good where I'm standing. Bay doors are fully open."

"Brilliant. Taking off in three... two... one."

There was a sharp force, pushing Skylark into the wall behind him and suddenly the view screen showed only space. From the common room, Binky cussed. Skylark grinned at the sound.

"This is Captain Gergiev," the comm. crackled. "I don't think I need to tell you to be careful out there. We'll see you back safe soon."

Skylark pressed the comm. button on his chest. "Aye, aye, Captain," he said. He patted Christie's shoulder. "Fly true, Officer."

"Yes, sir," Christie said.

Skylark left and joined the teams now gathered in the common room. Framboise was in the kitchen, opening cupboards and inspecting drawers. Skylark watched him a moment and shook his head.

"We all have our quirks," Wheeler said quietly. He toyed with the ring around his neck.

"Some are more obvious than others," Skylark noted. "How are you holding up?"

"Better. Not great. I don't think I'll be that ever again. But better."

"Good."

Wheeler smiled. "You are an enigma, Commander Skye," he said.

Skye frowned. "Pardon?"

"A street kid with a crazy IQ, who happens to get away with being a punk to every senior officer he meets, and gets out of the worst shit I've ever heard of."

"Nothing's been that bad," Skylark admitted.

"You lived through a meeting with a daemon. And you even managed to get life advice from him. The fuck are you? A Jedi Master?"

Skylark laughed. "You know what meeting the daemon taught me?"

"What's that?"

"It doesn't matter what corner of the universe you're from, we're all pretty much the same."

"And his daughter is fucking hot," Jack supplied.

Skylark blinked at her.

"You know, for an alien."

"Now I want to meet the daemon," Wheeler said with a smile.

"Let's just hope it's on friendly terms," Skylark said. "The tehoros could pick me up in full armour and toss me around like a fucking ragdoll. They're strong sons of bitches and I sure as hell wouldn't want to fight one."

Wheeler grunted. "Heroic death, though. Isn't that why we all signed up?"

Skylark's smile slipped. He let his gaze drop to the floor and pondered Wheeler's words a moment.

"Ladies and Gentlemen," Christie said over the comm. "This is your pilot speaking. We have arrived at our destination and are preparing to land. Please return your trays and seats to the upright position and thank you for flying Christie Air."

Binky glared at Skylark.

"Don't blame me," the commander said. "I had nothing to do with his assignment." He straightened. "All right, weapons check."

The teams ran through their regular pre-mission procedures.

They secured their helmets and made their way to the hatch at the back of the craft.

"Docking in five... four... three..." The craft creaked. "Two... one..." There was a slight jolt as the long-haul fighter docked.

"Docking successful, opening hatch."

The door slid open, revealing a long steel tunnel that looked intact. Skylark turned to Framboise. "Close the hatch behind you," he reminded the commander.

Team 6 moved forward as far as the end of the tunnel. Though the siren had ceased blaring, the throbbing red emergency lights continued their uneven pulsing. Everything else appeared normal.

"Tunnel is clear," Skylark reported back. "Opening station hatch." He keyed in the code. The light turned red and the console buzzed. Skylark frowned and tried again with the same result.

"Uh, Christie?" he said into his comm.

"Yes?"

"I need a manual override of the station's hatch."

"Alrighty, let me give it a go."

"Appreciated."

"That's nice."

After a moment, the hatch slid open.

"Thank you."

"Always a pleasure, Commander."

Skylark stepped into the station proper and stopped dead.

"Commander?" Binky asked from directly behind him.

"Jesus," Skylark breathed. He moved forward to the first available cover and knelt behind it, motioning his team through. They moved into position quietly.

"Commander," Jack said. "What exactly are we walking on?"

Skylark had no answer for her. Whatever it was, it was pink and rubbery, like skin, though it had started to dry in some places. Some sections had crumbled away entirely. Skylark pressed the comm. link on his chest.

"Captain, are you getting this?"

"I can see. What is it?" Gergiev answered.

"I couldn't tell you. It looks like skin, sir."

"Anything moving?"

"Not yet."

"Proceed."

"Yes, sir."

Commander Skye motioned his team. They moved through the cargo room, making sure anything that should not be moving was not moving.

"Clear," Skylark finally announced.

Teams 12 and 87 moved in.

"Whoa," Wheeler said as he stepped onto the skin-like covering on the floor. "The fuck?"

"Exactly," Skylark said.

"We're not in Kansas anymore," Framboise said. He moved to the door of the cargo room and waited for the hatch behind to close.

"Pressurizing," a mechanical voice said over the station's comms.

Framboise waited until the panel by the door turned green before entering his code. The panel flashed red and buzzed.

"For fuck's sake," he said.

"Got it!" Christie said before Framboise could ask. After a moment, the door slid open and Team 12 moved through.

"The stuff is everywhere," one of Team 12 said. "The walls and ceiling too."

"Proceed, Team 12. We're right behind you," Wheeler said. The teams entered the station and broke off, each doing their part of the sweep precisely as decided in the mess just two meals ago.

"I'm regretting breakfast," Binky said over the comm. link.

Skylark smiled. He tapped Spike on the shoulder and moved ahead. He opened a door to what was supposed to be Medical. He jumped back with a shout.

"Commander?" Jack said over the comm. "Commander, do you read?"

"I'm here, Jack," Skylark said. He shone his gun-mounted flashlight at the doorway.

"Gods," Doorman breathed.

"What is it, Skye?" Binky asked over the link.

"It's skin," Skylark replied. His stomach turned and he fought back bile.

"Like what's on the floor?"

"No. Like someone's skin pinned across the doorway."

Spike reached out and pressed the eyeless face. "Poor son of a bitch was flayed."

Skylark pressed his chest comm. "Captain?"

"I see it, Commander. Proceed."

Skylark took a shaky breath. "Yes, sir." He took his knife from its compartment in the side of the greave of his left leg and cut the skin down. He swallowed back the bile threatening to bubble up and walked forward.

"We're in Medical," he said. "I think."

It was impossible to tell if the room had once been the station's infirmary. Thin pink film stretched over every surface, making whatever was underneath unidentifiable.

"Sir," Doorman said.

"Yes?"

"Don't look up."

Naturally, Skylark looked up. He shone his flashlight on the ceiling and froze.

"Captain," he said into his long-range comm. "I think it's safe to say that there are no survivors."

"What is it, Commander? It's too dark to see."

"Skeletons, Captain," Skylark replied quietly. "Human. Affixed to the ceiling by their feet somehow."

"How many, Commander?"

"I'm counting two hundred or so."

"Commander?" Jack's voice said over the comm.

"I'm here."

"So, the kitchen has a bunch of Batman-wannabe skeletons on the ceiling."

"Yeah. Medical too. How many do you have?"

"Eighty? A hundred? Somewhere around there."

"Did you catch that, Captain?"

"I did. Proceed."

"Easy for you to say," Spike growled.

"You heard him," Skylark said. "Clear the room."

They had finished with Medical when Commander Wheeler's voice came over the comm.

"Teams 12 and 6, this is Commander Wheeler. Please come in."

"I'm here, Commander," Skylark answered. "What can I do for you?"

"We need you in the common room."

"On our way. Are you all right, Commander? Are you hurt?"

"No. But I need someone here to tell me I'm not hallucinating."

"What are you seeing, Commander?"

"I... really don't know, Ben."

"All right, guys," Skylark said. "Let's move."

The common room, the largest room in the station, was a combination of mess and recreation room, complete with a pool and water slide. At least it had been. Upon arrival, Skylark noted it had been turned into a macabre nursery.

Skeletons in the thousands hung from the ceiling along phlegmy chains. Thick, spongy white eggshells all, save one, sat popped open in tiny round craters all over the floor. Each cluster of eggs was arranged in hexagonal formation.

The pool remained but was now a sludge of blood and guts. At the far end of the room, made of the same pink skin-like substance that covered everything else, an enormous concave oval rose from the ground.

"I guess we've found everyone else," Doorman noted, staring up at the skeletons.

"I think it's safe to say that we're not dealing with anything humanoid," Skylark noted. He walked carefully over to Wheeler, who stood transfixed in the centre of the room.

"I feel sick," Wheeler said.

"You and me both."

"Commander, it's Jack."

"I read you, Jack."

"We're done our rounds, sir. Everything's clear."

"Yeah, I have a feeling whatever did this has moved on. I'm in the common room."

"On our way."

All three teams met in the common room.

"Fucking disgusting," Jack said when she arrived.

"Commander Skye?"

"Go ahead, Captain Gergiev."

"The scientists are ready to deploy. What's your status?"

"The station is clear, sir. I'm sending Team 12 out. Team 87 will escort the scientists from Dock 7 to my location. They're really going to want to see this."

"Sounds good."

Skylark turned to the waiting teams. "Team 12, you are relieved. Wheeler, the scientists are arriving soon at Dock 7."

"On our way," Wheeler replied. He took his team and left.

"I will be staying," Skylark told his team. "Anyone who wants to get back to USC Strategic *One* should go."

"We're staying," Binky said.

Skylark looked at each member of his team. No one budged. "As you like," he said with a shrug.

After twelve hours of consciously trying not to throw up, Skylark and his team followed the last of the scientists to Dock 7 and made sure they boarded safely before returning to the USC Strategic *One*, the last team to do so. As soon as the docking hatch closed behind him, Skylark removed his helmet. His team followed suit.

"You look green, sir," Jack said.

"You too, Jack," Skylark said. "You too."

"I need to hurl," she replied.

Skylark looked up at the hanger ceiling. "Ready when you are, Christie."

"We're already away, Commander," Christie replied through the comm.

"Maybe he can fly after all," Binky said.

Skylark nodded. Wearily they trudged up to the common room to join the others and sat in silence.

Dinnertime on the *Magellan* and no one on the teams, not even Binky, felt like eating. The three teams stared down at their plates, an island of silence in an otherwise noisy mess. Skylark broke the silence.

"Where's Jack?"

"In the showers," Binky said, pushing the food around his plate with a fork.

"For an hour?"

Binky shrugged and pushed his plate away. Skylark rose, patted him on the shoulder and left the mess.

He found Jack in the showers, curled into a ball on the shower floor, shivering. Her water allotment timed out long ago.

"Jack," Skylark said. He moved to her side and helped her into a sitting position. She looked up at him, her pale grey eyes filling with tears.

"All those people," she whispered.

Skylark nodded. He pulled her close and she burst into tears.

"Who knew you had a soft side," he said gently when her tears subsided.

"Tell anyone and I'll kick your arse," Jack said, prompting a short laugh from Skylark. They hugged for a while longer before Skylark helped Jack to her feet. He reached back and grabbed her towel from the railing outside the stall. She snatched it from him and wrapped herself up quickly.

"I've seen it before," Skylark said, smiling.

"Yeah, but on my terms."

Skylark conceded. "I think we're all going to bed early," he said. "I'll see you in the quarters."

"Yes, sir."

9

Team 6 lay in their respective beds aboard the *Magellan* and stared out at nothing, waiting for the lights to go out. Skylark had his hands behind his head and stared up at the ceiling. His left foot twitched back and forth. Of the five, only Jack had managed to fall asleep.

Skylark envied her. As always, she would be the first to recover from the shock of this mission. Always the first to get shock, but always the first to clear it from her system.

The lights dimmed.

"Finally," Spike said. He rolled over onto his side and closed his eyes.

Half an hour later, the lights went out. Skylark closed his eyes and dreamt terrible dreams of mutants tearing screaming children in half.

The smell of blood was in his nose when he woke. He sat up violently, lashing out at the shuffling figure beside him. He connected. The shuffling monster retaliated, slapping him hard across the face before it dropped to the ground.

The sharp pain woke the commander up properly. He blinked to find Jack on the ground, Spike kneeling next to her.

"Jack?" Skylark slurred. Then, "Shit! Jack!" Skylark leapt out of the bed and went to Jack's side.

"Piss off!" she hissed at him.

"Christ. Jack, I'm sorry."

Jack sat up with a groan. "Fuck you," she said. She leant against Spike, who held her protectively, struggling to breathe. Spike stared at Skylark.

"The fuck is the matter with you?" he demanded.

Skylark pulled away and sat back on his bed. He closed his eyes and rubbed his cheek.

"I'm sorry," he whispered lamely.

"I'm fine," Jack murmured to Spike. She looked across at Skylark. "You were dreaming," she said.

Skylark glanced at her and looked away again. What was he supposed to say?

"What, Commander? No quippy comeback?"

"Leave it, Jack," Binky said. He went to Skylark's bedside table and opened the cupboard. He pulled out a highball and a small bottle of scotch.

Skylark stared at him.

"Discovered it a couple of days ago," Binky said. "You really should check out your digs better, man." He poured a shot for Skylark and handed it to him.

Skylark silently accepted the glass with a hand that trembled so violently he nearly dropped it. He downed the scotch in one gulp. Binky moved to pour him another, but Skylark shook his head. He handed the glass to Jack. Binky poured for her.

"Not just a dream, then?" Doorman said.

Skylark shook his head.

"The skeletons?"

"I think that triggered it. I haven't had that nightmare since I was a kid."

"What dream?" Jack asked.

"What happened beyond the fence," Binky said. "Just like basic."

Skylark glanced at him and nodded.

"Jesus, sir."

"Would someone please tell me why the fuck my commanding officer punched my gut, without being cryptic?" Jack demanded.

Skylark stood. He reached into one of the drawers beneath his bed, pulled out a pair of hand wraps and was gone from the room without uttering a word. Everyone stared at Binky.

Sighing, Binky sat at the end of the bed. After a pause to collect his thoughts, he explained. When he and Skylark met, they had been in basic training. Skylark was a weedy kid of fourteen, and a punk to boot. Binky was Mr. Christian Binks, a rich kid of seventeen who had signed up just to piss off his parents.

Despite being a star athlete in school, Binky was unprepared for the toll of life in the military. His psychological distress translated into physical inability. He flunked his first course and quickly found himself as ostracized as Skylark.

Binky was ready to quit. Then, one miserable day on a full day hostilities course, in the pouring rain and mud, Binky fell behind the rest of his troop and couldn't find his way. Skylark came out of nowhere and dragged him to his feet.

"No one gets left behind," he had said, firmly.

And that was how their friendship began. The powers that be noticed and the pair were often matched during drills. They were later bunkmates, and that's when Binky noticed the dreams and the sleeplessness. It was one or the other.

Skylark never told him what they were about, precisely, but Binky learnt about Skylark's life before he was dragged into the military at eight. He learnt of the boy's night beyond the fence and rightly guessed that it was the cause of Skylark's issues with sleep.

Binky still did not know what happened when Skylark dreamt, but he knew there was no way it could possibly be good. Skylark had always had bad dreams, and that was that.

After Binky's story, Jack admitted that approaching him might not have been the brightest idea she ever had. She let Spike help her into the bunk beneath the one in which she had been sleeping. She was fairly certain that climbing was currently out of the question.

"Should we go find him?" Spike asked.

"No, man," Binky said. "He needs to be away from people when he gets like this."

Skylark punched and kicked the heavy bag hard. He had set the round timer for fifteen five-minute rounds, a minute break between each. He beat the bag so hard that his wrapped hands began bleeding halfway into round three. By round ten, the blood had started to drip and he noticed the pain even through his anger. He relied more on kicks and elbow strikes. Halfway through round fifteen, he fell to his knees, unable to breathe and feeling queasy. The swinging bag clipped his shoulder and he fell backwards. He curled into himself and, in spite of everything, fell asleep.

Commander Wheeler and Jack found him. They had met each other in the hall just after 0500.

"Hey," Jack greeted. "You seen Skye?"

"No. Why?"

"He, uh… he had nightmares last night and left 'cause we were all making him feel bad about it. You guys are friends, right? Maybe he went to talk to you?"

"Skylark doesn't talk," Wheeler said. "He's probably in the gym. Come on."

"You know, it's funny," Jack said. "He's been my commander for four years, and I still know nothing about him."

"He doesn't like to draw attention to himself. I've known him for ten years; he's still practically a stranger."

Jack smiled. "Maybe that's why he gets all the girls."

"Pardon?"

"He's a mystery. Nothing intrigues and frustrates a girl like a mystery."

Wheeler laughed. "No. He's broken, and every girl he meets thinks they can fix him. Only they can't. No one can. He's too close to the edge, and one day, he's just going to tumble right over it."

Jack scowled at Wheeler.

The commander shrugged. "That's what happens to bright stars, Jack. They burn out."

The pair stepped onto the platform that led down into the free train gym. The lonely, curled up figure of a shirtless Commander Skye greeted them. They froze.

"Commander?" Jack said. She raced down the stairs and ran over to him, ignoring the intense pain at her side. She knelt by Skylark's back and touched his shoulder.

"Commander?" she said.

Skylark's eyes fluttered open. "Jack," he said with a smile. He frowned when Commander Wheeler stepped into view.

"You were up for some late-night training, I see," Wheeler said.

"The fuck happened to you?" Jack demanded, catching Skylark's hands.

The commander's hand wraps were soaked in blood and it had left a thick pool slowly congealing on the floor beside the heavy bag.

"That happened," Wheeler said, pointing at the blood splattered heavy bag. He sighed. "Take him to Medical. I'll clean up here."

"Yes, sir!" Jack said. She wrapped one hand around Skylark and helped him to his feet.

"I don't need to go to Medical," he protested.

"The hell you don't. We're both going and they're going to be prodding my aching stomach and shit, so you don't get to complain. Come on."

Sighing, Skylark followed Jack up and out of the gym.

"Christ, Ben," Wheeler said as he gazed at the bloodied heavy bag. "You're not going to live past thirty-five."

The medic was not particularly surprised to see either Skylark or Jack. Commander Framboise was already asleep on one of the cots.

"What happened to him?" Skylark asked the medic.

"Severe alcohol poisoning," the medic replied. She grabbed Skylark's wrists, looked at his bloody, wrapped hands and then threw them away in disgust. She turned to Jack.

"And you?"

Jack lifted her shirt to reveal an enormous bruise on her abdomen. "Word to the wise," she said to the medic. "Don't try and wake an infiltrator having a bad dream."

"You did this?" the medic demanded of Skylark.

Skylark nodded.

"Good thing he didn't have a knife," Jack said, grinning.

The medic and the commander both levelled her with a glare. Jack's grin broadened.

"Then he went and punched his knuckles bloody," she said.

"All right, you first," she grabbed Jack by the elbow and marched her away to be examined. Skylark sighed and sat down on a chair near the door. He started to unwrap his hands.

"You're better off leaving those on for now," Wheeler said from the door.

Skylark looked up at him, stopped unwrapping and leant back in his seat. Wheeler took the seat beside him.

"Nightmares, huh?" he asked.

Skylark nodded curtly and Wheeler knew not to ask further. They sat in silence a while.

"How do you cope?" Skylark asked suddenly.

Wheeler grunted. "The truth? I cry. A lot."

Skylark smiled slightly.

"When's the last time you cried?"

Skylark shrugged. "I don't remember." A lie. "Before the streets." The truth.

"So, not since you were eight, at least."

"I guess."

"Christ, you really are a machine."

Skylark shrugged again.

"Going for tests!" Jack said brightly as she walked past the commanders, wearing nothing but a blue paper gown. Wheeler and Skylark watched her exit the room.

"Do you think she cares that she's stark naked in a gown that has no back?" Wheeler asked.

"I'm going with no."

"All right," the medic said as she wheeled a metal table over. "Let's look at your hands."

Skylark obediently put his hands on the table and the medic soaked them in saline solution and started to unwrap them. She glanced at Commander Wheeler.

"You need treatment too?" she asked.

"No."

"Good. Not interested in treating any more self-destructive freaks."

"Had a rough night?" Skylark asked.

"Fuck it," the medic said. She stood, brought over scissors and cut through the wraps instead of trying to unwrap them. Skylark winced as she pulled them back.

"Want a shot for the pain?" she asked.

The commander shook his head.

"Well lovely," the medic said. "I think I see bone. And to answer your question, Commander, I've been looking after a young computer engineer in Ward B who, since returning from the way station, has been unable to keep even fluids down. She's dangerously dehydrated. Sometimes she cries in her sleep."

"So do I," Wheeler said. "Sometimes."

The medic glanced at him.

"What the hell was up there?" she asked.

"Three thousand skeletons hanging from the ceiling and doorways made of human skin," Skylark said.

The medic paused and looked up at Skylark. She narrowed her eyes. "Bullshit! You're lying."

"Am I?"

She returned her attention to Skylark's hands. Exposed to the air, they started to sting. "Come over to the basin," she said.

She led Skylark over to a basin with a drain. Taking a large bottle from the cupboard above, she placed Skylark's hands in the basin and poured the solution in the bottle over his hands. The solution bit into the raw and bloody flesh and Skylark twitched. She did her best to wash the blood away.

"That'll do," the medic said. She dried Skylark's hands on a towel and reached for a different solution and a sterile cotton pad.

"Why do you do it?" she asked as she cleaned the wounds with the stronger solution.

"Do what?"

"Go to places like that. What made you sign up for infiltration, Commander?"

The commander shrugged. "It seemed a good idea at the time."

"And now?"

"And now it's my job," he said. "And if I don't do it, some other poor sod will have to, and they might not handle it as well."

"You call this handling it well?"

"This is because I hurt Jack," Skylark said. "She was right. It was damned lucky I wasn't holding a knife."

"You were having a nightmare. You can hardly be blamed."

"I should have better control."

"And must you always have control, Commander?"

"Yes." Skylark grinned wickedly. "Almost."

The medic smiled. "Well, it doesn't look like you broke anything, but you've shredded your knuckles. It's going to take a while for the skin to heal over. Bruising and swelling are going to render them unusable for the better part of a week." The medic smeared

Skylark's knuckles in a yellowish paste, placed a non-stick sterile pad over them and wrapped them firmly.

Reaching into the cabinet, she pulled out a fist full of non-stick pads and an unopened jar of paste. She placed them in a bag.

"This is all I can part with right now," she said, handing the bag to Skylark. "Clean and re-dress the wounds before bed every night." They walked to the door and the medic reached into the pocket of her smock. "There is a bar in the civilian section. Did you know that, Commander?"

"No. I didn't."

"I don't advocate drinking tonight, but my friends and I will be there tomorrow night after 1800." She handed Skylark the card. "Let me know if you'll be joining us."

"I will. Thank you, Doctor...?"

"LeBruin," the medic said.

"Doctor LeBruin." Skylark smiled at her and, with Wheeler in tow, left Medical.

"Unbelievable," Wheeler said.

"What?"

"She went from fire-breathing dragon to interested bed-mate in the space of a conversation. How the hell do you do it?"

Skylark grinned.

Commander Bennejin Skye spent the rest of the day in bed, putting ice over his wrapped hands, thinking. Jack returned shortly after lunch.

"Hey," she said. "Didn't think anyone was in."

"Why? Need me to go?"

"No."

"Listen, Jack," Skylark started.

"If you're thinking of talking about either the service hall or the ultrasound I had on my innards this morning, I would advise you to reconsider."

"I'm sorry."

"I know. Don't worry about it. I was an idiot for trying to wake you. It's Nightmare 101. I should have known better." Jack ascended the bunk ladder slowly and crawled into the bed. "And now I'm going to sleep it all off. Wake me up when we're back on Earth."

"Come in," Captain Gergiev said.

Commander Skye walked into the captain's office. "You wanted to see me, sir?"

"I did. Sit down."

Skylark obeyed.

"I've read your file, Commander."

"Hasn't everyone?"

Despite himself, Captain Gergiev smiled. He fetched two crystal glasses and a large bottle of expensive brandy from a cupboard beneath his desk. Skylark remained silent as the captain poured.

"Your psychological profile was especially interesting. Your childhood psychologist was particularly disturbed by you. You, apparently, were not a normal child."

"I did not have a normal childhood."

"So I've read. Did you really survive a night beyond the fence, Commander?"

"Yes."

"An initiation, I understand."

"Yes."

The captain grunted. He picked up a piece of paper from his desk, looked at it briefly then passed it to Skylark. "'Deeply repressed, psychotic tendencies.' That was the doctor's final report. He even went so far as to say that if you survived even one month away from his institution, he'd eat his hat."

Skylark put the paper down on the desk, unread.

"You don't want to read the report, Commander?"

"No."

"Why not?"

"It's not really my business what others think of me."

"What you really mean to say is that you don't give a shit what others think of you."

Skylark smiled but declined to reply.

"It's bullshit," the captain said, handing Skylark his glass.

"Sir?"

"This psychobabble. It's all bullshit. He could read you like he could read the future in the stars. Deeply repressed with psychotic tendencies may well be the clinical diagnosis, and it might even be frighteningly accurate, but you are good deal tougher than anyone guessed. Even Frank underestimated you when he dragged your sorry arse off the street."

Skylark looked down in to the brandy, frowning.

"You use interesting language, Commander."

"Sir?"

"With your team in mission. Your choice of words is very interesting."

Skylark scowled at the captain.

"You don't even realize you're doing it, do you?"

"Doing what, sir?"

The captain grinned. "It's not important. How are your hands?"

Skylark looked down at his bandaged knuckles. "Healing, sir."

"And Lieutenant Green is recovering?"

"Rapidly, sir. She's a tough girl."

"You look concerned, Commander. I'm not planning on court-martialling you over a nightmare."

"You know about that?"

"Not a lot happens on my ship without my knowledge, Commander."

"Is that a caution, sir?"

"Not unless you're doing something that requires it. Are you?"

"You tell me."

The captain smiled again. He drank his brandy and walked to the window. He stared out at the stars as they awaited the go ahead from Way Station S2-02. "It's beautiful, isn't it? I fell in love with the stars when I was a boy. It so much *cleaner* out here."

Skylark shook his head. "It's not. It's just as messy, just as complicated in space as it is anywhere else. It's just easier to hide it all in the dark."

"A cheerful thought."

Shrugging, Skylark said, "Sorry."

"It seems you are right, though. All kinds of things are hiding in the dark." The captain turned back to Commander Skye. "We are a day away from docking with the transit station. The Council wishes to be debriefed once we arrive. They've requested your presence."

Skylark's eyebrows shot up in surprise. "Why me, sir?"

"You've made a name for yourself, Commander. I imagine they want to know precisely what you saw and, I daresay, to assess the kind of man you are."

"You're cut from the same cloth," Skylark noted. He had meant to say it quietly, but the brandy was stronger than he expected and he was tired.

The captain looked sharply at Skylark, then laughed softly. "It's not often I'm caught out," he admitted. "You pick up on subtleties well, Commander. Ironic really. You possess little of your own."

"I don't have time for them," Skylark said. "Or a need. I'm a soldier, not a politician."

"No aspirations for when you retire from active service, Commander?"

"I don't expect I'll live to see that opportunity, Captain. Infiltrators rarely do."

The captain grunted. "I have work to do," he said.

"Yes, sir." Skylark stood. "Thank you for the brandy."

"Dismissed, Commander."

Skylark saluted and left the office. Just before he stepped out, the captain said, "Give my regards to Doctor LeBruin."

Skylark paused. He smiled a lopsided smile. "Yes, sir." Then he left, closing the door softly behind him.

Captain Gergiev laughed to himself, poured himself another brandy and walked back to his window to stare into space.

10

The war room was already occupied when Captain Gergiev and Commander Skye reached it. The captain knocked and entered without waiting for a response.

"You're late," Vice Admiral Hunt said. He waved away the salutes of the men and they found their positions around the table. Two of the three available seats were already occupied, so Commander Skye elected to stand behind Captain Gergiev.

They had arrived at the transit station half an hour behind schedule. Skylark had no time to shower and change, let alone eat. He was hungry and tired and wanted nothing more than to be on the shuttle that, at the moment, was taking Team 6 for some well-deserved rest and relaxation on Earth.

"Is everyone here?" Colonel Sandersen asked. He had taken the time to clean up, and looked sharp. Skylark could not fathom how the colonel had arrived before him.

"All accounted for," Vice Admiral Hunt said. "You may proceed."

Colonel Sandersen keyed in a code and the beams of a holograph shot up from the floor in the centre of the room. A figure stepped into view.

"Councillor Brand," Vice Admiral Hunt greeted. "A pleasure, ma'am."

"We are not accustomed to being kept waiting, Vice Admiral."

"My apologies. Captain Gergiev and his ship were delayed."

"Oh?" The holographic image turned to the captain.

"Traffic," he said. Skylark grinned.

"Let's get to the business at hand," the councillor said, turning back to the vice admiral. "We have received the pictures and the reports from the Strategic Teams and United Council scientists. It seems a little far-fetched, Vice Admiral. Space bugs?"

"It seems the likeliest explanation," a United Council scientist said from her position at the table.

The councillor turned to her. "You are certain it is not daemon?"

"Nothing is for certain, ma'am," the scientist said evenly, though she appeared annoyed. "We know almost nothing about the daemon. However, I am fairly certain they don't build nests out of the masticated skin of their targets. I'm not a daemon expert, of course."

"No indeed. The closest thing we have to that is Commander Skye," the councillor said. "Is he here?"

"Present, ma'am," Skylark said, stepping forward.

The image turned and looked critically at him. "You are Commander Skye?"

"Yes, ma'am."

"I have read your file, Commander."

"I've been hearing that a lot, ma'am."

"I am not impressed."

"I've been hearing that, too."

Vice Admiral Hunt cleared his throat audibly. He shot a poisonous look at Commander Skye, then at Captain Gergiev, who tilted his head and shrugged his shoulders, indicating that he did not bear the responsibility of keeping Commander Skye in line.

The holographic image of the councillor folded her arms and pursed her lips as she regarded Skylark coldly.

"And in your professional—and I use that term loosely— opinion, do you think the daemon are responsible?"

"No, ma'am," Skylark said. "Way Station S8-09 looked like a macabre wasp nest, ma'am. There is nothing I have seen nor anything in the, granted, little literature we have on the daemon to indicate they would have anything to do with that."

"Your report on your mission into daemon territory doesn't make it seem like you've seen much."

"Very true, but there is nothing insectoid about the daemon, ma'am."

"Perhaps they have cultivated some kind of insect to do their killing for them?"

"Had they done so, why would they start with a way station that is farthest away from where their enemy is currently settled? Our infrastructure is on Earth. Any half-intelligent foe would strike there first."

Again, Vice Admiral Hunt cleared his throat. Skylark ignored him.

"Commander Skye," the councillor said. "Do you have any idea who you are talking to?"

"Yes, ma'am."

"I suggest you keep that in mind."

Skylark's temper darkened. "You asked me my opinion, ma'am. And I gave it."

"He has a point, Councillor," a masculine voice with a British accent said. Another holographic image stepped forward.

"Councillor Fisher," Councillor Brand greeted. Fisher ignored her and instead observed Skylark in silence a while.

"You look a hard man, Commander," he noted.

"I've been in hard fights, Councillor," Skylark replied.

"Yes. I've read."

Skylark crossed his arms and kept his gaze steady. Councillor Fisher laughed. "And not easily cowed. I like that. So, you don't believe the daemon are behind this attack. It is a new species of alien, one that is insectoid."

"Not having seen one for myself, and not having analyzed the... stuff from the station, I cannot say for certain. But I suspect it is likely. The daemon are not the culprits this time." Skylark paused a moment. "You could, of course, ask them."

Dead silence fell over the war room. Vice Admiral Hunt rose to his feet. "Commander Skye," he growled.

"No," Councillor Fisher said, putting up one hand to tell the Vice Admiral to sit down. He did. Slowly. Glaring at Skylark.

"This is not the first time that a diplomatic outreach has been suggested. And, I daresay, it shall not be the last. The most recent push keeps coming from Britain's ambassador."

"You cannot seriously be suggesting we make contact with the daemon!" Councillor Brand interjected.

"As you can see," Fisher said ruefully, "consensus on the issue is far from being reached within the Council."

"They *invaded!*"

"I understand there are two versions of events, ma'am," Skylark said.

"That is not your concern, Commander," Brand retorted.

The figure of Councillor Fisher turned and glared at the figure of Councillor Brand. It turned into a holographic staring contest before Brand hissed, turned and left the stage, leaving only the holographic Fisher.

"Commander," Fisher said. "I am inclined to go ahead with a diplomatic outreach. If these new aliens have nothing to do with the daemon, then the threat is to both our species. It would be mutually beneficial to form an alliance to combat this new threat."

"Yes, sir. It would."

"Ambassador Clegg has insisted that he be sent. Something to do with his daughter, I understand. He will be accompanied by British military ground troops but has requested that you and your team join him. He thinks your presence will help with relations."

"Or it could really just piss them off," Commander Skye said. "I know I'd be annoyed if a pest I got rid of kept returning."

Councillor Fisher smiled. "This will not be optional."

"Noted, sir."

"Assuming I can get the Council to agree, we will send five other teams to escort you and the ambassador safely through mutant territory. Before I make my recommendations to the Council, are there any teams you feel are especially up to the task?"

"I want Team 87, sir."

"Just one?"

"Commander Wheeler is a capable commander, and his team is strong. As to the other four, it doesn't make that much of a difference. But I want 87 watching my back."

"Very well. I will do my best to sway the Council. In the meantime, I believe it is within my powers to grant you and your team extended shore leave pending the Council's decision." The holograph turned to Vice Admiral Hunt. "Make it happen, Hunt," he said.

"Yes, sir," the vice admiral said.

"Thank you, gentlemen," Fisher said. "This has been most—" He turned to Skylark. "Enlightening."

The holograph flickered and vanished and the war room sat in silence a moment. Captain Gergiev stood. "Well, that's that, then."

"Dismissed," Hunt said. Everyone stood and filed from the room. "Not you, Commander."

Captain Gergiev glanced at Skylark, who stood still, his expression impassive. Skylark's attention remained focussed on the vice admiral. When the last person filed out, the vice admiral shut the door and turned to Skylark. They watched each other for a moment.

"What the fuck was that?" Hunt demanded.

"Sir?"

"You were speaking to members of the Council, you piss-ant, not some boot-licking brat new to the USC!"

Skylark scowled. "Thank you, sir. I was unaware."

"Mind your tone, boy!"

"What exactly do you think I did wrong, Vice Admiral?" Skylark said. "I was requested to attend. My opinion was asked. I both attended and gave my opinion in the proper order and when asked. If you feel your toes have been stepped on, sir, take it up with the Council."

Close to losing his temper, Skylark marched past the vice admiral.

"You have not been dismissed," Hunt grated, turning to Skylark. Skylark paused, hand on the door handle.

"I believe I have, sir," he replied, before opening the door and marching from the room.

"Commander!" The vice admiral stormed after Skylark, catching him at the elbow and spinning him around. "You are lucky I don't haul your sorry arse to a disciplinary hearing."

"You are out of line. *Sir*." Skylark pulled away. "Touch me again," he said quietly, "and I'll break every bone in your arm."

"Are you threatening me, Commander?"

"Promising, Vice Admiral."

Skylark turned and walked rapidly away. He descended the stairs to the docking bay.

"Get me out," he snapped at a docking administrator. The boy jumped, turned and ran to find space on a transport to Earth. Before Skylark had time to calm down, he found himself in an empty transport, being brought to the USC Headquarters in Vancouver.

Once there, he stormed to his quarters, slammed the door shut and spent the rest of the day staring up at the ceiling, trying to empty his mind.

Team 6 spent much of their shore leave drinking. Doorman and Skylark, however, hiked the West Coast Trail, one of the few places of wilderness left in the world.

Skylark needed to get away from people for a while and Doorman was the perfect hiking partner—fit, diligent, and best of all, silent. Doorman, perhaps more than anyone else on the team, knew the value of silence and solitude. And he knew when his commander needed both.

Conversation was sparse over dinner and afterward at the fire. Mostly, they simply shared a beer and enjoyed the quiet of the trail.

By the time the fortnight-long hike was over, Skylark's mood improved. His shoulders were not quite as tense and he spent less time focussing on his breathing exercises. His return to base was celebrated with drinks in the USC base club Untied. Team 6 was on its seventh shot, when Vice Admiral Hunt approached, with an older, chubbier Ambassador Clegg.

Skylark's grin slipped when he saw the vice admiral approach. Jack looked over. "Brass-hole alert," she told the rest. The team gave a collective groan and Skylark stood. With neither himself nor the vice admiral in uniform, he was under no obligation to salute. He instead extended his hand to Hunt.

"Vice Admiral," he greeted. Hunt took it with a tight smile.

"Commander Skye. You remember Ambassador Clegg, don't you?"

"Yes," Skylark said. He extended his hand to the ambassador. "How is Gabriella?"

Ambassador Clegg smiled and shook the offered hand. "She'll be thrilled to know you remembered her name, Commander." He pulled a small photo of Gabriella from his back pocket and handed it to Skylark. He took it and smiled.

"She's a beautiful girl, sir." He handed the photo back.

"She is," Ambassador Clegg said. "In school in Switzerland at the moment."

"Switzerland?"

"Yes. An all-girl's boarding school. I didn't want her having any distractions from her studies."

Jack snorted into her beer and tried to cover it up by taking a long swig.

"I see," Skylark said, smiling at Jack despite himself. "Would you like to join us? I'm afraid we're already fairly gone, but we can catch you up, Ambassador."

Clegg smiled graciously. "That's kind, but no. I'm actually here to inform you that Fisher has managed to convince the Council to extend diplomatic relations to the daemon. They are anxious to get it over with as soon as possible."

"Ah."

"Party is over, gentlemen," Hunt said.

"Fuck you," Jack whispered. Hunt could not hear it over the music. Binky did hear. He coughed in an effort to disguise his laugh.

"You leave for Gate Compound 19 at 0800."

"Yes, sir," Skylark said. "All right everyone, last call. Bed in thirty."

"Thank you, Commander," Clegg said.

Skylark smiled at him. "Always a pleasure, Ambassador. Vice Admiral."

"Commander," Hunt said. He turned and led the ambassador out of the club.

"Ugh, I hate that man," Jack said. She stood and held up her beer. "Everyone up. First to finish gets the loser's breakfast."

Everyone stood, clutching their beers.

"Ready? One... two... go!"

Everyone save Skylark chugged what remained of their alcohol. Jack finished first, Doorman second and, in a surprise move, Binky last.

"Hah!" Jack said. "I get your breakfast."

"Skylark isn't finished!" Binky protested.

"He wasn't playing."

"Yes, I was," Skylark said. He put his beer down, unfinished. "Let's go."

The team walked from the club as upright as they could manage. Doorman had to help Spike, who kept listing to the right, and Binky weaved dangerously with every step. At the door to the club, Jack ran back to the table, chugged Skylark's beer, then ran to rejoin the group.

Morning was unkind to Team 6. They sat in miserable silence at the table nearest the door. The lights in the mess had headache-inducing rainbow halos that could only be seen by Team 6, and the din of the servicemen and women at breakfast ricocheted from every possible surface, landing painfully against their eardrums. Recruits served breakfast quickly, rushing between tables with plates of food. Skylark slid his over to Jack, who shrugged and emptied it onto her own.

Despite their wretched state, the team was armed and waiting for transport before the ambassador even arrived. Skylark raised his brows in greeting as the ambassador approached the platform alone.

"What happened to the militia, sir?"

"They're already at the compound, Commander," Clegg said. "I sent them ahead a few days ago."

"Ah."

"Ambassador, Commander," the docking administrator said. "We're ready to go."

"Thank you," Skylark said. He turned to his team. "Everyone in."

Team 6 entered the transport.

"After you, Ambassador," Skylark said.

"Thank you."

Without Christie to drive, the trip to the compound took the full two hours. After travelling in silence, the shuttle hatch opened to utter chaos. Medics in bloodied robes ran helter-skelter through the docking bay.

Team 6 and Ambassador Clegg were met at the dock by Canadian Army Captain Moore. He saluted smartly.

"Ambassador. Commander."

"At ease, Captain," Skylark said. "What the hell's going on here?"

"We were attacked last night, sir," the Captain said. "Muties tested the fence. Some got into the city. They didn't last long, but long enough to do some damage. Civilians, mostly."

"Where is Major Hallow?"

The captain hesitated. "He was bitten in the fight, sir."

Skylark straightened. "What? Where is he?"

"Medical, sir, but—"

Skylark turned to Ambassador Clegg. "Sir, permission to—"

"Go on, Commander. The mission will have to wait a while anyway."

With a brief nod, Skylark turned back to Binky, who said, "Got it, sir." He assumed command of Team 6 in Skylark's absence. Skylark brushed past the captain, who watched on with a displeased frown. Skylark outranked him, however, and he could do nothing to stop the man.

"Tell us where you want us, Captain," Binky said.

Medical was mayhem. Skylark's presence was largely ignored as medics rushed through the building from one case to the next. Skylark had to take one by the arm and haul her out of her run in order to be heard.

"Where is Major Hallow?" he demanded of her.

"Ward A, Room 7, sir," she said. She scurried off.

Vaguely familiar with the medical facility at the compound, Skylark found his way easily enough. Ward A was practically deserted, save for the bodies resting in the cots. Each room had four patients, almost all unconscious. Major Hallow had Room 7 all to himself. Skylark entered and went to the major's bedside. Frank Hallow had an IV drip and a machine designed to clean and recirculate his blood, but the major's black lips and tortured breath gave fact to the severity of his condition.

Sensing a presence, the major stirred. He opened his eyes.

"Sir," Skylark greeted.

"For God's sake," Frank said. "You outrank me now, Skye. I'm the one who should be saying 'sir.'"

"I give you leave to call me Ben," Skylark said, smiling slightly.

Frank laughed, which soon turned into a protracted, hacking cough. "I should stop smoking," Frank said, smiling. "It's going to kill me one day."

Skylark flashed a smile.

"They've been testing the fence for weeks," Frank said. "They're not just mindless freaks anymore, Skye. They're something else entirely."

Skylark nodded. "I noticed the last time," he said.

Frank reached up and Skylark took his hand.

"You look well," Frank said. "I'm glad."

He started coughing again. Skylark placed a hand on his shoulder.

"Stop fussing!" Frank grumbled.

"Yes, sir," Skylark said.

Frank laughed, then coughed. When the fit passed, he looked at Skylark. "Heard you had a run-in with Hunt."

"You could say that," Skylark admitted.

"The man's a prick. Always has been."

Skylark smiled.

"You impressed Captain Gergiev on S8-09. That's good. He's a good man. You'll want him on your side if you're going to butt heads with Hunt."

"I got the impression the captain did not much like me."

Frank laughed and coughed. "He likes to piss people off, Commander. He has a theory that people will show their true colours when they're drunk or angry. Angry is more fun than drunk for him, I guess." Frank started wheezing.

"Ben," he said.

Skylark shook his head. "You should rest, sir."

"Time's up for me, Ben," Frank said with a sad smile. "I want you to know what I said was true. I am proud of you. So proud."

Skylark's voice shook when he spoke. "Thank you, sir."

"Ben?"

"Sir?" Skylark frowned down at the major. "Sir?"

A blue light above the major's bed started flashing and a team of four medics rushed into the room. Skylark was pushed out, and so stood at the observation window as the medics fought to revive the major. After close to ten minutes of trying, the medics stood back. One looked at his watch, noted the time and left the room. He stopped moments before crashing into Skylark, as if he did not notice the broad-shouldered man in USC Strategic armour. Their eyes locked and the medic's face softened.

"I'm sorry," he said before moving on.

Skylark turned back to the window as the medics covered the major over with a sheet. One medic joined him at the window.

"He was a stubborn bastard, you know," the medic said. "He fought the night through after being bitten instead of coming straight to Medical. Saved an entire quadrant practically by himself. We could have saved him, but he got here too late."

Skylark said nothing. He stared at the sheet-covered bed.

"You're Commander Skye."

"Yes," Skylark answered absently.

"He spoke highly of you, Commander. I'm Michael Hallow." The medic offered Skylark his hand.

"Hallow?"

"His son, yeah."

"I'm sorry," Skylark said.

The medic smiled sadly. "Yeah. So am I. But, he'd have been pleased with all this. I have a feeling he didn't want to die a doddering old man in a home. He might even get a statue out of it."

Skylark smiled a little. He turned to the medic. "I could use a drink."

"Good, because my shift just ended and I'm parched."

Skylark found the ambassador later that night in Major Hallow's old office, yelling at Hallow's replacement.

"You have no idea how delicate this situation is!" he yelled. "You can't just start dropping bombs all over!"

"I have a population to protect," the major yelled back. "And I don't care if I take down a few daemon doing it!"

"You might regret it later," Skylark noted calmly from the door. He leant one shoulder on the doorframe and casually crossed his ankles.

"And who the hell are you?" the Canadian Army Major demanded.

"It's 'who the hell are you, sir,'" Skylark said. It was then the major noticed the stripes on Commander Skye's armoured shoulder.

"Yes, sir. Sorry, sir," he said immediately, standing to attention.

"At ease," Skylark said. "Now what appears to be the issue?"

"Sir, I've been ordered to bomb the mutie territory, sir."

"The scope goes well beyond their territory, Major. If the daemon are bombed, it's going to make it a whole lot more difficult to acquire their help," Clegg said.

"Help for what?" the major demanded, agitated again.

"That's classified," Skylark said. "But trust me, we're going to want the daemon on our side. So you're not going to bomb anything until we've spoken with them."

"Sir, if the muties attack again—"

"Thanks to the Council's generous reinforcements, you have double the personnel Hallow had. He managed to keep the city. If you feel you cannot do the same, I suggest you relinquish your command to someone more capable."

The major straightened.

"Now, you will refrain from bombing anything until the ambassador and I return from daemon territory."

"And in the likely event you don't return, sir?"

"Then I'll be dead, and I won't give a shit what you do. Are we going to have a problem?"

"No, sir."

"Good. Ambassador, I have been informed that the rest of the teams have arrived. I plan to have us out at dawn. I can walk you to your quarters if you like."

"Thank you, Commander." The ambassador shot a poisonous look at the major as he passed him and exited the office. Skylark nodded at the red-faced man standing in the office. "Major." And he left.

"Where have you been?" Clegg demanded as Skylark joined him in the hall. "I could have used that rescue an hour ago."

"Drinking," Skylark said.

"The major?"

Skylark pressed his lips into a thin line and shook his head.

"I'm sorry. I understood that he was quite fond of you."

Skylark shrugged. They continued in silence until the ambassador was delivered to his quarters. They said a brief goodnight, and Commander Skye retired to his quarters. He didn't bother taking off his armour. He sat on the bed, leant his head against the cool steel wall and waited.

The ambassador sat hunched over in the armoured personnel carrier, brooding. The daemon were notably hostile to any incursions into their territory. The likelihood that the entire operation would be for nothing and every party member involved killed on sight was high. Still, this was the best way to try and establish a functional, if not friendly, alliance with the daemon.

Hovering over the ground with a dull hum, the transporter matched the achingly slow pace of the British Army infantry that surrounded it. Inside the hold was a sealed container, containing the larval remains found inside the only unopened egg on Way Station S8-09.

Commanders Wheeler and Skye led the sizeable party through the streets of mutant territory. Skylark could feel the hostile gazes of the mutants as the group moved in the sunlight.

"Movement in the east," Wheeler reported.

"I see it," Skylark answered. "Keep sharp, everyone. These bastards have grown brains. Let's hope they're still allergic to the sun."

"Comforting," Jack said over the comm.

Skylark grinned. He turned his helmeted head in time to see something scurry between buildings. He shuddered. The pace was slow but steady and they reached their destination in five hours.

"Where is this symbol supposed to be?" Wheeler asked.

"The window," Skylark answered, looking at the hole where once the painted window had been.

"That one you're looking at?"

"The one that's not there anymore?" Skylark said. "Yup."

"Not a good sign."

"Nope." Skylark approached the building slowly. Something growled. He stopped and stepped back, lifting his weapon. Something moved at the door, and the slippery flash of two large eyes told him it was a mutant.

"It's a mutie," he said.

"Well, great. Did they get the daemon, then?" Binky asked over the comm.

"They'd have done us a favour," someone from Team 40 answered.

"Gods, I hope not," Skylark said. "We'll try for the apartment."

"Think she'll be there, Commander?" Jack asked.

"I hope so, because I'm all out of locations."

The envoy moved forward, following Skylark's lead to the apartment building where they had once been held captive. Though none of the windows were smashed, the place looked deserted.

"Maybe she's out shopping?" Binky offered helpfully.

Skylark halted the envoy and he and Wheeler approached the building. Sneaking a glance in through the front door, Skylark noted that it looked clear. Nodding at Wheeler, Skylark waited for him to open the door. They entered. Halfway up the stairs, the door slammed shut, pushed by the clawed hand of a mutant.

"Contact!" Wheeler shouted, firing at the creature.

Suddenly the place was flooded with mutants. Wheeler cleared a path to the door with a spray of bullets, but Skylark was cut off. Wheeler turned to help.

"Go!" Skylark yelled. "Go! Go!" He kicked in the nearest door and entered the apartment, which housed yet more mutants.

Wheeler, knowing he could not help Skylark, sprinted down the stairs and out of the building, trying to draw at least some of them off. The envoy opened fire on the first floor the moment Wheeler was clear. Seconds later, the second floor window shattered. Skylark tumbled out, a mutant clinging stubbornly to his armour. He rolled into the sun in an effort to shake the beast. Its skin smoked, but it hardly seemed to notice. It sat on his chest and scratched desperately at his helmet. Skylark elbowed it in the face and seconds later, a glowing blue blade burst through its chest.

The mutant keeled over. In its place, a tall daemon stood, glowering down at Skylark, its eyes glowing blue. Two glowing blades protruded from its wrists, crackling with electric heat. The daemon snarled something at Skylark, picking him up and holding him high.

"Hold your fire!" Skylark snapped over the comm. when the envoy reacted.

"Sir?" Jack asked.

"I said hold your damned fire!"

A group of seven daemon, more than enough to cut through their group of thirty, surrounded the envoy. The mutants that had been tracking the party had fled. The daemon holding Skylark aloft reached up and took a hold of Skylark's helmet. It snarled something again and started to squeeze. Skylark struggled against the pressure.

"Ben?" Wheeler said.

"Hold your fire!" Skylark said again.

A loud barking command from another daemon drew everyone's

attention. The daemon holding Skylark stopped squeezing. There was a brief argument, then the daemon holding Skylark tossed him to the ground. Wheeler ran to his position and dragged him out of reach before helping him to his feet.

"You all right?" he asked.

"Fine, I think," Skylark answered, struggling to keep his feet. "Team 6, weapons down."

"I don't think that's a good idea, sir," Doorman said.

"I said, weapons down." He slowly placed his own gun on the ground and straightened. Very hesitantly the rest of Team 6 did the same.

"Are you sure that's a good idea?" Wheeler said.

"Nope. If this doesn't work, Wheeler, you get everyone out of here. You understand?"

"What are you going to do, Skye?"

"Attempt to make peace." Skylark took a step forward, then removed his helmet.

"Skye," Wheeler said, his tone informing Skylark that the commander of Team 87 did not think much of this plan.

The daemon who had grabbed Skylark snarled and the blades at his wrists lengthened. Skylark stopped walking forward. He spread his arms with his palms facing out, indicating he was unarmed.

Jack removed her helmet as well. Taking their cue, the rest of Team 6 removed theirs.

The daemon said something and raised his arm to strike. Skylark closed his eyes, waiting for his head to be lopped off, but a rapid movement and a heavy thud forced them open again. One daemon had taken Skylark's would-be executioner to the ground, and now stood defensively between him and Skylark, saying something. Its deep voice growled a low threat. Another argument ensued, but at length, the protective daemon won. The first daemon stormed off. The other turned to face the commander.

Commander Skye let out a shaky breath.

"You stupid," the daemon said. He narrowed his eyes. "But brave. Why come?"

"We are escorting an ambassador," Skylark said, turning back to indicate the hovercraft.

The daemon cocked his head with a frown. "No good," he said. "Don't speak."

Skylark smiled. "We need to speak with the tehoros."

The daemon blinked. He bent down and looked Skylark in the eye. It was then that Skylark noticed the blue hue of the daemon's eyes was nearly a match for his own.

"Tehoros gone," the daemon said slowly.

"What?" Skylark was genuinely surprised. "What happened?"

The daemon shrugged. "Don't know. Went." The daemon indicated a walk with two fingers of his right hand. "Never came back. Poof. Disappeared. We thought you."

Skylark swallowed. "No. It wasn't us," he said. He was not likely to have any familiar faces at this meeting. It would be an issue. "His daughter?"

"Daughter?" The daemon straightened and pondered on Skylark's meaning a while. "Ah! Girl-child. Daughter, yes?"

Skylark nodded. "Yes."

"Daughter Tahorah now." The daemon puffed up with pride. "Strong! Brave! You see her, yes?"

"If she will. Yes."

"Come. I take you. Bring ambassador. And only—" The daemon lost the ability to talk and simply mimed the removing of helmets. Skylark nodded in understanding.

"Team 6," he said. "That means you."

Jack reached down to pick up her gun, but the daemon put up his hands. "No weapons. Weapons bad. Meaning death. No weapons."

"Put it down, Jack," Skylark said.

"Yes, sir," she said. She let go of the gun slowly and stood, offering a small, sheepish smile.

"Transport, you still good to drive?" Skylark asked into the comm. link at his chest.

"Good as gold, sir," the driver said. "But I'm sure going to miss the escort."

"You and me both." Skylark turned to Wheeler. "You get everyone to safety."

"Yes, Commander."

"I'll see you soon."

"I sure as hell hope so." Wheeler and Skylark grasped hands momentarily before Skylark turned away.

"All right, Team 6. Let's go."

The transport floated away from the group and Team 6 took up position in a protective circle around it. The daemon formed a circle around them and they marched forward. The long strides of the tall daemon meant Team 6 and the transporter had to jog to keep up. The daemon who had spoken to Skylark kept looking back. At length Skylark spoke up.

"Why do you keep looking at me?"

"You are Chieftain, yes? Came for lost girl, yes?"

Skylark blinked in surprise. "Yes," he said guardedly.

"Your face is known to us."

"How?"

The daemon grinned. "Tehoros showed. He said you sad."

"What's that supposed to mean?" Binky said.

Skylark shrugged. "We must look pretty pathetic," he said. "The tallest of us only comes up to their shoulders."

Binky grunted and fell back.

"Is sad bad?" the daemon asked, after noting the exchange.

"Depends," Skylark said.

"What is 'depends?'"

Skylark opened his mouth to try and explain, but found he could not without a reference, so he moved his hands up and down like an old-fashioned weigh scale, hoping that would be sufficient. It was not. The daemon scowled.

"Tahorah explain," he muttered.

Skylark grinned. "Let's hope," he answered.

It was another two hours of travel through the eerie abandoned city before the team crested a hill at the city's edge. The daemon citadel rose from the plains that began at the base of the hill. A landed daemon spaceship sat in plain view. The citadel was a massive, conical creation surrounded by lush gardens. A thick forest stood to one side. Beyond it spread a plain upon which a large herd of bison grazed. From the grass on the plain rose the ruins of several buildings, now nothing more than twisted metal spires covered in vines.

"Whoa," Binky said. "Unexpected."

"Come," the daemon said. "Almost home."

"It's beautiful," Jack murmured.

They marched down the steep slope into the valley. As they entered the carefully tended gardens, daemon straightened from their work and blinked in surprise at the new arrivals.

At the entrance to the grounded spaceship, the daemon in charge was stopped and questioned closely. The two daemon guards, wearing armour that was similar in function, if not design, to the USC Strategic armour, peered closely at Commander Skye.

"Famous across species," Binky said, patting Skylark on the shoulder. "You dog."

Skylark smirked. "I'm not entirely sure that's a good thing."

After a long conversation, the daemon leading the group turned.

"They want open ambassador."

Skylark frowned. "What? Oh! No, that's not the ambassador. That's the transporter."

"Not ambassador? But you said—"

Skylark smiled. He turned to the transport. "Open up," he said.

Hearing a driver sigh over the comm. turned Skylark's smile into a smirk. The side of the transporter slid open. Ambassador Clegg nervously stepped out. Skylark indicated for him to approach. Blinking in the sudden light of day, Clegg straightened, fixed his suit and walked forward. He smiled, but Skylark could detect uncertainty behind the smile.

"This," Skylark said, "is the ambassador."

The daemon cocked his head, then lowered himself down to look the ambassador in the eye. "Ambassador title?" he asked, looking back at Skylark.

"Yes."

"Ah." The two guards had gone to the transporter and were now peering inside. One pulled his head out and wrinkled his nose. "Man stink," he said. Then he said something rapidly in his language and pointed inside the transporter.

"What is box?" the daemon translated.

"It contains a specimen," Skylark said. "That we think you should see."

The daemon scowled. "No good," he said, plainly frustrated. The guards expected an answer. So the daemon spoke again. "Is it bad?"

"Very," Skylark replied. "But it is not dangerous." He spoke slowly.

The daemon nodded slowly and translated what he thought he understood to the guards. The guards narrowed their eyes. After a pause, one spoke. The daemon standing with Skylark nodded.

"Only ambassador and chief," he said. "Others stay."

"Hell no," Binky said.

"Binky," Skylark said.

"Nuh-uh. I am not letting you in there without someone watching your back."

"I'll be fine Binky. I'll leave the comm. on. You'll be able to hear everything."

"I don't like it."

"Neither do I, but it's not like we have much of a choice now, is it?" Skylark turned back to the daemon and nodded.

"Come, then. Others—" the daemon scratched his head, then waved his hand vaguely in the air. "Laze."

Skylark turned to Binky and grinned. "You heard the man. Laze." And then he was off, following the daemon and the ambassador into the citadel.

11

A thin strip of blue-coloured grass divided the ramp into the daemon spaceship-turned-citadel in half. Skylark noted it in silence, curious as to how the alien grass could possibly survive in such a high traffic area, let alone the journey through space the daemon took to get here.

It took Skylark a moment to adjust to the dim light of the interior of the citadel. When his eyes found focus again, he thought he was staring into a cave. The interior of the ship appeared to be sculpted clay with strange, alien plants hanging from various crevices. Bioluminescent blob-like creatures provided much of the lighting, along with two large windows further in. They wandered over the ceiling trailing glowing, mucus-laden arcs. Skylark watched them a moment as he walked, almost tripping over his own feet in the process.

Inside, a large gathering of daemon were having what appeared to be a heated discussion. The daemon leading the ambassador and commander motioned for them to stop. He listened in on the argument a while before turning to Skylark.

"You stay," he said. "I must go—" He clicked fingers as he scrambled for the correct word. "Pronounce!" The daemon flashed a quick smile, pleased with himself, and vanished into the crowd.

"I think he meant announce," the ambassador said.

"I wasn't about to correct him. Were you?"

"No. I suppose not."

Skylark observed the scene a moment. The tall, muscular daemon were clustered together, but obviously divided into two camps, each side screaming at the other. If there was some kind of arbiter for this discussion, they were nowhere in sight.

The daemon who had led Skylark and the ambassador to the citadel disappeared into the crush of angry daemon bodies. The argument continued for a moment longer before an eerie hush fell over the group. One by one, the daemon turned to peer at the intruders standing awkwardly at the top of the ramp.

The daemon who had led the humans reappeared.

"Tahorah will see you," he said. "Come."

"Lead the way, sir," Skylark said.

Swallowing hard, Ambassador Clegg walked forward, Skylark half a step behind at his right shoulder. Knowing the highly skilled soldier in thick USC armour was nearby gave the ambassador courage to walk tall as the sea of daemon parted before him, their glowing blue eyes fixed upon him and their expressions openly hostile.

At last, the daemon who led them stood aside, revealing the woman who had once occupied the apartment from which Skylark had narrowly escaped some hours before. Skylark recognized her long, raven black hair and ghostly white skin. Her frame looked impossibly small and frail compared to the company she kept. Red lips pursed as she cocked her head, and violet eyes sparkled with a mixture of mischief and curiosity as she watched the two men approach.

She looked familiar, but a great deal had changed, as well.

Her left cheek now sported an angry red line; a scar newly healed. And she now wore the same golden, broken circlet her father once had. How it remained on her head was a mystery to Skylark; the two halves of the broken circlet did not touch at either the front or the back.

Two gold rings, much smaller than her father's had been, dominated her unclothed forearm. Her clothing might well have come from any store in the free world; tall boots worn over trousers and a sleeveless, form-fitting top, though the materials were not the synthetics typical of most, save the most expensive, fashions.

Standing before a roughly hewn stone table, the tahorah watched their approach with interest, but declined to speak until well after the silence became uncomfortable.

"You are not expected," she said, her accent light and lilting.

"We apologize if it is inconvenient," Ambassador Clegg replied smoothly.

The tahorah cocked her head to the side and assessed the ambassador. Her piercing gaze made the tall, greying man nervous. He fought the nerves but could not hide the slight sift of weight that belied his racing pulse.

"Your ship is interesting," the ambassador said.

"The lower floor of the citadel was built to mimic the homes of the daemon. The upper sections are," she cocked her head the other way, "more functional."

"I see." Hoping to pick up some cues as to how he was supposed to behave, the ambassador paused. When the pause became oppressive, he said, "Well, let's get to the business at hand, shall we?"

The tahorah raised her hand, silencing him. "I will not treat with you," she said. "You lost your own daughter. I cannot trust such a man."

"How did you know...?" Ambassador Clegg asked.

"If your species was hoping to begin on good terms, they would send Gabriella's father. His thanks would, perhaps, mollify the rage the daemon feel against your kind. It is also, I think, why they sent the chief, since his face is known to us."

Skylark smiled slightly. "Clever," he said beneath his breath.

"Also," the tahorah continued. "She has your eyes."

Ambassador Clegg smiled slightly. "You flatter me. Nothing so beautiful came from me. She looks like her mother."

The tahorah cocked her head again. Her bird-like mannerisms and exotic appearance brought to Skylark's mind images of a bird of paradise. The keen intellect behind her violet eyes, however, gave her a decidedly corvid air.

"I, uh—" Ambassador reached into his pocket. "This is highly irregular, I know," he said. "But she made me swear I would give you this." He extended his hand, now holding a school photograph of Gabriella.

One of the daemon snatched it from him, looked down at it, then passed it to the tahorah. The woman took it. Her features softened the moment she saw Gabriella's image smiling back at her.

"She has grown," she said softly.

"Yes," Ambassador Clegg said.

The woman looked up at the ambassador again.

"She often spoke of you," Clegg said. "She told me you were the most beautiful woman she'd ever seen. I can see she was not exaggerating."

The tahorah frowned slightly, then smiled. "Tell me, Ambassador," she said. "Are your women easily susceptible to flattery? Can they not see it for what it is?"

Ambassador Clegg had no answer. He stared at the woman, who folded her arms and stared back at him expectantly. Skylark would be lying to himself if he did not admit that he enjoyed seeing the politician squirm in discomfort. Having heard enough of his silence and his discomfort, the tahorah leant back on the desk.

"I will not treat with you," she repeated. "But I do not think you would have risked your life in daemon territory if your message was not of vital importance. Therefore, I will treat with the chief."

All eyes fell on Skylark, who stood stunned. It was his turn to feel intensely uncomfortable.

"Uh," he said. "I am not a diplomat."

"Good," the tahorah said. "I have little patience for meaningless flattery and less patience for lies and intrigue. A soldier does not mince his words. Step forward."

Glancing briefly at the ambassador, who nodded, Skylark moved forward, acutely aware that all the hostility in the room was now directed at him. After a moment of the tahorah's discomforting assessment, she beckoned him closer.

"Come," she said.

One of the daemon growled something quietly at her, but she dismissed his concerns with an easy wave. The daemon stepped back but kept his narrowed eyes on Skylark. The tahorah led Skylark to the back of the room, where a grand double staircase led upwards to a balcony. Without hesitating, the tahorah walked up the stairs.

Skylark followed, wanting desperately to ask questions, but sensing it would not be appropriate to speak now. The air at the top of the stairs shimmered slightly. The tahorah passed through without hesitation. Skylark did hesitate. He stared at the shimmering air before him, lost in the rainbows that flickered across the space.

Sensing Skylark was no longer behind her, the tahorah turned. She placed one hand on her hip and arched her brows at him. Smiling slightly, Skylark stepped through.

The balcony served as a divider between the meeting hall and an extraordinary garden. Bioluminescent plants filled the dark cavern-like space, some sharing surprisingly similar forms with plant life native to Earth. Bioluminescent, six-winged butterflies flitted between the glowing flowers.

"Those in the hall, they can see us," the tahorah said quietly, staring out over the garden. "But they will not be able to hear us. Our conversation will be private."

"Not quite," Skylark said. He tapped the comm. link in his ear, smiled and disconnected it. "There. Now it will."

The tahorah smiled. She turned back to the garden in silence. After a moment, she glanced across at Skylark, who had become absorbed by the garden.

"You wear new stripes, Chieftain," she said, tapping on Skylark's armoured shoulder.

"So do you," Skylark said. He reached out and briefly touched the tahorah's scarred cheek, pulling back his hand rapidly so the touch did not look like a caress.

"Keeping the tribes in line has been..." She paused and tilted her head. "A battle."

Skylark nodded. "I heard your father has disappeared."

"Yes? Well, the majan talks too much."

Skylark laughed a little. They both watched the garden.

"We thought that perhaps it was your people," the tahorah said.

"It wasn't us," Skylark answered.

"That you know."

The commander nodded. "That I know."

"It has been two and a half years. Every day I awake hoping I will see him again. Every day I am disappointed. But I cannot help but hope." The tahorah sighed. "I do not think that your people have him, with your knowledge or otherwise. If so, why would you wait so long to make your demands? No. He is gone elsewhere."

"Have you perhaps... have you given thought to the—"

"To what? Your not-humans between your fence and the citadel?" The tahorah looked down at her hands. "He would not have gone there alone. He was stubborn, and very proud. But he was not stupid."

"But they might have…"

"I have thought it too," the tahorah admitted. "But we could find nothing to say it was so. His disappearance is a mystery."

"I'm sorry."

"You sound genuine. He mentioned you, you know. Some months after you returned to the fence."

Skylark raised his eyebrows.

"You should be flattered. It means you were on his mind for months. He does not speak of anything he has not thoroughly thought through. He would say things seemingly out of the blue weeks even months after the discussion on the subject had closed. It would drive my mother insane."

"And what did he say?"

"'The chief is sad.'"

Skylark scowled. "There is something he said to me, that night. It's meaning has plagued me ever since."

"What was it?"

"'I have seen you.'"

The tahorah smiled. "Ah. There are several meanings for that. There is, as you would recognize, that he sees you standing there. He has noticed you and knows of your presence. It could be that he has guessed your motives, though you've tried to disguise them. But I suspect that he meant neither."

"What did he mean, then?"

"That he sees you," the tahorah said. She smiled when Skylark pressed his lips into a thin line. "I cannot explain what it means except to say that it goes deeper than seeing with your eyes. It's seeing with your heart into another's heart."

"That still means nothing," Skylark said with a smile. "But I appreciate the effort."

The tahorah laughed. "Perhaps one day you will understand."

"I doubt I have that depth." Skylark met her gaze and found himself trapped in it. Her violet eyes held him in thrall. Though he knew that staring so long was rude, he found he could not turn aside. It was the same intriguing, captivating gaze as the tehoros had possessed. It slowly dawned on him that the tahorah was attempting to "see" him in the way her father had. He broke his gaze and turned back to the garden, feeling suddenly drained.

"Why have you come, Chieftain?"

"Chieftain," he echoed, smiling softly. "That's a new one. Majan called me that."

"The majan," the tahorah corrected gently. "It is a title, not a name."

"Oh. My apologies. What is his name?"

The tahorah looked sidelong at Skylark and shook her head. "It is not for me to tell."

Skylark frowned at her. "I don't understand."

"Names are sacred amongst the daemon, Commander. They are not given, but earned."

Skylark turned and looked over the garden again. "Bennejin," he said suddenly. "My name. It's Bennejin Skye. Formally, I would be Commander Bennejin Skye. Most everyone calls me Skylark, though. A very few call me Ben." He turned to face the tahorah, who looked at him with her head cocked to the side, a slight frown on her face.

"You saved a lost girl from the muties," he said softly. "Then you saved me from your very irate father, and helped ensure that my team and I, and that little girl, got home safely. I think you've earned my name."

The tahorah smiled. It was a genuine smile, one that lit her violet eyes and sent them sparkling in the dim light of the bioluminescent garden. "I am flattered, Commander," she said, matching his soft tone. "But, I believe, such was your intent."

Skylark grinned suddenly. "You are a difficult woman to fool."

"And you are an easy man to read. Yet I find myself inexplicably willing to hear your cause."

Her saucy smile made Skylark laugh. "Then why do I feel like I'm the one being played?" His smile slipped a little. "What you said was true, though. We do come on vitally important business."

"Then state it, and let's return to the awaiting crowd, who must by now be surely wondering what it is we are saying."

With a sigh, Skylark turned his back on the garden. He leant against the rails and folded his arms. "Two weeks ago, our outermost way station was attacked."

"Way station?"

"They're artificial wormhole generators. They can facilitate the rapid transit of star ships through these wormholes pretty much anywhere we want in the galaxy. What used to take years now only takes hours. Way Station S8-09 was on the outermost stretch of our galaxy, and was being fitted to create longer, larger wormholes so that we might start exploring other galaxies."

"And it was destroyed?"

"No. Everything remains intact. But all three thousand and some souls on board were killed."

"And you thought it was the daemon?"

Skylark shook his head. "No. Not from what I saw. Though, I will freely admit that the Council did not see it that way at first."

"You were there, Commander?"

Commander Sky nodded. "Some time after the attack." He closed his eyes briefly and declined to speak more.

"Do you have some idea as to who attacked you?"

"A very vague idea of what," Skylark said. "But it's more a concept at the moment. Honestly, we were hoping that you might be able to shed some more light on whom, or rather, what did this. The ambassador has a file with all the data we've managed to compile from our visit to the station. Will you look at it?"

"I do not like that man," she said, pursing her lips.

"I don't blame you. He's a politician. But he knows what the Council wants. I'm just here to try and make sure he doesn't get killed."

"You do not know what your own council wants?"

"I know only what I'm paid to know, Tahorah."

"Your people's secrecy is troubling," she said.

"Yes," Skylark agreed. "It is."

The tahorah sighed. "Very well. I will listen to your ambassador. But I have one request, Commander."

Skylark raised his eyebrows at her.

"You tell me the truth. Always."

"I have thus far."

"I will have your word, Commander."

Their eyes met again. Again it felt as if Skylark was plummeting into her gaze only to drown in a sea of purple. It was as if his very soul was trying to claw its way out of his body through his eyes so that it might find a new home in the tahorah. The sensation very nearly overwhelmed Skylark and his knees buckled slightly. The tahorah broke her gaze.

"You have my word, Tahorah," Skylark croaked.

Satisfied, the tahorah led the way back to the meeting chamber. The ambassador cast an enquiring look at Skylark, who could only shrug at him.

"Ambassador," the tahorah said brusquely. "I have been convinced by the commander that you have come with important information that I ought to hear. He also assures me you are a man of worth, who values your word."

Ambassador Clegg glanced at Skylark, who kept his face impassive. "Yes," he said at length.

"You should know, the daemon are not fond of you and your kind. Play them false, and they will happily obliterate you."

The ambassador blinked in surprise, then scowled. "It is generally thought unwise to begin diplomatic relations with a threat," he said.

"That particular crown belongs on your head, ambassador," the tahorah replied.

"I beg your pardon? You invaded!"

"The daemon came looking for aid. For three days they waited for you, the host, to approach. You sent missiles as your emissaries, Ambassador."

The ambassador took a deep breath to calm his temper. "The war was regrettable," he said.

The tahorah raised her eyebrows but declined to comment. Instead, she waited for the ambassador to collect his thoughts and begin his speech.

"I... we recently lost over three thousand people in an unexpected stealth attack on our outermost post. I will not lie. At first the Council thought that the daemon were responsible. But after Commander Skye and his teams returned, we realized that the attack was perpetrated by someone or something else; something we are entirely unfamiliar with." The ambassador produced a small tablet from his pocket. He keyed in his code and set the tablet on the table in front of the tahorah. A holograph immediately began displaying the images the scientist and teams had taken while on S8-09.

"What you're seeing are images from the station."

"What is that?" the tahorah asked, pointing at one photo that was almost entirely pink.

"Skin," the ambassador said. "The crew of the station were flayed. Their skin was pulped and mixed with digestive juices, then used to line almost every surface inside the station."

The tahorah's eyes grew wide. She looked at Skylark. "Is this so, Commander?"

"I'm assuming so," he said. "I am not a scientist. I didn't analyze the stuff. But it sure felt like skin walking on it."

The tahorah returned her attention to the ambassador. "Continue."

"The largest room in the station," Ambassador Clegg explained as the image flashed up. "It was converted into a hatchery. The majority of the crew were found there, stripped to the bone and hung upside down from the ceiling. We're thinking we are dealing with an insectoid race and were wondering if your people have any dealings with something similar."

The tahorah scowled, searching her mind. "I have no memory of such things."

"We have the remains of one the creatures in its larval stage. It was very near hatching, we think. Perhaps seeing it would help?"

"Perhaps. Show me."

Skylark plugged in his comm. "Binky, bring in the box."

"Yes, sir."

Moments later, the rest of Team 6 entered, carrying the coffin-sized box on their shoulders. They lowered it gently and opened it. The escaping cold air from the box flowed over the edges in a sinking cloud of vapour. Curious, the gathered daemon stepped closer, vying with one another for a good look. Taking the corners of the fabric wrap that covered the larva, Team 6 lifted the creature out and laid it on the ground. They flipped the material open.

The daemon stepped backwards in unison when the translucent beetle-like creature was revealed. All except the tahorah. She rolled her eyes and muttered something darkly beneath her breath. Skylark tried to conceal his smile at her derisive tone by turning his head and bringing his hand to his mouth to cough.

Approaching cautiously, the tahorah touched the thing with the toe of her boot. She knelt down for a closer look.

"'I'll keep the comm. on,' huh?" Binky muttered as he took a place next to Skylark.

"Sorry," Skylark said.

"It has teeth," the tahorah said after a careful examination.

"Yes," the ambassador said. "Most of them sharp, indicating that they're likely predators."

"It is taller than I."

"Not difficult," Skylark said.

Everyone turned to look at him in surprise. Despite the fact that he had spoken truly—the tahorah was surprisingly petite, coming up to Skylark's cheek at most—saying anything was stepping farther out of bounds than usual.

If the tahorah found it rude, she did not say so. She flashed a quick smile, then stood. She frowned.

"I am sorry, Ambassador. I do not know this creature."

"Ragnar," someone said from the back.

Everyone turned and an elderly daemon woman walked proudly forward, leaning heavily on a cane. The daemon respectfully stood aside as the daemon woman marched through. Deeply scarred and ancient, and standing taller than many of the daemon men, Skylark guessed that she was a war hero. The ancient daemon stopped and pointed the butt of her cane at the larva.

"Ragnar," she said again.

"Ragnar?" the ambassador asked. He looked to the tahorah, who frowned deeply.

"The memories I have are vague at best. The name is mentioned in children's songs, and perhaps a story where a ragnar queen tries to trap children, but there are no descriptions of them and there is nothing of them being real in my ancestral memory."

"Ancestral memory?" Skylark asked.

The tahorah smiled at him. "Yes, the memory each of us are born with. For the daemon, it can stretch back as far as a hundred generations, depending on the lineage."

"Intriguing," the ambassador said. "How is such memory acquired?"

"We are born with it," the tahorah said slowly. She was deliberately evading the question and for the sake of the current mission, the ambassador let it drop.

The tahorah turned to the daemoness and they spoke in their language for a long time. Clearly both sides ended up frustrated so the daemoness raised her hand.

"Mihir," she said.

The tahorah cocked her head thoughtfully before nodding. She scrambled onto the table. Both the tahorah and the daemoness faced each other. They placed their right palms against each other's left temples, and their left hands on the other's right shoulder. They touched foreheads and after a short time, closed their eyes. The chamber fell deathly silent and the mood changed drastically from tense restraint to a reverent silence.

After approximately five minutes, the two broke apart. The tahorah blinked rapidly, then screwed up her nose.

"Ew," she said.

The daemoness broke into a wide smile. She affectionately tucked some of the tahorah's hair behind her ear and nodded. Stepping back, she allowed the tahorah to scramble off the table.

"What was that?" Binky asked Skylark.

"Whatever it was, it was kinda hot," Jack said.

Skylark and Binky looked at her.

"What?" she demanded.

After a pause to collect her thoughts, the tahorah turned to the ambassador. "The grebar's ancestral memory is long; longer than most. Even still, her memories are vague and uncertain."

"Is that what just happened?" Skylark asked. "Memory transferal?"

"In essence, yes," the tahorah responded. "It is called Mihir—soul sharing."

"And what did she show you?" the ambassador asked.

"When the daemon were young and had not yet looked to the stars, the home world came under attack. The creatures were insect-like. For the most part, they hunted daemon and other non-vegetation for food. Some, however, they would..." The tahorah frowned and cocked her head, trying to figure out an adequate explanation. "They would make fighters?"

"What do you mean 'make fighters?'" the ambassador asked.

"Of daemon?" Skylark interjected.

"Yes," the tahorah said. Deciding that Skylark would perhaps be a little less dense, she began talking to him. "Of daemon. They would change them, make them obedient to the hive queen like bees."

"How?" Ambassador Clegg asked.

The tahorah shrugged. "There is no memory of the method. But, there is some of their social structure and behaviour and of the mindless fighters they created. In the grebar's memory, this time was known as the dark days."

"How did the daemon survive?" Skylark asked.

"War," the tahorah answered. "Almost hopeless. But in the end, the creatures left. Perhaps daemon proved too difficult a food source." The tahorah smiled at this.

"I can't imagine why," Skylark muttered.

Hearing, the tahorah laughed. "Perhaps that victory is the source of daemon pride."

"How were they defeated?" the ambassador asked.

Shrugging, the tahorah said, "That memory has been lost."

"Helpful," Binky said. Skylark glared at him.

"The memories are not good. If this creature is the same as the ones the grebar remembers, then all are in grievous trouble."

"Is there anything you can tell us about them?" Skylark asked. "Even some knowledge of their behaviour would help a lot."

The tahorah nodded. "Well, you see for yourself that they are insects, of a kind. However, they behave more like a… what is it called…? Virus. They move to a source of food, mine it until there is nothing left, then move on to the next available food source. They operate in similar fashion to bees. There are queens in each hive that are responsible for directing the behaviours of their workers and soldiers."

Skylark grew thoughtful. "So, the best way to stop them is to strike at the heart. Kill the queen."

"And then what?" the ambassador asked.

"Without a queen controlling them? Who the hell knows? How are they able to travel, Tahorah?"

"I do not know," the pale woman answered. "I know of nothing living that can survive space. Perhaps they have vessels like we do."

"Would they have that kind of intelligence?"

"Wasps and bees build homes. Ants can make rafts," the tahorah answered. "I do not see how these ragnar would be any different."

"Yo," Binky whispered to Skylark. "How come she knows so much about Earth?"

"I read," the tahorah answered, cocking her head at Binky and smiling softly.

"Oh," Binky said, shifting awkwardly under her curious purple gaze. Skylark laughed quietly.

"I fear, Ambassador, that this puts us in the awkward position of trying to like each other," the tahorah said, shifting her intense attention away from the lieutenant commander. Binky sighed in relief.

"I do not find that especially awkward," Ambassador Clegg said, smiling. "And I am authorized to speak on behalf of the Council."

"And what are the Council's terms?"

The ambassador folded his arms. "We're prepared to offer you refugee status on Earth," he said.

The tahorah waited, expecting more. When none was forthcoming, she smiled slightly.

"The daemon have already won their land, Ambassador. And as your previous war made plain, you would have a great deal of trouble moving any single one of us."

"I take it you have a counter offer?"

"For access to daemon knowledge and technology and for our full cooperation in defence of Earth, we require that daemon territories already won are officially recognized. Also, room must be made for the daemon on your Council, and daemon warriors integrated into Earth's defence forces."

"That is quite a list," the ambassador said. "Not to mention the fifteen million or so Canadians who will not be getting their homes back."

"Considering that many daemon will likely die in defence of this planet, it seems only fair that the daemon share in its bounty and its governance," the tahorah answered.

"And if we refuse?"

"Daemon ships are fully functioning closed ecosystems, Ambassador," the tahorah said. "Should these ragnar ever come to Earth, we will return all your lands to you and journey once again to the stars. We can live there a long while as we search for a new home. And you will be left to fight this threat alone."

"You are a tough negotiator, Tahorah," the ambassador said with a frown. "This is well beyond my power to grant. I will need to discuss this with the Council."

"You may. I will wait."

"In the meantime," Skylark said, noticing the length of the shadows outside. "The envoy is currently entrenched in mutant territory. I would like permission to return to them and assist in the fire fight that's about to happen."

The tahorah looked at him a moment before responding. "We will have your envoy escorted to safe ground, Commander," she said at length. "I will send out the majan and a company of warriors."

"Thank you, Tahorah," Skylark said. He pressed the comm. button on his chest. "Wheeler, this is Skye. You still there?"

"Still here, Ben. We're getting a lot of movement over here. How goes it at your end?"

"Very interesting. I'll fill you in later. For now, you should probably start heading east. You will rendezvous with a team of daemon majan. They will escort you to safe ground."

"Thank fucking God."

Skylark grinned. "I'll see you soon, John."

"Wheeler out."

"Forgive me, Tahorah," the ambassador said. "Is there somewhere I can converse with the Council in private?"

"Of course, Ambassador. Follow me." The tahorah led the ambassador up to the balcony where she and Skylark had their lengthy discussion. They exchanged a few words and the tahorah left him to his business. She returned to the meeting room and addressed Commander Skye.

"The sun will set shortly. I do not think negotiations will be concluded before tomorrow. I can have pods set up for you and your team."

"Pods?" Skylark asked.

"Portable chambers, Commander."

"Ah." He turned to his waiting team, who shrugged as one. "I appreciate your hospitality, Tahorah."

"It is only proper. I am the host. Come." The woman led Commander Skye and Team 6 out of the grounded ship and into the sunlight. She paused to turn her face to the sun and smiled. Then she motioned one of the guards to her. They spoke briefly and the guard broke off to prepare.

"The majan will return to escort you to your pods once they are prepared. I must return to my own council. There are domestic issues that require resolution."

"Of course. Thank you again." Skylark smiled at her and she offered a small one in return, but her eyes remained frighteningly intense. Not long after, she disappeared up the ramp and, judging from the sudden din, the argument from earlier in the afternoon resumed.

Skylark walked to the edge of the small paved area before the ramp and looked out over the garden. Binky and the rest of Team 6 moved over to the transporter and struck up a conversation with the driver.

12

"Beautiful, isn't it?" a deep but distinctly feminine voice said.

Skylark glanced across at the grebar who had joined his vigil at the edge of the garden as silently as a stalking cat. "I will be sorry to leave it behind."

"You expect the Council to reject your terms, I take it," Skylark said.

The grebar nodded. "I have not high hopes for your species. The tahorah's mother notwithstanding, there has been little I have seen that I admire."

Skylark grunted. "To be fair, you haven't seen an awful lot."

"Perhaps not." She looked at Skylark with the same curiosity the tehoros had done four years ago. "My son was intrigued by you."

"Your son?"

"The tahorah's father."

Skylark started. "You're her grandmother?"

"Yes."

"Oh."

"You seem apprehensive suddenly, Commander."

Skylark said nothing. He turned his attention back to the gardens. "What was your home land like?" he asked suddenly.

"Much like this," she said, waving her hand. "But the grasses were blue and purple, not green. And we did not build. We lived in caves formed many eons ago by water and fire."

Skylark looked surprised.

"You are wondering how cave dwellers could ever be advanced enough to create ships capable of rapid space travel, yes?"

"Yes, actually."

The grebar laughed. "Dwelling in caves was a deliberate choice. To build where adequate shelter had been provided was wasteful. To a daemon, land is precious. You do not spoil it. And our land was beautiful. Forests grew in the caves, glowing like our own garden in the ship. Outside was dominated by blue grasses and trees in purple and gold. We lived in paradise."

"Why did you leave?"

"War," the grebar answered. "There were twelve tribes, and each tribe had many, many clans. The tribal leaders held council, much like you do now. But one had been corrupted by his power. He felt the tribes were too disparate. He dreamt of uniting all daemon under his banner and his alone. But we are not easily swayed, and we distrust such concentrated governance. One man with all the power can sometimes be a good thing, if that man is honourable and just. Most often, it becomes an evil thing and all are subjected to the cruel whimsy of whoever sits in power.

"At first, diplomatic solutions were presented. But it was not enough. The councilman would not settle for less than complete control. He gathered his tribe, the most numerous of all the tribes and, one by one, destroyed the other tribes. We were blind to his deeds. The Council seldom met, and such terrible evil was beyond our comprehension. By the time the rest of the Council were alerted, there was no option but war.

"We won in the end, but at great cost. Our paradise was lost and few of us were left. What remained of the tribes scattered, each seeking peace in a new world. What became of them, I do not know. They are now too far away to sense, if they live at all."

"You fought in that war?" Skylark asked.

The grebar nodded sadly. "I lost my family in that war. When it was over, I had only myself and my infant son. I led our tribe until the tehoros was old enough. He grew into manhood amongst the stars and all he knew of his birthplace were the bittersweet memories I passed to him. I wish he could have known it better."

Skylark observed the grebar's face a moment. Her expression remained impassive, though tears rimmed her blue eyes.

"I'm sorry," he said gently.

The grebar waved dismissively in the air. "What's done is done.

There is no going back. Bah! Listen to me. I have become an old woman!" The grebar smiled.

"And what of you, Commander? What of your home?"

Skylark thought briefly of his hellish life before the USC. He shook his head. "The closest thing I have to a home is the USC Headquarters," he said.

"Were you born there?"

Skylark pressed his lips into a thin line. "No," he said, hoping his flat tone would be enough for the grebar to understand that he did not want to discuss it.

"I see," she said simply. The intense curiosity behind her gaze returned.

The arrival of the majan informing them that the accommodations for Team 6 were prepared broke her observation, for which Skylark was supremely grateful. The grebar dismissed the majan. The warrior bowed and returned to his post at the ramp.

"Come," the grebar said. "I will escort you."

"Thank you," Skylark said.

He motioned for Team 6 to fall in and they walked through the gardens in silence for some time. At the edge of the garden, six small round mud huts had been erected, complete with thatched roofs. There was enough room for a bedroll. Inside, hanging from the ceiling was a glowing blue bioluminescent lamp.

"Quaint," Jack said, smiling. "Like something out of Sub-Saharan Africa."

"As I understand it," Skylark said, "they're not keen on building."

"So why'd they build spaceships?" Binky asked.

Skylark shrugged. "Because there are no caves in space."

The grebar chuckled at this, especially since Binky looked so utterly confused. The ancient daemoness turned to Skylark. "I shall leave you to your rest. When you are ready to sleep, you can place the lamps on the hooks on the outside of the doors of your pods."

"Thank you, Grebar," Skylark said.

The daemoness cocked her head and smiled. "You are welcome, Commander." She turned and, still smiling, made her aching way back to the daemon ship.

Skylark watched her leave, before turning to his team. They observed him with identical enquiring expressions. He grinned but refused to elaborate. He simply shrugged at them, found a spot on the grass on which to sit, and stared out towards the setting sun as it shone golden light onto the backs of the grazing bison. The rest of the team joined him. They simply sat and enjoyed the quiet peace until the light faded and they retired to sleep.

The quiet of the night, broken only by the buzz and chirp of insects, the murmuring of a breeze and the occasional distant bellow of a bison was wholly unfamiliar to everyone in the team. Team 6 was so accustomed to the constant hum of the ships, the low murmur of the crew or the traffic of Vancouver that the silence of the world away from the USC made for a difficult sleep.

Skylark did not sleep at all. He sat with his back against the wall of his pod, his eyes closed, trying to empty his mind. When the first bird called from the grass, he stood and left his pod to watch the rising sun.

Ambassador Clegg also received very little sleep. He and the tahorah were deep in negotiations all night. The small, pale woman seemed to have boundless energy and her aggressive bartering never let up. Clegg had to retire the argument to the Council. Their careful diplomacy only shed light on their dislike of the tahorah, her demands and the daemon as a whole. But even they were worn down by her tireless insistence.

In the end, a satisfactory agreement was reached. Assuming victory in the coming war, the daemon would keep their hard-won lands until a suitable home-world could be located for them. Humanity would do everything in their power to help them find it. Their current location would be kept as an embassy for daemon ambassadors to Earth once they found a new homeland.

The USC would be expanded to include the daemon, provided that the daemon maintain certain conditions of conduct. The conditions were agreeable to the tahorah, who made a point of explaining that most, if not all, were already practiced by the daemon. Daemon agents would be incorporated into the USC personnel, with USC Strategic teams now numbering six members to accommodate the influx of soldiers. In an unusual compromise, the tahorah agreed that any daemon entering the USC be subjected to testing for preparedness. At the same time, USC training was to be altered to accommodate daemon training methods.

The admiral of the USC and the tahorah's own military advisor agreed to a meeting to devise a new training curriculum that would benefit both species.

The daemon also demanded that their equivalent of fighter pilots remained under the sole command of the daemon commander-in-chief in much the same way the representatives of the USC regions still had command of military forces of their own.

The changes in the structure to the USC were unprecedented. The Council admitted that they were at a loss as to where to start. The tahorah reminded them that time was of the essence. A place on the Council, the meeting of the two military commanders, and integration into USC Strategic would have to happen soon. The rest of the integration of daemon troops into the USC military would be better if done slowly.

To help facilitate the necessary changes, the tahorah offered to meet with the Council in person, accompanied by her personal guard, the majan. The offer was not done lightly. As leader of the daemon, she knew she was vulnerable. Should the Council take this opportunity to try and take her captive, or kill her in an effort to rid Earth of its newest residents, escape would be difficult; not impossible, she trusted her skill and the skill of her majan well enough, but difficult.

However, the evidence presented to her satisfied her that both species faced a genuine threat and any attempt on her life would be extremely foolish of the Council. At least, such was her case in the argument she used against her advisors in the conclave that followed. Though the ambassador understood nothing of the argument, it was perfectly clear to him that the daemon were deeply fond of their petite, pale leader, despite the obvious difference between herself and them. More to the point, they were suicidally protective of her.

In one of their many private conversations that night, the ambassador made it clear to the Council that crossing the tahorah could be catastrophic. He warned them of the volatile nature of the daemon. His warnings gave them pause and, sensing their hesitation, the ambassador's heart sank. They had been planning something he was not privy to.

At length, Councillor Brand simply said, "Noted, Ambassador. Thank you."

Dawn came and went. At last, with everyone save the tahorah exhausted, the final arrangements were made. The Council members themselves would be at USC Headquarters, Vancouver to greet the tahorah in person. The USC teams would be briefed on the change in their structure and a general press conference would be held to inform the world about the first ever Intergalactic Council of Nations, created from what was once the United Council.

Satisfied, the tahorah concluded the meeting, and permitted the ambassador time to sleep at last. The following morning the envoy would begin their journey through mutant territory to Gate Compound 19.

Team 6 were informed of the details by the grebar, who seemed to enjoy conversing with them. Her presence was matronly and kindly, but the team was always aware of the steel beneath her warmth. The daemoness, though ancient and aching, could still kill them all in a heartbeat. Skylark watched on as the team tried to teach her to play craekers. Her shrewd mind acquired the rules quickly, but she acted well, and so they were all convinced that beginner's luck had lost them the first three hands.

The grebar slyly winked at Skylark, who replied with a grin, before sinking back into his thoughts.

After only two hours of play, the grebar had soundly thrashed them. She turned in her cards with a cheeky smile and left to join Commander Skye as he watched the bison herd in the distance.

"It is an interesting game," she said.

"We're always finding unique ways to entertain ourselves," Skylark answered.

"That is good. Play increases the capacity of imagination, which increases the capacity for innovation. It is good for the mind."

Skylark smiled. "I'm not sure it's helping them," he said, nodding his head towards his team, who had dissolved into an argument about whose turn it was to cut the deck. The grebar laughed.

"May I ask you a personal question, Grebar?" Skylark asked.

"Of course, though whether I shall answer is a different matter entirely."

Skylark smiled. "The tahorah's mother. Did you approve?"

The grebar cocked her head. "You are wondering if we feel the same natural hostility towards otherness as is so often displayed by your kind."

"Not in so many words, but yes, I suppose."

"Hostility is perhaps not the best word to describe it. I was disappointed when we could not treat with you when first we came. But I cannot blame you. You are a younger species and had some very strange ideas about how important you were in the grand scheme of things."

Skylark smiled at this. "Some of us still do."

"I figured as much. The tahora's mother was special, though. I saw her, and I liked what I saw. I understood immediately why the tehoros chose her. She had a good light."

"A good light?"

"Yes," the grebar said. "Our eyes are more sensitive than yours, I suppose. Every living thing has light. It surrounds them and fills them, and each light is unique. The patterns are similar. I can, for example, tell the difference between a tree and a bird because each has a different sort of light. And each species of bird has more subtle differences, each individuals of a species yet more subtle differences, but still discernable. And the tahorah's mother had a good light—pure and gentle and warm."

"Can the tahorah see this light?"

"Oh yes. She is daemon, even if she doesn't look it."

"She doesn't look human either. Not exactly."

"Ah yes, there are differences. Her skin, so ghostly white, and her violet eyes. I had never seen eyes in such a hue. It is odd, for both her father and mother had eyes of clearest blue."

"I'm surprised that her mother could, you know."

"Conceive? It was unexpected. Still, our phenotypic expressions are similar enough. Perhaps there is enough true genetic similarity to make such a thing possible with each interspecies coupling. Or perhaps our little tahorah is simply special."

Skylark smiled. "I wonder if that question will ever be answered."

"Perhaps, now that this new treaty is being created."

"That doesn't upset you?"

"Should it?"

Skylark shrugged. "I guess I'm just used to dealing with people.

Human people, I mean. Some of them still get upset if their children marry another ethnicity. I cannot imagine how they'd react if their child became involved with another species entirely."

"And would it upset you, Commander, if a child of yours became involved with one of us?"

Skylark grinned. "A child of mine? I doubt I will ever have to cross that bridge, Grebar."

The daemon cocked her head at the commander, her large blue eyes revealing nothing other than careful consideration. She pursed her lips. "You are intriguing, Commander," she said at last.

"People keep saying that."

The grebar flashed a smile. She sighed as she looked over the grasslands. "Will you make me a promise, Commander?"

"That depends, Grebar."

The elderly daemoness looked seriously at Commander Skye. "Keep her safe? My granddaughter is all that remains of a once flourishing and noble bloodline. If she dies, she takes with her our entire history. And," the grebar smiled. "I am very fond of her."

"I will do what I can, Grebar." Skylark's eyes met the daemoness's and they locked gazes. After a time, the grebar nodded and turned back to the setting sun.

"I believe you will," she said quietly. "I must return. The tahorah will need some help. Until the morning, Commander."

"Until tomorrow, Grebar," Skylark answered.

The grebar turned and made her meticulous way through the garden.

"What was that about?" Binky said.

"A grandmother's concern," Skylark answered. "Tell you what, I'll be glad for my own bed."

"I dunno," Spike said, leaning back on the grass where Jack and Doorman sat, discussing a book. "It's nice here. I reckon I could live here a while."

Skylark smiled. "It is peaceful," he agreed.

"And to think, I was expecting a desolate wasteland. Isn't that where all evil things live? I guess they can't be as evil as the history books say."

"I guess not," Skylark agreed.

"Craekers, Commander?" Jack asked.

"Sure. Why not?"

Team 6 sat on the grass and played cards until it was too dark to see.

Skylark slept that night, though he wished he had not.

13

Team 6 were summoned to the citadel before sunrise. The transport drivers waited, leaning against the bonnet of their hovercraft. They nodded their greeting as the team passed, too tired to speak.

Moments later, the ambassador exited the citadel, the box containing the ragnar specimen carried by two majan. At the ambassador's request, they loaded it into the transporter and left again.

"Everything all right, Ambassador?" Skylark asked.

"I sure as hell hope so," Ambassador Clegg answered. "Things will be getting very interesting in the USC."

Commander Skye raised his brows in query, but Ambassador Clegg simply shook his head. He turned back to the citadel, drawing Skylark's attention to the ramp. Seven daemon majan in full armour strode down the ramp, headed by the tahorah who wore a much smaller replica of daemon armour. Unlike her majan, she had not yet put on her helm.

Daemon armour looked surprisingly similar to USC armour, though the design appeared less bulky and much more flexible, allowing for a range of motion that made Skylark envious.

"Christ," Binky said. "They really do look like their namesake in that armour."

Skylark smirked. "Is it wrong that I really want a set?"

Binky laughed. "It is pretty badass."

"We are ready to go when you are, Ambassador," the tahorah said.

"We should probably get started then," Ambassador Clegg said. He opened the door of the transport and stood aside to permit the tahorah to pass. She cocked her head and smiled.

"Thank you, but I would much rather walk."

"As you wish," the ambassador said. He clambered into the transport and a driver shut the door.

The tahorah turned to Skylark. "We will travel to your envoy's position first, and then move across the dead city to your gate compound."

Skylark raised his brows. "You're coming?"

"Yes, Commander. I have business with the Council."

"Are you certain that's a good idea?"

The tahorah smiled at him. "It would be especially foolish for the Council to try anything, Commander," she said. "Do you think they would risk it?"

"In truth, I wouldn't put anything past the Council. I trust them about as far as I can throw them."

"It is a good thing they sent the ambassador to treat with me then. Your lack of faith in your own species is disturbing."

Skylark shrugged. "I trust my team. As to everyone else, well..." Skylark left it hanging.

"I understand," the tahorah said, her slight smile never leaving her face.

Skylark felt as if he was being mocked. He turned and noted the thin line of light that announced dawn. "We should get going if we're to arrive at the compound while there is still sunlight."

The tahorah nodded. She said something softly to one of her majan, who, Skylark noticed, looked older and more senior than the others. He rightly guessed that that particular majan was the advisor who would be working with the admiral on a new USC curriculum. Together, they took point. The tahorah nodded at them, indicating Skylark should follow. Just before he turned to lead his team, Skylark glanced at the top of the ramp where the grebar stood.

The daemon, looking every bit as drawn and concerned as any grandparent would, nodded at Skylark. Skylark nodded in return, then led the way behind the two majan, leaving the citadel, and the worried matron, behind.

They found Team 87 and the group of British infantry playing craekers with the daemon majan who had been sent to protect them. Most of them were grinning as they played their hands.

The two majan leading Team 6 and the tahorah exchanged a glance. Unnoticed, they halted and watched a moment. Skylark pressed the comm. button in his chest plate.

"Good morning, Commander Wheeler," he said, unable to keep the smile from his voice.

"Ben!" Commander Wheeler said over the link. "What's happening? Oh. Never mind. I see you."

Skylark laughed as the players hurriedly put away their cards and stood to attention. Skylark and Commander Wheeler greeted each other by clasping hands.

Skylark grinned at him. "You've been busy I see."

"They've gone mad for the game," Wheeler said, indicating the majan. It was then he noticed the tahorah.

"Tahorah," Skylark said, standing aside. "This is Commander Wheeler, leader of Team 87."

"Commander," the tahorah greeted. She walked forward and extended her hand, cocking her head as she looked intently at him.

"Tahorah," Commander Wheeler said, shaking her hand firmly. Despite her small hands, she had a firm grip.

"We will be escorting the tahorah and her guard to the Gate Compound," Skylark explained.

"We are?"

"She has business with the Council."

"I see." Wheeler looked back at his men. "We're ready to go."

"Good."

"I suggest you lead from here, Commander," the tahorah said to Skylark, "as you know the precise location of the compound."

Skylark shrugged. "All right." He cocked his head and the group moved out.

The sun shone brightly as they moved, and Skylark felt in good spirits. He and Wheeler casually walked the short distance between safe ground and mutant territory.

Wheeler glanced back at the tahorah, who walked surrounded by her massive guard.

"What's the deal with her?" Wheeler asked.

Skylark shrugged. "She's their tahorah. It means All-Queen, I'm guessing."

"What happened to their All-King?"

"He's missing."

"Oh." Wheeler looked back.

"Stop it, John. You're going to give her a complex."

"She's not what I expected. Shouldn't she be seven feet tall and black as night?"

Skylark grinned. "You would think so, wouldn't you?"

"She's actually quite pretty."

"You seem surprised."

"Well, admitting an alien is attractive feels odd."

"It is odd."

"You don't find her pretty?"

"She's beautiful," Skylark said. He stopped walking, indicated a broken window and immediately put on his helmet. The others followed suit and soon they were moving forward with caution. All conversation about the attractiveness of alien species ceased as Skylark and Wheeler let their training take over. Thanks to the early start and full sun the entire trip, they arrived at the Gate Compound without incident.

Canadian Army Major Chapdelaine, who looked not a little afraid of the fully armoured giants gathered behind the ambassador's envoy, greeted the group in the courtyard. When the ambassador exited the transport, the major saluted.

"We were informed of your imminent arrival last night, Ambassador," the major said. "There should be plenty of room to house you for the night. A transport is not due to arrive until tomorrow morning."

"Thank you, Major," the ambassador replied. He ushered the helmeted tahorah forward.

"This is the tahorah, leader of the daemon," he introduced.

The tahorah removed her helmet. The major saluted smartly after recovering from his initial shock.

"It is an honour, ma'am," he said.

The tahorah smiled at him. "Thank you," she said simply. "If it is not inconvenient, I should like to share my room with my guard."

The major looked over at the monstrous aliens in their intimidating armour.

"I'm not sure we have any beds long enough," he said.

"That is fine. A clear floor will do."

"I will see what we can do, ma'am."

"I would appreciate it."

"I will leave it to Docking Administrator Anders to see that you are comfortable. Dinner is served at 1830." The major saluted smartly again and, dismissed by the ambassador, marched rapidly away.

Skylark flashed a wolfish grin.

"Poor, terrified bastard," Wheeler said, voicing the thought behind Skylark's grin.

Docking Administrator Anders approached, saluting.

"Ambassador, the major has made available his private study for you and your guest to relax while preparations are being made. The teams and infantry are invited to the officer's mess for coffee if they like."

"Thank you," the ambassador said.

"Forgive me," the tahorah said. "But my guard?"

Anders looked up at them helplessly. "They were not mentioned, ma'am," he said. "I am sure they would be welcomed in the officers' mess. There is not room for all of you in the major's study."

The tahorah turned to her guard and noticed they were yet to remove their helms. She placed one hand on her hip and glared at them until they did so. One smiled sheepishly at her and she rolled her eyes. She relayed the invitation to them. One glanced at Anders with a scowl. He spoke to his tahorah in a low voice. The tahorah answered, her voice soft and calming. At length, the daemon nodded.

"Do not like," he said.

"I know," she replied. She smiled up at him and the daemon shrugged helplessly. The tahorah turned back to the docking administrator. "That will suit," she said. The docking administrator nodded. He turned to Skylark, almost pleading.

"Commander," he said.

"I know the way," Skylark replied. "I will take them."

Anders relaxed with a barely audible sigh. "Thank you, sir." He turned back to the ambassador and the tahorah. "Please, follow me."

The tahorah and the ambassador spent the night talking quietly in the major's study. Things were much more tense in the officers'

mess. The majan were given a very wide berth by most everyone. The British infantry, suddenly very aware of the otherness of the daemon opted to sit with the teams, with the exception of Teams 6 and 87 who, following Skylark's pointed display, joined the daemon guard. Still, they sat uncomfortably, dwarfed by their companions and feeling vulnerable. One of the daemon, having refused the coffee, watched Skylark drink it with interest.

"Want some?" Skylark asked, offering his mug to the daemon.

Hesitantly the daemon took the mug. He sniffed it, raising an eyebrow at Skylark.

"It's good," he said.

The other daemon watched in apprehension as their fellow majan took a sip. The majan screwed his face up.

"Fruv," he said handing the mug back to Skylark, still pulling a face. "Fruv!"

Skylark laughed, signalled a private, and asked for a glass of water. The majan drank it down, trying hard to cleanse his tongue of the bitter taste.

"It's not fair," Binky said. "Skylark takes it strong and black. Here. Mine has sugar." He offered his mug to the daemon, who pushed it away shaking his head violently.

Skylark laughed again, prompting some of the daemon to do so as well. Shaking his head, Skylark reclaimed his mug and drank his coffee. The majan watched him with an incredulous expression.

"How?" he demanded, pointing at Skylark's now empty mug.

Skylark shrugged. "An acquired taste, I suppose."

The majan looked at one of his own for clarification. One helpfully translated and the daemon returned his attention to Skylark. He shook his head. "Fruv," he said in disgust. "Bitter."

"Fruv means bitter?" Skylark asked. The daemon nodded and Skylark grinned.

What followed over coffee and then dinner were Skylark and the daemon exchanging vocabulary. They grinned and guffawed with one another as both sides struggled with pronunciation and translation. Before long, the rest of Teams 6 and 87 and the rest of the majan were engaged in trying to learn one another's language.

The officers' mess continued to speak in hushed tones, looking over at the animated group with marked distrust. Skylark noticed, as did the majan. The only thing that kept the peace was Skylark's obvious and determined ignoring of the USC and MP personnel in the mess.

Alone in the large room provided for the daemon and the tahorah, a different discussion took place.

"I do not like them," Majan Sarcen growled to his queen. "They are small in mind as well as body."

"They are not all so," Majan Butan said. "The dark commander is good. He has a good light."

"It is broken," Sarcen said. "You cannot trust a broken light."

"But it is still good," Butan insisted.

"Butan is right," the tahorah said. "You cannot judge the entire species on the actions of a few."

"But you can on the broken light of one?" Sarcen countered with heat.

"Calm, Sarcen," the tahorah said gently. "I see you."

"They will turn us ill."

"Perhaps."

"We could just leave."

"I do not want to leave," Butan said. "This is home now."

"It is in their best interests to keep their word, Sarcen," the tahorah said. "We must trust that they so see it."

"I cannot trust," Sarcen said.

"Try."

That was the end of the argument. Sighing, Sarcen sat next to his queen and wrapped an arm around her. "I worry for you," he said. "You are good."

The tahorah smiled and rested her head against Sarcen's powerful frame. "So are you," she whispered. Moments later, she was asleep and the majan settled in for a sleepless night of guarding.

Due to complaints by the personnel who frequented the officers' mess, the daemon were treated to a full breakfast in bed under the pretence of offering them extra time to rest. None of them were fooled, but they accepted graciously, pleased to be away from the glares and whispers of the personnel of Gate Compound 19.

They remained in the room, relaxing until they were summoned at 0815. The transport was soon to arrive.

"Missed you at breakfast," Skylark greeted Butan with a grin as the daemon arrived on the docking platform.

"Made eat room," Butan answered hesitantly.

"They ate their room?" Binky asked.

Skylark rolled his eyes at him. "Shame," he said to Butan. "There was good coffee."

The daemon pulled a face and Skylark grinned.

Ambassador Clegg arrived moments later, looking tired. He smiled slightly as he approached.

"I'm to bid you farewell here," he said. "The Council wants me back in Britain to watch over the election. I'll be flying out tomorrow."

"We were looking forward to your company," Skylark said, extending his hand. "I believe you are one of the few politicians I can stomach."

The ambassador shook Skylark's hand and offered a warm smile. "I am pleased," he said.

Skylark grinned. "Tell your daughter I said hello."

Ambassador Clegg wrinkled his nose. "She'll be saying your name until the cows come home." He shook his head. "I'll pass along your greeting." Turning to the tahorah, he extended his hand. "I wish you luck," he said. "Be especially wary of Councillor Brand. She is not an easy woman to please and her dislike of the daemon is legendary."

"I will bear that in mind, Ambassador. Thank you."

"It looks like the first transporter is here."

Everyone turned to look. Sure enough, the hovercraft had alighted smoothly on the docking rails and was approaching the buffer with caution. Skylark caught Binky's eye.

"Thank God," the lieutenant commander mouthed.

Skylark grunted, actually disappointed. No Christie.

"Good morning," the pilot greeted cheerily as the door opened. She remained seated. "I have room for two teams today."

"The tahorah should go first," Wheeler said.

"Agreed," Skylark said, as another transporter alighted the rails on the other side. He turned to the tahorah and indicated the transporter.

"I think your guard will take up most of the room," he said. "Team 87 and 6 will follow in the next transport."

The tahorah nodded, though she looked apprehensive. Skylark pulled out an old short wave radio. "We'll be right behind you," he said, handing her the radio. "If you feel you are in danger, you can notify me with this."

The tahorah took it. "Thank you, Commander. I trust I will not need to." She clipped it to her armour all the same, then boarded the transport, followed by her majan. Butan looked back at Skylark, grinned, then vanished from view.

"I think you have a friend, Commander," Wheeler noted.

Skylark grunted. He patted Wheeler on the back and entered the newly arrived transport with the rest of his team. Team 87 joined them and before long, they were zipping along the lower path towards USC Headquarters, Vancouver.

They arrived in a little under two hours, and just seconds behind the tahorah. Aware of her precious cargo, the driver of her transport had taken extra care. Both transports opened their doors simultaneously.

Skylark and Wheeler kept their teams near the transport as the majan and their tahorah alighted at the foot of the stairs to the tall, ultra-modern USC base in the centre of Vancouver. Waiting there were all five Council members. One stepped forward as the tahorah cautiously approached. He extended his hand.

"Good morning, Tahorah," he greeted with a smile. "I am Councillor Fisher, representing Europe on the Council. Allow me to introduce you?"

The tahorah took Councillor Fisher's hand. "An honour to finally meet you in person," she said. "I would like an introduction."

Councillor Fisher offered his arm to the tahorah, who took it. He led her to the waiting councillors.

"This is Councillor Mpho Tsutume, representing Africa."

The tall, elegant black woman wearing a brightly dyed and patterned long sleeved robe and hat shook the tahorah's hand and smiled.

"Hello," she said in a deep voice touched by a musical accent.

"Hello," the tahorah replied.

"Councillor Lao Mingh, representing Eurasia," Fisher said. "Councillor Brand, representing the Americas. And this is Councillor Ngu, representing Australasia."

The tahorah greeted each one in turn. She turned and beckoned one of her majan.

"This," she introduced, as the daemon stepped up, "is the chtakah, the chief military advisor. He has come to meet with the admiral of the USC to discuss the integration of daemon warriors."

"Ah, yes," Fisher said, slightly taken aback by the immense size of the daemon standing before them.

Councillor Tsutume stepped forward and welcomed him very warmly. "You do not look so different from my brother," she said.

The daemon cocked his head as he regarded her. "Perhaps in some distant past, we are kin."

Mpho smiled. "It might be so."

Councillor Brand snorted and both the tahorah and the chtakah turned to her. The tahorah had the good grace to keep her features impassive, but the chtakah could not care less about politics. He narrowed his eyes at her.

"Uh, we have prepared an honourary luncheon to welcome you and your entourage to the USC base on this historic day," Fisher said quickly, in an effort to break the tension. "I can have you shown to your quarters so that you can prepare."

"Thank you, Councillor," the tahorah said. She looked back. "I trust arrangements have been made for my majan?"

"Yes. Of course. We were informed of their arrival and have prepared a section of the base for them. I will turn them over to the very capable care of the USC personnel. I will show you and the chtakah to your quarters."

"Thank you, Councillor Fisher." The tahorah turned back to her majan, offered them an apologetic smile and followed Councillor Fisher into the building, with the chtakah following.

One of the majan growled. A gruff American Army Major marched up to them, saluted, then stood at ease.

"I can show you to your quarters," he said.

The daemon looked at one another.

"Can they understand him, do you think?" Wheeler asked Skylark quietly.

Skylark folded his armoured arms across his chest and grinned. "This could get interesting."

When the daemon did not move, the major frowned. "Follow," he said slowly, as if talking to children. One daemon folded his arms.

"No," he said.

Another turned and looked at Skylark. He pointed. "Him," he told the major. "Follow him."

The major scowled. "No, I'm not going to follow him. My orders were to take you to your quarters. Now, please follow me."

The daemon looked at each other, not yet comfortable enough with English to comprehend the major. Skylark started laughing. He walked over to the major and patted the confused man on the shoulder.

"Lead on, Major," he said.

"Yes, sir," the major said, turning away.

"Beds," Skylark told the waiting daemon. "Come." And he turned and followed the major. The daemon then started walking, not cowed in the least by the stares of everyone they encountered.

"I'm sorry, sir," the major said as he walked. "Was I unclear?"

"Not at all," Skylark said. "Unfortunately, few of them speak English and more unfortunately, we fired missiles at them when they came visiting. They are not overly prone to trusting humans."

"They trust you, it seems."

Skylark shrugged. "They've been around me for a couple of days."

The major looked back and snapped his head forward again. "They're huge!"

"Very," Skylark agreed. "And strong as hell. One nearly crushed my helmet with my head still inside using just one hand."

The major's eyes went wide.

"It's not a lie," Skylark said. "Where have they been placed, incidentally?"

"Ambassador Clegg sent word that Team 6 had formed a tentative relationship with the tahorah's guard, so we placed them in the spare rooms on your floor. Is that an issue, sir?"

"No, Major. It's a very good idea."

The south tower of the USC Vancouver base had been given over to the USC Strategic Division entirely. The teams lived there when not on mission and there were provisions should the team wish to entertain. The building soared, with 100 floors, the bottom one given over to a massive shopping centre with restaurants and a nightclub. The next four floors were used as offices. The United Space Corps Strategic Division had all its bureaucracy on those floors. The rest of the building housed the teams. Team 6's quarters were on the ninety-fourth floor.

"Are you not concerned that they will be dangerous, Commander?" the major enquired as they entered the building.

Skylark nodded at the security guards, who did not notice. They stared slack-jawed at the daemon, despite being warned of their arrival.

"Staring is rude, Clarke," Skylark quipped as he passed.

"Yes, sir," the security guard named Clarke said absently. He did not stop staring.

"To answer your question, Major, I believe that they are extremely dangerous. If we give them a cause to be."

The major nodded. He passed his key over the elevator panel and waited.

"Commander?" one of the majan asked.

"Yes?" Skylark answered.

"What?" The daemon pointed at a stuffed toy in the window of one of the shops.

Skylark smiled. "Toy."

The daemon cocked his head. "Toy?"

Another daemon growled something and the first smiled. "Ah!" he said. "For children!"

"Yes," Skylark answered.

The daemon turned and examined the stuffed toy through the window. Skylark returned to the major, who looked between him and the daemon with wide eyes. "Where is the tahorah sleeping?" he asked.

"The Council thought it best to house her and her advisor in the building proper. I believe she has been given an ambassador's suite." The major observed Commander Skye's sombre expression. "Is that a problem, sir?"

"It might be," Skylark said. "The majan are the tahorah's personal guard. They're going to get agitated if she stays from their sight for too long."

"Oh."

"I'll see what I can do," Skylark said. "But if possible, I'd like to speak to the Council about making an arrangement."

"Like what?"

"At least one of her majan should be permitted to stand guard over her in the night. They've been doing it since we've set out and the rest will believe she is unharmed if they hear it from one of their own."

"I will send in the request to Vice Admiral Hunt immediately."

Skylark winced. "Is there no one else, Major?"

"No, sir. Vice Admiral Hunt was selected by the Council to oversee the tahorah's visit. Why?"

"No reason," Skylark said as the elevator doors swung open. Then under his breath he muttered, "Shit."

It was a very tight fit in the elevator. The major was very uncomfortable, squished against the keypad by his own desire not to touch the daemon. The daemon observed the elevator carefully. They watched the rising numbers displayed on the door in silence.

"Beds high," one daemon muttered.

Skylark smiled. Another daemon noticed and grinned. After an awkward few moments of silence, the doors slid open smoothly to reveal the peach marble foyer of the ninety-fourth floor. Skylark led the way out.

"Us," he said pointing to the door on the right. "You," he said pointing to the door on the left. He walked over to the door and opened it.

One daemon peered in. He stared down a hall with six doors on either side. The tunnel opened out to a sizeable open concept living room, dining room and kitchen. The daemon walked cautiously into the hall, went to the first door and opened it. He brightened and turned back to his fellow majan.

"Bed," he said, pointing into the room.

The majan poured into the hall like a flood. Skylark followed, watching with a soft smile as the daemon began to explore the apartment. He peeked into one of the rooms to find that the beds had an extra two feet of length attached, giving the daemon enough room to lay comfortably. Barely. He smiled and nodded at the major.

"Nice touch," he said.

The major smiled. "I hope it holds. Those ends were welded on in a hurry."

Skylark grinned. "We'll find out soon enough."

There was much discussion amongst the daemon as they selected their rooms and then explored the kitchen and living room.

One daemon turned back and looked at Skylark. "You?" he asked pointing to the wall that separated the team's apartment from the guests' quarters.

Skylark nodded. "Come," he said.

The daemon's face brightened and he followed Skylark to the team's quarters. The set up was much the same as the guests' quarters except that Skylark, as Commander, had a sizeable room behind the kitchen with its own shower and a large balcony.

The daemon blinked in surprise at the room. "For Commander?" he asked.

Skylark nodded. "Yes."

The daemon smiled. He watched as Skylark passed his hand over a sensor. The wall opened and an armour mannequin rolled forward.

"What?" the daemon asked, pointing at it.

Skylark smiled and started to remove his armour, placing it on the mannequin.

"Ah!" the daemon said. "Good!"

Skylark nodded. Once out of his armour, he passed his hand over a different sensor and a full closet opened. He took out his USC jacket and standard issue boots and dressed in them. The daemon watched him a moment.

"You," the daemon said. "I like."

Skylark blinked in surprise.

"Commander good," the daemon said.

A slow smile spread across Skylark's face. "You're not half bad yourself," he said. The daemon cocked his head with a frown and Skylark tried again. "Majan good also."

The daemon grinned. He extended his hand. "Butan," he said. "Name."

"Butan," Skylark said, smiling. "I'm Ben."

"Better Commander around others," Butan said with a frown. "Names taken lightly by you."

Skylark nodded. "It is better you call me Commander around others."

Butan nodded, then smiled. "No armour?"

"Not today."

"Then we dress also."

Skylark nodded and Butan left. The major appeared at the door of Skylark's personal quarters.

"The ambassador was right. You do seem to have a way with them."

Skylark shrugged. "My guess is they can sniff out bullshit faster than a caffeinated dog. And politicians are full of bullshit."

The major smirked. A sound at the door turned his head and he immediately stood to attention. "Vice Admiral," he greeted, saluting.

"Fuck," Skylark muttered. He stood at attention and saluted as the vice admiral entered the room.

"You made it out alive after all," Hunt said. "Again."

"You sound disappointed, sir," Skylark said.

Hunt smiled slightly. "Surprised. I've actually come to check on the aliens."

"The daemon are making themselves comfortable in the guests' apartment, sir," Skylark said.

"I understand you can interpret?"

"I don't know the language, sir," Skylark said. "But I can guess fairly accurately."

"Good. You are to accompany me."

"Yes, sir."

"Major Drew?"

"Sir?"

"You are dismissed."

"Yes, sir."

The major turned and exited the apartment hurriedly. Without a word, Vice Admiral Hunt turned and left the apartment. Skylark followed. They met the rest of Team 6 in the foyer.

"Sirs," Binky said as he snapped to attention and saluted.

"At ease," Vice Admiral Hunt said as he breezed past them. Binky raised his brows at Skylark, who followed Hunt. Skylark shook his head and indicated for them to proceed into the apartment.

Shrugging, Binky led the team in. On her way, Jack stuck her tongue out at the vice admiral. Skylark caught it in the mirror. He tried very hard not to laugh. Hunt stopped at the door of the guests' quarters and indicated for Skylark to proceed.

Skylark knocked twice. Butan opened the door. He smiled at Skylark, who returned it with a tight one of his own, before noticing the vice admiral. He narrowed his eyes.

"Who?" he demanded.

Skylark desperately wanted to turn back to observe the vice admiral's expression, but refrained. "Majan," he greeted formally. "This is Vice Admiral Hunt."

The daemon majan scowled.

"My commander," Skylark said.

The scowl did not lessen. "Commander's commander?"

"Yes."

Grudgingly, Butan stood aside, permitting the vice admiral and the commander into the apartment. They made their way to the living room, where one majan, already having removed his armour, stood watching the traffic from the window. The majan turned when he noticed the reflections of the visitors in the glass. He observed them both with a scowl, taking careful note of Skylark's body language. It indicated a reluctant acceptance of the vice admiral's superiority.

To his credit, Vice Admiral Hunt did not flinch under the majan's stern blue gaze. The majan turned to Butan and said something. Butan nodded and vanished into the hall, knocking on the bedroom doors. One by one, the majan, in various stages of armour removal, entered the living room. They gathered behind the majan at the window, their collective attention on the vice admiral.

Hunt cleared his throat. "I would like to formally welcome you to the USC Headquarters, Vancouver," he said.

The daemon looked at each other.

"I am Vice Admiral Hunt."

The dressed majan looked at Skylark. "Vice admiral title?" he asked.

"Yes," Skylark said. "A very high ranking title."

The majan nodded. He turned his gaze back to the vice admiral before explaining to the majan in his own language. One grunted, but that was all the reaction the vice admiral received.

"You are?" Hunt asked.

Skylark cleared his throat. "My apologies, sir," he said. "Names are considered sacred amongst the daemon. It is not polite to ask it."

Hunt turned to Skylark, his expression telling the commander that the vice admiral was trying to figure out if he was joking.

"Then what do I call him?" Hunt said at last.

"It is proper to refer to him by his title, sir."

"Which is?"

"Majan, sir."

"Are they not all majan?"

"Yes, sir."

"Then how do I make it clear which one I'm speaking to, Commander?"

"You look at the person to whom you're speaking. Sir."

Hunt narrowed his eyes at Skylark, then turned back to the waiting crowd of majan. He cleared his throat.

"I hope you find your accommodations to your liking?" he said.

The majan grunted. "It is... good." He said. Vice Admiral Hunt smiled.

"But," the majan continued. "No room for the tahorah."

Hunt blinked. "The tahorah will not be staying here," he said.

Immediately, all the majan tensed and the designated spokesman growled. "Not good," he said. "Majan guard Tahorah."

"I am sorry," Hunt said. "There simply is no room for you where the tahorah is staying."

The eyes of the majan started to glow and the vice admiral reached for the firearm he had concealed at the small of his back. Skylark moved to stop him.

"I would strongly suggest you try diplomacy first, sir," Skylark said softly. "We'll both be dead before you get a single shot off."

"They are threatening me, Commander," Hunt hissed back.

"No, sir. They are presenting their discontent."

Hunt turned back to the majan and swallowed. "Perhaps we can come to an arrangement?" he said.

The lead majan cocked his head, but his eyes did not cease their hypnotic glow. "We guard Tahorah," he growled.

"Yes," Hunt agreed. "Perhaps we can find room for you in the ambassador's suite."

The glowing eyes turned to Skylark. "Tahorah with Ambassador?"

"No," Skylark corrected. "She's with the chtakah. The ambassador suite is a room, a very big room with a bed. Suite means big bedroom."

The majan cocked his head, deciphering Skylark's words. "Majan must guard," he said.

Skylark nodded. "I agree. Suite is big, but not big enough for all six of you. Perhaps two at a time?"

"Like at city of dead?" the majan asked. "Sun watch, star watch?"

"Yes," Skylark nodded.

"Rest stay here?"

"Until it's their turn, yes."

The majan considered a moment, then his eyes ceased to glow. "Agree."

"Thank God," Skylark breathed. To the majan he said, "Good. I apologize. Our people do not know you."

"Accepted, Commander," the majan said. The scowl he had used when observing the vice admiral was replaced with a curious expression now that the majan was observing Skylark. "But only for Tahorah."

Skylark nodded. He understood perfectly. Humans were the enemy.

Vice Admiral Hunt looked between Skylark and the majan.

"This needs to be cleared," he told Skylark sharply.

"Then, sir, I suggest you clear it. This is a massive compromise for them and to refuse it would cause more problems than we can adequately deal with at present. Sir."

Hunt glared at Skylark but nodded. "Since they seem to listen to you, Commander, you are appointed as mediator. I will inform you of the Council's decision as soon as it is made."

Skylark nodded. "Yes, sir."

"Good." Hunt turned back to the majan. He smiled tightly. "I must go and make arrangements. If you require anything, please see Commander Skye. He will be looking after you."

The majan looked between Vice Admiral Hunt and Commander Skye before nodding. "Thank you, Vice Admiral," he said.

"You are welcome, Majan," the vice admiral replied. He excused himself and left rapidly.

Skylark watched him go with pursed lips. They split into a smile when Butan growled, "Him, I do not like."

"Neither do I," Skylark said. "Hungry?"

The majan looked at one another before their spokesman nodded. "Yes," he said.

"You are welcome to come over to our kitchen," Skylark said, speaking carefully so that he could be fully understood. "I smell Spike's cooking."

The majan nodded. "Good. We come."

"As soon as you like," Skylark said before excusing himself.

The majan named Sarcen watched him go with a curious expression. He turned to Butan and said, "He's growing on me."

Butan grinned.

"Now everyone change. We will not threaten our hosts by accepting their food in armour." The majan left and Sarcen sighed. He turned back to the window.

14

"Hey, hey!" Spike greeted from the kitchen as Skylark entered the apartment. "How did things go with the brass-hole?"

Skylark grinned. "Not as good as they could have, much better than expected. Is that steak?"

"Yes, sir!"

"How many do you have?"

"Six. Why?"

Skylark pulled a face. "Jack!" he called.

"Sir?" Jack said, sticking her head out of her bedroom door.

"Can I ask a favour?"

"Depends."

"We're expecting guests for lunch today. Can you run downstairs and pick up some wine and about twenty more steaks?"

"Why do I have to do the shopping?" Jack asked as she disappeared back into her room.

"Because you're the woman," Spike yelled from the kitchen.

"Fuck you," Jack yelled back, though she was laughing. She stuck her head out the door again. "As if you even know what that is."

Doorman laughed quietly from his place on the couch.

"Please, Jack," Skylark said.

"Fine," Jack said. "But only because you said 'please.'" She vanished back into her room and emerged moments later wearing a long sundress. Everyone stared.

"You're burning the steaks," Jack said.

"You're wearing a dress," Spike replied.

"What?" Binky demanded from his room. He stuck his head out of his door. "Holy shit."

"What? You've never seen a girl in a dress before?"

"I've never seen you in a dress before," Spike said. "You look good."

Jack grinned. "Thanks, Spike. I'll see you guys in a few." She turned before she reached the door. "Is there anything else you need, Skylark?"

Mute, Skylark shook his head. Jack flashed a smile and left.

"She's actually really hot," Spike said.

"You just noticed?" Doorman asked.

"Yeah, well, she's never worn a dress before," Spike said. He sighed. "Too bad she's a lesbo. None of us will ever know."

Skylark remained silent.

Moments later, the daemon arrived. Butan knocked timidly on the door with exactly the same rhythm that Skylark had used on their door.

"Come in," Skylark called. When Butan stuck his head in, Skylark smiled. He beckoned the daemon in and continued to set the table.

Butan entered, followed by the majan that appeared to be the leader and the rest of the majan. They gathered at the end of the hall and watched the team make preparations.

"Make yourself at home," Skylark said, waving vaguely in the air.

"At home?" Butan asked, frowning.

"Yes. Uh, it means pretend you are home. No need to be formal."

Butan paused to puzzle through Skylark's words, when the majan leader said something.

"Ah!" the majan all answered, almost in unison. They entered the living room and found a place to sit or stand. Doorman jumped up.

"Can I get you a drink?"

Butan looked at him. "What?"

"A drink. You know," Doorman mimed drinking.

"No," Butan said. "What drink?"

"Oooooh! Well, we have water, of course. Wine. Beer. Juice. Actually, do we have juice, Skylark?"

"I don't think so."

Doorman turned back to the majan. "Sorry, no juice."

"What is beer?" Butan asked.

Doorman grinned. He went to the fridge and pulled out a bottle. He popped open the lid and handed it to Butan. Butan sniffed it, frowned and sipped. He tasted it slowly, then sipped again. Still frowning, he shrugged and passed it on.

"Fruv," he said. "Gae hym."

One by one the majan tried the beer. Doorman watched, more and more amused. Finally, one said. "Yes." He held up the beer bottle.

"We have a winner!" Doorman said. He reached into the fridge, pulled out a fresh bottle and handed it to the majan.

"Thank you," the daemon said.

"You're very welcome."

"What is wine?" Butan asked.

"Hey," Jack said from the door.

"Just in time," Doorman said. "Wine?"

Jack smiled. She put her bag of groceries on the kitchen counter and pulled out three bottles of wine. "I got two reds and a white. Here are your steaks."

"And what is all that," Doorman asked, pointing to the still full bag.

"Stuff for a salad," Jack answered.

"Salad? Really?"

"How you lot don't have scurvy is beyond me," Jack said.

Doorman laughed. He picked up a bottle of the red and the white. "Red or white?" he asked Butan.

The majan looked between the bottles then shrugged. "I do not know. Which is good?"

Doorman grinned. He poured a glass of each and handed them both to Butan to try. The daemon sipped them both, frowning, before passing them on.

"White," he said.

Doorman nodded. He poured a fresh glass. Most of the daemon selected the white. The majan leader demanded only water.

"And you, Commander?" Doorman asked.

"Red, please."

"Yes, sir." Doorman obliged, bringing Skylark his glass of red wine.

"Thank you," the commander said. He sipped. "Mm. Good choice, Jack."

"I knew you'd like it."

"What?" Butan asked, pointing at the steaks in the skillet.

"Steak," Spike said.

Butan cocked his head. "Don't know."

"Uh, beef?"

Butan shook his head.

"Cow," Spike said.

Confused, Butan looked at Skylark. "Cow?"

"Here," Jack said. She went to a cupboard and pulled out a cookbook with the picture of a cow on the cover. She pointed at it.

Butan's eyes went wide. "You eat animal?" he demanded.

Team 6 froze. "You don't?" Spike asked carefully.

Butan frowned and shook his head.

"Uh-oh."

"It's all right," Jack said. "We have potatoes and rice. I can whip something up."

"Thank you, Jack," Skylark said, smiling softly.

Butan looked down at his drink. "Animal?" he asked, pointing at the glass.

"No," Skylark said. "Plant."

Butan relaxed. "Good."

"Vegetarians, huh?" Binky said. "Wow."

Skylark shrugged. "My fault. I should have asked."

"Not offended," the majan leader said. He offered a small smile to Skylark. It was not lost on the commander the significance of that smile. Of the majan, he had been the most openly hostile.

"Great, so now we have a tonne of steak," Spike said.

"Good," Binky said. "I'm hungry as hell."

"Yeah, I'll have seconds," Jack agreed.

"Me three," Doorman said.

"Alrighty then, I'll cook them all up." Spike smiled and set to task.

Lunch felt oddly comfortable, despite the massive aliens that crowded the space, finding wherever there was room to sit and eat. Butan was the most social, making great efforts to understand and be understood. The other majan tried as well, but not to the same extent. Skylark leant against the wall in the living room and watched. Eventually, the majan leader approached.

"You do not eat much, like the others," he noted.

Skylark smiled slightly. "I eat enough to satisfy."

The majan grunted. He watched the daemon guard and Team 6 interact. "You have surprised me, Commander," he said at length.

"How so?"

"You are reserved, but not hostile. Others like you have proved... less."

Skylark grunted. "Humanity as a whole has proved disappointingly small-minded." He nodded towards Binky. "It was not so long ago that men who looked like me owned men who looked like him."

"I have read much to that effect," the majan said. He formed the words slowly and deliberately, concentrating hard on his word selection. "The tehoros was optimistic about you. I thought it was bias."

"Because of the tahorah's mother?"

"Yes. She was good."

Skylark smiled. A loud laugh turned his head and he watched as Jack, grinning, knelt on Binky, pinning him to the ground.

"Ow! Ow!" Binky said. "All right! All right! You win!"

Laughing, Skylark shook his head.

The majan cocked his head at Skylark. "You are different from them." He waved in the direction of Team 6.

"Oh?"

"Your light," the majan said. "It is different."

"Are not all lights different?"

"Yes," the majan conceded. "But yours is more different."

Skylark smiled slightly. "I wish I could see this light that I've heard so much about."

The majan shrugged. "Perhaps one day. Daemon were not always able to see. It was..." He cocked his head as he tried to figure out a word. "Cultivated."

"The grebar had mentioned so."

The majan grinned. "The grebar enjoyed your company, Commander. That is main reason I did not kill you."

"Thank you, Majan," Skylark said. "I appreciate that."

The majan laughed. "I hope more are like you."

"Thank you," Skylark murmured.

Three sharp knocks at the door disturbed the gathering.

"Got it," Doorman said. He ran to the door.

"Commander," he greeted Commander Wheeler.

"Hi," Wheeler said. "Is Ben in?"

"Commander," Doorman called back.

"Come in, John," Skylark said. He moved to the kitchen. "Can I offer you a drink? Beer?"

"No, thank you," Commander Wheeler replied. "I'm here on official business."

"Shame."

"Vice Admiral Hunt said he spoke with the Council. The tahorah had also expressed concern about her separation from her majan. Your compromise was mentioned and she found it agreeable. The guards are to be escorted to and from her accommodations by members of your team at 0600 and 1800 precisely."

"That is reasonable," Skylark said. "Thank you. If you happen to see the vice admiral, please let him know that we will carry out his orders to the letter."

Commander Wheeler nodded. "Can I speak with you? In private?"

The urgency behind Commander Wheeler's words raised Skylark's eyebrows. He nodded and led Commander Wheeler to his private quarters. He closed the door softly and turned to Wheeler.

"How can I help you, John?"

"What did you do?" Wheeler asked.

Skylark scowled. "Pardon?"

"To the vice admiral? He was practically foaming at the mouth."

Lost for words, Skylark stood in silence. He sighed and explained the majan's request, the vice admiral's near brush with disaster, and his own intervention. By the end, Wheeler was shaking his head.

"Hunt's a bastard," he said at last. "Look, he hates your guts, Ben. You need to be careful around him, all right?"

Commander Sky shrugged. "It won't matter what I do, John. The man's going to hate me all the same."

"Yeah. I know. But all the same, watch your step. You've got a friend in Councillor Fisher and a few of the officers. But amongst the flag officers you're not so well loved."

"Noted. Thank you, John."

"You're a good soldier, Ben, and a better commander. The USC needs men like you. I want to make sure you stay."

Skylark smiled. "Thank you."

Commander Wheeler nodded. "I should get back or I'll lose my turn."

"Sure I can't interest you in a drink?"

"Certain. I'm finally winning a game of craekers. I don't want to give that up." Wheeler grinned impishly at Skylark.

"I won't keep you then," Skylark replied, laughing. He walked Commander Wheeler to the door of the apartment and shook his hand. "Thank you again, John."

"Always," Commander Wheeler said. He smiled and left.

"What was that about?" Binky asked when Commander Skye shut the door.

Skylark simply shook his head and went back to retrieve his wineglass. The party atmosphere had returned by the time Skylark reappeared. He noted the majan leader's curious gaze and drifted over to talk to him.

"You are concerned about something," the majan noted.

"I am," Skylark said. He shook his head and changed the subject. "The tahorah has requested at least one guard in day and night shifts. One of the team is to escort the guards to and from her accommodations."

The majan nodded. "I shall go first. There is much I wish to discuss."

"I figured as much. I will take you."

"Good." The majan went back to the party to relay news of the tahorah's request. It made the daemon guards grin. Skylark watched a while before retreating into his thoughts.

15

"They did not mistreat you?" Sarcen asked his queen as soon as Commander Skye exited the suite.

The tahorah smiled and shook her head. "I am told you are staying with the chief?"

"Yes. His team live together like a clan, but they are not family. They have spare rooms in their house. It is a high house. Where is the chtakah?"

"Still in talks with the USC admiral. They appeared to like each other well enough."

The tahorah smiled. She took up her mother's brush and started combing her hair.

"Let me," Sarcen said. He took the brush from her and gently ran it through her black hair.

"Hair," he said. "It is strange. Even the chief shaves his down to almost nothing."

The tahorah laughed. "That is his business. I like mine."

Smiling, Sarcen combed her hair in silence. "Tahorah," he said suddenly. "What now?"

"The government here is complicated," the tahorah said. "Each country has representatives in separate councils who decide what each councillor on the United Council must decide. The United Council does not represent countries, but regions. It runs one military, the United Space Corps, but each country has their own armies as well." The tahorah shook her head. "I cannot understand how they ever get anything done."

Sarcen snorted. "They are primitive. Did you know they eat animal?"

"Yes, Sarcen. That means they are hungry, not primitive."

The majan pulled a face. "And the ragnar?"

"They know less than we. It is certain that it is wiser to work together now, though. Finally, Father's dream. I wish he were here to see it."

Sarcen stopped brushing the tahorah's hair and wrapped his arms around her. "You make him proud. You make us all proud."

The tahorah leant back onto Sarcen's chest. "Thank you," she whispered.

Sarcen held her until she fell asleep. Laying her gently onto the bed and covering her in blankets, he took up his post at the door. There, he stood in silence until Binky arrived with his replacement.

Skylark returned to the apartment to find Team 6 gathered around the television. "What's going on?" he asked.

"News," Spike said. He turned up the volume.

"…And rumours that an emissary of the alien invaders has arrived at the USC Headquarters in Vancouver have been confirmed this evening in a statement released by USC Admiral Gregory Brooke. The statement reads that 'a diplomatic conference is currently being held for the mutual benefit of both species.' Admiral Brooke continued by saying he has high hopes that both species can find a mutually agreeable solution to their current situation."

Skylark sat down on the couch and listened eagerly.

"The news has prompted several riots in the Canadian refugee camps in Detroit, though Mr. Duncan Schwartz of the Society for an Inter-Species Alliance says that the talks are long overdue and that he believes humanity as a whole will benefit from the conference."

The news cut to an interview with a portly German man who rambled on in a thick accent about his incredible hopes for a peaceful intergalactic society.

Skylark grunted and stood. "What's for dinner?" he asked.

"Leftovers," Spike said.

Skylark raided the fridge, ate quickly, then retired to his room to read. Outside, he could hear his team talk in low voices. He fell asleep still holding his book.

The conference, such that it was, took just over a week to conclude. The details of the alliance were settled, finalized, and sealed with the signatures of everyone involved. Both Councillor Fisher and Councillor Tsutume were pleased with the result. Councillor Brand had proved difficult but bowed under pressure.

Following the conference, all USC Strategic teams were summoned to a massive lecture hall. They sat, chatting while they waited for the briefing to start. The buzzing hum of their talk ceased as a large group of daemon arrived. Nearly one hundred fully armoured warriors strode through the auditorium doors, with one daemon leading. Skylark recognized him immediately. He nodded his greeting. The majan nodded back and the daemon found seats in the back of the hall. It was not long before noise returned to the auditorium.

"Wonder what's going on," Binky said.

"We'll find out soon," Skylark said. He waved at Commander Wheeler and Team 87 as they arrived. Wheeler walked to him and they shook hands.

"Room for us, Commander?" he asked.

"Absolutely. Binky, move down."

Team 6 stood and moved in several seats to make room for Commander Wheeler and his team. They sat and the lights dimmed. The auditorium fell silent as Admiral Brooke, the members of the Council, the tahorah, and the chtakah walked across the stage. The teams stood to attention.

"As you were," Admiral Brooke said into the podium's microphone. The teams sat.

"Good evening, USC Strategic." The admiral smiled at the crowd. "As you are uniquely aware, our species and our planet face a brand new threat. A new, possibly virulent species of hostile alien has been discovered. It attacked Way Station S8-09. All three thousand souls on board were lost.

"In light of this tragedy, and the nature of the threat, the United Council has reached out to our former foes and we have reached an agreement that has satisfied both parties."

Councillor Brand cleared her throat and was ignored. Skylark's lips twitched with the threat of a smile.

"However, it means changes to the USC of an unprecedented

magnitude. Many of these changes will be phased in to minimize disruption. As the front line of this fight, Strategic does not have the luxury of time.

"As of this minute, all USC teams will be expanded to six members. That new member will be a daemon warrior."

The auditorium erupted in expressions of surprise or protest. The admiral clenched his jaw and stood back from the microphone. The hall fell silent again. Skylark and Wheeler glanced at one another.

"Command of each team remains with the trained infiltrators who were promoted to the position," Admiral Brooke continued, once the hall settled. "That said, we are integrating the daemon into USC personnel. It is expected that, in the future, command may fall to one of them. If you make this a problem for the USC," the admiral said, "I will make it a problem for you."

Skylark grinned. "I like him," he murmured to Wheeler. Wheeler snorted.

After a pause to get his point across, the admiral continued his speech. "The daemon are also maintaining their own forces under sole daemon command. I expect that all USC personnel will go out of their way to ensure that relations with the daemon remain smooth. Make no mistake, we *will* need their help.

"The mandate of the USC was always to protect Earth. And we will continue to do so until the bitter end. USC Strategic commanders, you are to report to the Admiralty Floor at 1830 for a formal dinner. It is not optional. That is all. Dismissed."

Noise erupted from the soldiers as the delegation left the stage. Skylark and Wheeler remained sitting, as did the daemon warriors until the auditorium was largely empty.

"Interesting," Skylark said.

"Another member?" Binky asked. "We do good with just us."

"That we do," Skylark said. "But I'll be lying if I didn't think a daemon will be damned useful."

"Come on," Wheeler said, standing. "We should dress in our formals if we're dining with the admiralty tonight."

Skylark grunted. He stood. "Let's go, then," he said. He led the way up the stairs only to be confronted by the majan leader.

"Did you know?" he demanded angrily.

"Did I know what?" Skylark asked. "About our extra teammate? No."

The majan searched Skylark's eyes before relaxing slightly. "I do not like," he said.

"Many of the teams feel the same," Skylark said. "It seems we're both going to have to do some growing."

The majan laughed suddenly. "I am chastized," he said. "We will serve well. But it is for Tahorah."

"Just don't tell that to the other commanders and everything will be fine."

"Hah!" The majan grinned and nodded. He left the room, the daemon following. Skylark recognized Butan amongst them. The daemon met his eye and gave a sheepish smile. Skylark smiled back and began walking again.

At precisely 1830, the massive door to the Admiralty Floor of the USC Headquarters, Vancouver swung open, revealing an enormous dining room with a suitably enormous table. On the right, a cavernous marble fireplace sheltered the blaze which leant a flickering golden glow to the room. Wheeler and Skylark immediately stood from their places on the sofas in the foyer as the admiral appeared at the door, smiling.

"Welcome, Commanders," he said cheerily. "Please, come in." He stood at the doors and greeted each commander as they filed past. He paused a moment when he got to Skylark.

"Commander Skye," he said, taking Skylark's hand in a firm grip. "I've heard a lot about you, son."

Skylark smiled. "I understand that not all of it is good."

The admiral smiled, his brown eyes dancing. "We'll talk on that later, I have no doubt."

Skylark nodded and walked on. He frowned, not sure if he should be concerned. He looked around and paused midstride as he spied Captain Gergiev speaking to Vice Admiral Hunt. The captain smiled at Skylark, excused himself and approached.

"Commander!" he greeted warmly. "It is good to see you!"

"Captain," Skylark said. Then he noticed the new lapels. "I beg your pardon," he said. "Commodore. Congratulations on the promotion, sir."

Gergiev grinned. "Thank you, Commander. It came as a shock." He lowered his voice. "It's usually only prigs who get to be flag officers."

Skylark grinned and tried very hard not to look at Vice Admiral Hunt. A young private in formal uniform carrying a tray of drinks walked past. Commodore Gergiev snatched one up and handed it to the commander.

"I understand, Commander, that you have managed to form something of a bond with our newly made intergalactic allies."

"I'm not sure that a bond is the correct way to phrase it," Skylark said. "It's more of a mutual respect."

"Is it?"

"To be honest, I'm not sure how mutual it is," Skylark said with a smile. "But I sure as hell have a healthy respect for them."

Commodore Gergiev laughed. He noticed another officer and excused himself. Skylark stepped back to create space for the commodore to pass. He took a sip of his brandy and watched the room. All the flag officers were present, though only the newly made commodore and the admiral seemed comfortable mixing with the regular officers.

"I feel out of place," Commander Wheeler said quietly as he came to stand by Skylark.

Skylark nodded. "You're telling me. I was born in the ghetto at the fence."

"It's the same shit," Wheeler said. "It's just wearing perfume."

Skylark grinned.

"Have you seen the seating plan, Ben?"

"There's a seating plan?"

"The Council will be here. And so will the tahorah and the chtakah. I said that right, right?"

"I believe so," Skylark answered.

"You're sitting beside the admiral."

Skylark blinked. "I am?"

"According to the fancy gold lettering that spells your name on the seating card, yes."

"Well, shit."

Wheeler laughed and clapped his friend's shoulder. "Better be on your best behaviour."

Shaking his head, Skylark took another sip of brandy. "I could really use a beer," he mused.

"Later tonight, if we're not too late, we'll head out to Untied."

"Deal," Skylark said. It had been a long time since Skylark had set foot in the nightclub at the base.

By and by the councillors arrived, shortly followed by the tahorah and the chtakah. The chtakah wore an ankle-length black robe with a high mandarin collar. The collar and sleeves were embroidered in gold.

The tahorah wore a simple lavender gown underneath a full-length, sheer white, long-sleeved robe. The robe was richly embroidered in deep purple and gold. Her dark hair was tied up away from her face in an intricate braided design.

The admiral greeted them both warmly. He offered his arm to the tahorah, who took it graciously, and whisked her away to make the rounds. The chtakah scanned the room, met Skylark's gaze and approached.

"You are Chief," he said, extending his hand. Skylark took it.

"Commander Skye," he said.

The chtakah grinned. "You look different without armour."

"So do you."

The chtakah grunted. He turned to watch the tahorah a moment. "She did well," he said. "Stood strong against much."

"You sound almost surprised, Chtakah."

The daemon glanced sidelong at Skylark. "The tahorah is much like her mother. Her heart is gentle. It is sometimes difficult to remember she is strong." He shook his head. "But, she has her father's temper."

"Why did you agree to the alliance?" Skylark asked suddenly. "You could have just left us to our fate."

"And what good would that do us? Yes, we would avoid the ragnar for a time. But they would find us eventually. Or perhaps something worse will. And then what? Who would there be to come to our aid? No. It is better to make friends than enemies."

"I'm not sure friendship is the right word."

"Not yet, Commander," the chtakah smiled. "But time is a patient master."

"It's a pity about his students," Skylark answered. The chtakah laughed. It was a deep, rumbling sound.

"The majan tell me you are good host," he said after he finished laughing.

Skylark shrugged. "Even though I tried to feed them meat?"

"You did not know." The chtakah turned and faced Skylark, his expression earnest. "They say you are good. One has told you his name. That honour must not be underestimated."

"I am grateful," Skylark murmured.

"Perhaps, one day, you will earn mine."

Skylark flashed a grin. "That would be nice."

"Ladies and gentlemen," the admiral said, his booming voice jovial. "I am informed that dinner is ready. Please find your seats."

Skylark found himself seated between the admiral and the chtakah. The tahorah sat on the far side of the admiral, with Councillor Fisher beside her.

"I hope you don't mind," the admiral said cheerfully to Skylark. "It will be a vegetarian meal this evening."

"I'm looking forward to it," Skylark replied. "It's been nothing but steak for a week at home."

The admiral grunted a laugh. "You have an interesting file, Commander Skye," Brooke noted. "It made better reading than my wife's most sordid novel."

"Having lived it, Admiral, I assure you it's nothing special."

The admiral grunted. "I imagine not. Still, it has made for good reading. Your reports, especially. Short and to the point. I like that."

Skylark smiled. "I've always despised writing those."

"And I've despised reading them," the admiral admitted. Skylark laughed.

"Sending you to treat with the tahorah was one of Clegg's better ideas, it has to be said."

"I had my doubts, sir," Skylark admitted.

"So did I."

Skylark grinned. He found the admiral's honesty refreshing.

"It seems you are something of a loose cannon, Commander."

"No, sir," Commander Skylark said. "I'm ordered to do a job, and I do it."

"Well, you get ample points for flair."

"Is the commander such a problem?" the tahorah asked, smiling at Skylark.

"He gets the job done," the admiral said. "His team is the most successful in USC Strategic history. He does have a habit of frustrating his superiors, though."

Skylark said nothing. Instead, he took a sip of wine.

"Have you any idea how you're going to divide the daemon warriors, Chtakah?" Skylark asked in an effort to change the subject.

The chtakah shook his head. "My main concern is where to place the tahorah," he said.

Skylark's brows shot up in surprise, then down in a confused frown. "I don't understand. Is she not your leader?"

"Yes."

"Should she not be on the Council?"

"No," the tahorah said. "That will be the grebar. Our councillor will be much like your own, Commander. An emissary."

"Then surely you'll return to the citadel and command from there?"

"That will be the chtakah," the tahorah said. "Since he has experience in matters of warfare."

Skylark frowned at her. "I would have thought that you would be the commander. The citadel is surely the safest place for you."

"It will not do," the chtakah said. "One cannot command until one has been commanded. The tahorah must first learn what war means before she can effectively stage one. To let her try before she has learnt would be unwise."

"But she might die!"

"Astute," the tahorah said, teasing.

"Yes," the chtakah said.

Skylark shook his head. "I'm sorry," he said. "I'm having difficulty with this concept. I am used to rulers being protected at any cost."

The admiral sat back with a smile. "I had this argument already," he said. "This is entertaining."

"If the tahorah shirks her duty in war, she will not be respected.

If the tahorah cannot be respected, she will not be obeyed," the chtakah explained patiently.

"And if she dies in battle, you will be left without a leader."

"In that case, a conclave will be held to elect a new leader."

"I thought it was hereditary."

"It is, but in cases where the death signals the end of a bloodline, a new tahorah will be elected."

"Not a tehoros?"

"Not unless it is a tehoros with no living heirs."

"I see. So the gender must match."

"Yes."

"Why?"

The chtakah smiled. "Tradition."

Skylark grinned. "A good reason," he said.

Conversation floated onto more pleasant topics. In the course of the evening, Skylark learnt that the chtakah had been in the war against humanity and had proved himself a prodigy. His position, the daemon equivalent of the admiral of the USC, had been well earned.

No amount of careful enquiry could induce Skylark to speak much of himself. As far as the tahorah and chtakah were concerned, Skylark was an orphan, taken into military life from the streets when he was eight. He had known nothing but life in the military, and remembered very little of his life before that.

Skylark knew full well that neither the chtakah nor the tahorah were convinced. The tahorah, especially, observed Skylark with her intense, violet gaze. Still, Skylark refused to reveal more, pressing his lips into a thin line to emphasize the fact that he did not wish to discuss his past further.

It took three attempts at different avenues of conversation on his part before the chtakah would let his past lie. Even then, it took an interjection from Commander Wheeler, who had been listening from his position two seats from the tahorah. He leant in and said, "I spent two years with him in flight school. I've known him for ten, and you now know as much about Commander Skye as I."

The admiral looked at Skylark in surprise, but did not push the issue, though he was now more inclined to agree with Skylark's childhood psychologist. Skylark was deeply repressed; a man on the edge.

Dinner finished and Skylark found himself deep in conversation with the admiral, Commander Wheeler and the chtakah. The tahorah had retired to a chair and stared blankly at the fire, giving the appearance of her mind being elsewhere. But she listened closely.

"Be honest, Commander," the admiral said.

Skylark sighed. "I am not certain that most are ready. The war ended not that long ago. Some were too young to fight. But many of the senior officers were not. There is a great deal of ill will against the daemon, especially amongst the Canadians. Orders will be carried out, sir. But there will be a great deal of tension."

"And do you not resent us, Commander?" the chtakah asked.

"I was not yet born when the war ended. I don't remember a time when you weren't here, Chtakah. And your presence had very little to do with my world until I learnt about you in military school."

"You do not blame us for the formation of the ghetto at the fence, where you were raised?"

Skylark gave a soft smile. "I believe each man is responsible for his own actions. You did not build the ghetto. We did. It was not you that formed the drug lords, the gangs, and the lynch mobs. We did."

"I fear you are rather unique in that opinion," the admiral said. "I say that without blame," he said to the chtakah.

The chtakah inclined his head.

"I fear so too," Skylark said. "It will take a great deal of effort on everyone's part to ensure this is a smooth transition."

"Perhaps it will not be so terrible," the chtakah said.

Wheeler scoffed. "Humanity has enough trouble accepting its own," he said bitterly. "I am sorry, Chtakah, but I do not share your optimism."

The chtakah cocked his head at the commander. He observed him with the same curiosity that Skylark had often been subjected to. Wheeler shifted uncomfortably under the intense gaze. At length, the chtakah nodded, as if confirming something to himself, then turned to the admiral.

"I fear the commanders may be correct. I have sensed deep hostility in the Council, as well as several of your officers."

"I will not let it get out of hand, Chtakah," the admiral assured him. "Personnel have been notified of the severe penalties any disturbances will bring down on them."

The chtakah sighed. "I find I regret our war. In different circumstances, I am sure we might have been good friends."

"We might yet," Skylark said with a tight smile. "Some of us anyway."

"Which reminds me," the admiral said. "I would have your daemon candidates go through a six week intensive course. They need to know how the USC Strategic Division operates in the field. I hope they can acquire our language as quickly as you."

"It should not be difficult."

The admiral grunted. He turned to the commanders. "There is little else left to discuss. With everyone else in bed, I suppose it is only fair to let you sleep. Dismissed, Commanders."

"Thank you, sir," Skylark said. He and Wheeler exited the dining room together.

"That," Wheeler said as they crossed the grounds to the Strategic tower, "was weird."

Skylark smiled. "Is every dinner like that do you suppose?"

"They're flag officers. Of course it is."

Laughing, Skylark shook his head. The commanders parted ways on the twentieth floor of the Strategic building. As he left the elevator, Wheeler turned to Skylark.

"Did you notice Councillor Brand and Vice Admiral Hunt at dinner?" he asked.

"No."

"We're in for trouble, Ben. Stay sharp."

"You too, John."

"Goodnight."

"Goodnight."

The doors of the elevator slid closed. Skylark leant back against the railings in the elevator and pondered Commander Wheeler's words.

16

Amar Gregorvich grinned as he put the drill in its storage container. He looked with satisfaction at the progress he had made. In just two months, the Space Monkeys—a team of highly trained asteroid miners—had dug deep into the rock, extracting enough iron to make a small fortune. Fraggle, the company responsible for asteroid mining, would be keeping its shareholders extremely happy this quarter.

"Not getting a response from the station," Ali Almatwali said, his Egyptian accent making it difficult to understand over the comm. link.

"Probably another solar flare, like last week," Amar said. "Come on. It's dinner time and I'm hungry."

The pair walked carefully from the mineshaft, their magnetic boots the only thing keeping them pinned to the asteroid. They clambered into their buggy and headed towards the station that had become their home.

Orbiting outerworld planet PX8X, the enormous asteroid had been targeted by Fraggle for its rich iron and titanium deposits. Wormhole travel had made it easy, fast, and cost effective to ship the raw ores to the processing plant in orbit around PX18M. The ships delivered their cargo and returned in a matter of hours. The refined material could then be sent to Earth, a journey that only took weeks. The miracle of artificially created wormholes, known fondly as slipstreams, had made billionaires of the daring.

Ali kept trying the comm. The station did not respond.

"Relax," Amar said. "We're almost home."

The station came into view as they rounded a spiralling peak jutting from the surface of the asteroid. Nothing looked amiss. The lights were on, sending glittering shafts of light and shadow all around.

Amar parked the buggy beside the ladder leading into the station. Out of habit, they left the hatch open when they left to work in the mine. It saved them some time upon their return not to have to fumble with the key code in their thick space mining suits. Ali closed it tightly behind him as he entered the pressurization chamber.

"Pressurizing," a mechanical voice said. Ali and Amar waited patiently until the lights in the chamber came on and the door to the station proper slid open.

"Hallelujah," Ali muttered. He and Amar slipped out of the spacesuits and entered the station.

"Where the hell is everyone?" Ali asked.

The normally busy hallway was silent.

"Probably watching the news. Did you hear about the secret meetings that were happening with the aliens?"

Ali grunted. He turned around to make his way to his quarters and froze. He reached out and tugged on Amar's sleeve.

"What?" Amar demanded. He noticed Ali's suddenly pale face and turned.

His eyes met twelve others, all in the same grotesque head. The pincers in that head clicked.

The men screamed.

Skylark and Wheeler, along with Teams 6 and 87, stood in the bleachers and watched as the one hundred daemon warriors trained. Personal firearms were new to them, but they did not seem to have much difficulty learning to use or care for them.

"Like for ships," Skylark overheard one say to his friend. "But for you."

Wheeler watched everyone train in fascination. Skylark's eyes were continually drawn to the tiny pale woman in the group. She looked so small and dainty amongst the pack of tall, muscular warriors it might have been tragic. That she consistently outperformed most of them made it comical.

Her hand-to-hand combat performance proved especially

impressive, making up for her lack of size and strength with devastating speed and exceptionally clever tactics. Only the majan leader managed to beat her. The teams watched as she tossed around the daemon warriors with effortless grace. She was bested only the once that Skylark saw.

"There is good reason she is still tahorah," the chtakah said. He had appeared in the bleachers to stand unnoticed beside Commander Wheeler. He spoke to Commander Skye. "I taught her myself; a unique challenge. Much had to be adapted to suit her size."

"You taught her well," Skylark said.

"The admiral tells me that testing team compatibility will begin soon. I hope there are few problems."

"Team compatibility, Chtakah?" Wheeler asked.

"Yes. He wishes to move daemon through teams to test how they will function together. Training drills. Is that what you call them? They will start soon."

Skylark grunted. "That should prove interesting."

"I am told my warriors are up to standard. What does that mean?"

Skylark grinned. "It means they can do everything we can."

"Probably better," Wheeler said.

The chtakah grinned. "You underestimate yourselves."

"Do we? Look at you. Now look at us. Most of us are a good foot shorter than your shortest warrior, and all of us are at least half their mass."

"Ah, physically," the chtakah said. "But there is something in your light, Commander. Humanity has great capacity. More than your small frames would suggest. In a fight, you would be a match."

Wheeler smiled slightly. "I believe you just complimented us, Chtakah."

"Yes," the chtakah said. "But it is not flattery."

"Is there a difference?"

"Yes," Skylark and the chtakah said in unison. They exchanged an amused glance, then turned their attention back to the training daemon.

Before the six-week training period was complete, all the team commanders had followed Skylark's example and watched the daemon warriors train. Many brought their teams to watch as well. Quiet discussions arose amongst them; too quiet for Skylark to eavesdrop upon from where he sat in the bleachers without being horrifically obvious. He hoped, however, that the commanders and teams could all see and were discussing the value of the daemon that was so obvious to himself.

One hundred days training with the daemon followed. All day, every day for one hundred days, each team drilled with a new daemon. Skylark enjoyed his days with the majan. They were smart and, because they knew and trusted Skylark, obedient. Butan proved especially eager to please. At the end of each day, Skylark insisted that the daemon on their team sit with the team for the evening meal. On the first day, he was the only commander to do so. On the second day, in a silent show of solidarity for a commander who was quickly becoming the centre of malicious gossip amongst non-Strategic USC personnel, Commander Wheeler also made it a requirement for his team. By the end of the hundred days, almost all commanders were requiring it.

Day one hundred saw Team 6 matched with the tahorah. Unlike Butan, who had been easy with his smiles and even attempting to joke, the tahorah was quiet, serious, and extremely focussed. Wheeler had described her as coldly professional when he discussed his day with her over a quiet beer on Skylark's balcony. It proved to be a very accurate description.

Skylark did not blame her. She had a plethora of prejudices working against her. Not only was she a woman, but she was more petite than most women entering the USC, and an alien to boot. In truth, considering his own team's constant back talk and bickering, her polite, aloof demeanour was refreshing.

The tahorah was no more open during dinner.

"You did well," Skylark noted as the private serving dinner placed a plate of food before the commander.

"Thank you, Commander," the tahorah said.

"Everyone did," Skylark continued conversationally. "I don't envy the admiral and the chtakah, who have to make their decision soon."

"Our warriors know their place. The commander will not change that."

"Not true," Jack said. "The commander makes all the difference. A good commander inspires confidence. They're someone you can trust explicitly. Commanders like that are a rare breed."

The tahorah smiled slightly but did not speak further. She ate quietly and, because she did not talk much, was first to finish. She watched the commander and his team interact until Skylark noticed she had stopped eating.

"You don't have to stick around if you don't want to," he told her gently as Spike and Jack argued loudly about the current state of their game of craekers.

The tahorah hesitated.

"Go on," Skylark said.

"Thank you," the tahorah murmured. She stood and left, walking quickly.

Skylark watched her leave the mess and turned back to his team. His eyes met Binky's.

"What?" he demanded.

"Nothing," Binky replied with a smile that said that it was most certainly something.

Skylark narrowed his eyes at his lieutenant commander. Binky innocently smiled back at him.

The tahorah crossed the campus of the USC base, her mind on Jack's words and the chtakah's lessons. She did not notice the gang of fourteen USC privates dogging her steps until she nearly ran into a fifteenth man, who blocked the passage from the central tower to the barracks the daemon shared with the new recruits.

The tahorah smiled an apology. "Pardon me," she said, moving to step around him. The private blocked her path.

"Where are you headed?" he asked.

The tahorah frowned. "To bed," she said slowly.

Snickers alerted her to the presence of the men behind her. She turned her head and counted. Fifteen in total. She turned back to the man before her and saw two more had appeared from around the corner. Seventeen.

"Stand aside," the tahorah said softly. Her pulse raced and the hairs on the back of her neck stood on end.

"Come on," the man said. "We just wanna talk."

"Perhaps later."

"Oh sweetie," the man said, prompting yet more snickers from the gathered crowd. He stepped forward. The tahorah refused to back down. She set her jaw and squared her shoulders.

"It's cute how you think you have a choice," the man said. "You should relax. It'll hurt a lot less." He grabbed for her.

Cadet Scott Pierce scrambled up the tree with his apple. He had snuck away from the military school that stood adjacent to the USC base. Most of the students were in the mess the school shared with USC personnel. Pierce couldn't stand the noise and the press of bodies. He never could. He needed quiet for a time.

The tree was his favourite spot. He often came here to read or relax away from his asinine classmates. He had never been seen or, at least, no one ever paid him any notice. He settled on his favourite branch and took a large bite of his apple, glancing around as he did. He froze when he saw the rabble of men surrounding a young, pale woman with black hair Pierce knew to be the leader of the daemon.

He knew what he was seeing, and his stomach dropped. He stared, unbelieving, until the fight started. Swearing, he scrambled down the tree and ran towards the group. Then he stopped. What could he possibly do? He was all of fourteen, and skinny to boot. But he knew who could do something about it. He had been gossiped about almost nonstop in school and various lecturers referenced him as either a shining example or the worst possible kind of cautionary tale.

Pierce turned and sprinted for the mess in search of Commander Skye.

"Commander!" he called as soon as he spotted Commander Skye, grinning with his team in the mess. He was unmistakeable, with his blue eyes and dark hair shaved close to his pate. Pierce ran forward. "Commander Skye!"

Commander Skye turned and raised his eyebrows. Someone from Team 56 grabbed the boy's arm. "You should know better than to disturb the officers in the mess, boy," he growled.

Pierce struggled. "Let me go!" he said.

Commander Skye was up and in front of Pierce immediately. "Let him go," he demanded.

Remembering his place, Pierce immediately saluted.

"Commander, they're attacking her!"

"Attacking who?" Binky asked, having stood and moved behind his commander. But Skye knew immediately.

"Where?" he demanded.

"Smoker's Alley, sir."

Commander Skye moved, leaving the mess at a sprint. Team 6 followed immediately.

The fight was still going when Skylark arrived. Had it been anyone else, Skylark was certain they'd be unconscious on the ground by now. The tahorah was still up and fighting.

Skylark paused only briefly before he jumped into the fight. His arrival prompted some of the attackers to flee. When Skylark reached the tahorah, she had been tackled to the ground. It took five men just to keep her pinned there. Skylark grabbed the man who knelt on top of her and slammed him hard against the wall. The rest of the team took out the others.

"What the fuck do you think you're doing?" Skylark spat at the private.

"Fuck you, you fucking traitor," the man spat back.

Skylark delivered a backhand that sent the man to his hands and knees. The commander picked him up and slammed him against the wall again.

"Do you have any idea what you're doing, Private?" he demanded. "Do you have any idea what's out there? You do something to jeopardize this alliance, and you are damning humanity to face this fight alone and it's a fight we will not win." He slammed the man back again. "Now who's the fucking traitor?" he growled.

The USC Military Police arrived. Skylark threw the man to the ground in disgust. "Get him out of my sight," he growled at the MP before going to the tahorah, who struggled to stand. She pushed him away.

"Get away from me!" she snapped. She tried to stand again.

"Jack!" Skylark barked.

"Got it, sir," Jack said. She ran to the tahorah and put one arm around her. "Come on," she said gently. "Let's get you to Medical."

"I can walk," the tahorah protested weakly.

"I know," Jack said softly. "And I'm here to make sure you do."

"Thank you."

Jack smiled. They moved as quickly as the tahorah's battered body could manage. The MPs were pushed aside. The tahorah would let no one else touch her.

Skylark watched them go, his expression so fierce, it took the gathered MP some courage to approach.

"What happened, sir?" an officer asked.

Skylark noticed Cadet Pierce standing a few feet away, watching. He ignored the MP and walked to him. Pierce stepped backwards, looking a little terrified.

"Your name, Cadet?" Skylark asked.

"Pierce, sir," the cadet answered. "Scott Pierce."

"You at the military school, Cadet Pierce?"

"Yes, sir."

Skylark looked him over. Tall and scrawny, as Skylark had been at his age, he nevertheless showed a great deal of courage and initiative in coming to the commander for help.

"Find me when you graduate," he said. "I'll see about getting you a job."

Expecting a severe reprimand for being where he shouldn't, Pierce looked stunned. "Yes, yes, sir," he stuttered.

Skylark smiled. "You'd better get back to the Cadet Barracks. If you are reprimanded, send your commanding officer to me."

"Yes, sir." Pierce saluted and ran off.

Skylark watched him disappear into the dark before turning back to deal with the waiting MPs.

Jack sat on the tahorah's cot in the medical bay and swung her legs girlishly. The tahorah sat in silence, perfectly still. They waited for the medical officer to return with news. It had been a long wait, and another hour of testing.

"Well," the medic said as he walked into the room, flipping pages on his electronic chart. "It looks like you'll be just fine." He smiled at the tahorah. "You'll be sore for about a week or so, and I would advise you to refrain from heavy training during that time. And, if it's all the same to you, I'd like to keep you overnight for observation, just to make sure."

The tahorah nodded absently. The medic placed his hand on her shoulder. "I am sorry." Knowing he was not wanted, and having more patients to treat, the medic left.

Jack and the tahorah sat in silence for a while. The tahorah began to shake. Noticing, Jack wrapped her arms around her and pulled her close.

"It's going to be all right," she soothed.

"I don't understand," the tahorah said, moments before breaking down and sobbing.

"Yeah, well, I do," Jack said. "They're fucking arseholes. You didn't do anything wrong. You just had the fucking audacity to be a girl, and better than them at pretty much everything, and an alien. It must have really pissed them off that an alien *and* a girl was better than them. And they made the mistake of thinking that because you've an angel's face and a small frame they could bring you down. And you kicked their arses. Hard. Atta girl."

Despite herself and her tears, the tahorah giggled. Jack smiled. She held the tahorah close for a moment longer. The tahorah pulled away and looked at Jack, searching the lieutenant's grey eyes with her uncomfortably intense gaze.

"How did you cope?" she asked at last.

Jack blinked in surprise. "How did you know?"

A slight, sad smile touched the tahorah's red lips. "Your light."

"Yeah. Skylark mentioned something about you guys seeing that." Jack sighed. "It was my dad," she said, settling in beside the tahorah again. She drew her knees up to her chin and hugged them. "After I came out. I knew he could be an arsehole, but, well, no one expects the Spanish Inquisition. I told him I was gay and he just flipped. I was sixteen. Mum cried in her bedroom but didn't do anything to stop him." Jack rubbed the back of her neck.

"I ran away that night; signed up to the USC. It was better than the streets, you know? And, really, I wanted to make sure that if that fucker ever came for me, I could kick his fucking arse straight to hell." Jack grinned. "And now I can." She glanced over at the tahorah, who watched her with wide eyes, tears streaming in silent rivulets down her cheeks.

"Hey," Jack said. She wiped the tahorah's tears away. "None of that. I'm all right. I'm all right now."

"How?" the tahorah whispered.

"Skylark had a lot to do with it," Jack said. "I hated every man I ever met since my dad. But Skye's special. At first it was a grudging respect. Then I started liking the bastard. Now he's family. I'm not going to lie. A lot of guys are complete arseholes. But not all of them. He helped me see that."

The tahorah leant over and wrapped Jack in a tight hug. Jack smiled and replied in kind.

"Don't tell him I said that," she whispered. "He'd never let it lie."

The tahorah giggled again. She pulled away, smiling, then kissed Jack on her forehead. "You are good," she said.

"Thank you, Tahorah."

"Naschari," the tahorah said quietly. "My name is Naschari."

Realizing the profound honour that was just bestowed upon her, Jack smiled brightly. She reached out and touched Naschari's scarred cheek. "You should rest now," she said. "I'll come visit you after breakfast."

Naschari nodded. She allowed Jack to help her into the bed.

"Sleep well, Naschari," Jack said. Naschari squeezed Jack's hand briefly before closing her eyes. Jack walked quietly from the room—And straight into Skylark.

"Sorry," Skylark said.

"Was heading to the sheriff's office," Jack said, grinning. "Looking for you."

"How is she?"

"Bruised," Jack answered. "Angry, upset, you know. All the warm and fuzzies that come with sexual assault."

Skylark grimaced.

"She'll be fine," Jack said. "She's a tough little nut. Anyone softer would have been jam by the time we reached them."

"She gave them a good beating," Skylark said with a grin.

"She did. Now come on, I think we've earned a drink, don't you?"

"Thank you," Skylark said. "For looking after her."

Jack shrugged. "I had a good teacher. Now come on. I think Sarah's working the bar tonight, and I really want to get laid."

Celebrations were, unfortunately, postponed for Commander

Skye. He never even made it to the door of the Strategic nightclub, Untied. A young corporal intercepted him.

"I'm sorry, Commander," the corporal said. "Admiral Brooke has requested your presence in his study."

Skylark sighed and rolled his eyes. He turned to Jack and offered an apologetic shrug. "Have fun," he said.

"I will," Jack replied, flashing an evil grin. She entered the club and Skylark followed the private, who showed Skylark the door, then left. Pausing to collect himself, Skylark knocked twice.

"Come in," the admiral said, his voice cheery. Skylark did as he was told.

"You wanted to see me, sir?"

"Yes, I did. Come in. Sit down."

Noting Vice Admiral Hunt's presence, Skylark sat.

"You look sombre, Commander," Brooke noted. "Is something the matter?"

"There was an incident on the base this evening, sir," Skylark answered.

Admiral Brooke's eyebrows rose, but Hunt waved his hand dismissively. "Boys just being boys, I expect," he said.

"Are you suggesting that boys are naturally rapists, sir?" Skylark asked coldly. "Because that offends me."

"Rape?" the admiral demanded.

"No one got raped," the vice admiral said.

"Because I was there to intervene," Skylark replied, rising to his feet, his muscles coiled in preparation for a fight. He glowered at Hunt. "And the only reason it got that close was because the tahorah had the wherewithal not to create a diplomatic disaster by killing anyone."

"The tahorah?" the admiral asked.

"From what I understand, those men were brutally beaten."

"Those men are lucky to be alive," Skylark growled. "I would not have shown her restraint had I been in her situation."

"Would you both shut up!" the admiral roared, standing. Skylark and Hunt snapped to attention. "Now," Brooke said, forcing calm into his voice. "Commander Skye, what happened?"

"The tahorah was attacked on her way to the barracks after dinner, sir," Skylark said.

The admiral turned to Vice Admiral Hunt. "Is this so, Vice Admiral?"

Hunt hesitated.

"Is. This. So?"

"Initial reports suggest so, sir," Hunt said.

Skylark closed his hands into fists and clenched his jaw. To avoid starting a brawl with the vice admiral, he stared hard at the wall behind Admiral Brooke's desk. The admiral sank slowly onto his chair. He looked at Skylark.

"Is she all right, Commander?"

"Injured, sir. She is in Medical. They're keeping her overnight for observation."

"Christ." The admiral turned to Hunt. "I want the reports on my desk. Yesterday. I need all the information before I announce this cluster-fuck to the chtakah. How is it you were alerted to the incident, Commander Skye?"

"A young cadet from the school approached me in the mess, sir."

"His name?"

Skylark hesitated. "Pierce, sir. Scott Pierce. He observed the mobbing from the tree near Smoker's Alley."

"He shouldn't have been out," Vice Admiral Hunt muttered.

"It was a good thing he was," Skylark growled, not looking at Hunt.

"You are dismissed, Vice Admiral," Brooke said. "Those reports."

"Yes, sir," Hunt said. He stood to attention, saluted and left the office.

"Sit, Commander," the admiral said gently. "You're making me agitated."

Skylark sat, but the tension did not leave his body. Admiral Brooke observed him a moment.

"And here I was, going to offer you a drink as a congratulations for a smooth one hundred days of daemon integration," Brooke muttered.

"I'll take that drink, sir," Skylark said with a small smile. "If it's still being offered."

Brooke laughed. He nodded and poured Skylark a large helping of brandy from the decanter on his desk.

"Thank you," Skylark said as he took the glass.

Brooke sighed. "Why is it that you are around whenever something goes wrong, Commander?"

Skylark shrugged. "It's just good luck, sir," he said.

Brooke laughed. "Never accept a promotion, Skye," he said. "All the headache and none of the fun." He shook his head.

"I noticed you observing the drills," Skylark said, changing the subject. "Any idea how you're going to match up the daemon?"

"Actually, I was going to let the commanders decide. They were in the drills. They could see better than anyone which daemon responded best to their team. I was going to start with Team 1 and work my way up. But, given tonight's events, I'm letting you have first pick."

Skylark raised his brows. "Thank you, sir." He sipped his brandy and leant back in his chair. With Hunt gone, he felt the alcohol work out the tension in his shoulders.

"Am I supposed to guess, Commander, or are you just going to tell me?"

"Who I want on my team, sir?" Skylark smiled. "I have three choices, actually."

Brooke raised his eyebrows.

"The leader of the majan," Syklark said. "If I can't have him, I'll take… uh… I'll point him out, and either of them only if I can't have the tahorah."

Brooke did not conceal his smile. "The tahorah? Why her?"

"She's good. Very good. I observed the daemon training before the drills. She is better than most of her own warriors. And we have enough trust between us, I think, to make it work."

"Is that all?"

Skylark sighed. "And because after tonight, I'm not sure she'll be very safe."

Brooke observed Skylark in silence.

"She can take care of herself," he continued, compelled to explain under Brooke's stern gaze. "But she's small and will be continually underestimated. It could spell disaster if she ever loses her temper."

"I find these reasons adequate. I will relay your request to the chtakah. Be aware, however, that the nature of her position affords her the luxury of choice. She may decline."

Skylark nodded, then grinned. "Then I get one of the other ones," he said. "And that would suit me just fine." He finished the brandy.

"Very well. Dismissed, Commander."

Skylark stood and saluted. "Thank you for the drink, sir."

Brooke grunted and waved Skylark away.

17

Skylark entered Medical shortly after breakfast. Jack had gone ahead. Skye visited one of the stores in the first floor of the Strategic tower of the USC Headquarters to pick up some flowers en route.

When he arrived at the tahorah's room in Medical, Jack was nowhere to be seen. The tahorah was sitting in bed, her back supported by multiple pillows, her eyes closed. A purple bruise dominated the right side of her jaw, stretching to below the line of her gown's collar.

She opened her eyes as the commander approached. "Commander," she greeted.

Skylark smiled slightly. He walked to the bed and placed the plant he held on the bedside table. The tahorah stared at it.

"How are you feeling?" Skylark asked.

"I ache," the tahorah replied. "But I am not angry anymore."

"Where's Jack?"

"Getting tea. What is that?"

"An orchid," Skylark said. "It's for you. I thought it might cheer you up."

"Is, is it glowing?"

Skylark smiled. "It's hard to see in this light though. The florist said they have managed to add bioluminescence into the fertilizer without harming the plant. When it starts losing its glow, you just add more."

"It's beautiful." The tahorah reached out and touched the petals of one of the blossoms gently.

"I saw it and thought of the garden in the citadel," Skylark said.

The tahorah looked up at him and smiled. "Thank you," she whispered.

Skylark smiled. "Listen," he said. "About last night—"

"I should apologize, Commander," the tahorah said. She looked down at her hands.

Scowling, Skylark asked, "What? Why?"

"I should not have snapped at you as I did. I—"

"Shh," Skylark said. He placed a comforting hand over both of hers. "You did nothing wrong."

"You were trying to help."

"Given what you went through, a little anger is more than reasonable."

The tahorah attempted a smile. It became a grimace. "I was still wrong. I should have better control."

Skylark shook his head. "You have more than I would have thought possible."

The tahorah sighed, fighting against the tears that threatened to spill. "All my life, I have been surrounded by people twice my height and more than three times my mass. I have never been made to feel so small." The tears spilled despite the tahorah's best efforts.

Skylark sat on the bed beside her and wrapped his arms around her. "I'm sorry," he whispered. The tahorah leant into his muscular chest as her shoulders shook with the effort of containing her grief.

"Tahorah," Skylark said gently. "The admiral is allowing the team commanders to select the daemon they want on their teams." He pulled away and smiled at her. "There is a place for you on my team, if you want it."

"Thank you," the tahorah said quietly. "I will think on it."

Skylark nodded. He brushed the bruise on the tahorah's face gently, then stood. "I should go," he said.

The tahorah nodded. "Commander," she said as he reached the end of the bed. Skylark turned to her.

"Thank you."

The commander offered his lopsided smile and left in a hurry, meeting Jack at the door of the room. Jack gave a secretive smile and Skylark narrowed his eyes at her.

"You great big kitten," Jack murmured, laughing. Not waiting for a retort, she walked into the room and handed the tahorah a cup of tea. Skylark rolled his eyes in irritation and returned to his apartment.

It took five majan and the chtakah all their strength to restrain Sarcen as he struggled to free himself and embark upon a murderous rampage. The enraged majan only stopped struggling when the tahorah walked through the door. She broke the tension when she burst out laughing.

"It is not humorous!" Sarcen growled.

"No," the tahorah said, still laughing. She walked forward and wrapped her arms around Sarcen. "No, it's not. I'm sorry you're angry."

"Why are you not?" Sarcen asked, plainly confused. His limbs now free from his fellow majan, he pulled the tahorah close.

"I was," the tahorah admitted. "But I am not anymore."

"We should kill them all!" Sarcen growled. The tahorah laughed again.

"No," she said. "Not all. We need friends if we are to fight the ragnar."

"We can find others."

"Can we?" The tahorah pulled away. She reached up and touched Sarcen's cheek fondly.

"Ones that will not hurt you."

"They also saved me, Majan," the tahorah said quietly.

Sarcen scowled.

"The chief and his team. They came when they learnt I was in danger. They are not all evil."

Sarcen blinked in surprise, taking time to process the new information. He pulled his queen into a hug again. "Then we take the chief with us, and kill the rest." The threat was empty, as the tahorah well knew. Skylark's involvement in the incident had mollified Sarcen's rage enough that he could now be reasoned with.

The tahorah smiled. "Maybe one day."

Sarcen sighed.

The USC Strategic team commanders gathered on the stage as

ordered. The mood was slightly sombre as a week ago the entire USC had been shaken with the scandal of the attack on the tahorah. Twelve privates now languished in the USC prison awaiting their dishonourable discharge papers to be processed before they were removed to a civilian prison near Gate Compound 4. A further eight privates were currently under investigation.

For now, however, the team commanders tried their best to focus on the matter at hand. They sat in order of their team number on the tiered stand on stage. Their team members and the one hundred daemon warriors soon to be their new teammates sat in the audience, mumbling amongst themselves in a dull drone. Various USC and civilian dignitaries occupied the front two rows of seats in the auditorium.

Skylark was in the sixth seat of the front row on stage. He desperately wished he wasn't. Being in front of so many people, many of whom were very important, made him slightly nauseated. Only the fact that he could see Jack and Spike trading bets on whether or not he would be ill kept him in his chair.

The auditorium full, the admiral and the chtakah strode across the stage. Silence fell.

"Ladies and gentlemen," Admiral Brooke said, speaking into the microphone. "I'd like to bid you a good morning. It has been an interesting four months. I am pleased with the progress of our new USC personnel and I am proud of USC Strategic, mostly, for their continued diligence in achieving something that none of us were sure would be achievable."

A small smattering of applause made its way through the audience.

"I am pleased to announce that the process is over, and we can move forward now with confidence. Our team commanders have selected their new team members. I hope you will now join me in welcoming them to USC Strategic."

Skylark shifted in his seat. He felt genuinely nervous. He had not been informed of the tahorah's decision prior to the ceremony. He also did not know if he would be getting either his second or third choice. None of the commanders knew. The admiral had not sent word and there had been little opportunity to speak with him.

Skylark suspected that the admiral had been deliberately avoiding him.

"Daemon warriors, when your call sign is announced, please come onto the stage to greet your commander formally."

Skylark stared down at the USC Strategic pin in his hand. He would pin it on his daemon's lapel and that would be the formal acceptance of the daemon into his team.

"Saracen," Admiral Brooke said.

Sarcen stood and walked onto stage. He clasped hands with the admiral briefly before moving on to the commander of Team 1. It was amusing at how high Commander Speedman had to reach in order to pin the daemon's new insignia on his lapel.

"Welcome to Team 1, Saracen," Speedman said.

"Thank you, sir," Sarcen replied. The pair walked off stage to join Team 1 sitting in the audience at the back of the auditorium.

The admiral went through the next four call signs slowly. "Doc, X-Wing, Vamp, Jazz."

Skylark looked down the stage to find the tahorah standing next in line. He concealed a smile as the admiral called her forward. "Tahorah."

She walked boldly forward and took the admiral's hand. Skylark stood as she approached him. She stopped in front of him and saluted. Wearing a USC uniform, with her dark hair pulled back in a regulation style, it was easy to forget that she was an alien. Skylark saluted in return. He pinned the USC insignia onto her lapel.

"Welcome to Team 6, Tahorah," he said.

The tahorah smiled. "Thank you, sir."

Feeling relieved, Skylark led her off the stage to his team. Jack jumped up to give the tahorah a hug.

"Thank God," she said. "I'm glad you said yes!"

"Thank you," the tahorah said. She settled beside Jack and Skylark and watched the rest of the ceremony with interest. Butan, Skylark was pleased to note, joined Team 87.

"That is good," the tahorah said when she saw. "He liked the commander."

"He seemed an easy man to please," Skylark noted.

The tahorah smiled. "You would be surprised."

The audience had largely stopped paying attention by the time the last thirteen names had been called. Only fear of reprimand stopped them from talking through the ceremony.

At last, Admiral Brooke turned to the audience. "That concludes the formal section of today's ceremony. I'd like to invite the guests and teams to a luncheon on the lawn."

Thunderous applause filled the hall, and the admiral walked from the stage with the chtakah at his side.

"So," Spike asked. "Are they best pals now, or what?"

"They have a healthy respect for one another," Skylark said.

"Gods," Doorman said. "Let's get some food. I'm starving!"

"I second that," Binky said.

Team 6 filed out of the auditorium.

Later that evening, the tahorah found herself in the spare room in Team 6's apartment. She looked around the room from the door. She was greatly relieved to find it private, unlike the shared sleeping space in the barracks. There was room enough for a double bed with a bedside table, a dresser and a small table with two chairs.

Smiling, the tahorah walked forward and placed her orchid on the table before walking to the dresser. It took her very little time to unpack her duffle bag. She had brought few clothes with her.

Her armour was another matter. It took some exploring before she found the correct panel for the armour mannequin. Once everything was tidied away, she sat on the end of the bed.

"Everything all right?" Skylark asked from the door.

The tahorah glanced up. "Yes, Commander. Thank you."

"We're not in the field, Tahorah. Skylark will do, or Ben if you prefer."

"What do you prefer?"

"I prefer my team is comfortable enough to speak their minds in my presence. Call me whatever makes you comfortable."

"So, Commander, then."

Skylark smiled. "We're headed downstairs to the club. You best get dressed."

"The club?"

"The nightclub."

"Oh, I don't think—"

"You're coming," Skylark said. "You're the reason we're celebrating."

"Oh."

"Consider it a bonding exercise."

"Yes, Commander."

Skylark smiled and left the doorway. Feeling utterly lost, the tahorah went to her dresser and searched for some suitable clothes.

Team 6 gathered in the living room, enjoying a beer when the tahorah walked in.

"Oh, no!" Jack said. "No. You cannot go clubbing wearing that."

The tahorah looked down at her gown. "I have nothing else."

"Oh, sweetie." Jack walked forward and took the tahorah's hand. "Come with me."

The boys watched on in amusement as Jack dragged the tahorah to her room. Jack stuck her tongue out at them before slamming her door shut.

"Hey," Spike asked. "You think they're making out in there?"

Skylark slapped the back of Spike's head lightly. Binky and Doorman laughed. Their laughter stopped suddenly as Jack stepped out of her room, closely followed by the tahorah.

"You laugh, I will hurt you," Jack warned, before she stepped aside.

Nervously, the tahorah stepped forward. She wore a dark teal cowl-necked shirt that had no sleeves, nor a back to speak of, save three strips of sequinned fabric that kept the thing on. Tight black jeans with tall black boots finished the outfit. Her long black hair had been pulled back into a high ponytail, revealing a long, elegant neck.

"I was going to do her face," Jack said, if only to fill the sudden oppressive silence. "But she's so pretty she doesn't need makeup."

"No," Skylark said, the first to recover from shock. "She doesn't." He looked directly at the tahorah. "You look beautiful."

The tahorah looked down at the floor to hide her blush. "Thank you," she murmured.

Jack grinned and looked between the stunned expressions of the three men in the lounge room. "You lot ready to go, or what?"

"Yeah," Binky said, rousing himself so suddenly it looked like a spasm. He stood. "Let's get going."

Everyone else stood and Team 6, led by Jack, made their way to the elevator.

"Oh. My. God." Binky mouthed to Skylark. Skylark grinned.

The club was loud, as always. Team 6 gathered around a high table designed for standing against rather than sitting at. Jack bought the first round—tequila shots. After the fourth round, the tahorah was compelled to dance. She, Jack, and Spike took to the floor while Skylark, Doorman and Binky looked on.

"I don't care if she's an alien," Binky said. "She's fucking hot."

Doorman grunted his agreement, then turned to Skylark. "Beer, sir?"

"Please," Skylark said.

The evening, judged a success by the way the tahorah, Jack, and Spike stumbled from the club laughing breathlessly, ended moments before the sun came up. Team 6, all a little worse for wear, stumbled to their apartment in a loud gaggle. Even the tahorah, who had been so reserved just hours ago, joined in the excited babble, her bubbling enthusiasm no doubt aided by the copious amounts of alcohol she had consumed.

Skylark, as Commander, did his best to maintain some semblance of sobriety. Though tipsy, he was nowhere near as plastered as the rest of his team. As such, he could observe them in private amusement.

"You're all going to regret this in the morning," he said.

Jack stuck her tongue out at him. "Totally worth it," she said. "Who knew our little alien could dance?"

"Psht," the tahorah said. "You think you are so special. Everything dances."

Skylark laughed softly, the laugh became much louder when the elevator doors opened on the ninety-fourth floor and Spike spilled out of the elevator onto the foyer.

"Come on, little bro," Doorman said, picking his brother up. "Let's get you to bed."

"Screw you," Spike mumbled.

Binky laughed so hard he could barely walk. Skylark wrapped an arm around his heaving shoulders. "Come on, Binky," he said. "Up you get."

Binky straightened and, still laughing, made his way to his quarters. "That was a good night," he said.

"It was," his commander agreed.

"Goodnight."

"Night, Binky. Sleep well."

Binky was snoring before Skylark shut the door. The commander went to the kitchen. He could hear Jack and the tahorah giggling in the tahorah's room as he filled a pitcher of water.

The giggling stopped and Jack left the room. She came into the kitchen to fill herself a glass of water.

"Hey," she said.

"Hey," Skylark replied.

"That was awesome. You should've come dance."

Skylark shook his head. "I don't dance."

"Unless it gets you laid, right?"

Grinning, Skylark picked up the tray he had prepared. "Even then, there's not so much dancing."

Jack rolled her eyes. She downed her glass in three easy gulps, then kissed Skylark on his cheek. "Goodnight, Commander," she said.

"Goodnight, Jack."

Skylark watched her skip to her room and vanish inside. He shook his head and walked to the tahorah's room. He knocked.

"You dressed?"

"Yes," came the muffled response.

Skylark entered to find the tahorah sitting on her bed, massaging her bare feet. "They hurt," she said. "I have not danced for so long before."

"You did very well," Skylark said. He poured her a glass of water and dropped an effervescent tablet into it. The water bubbled furiously, turning lurid pink.

"What is it?" the tahorah asked, accepting the glass from him.

"It's a vitamin drink," Skylark said. "Drink it down. You'll be thanking me in the morning."

The tahorah raised the glass to her lips. She looked speculatively up at Skylark before drinking the glass down. She pulled a face. "Tastes fuzzy."

Skylark laughed. He refilled the glass and placed it on her bedside table, along with the pitcher of water.

"You'll probably wake in the night. Drink a glass of water before you go back to sleep. It'll help with the headache in the morning."

The tahorah smiled. She reached out and, taking Skylark's hand, pulled him down to kneel before her. She cocked her head as she observed his face. Leaning forward, she whispered, "Thank you, Commander." She kissed him.

The tahorah pulled away. "You are good," she said, looking him in the eye.

Skylark managed a smile, though his face didn't seem to be working properly. He helped the tahorah between the blankets of her bed. She smiled up at him, then fell asleep.

Skylark remained kneeling by the bed a moment before slowly standing. In a daze, he picked up the now empty tray and exited the room. He paused at the tahorah's door, looking back before he gently closed it. He walked to his quarters, placing the tray absently on the kitchen counter as he passed.

He entered his quarters and prepared for bed. He knew he should have felt uncomfortable at that kiss. He knew that it may well be a bad sign. Relations between team members was a punishable offence in the USC. As it should be. It made things unnecessarily and often dangerously complicated.

Skylark threw his shirt into his laundry basket and picked up his toothbrush. He frowned down at it a moment, trying to get his stunned brain to function, before he applied the toothpaste and scrubbed his teeth.

When later he lay in bed, he thought of the tahorah. Skylark convinced himself later that she had meant to kiss his cheek, as Jack had done, but missed slightly, getting instead the corner of his mouth. In the moment, though, it did not feel like one of Jack's affectionate pecks. It was a gentle caress, soft and sweet, but far from innocent. He reached up and touched the corner of his mouth where the tahorah's lips had landed. It still tingled.

He fell asleep smiling.

Morning was unkind to Team 6. Skylark had risen early to prepare for the deluge of whining team members. He moved around the kitchen preparing his famous hangover cure—a large pot of pho. He didn't care to keep very quiet. Jack was out first. She glared at

Skylark, who smiled impishly at her, before flopping dramatically on the couch.

"Good morning," Skylark said.

Jack grunted.

Binky was out next, headed straight for the bathroom where he emptied his stomach. Skylark laughed at him when he dragged himself out again.

"Shut up," he growled, collapsing on the armchair.

Skylark let his soup simmer and fetched glasses of vitamin water for Jack and Binky. They accepted them, barely even managing a grunt in thanks. Next out was Doorman, though he only went to his brother's room, carrying his rubbish bin. He remained in the room for a while before joining the rest in the lounge. Though tired, Doorman had never been much of a drinker, so he did not suffer the unfortunate fate of the rest of his team.

"Ah," he said. "Commander's famous hangover cure."

Skylark grinned. "Vegetarian today. It'll be ready soon. How's Spike?"

"Not so great. He probably won't make it out of bed until this afternoon, if then."

Skylark grunted.

"What about our newest member?" Doorman asked.

"Still sleeping. I'll wake her when the soup's ready. Did you want a coffee?"

"That would be great. Thanks."

No sooner had Skylark handed Doorman his coffee than the tahorah opened her door. She had dressed in her casual uniform, her hair still pulled back. Though her eyes were red and a little swollen, she didn't appear to be having the adverse effects that so afflicted Binky, Jack, and Spike.

"Good morning," Doorman greeted pleasantly.

"Good morning," the tahorah answered. She pulled a face at the sound of her own rough voice. "I've swallowed a hunnte."

"A what?"

"A hunnte. It's a..." She cocked her head. "An animal," she finished lamely, unable to come up with an Earthly comparison.

"I'll take your word for it." Doorman sipped his coffee.

"Do you want a coffee, Tahorah?" Skylark asked.

The tahorah frowned and shook her head.

"Breakfast will be up soon."

Pulling a face, the tahorah moved to sit on the couch. Refusing to budge, Jack simply lifted her legs in order to make room. The tahorah took them, sat down and placed them on her lap. "I feel tired," she said, closing her eyes.

"You're doing a damn sight better than the other three," Doorman noted. The tahorah smiled.

Sounds of violent retching echoed down the hall from Spike's room. The tahorah looked across in alarm.

"He'll be fine," Doorman said. "Just needs to purge his system."

The tahorah looked unsure, but since no one else seemed overly concerned, she did not move.

"All right," Skylark said moments later. "Soup's up. Everyone at the table."

Groaning, Jack and Binky rolled out of their seats and staggered to the table, Doorman and the tahorah following. Skylark served them all a large helping of the pho. They ate slowly, except for Skylark, who was hungry.

Spike groaned loudly from his room.

"Baby," Doorman growled. He finished his soup quickly and gathered soup and water for his brother. He rolled his eyes at Skylark who smiled in response.

"There was water in my room," the tahorah said to Skylark. "Was it you?"

"You don't remember?"

The tahorah shook her head. Skylark was unsure whether to be relieved or disappointed. He nodded. "That was me. Best way to recover from a heavy night is to hydrate."

"Thank you, Commander."

"You're welcome."

"Such a fucking gentleman," Jack said. "Where was my water?"

"You ought to have known," Skylark answered. "This is new for the tahorah."

Jack rolled her eyes.

The apartment fell quiet after breakfast. Doorman and the tahorah cleaned up before they returned to their quarters. Jack and Binky retired to bed immediately following breakfast.

That left Skylark alone. He spent the afternoon at rest, alternatively reading and snoozing in the sun on his private balcony, enjoying the silence.

The phone in Skylark's quarters buzzed at 0200 the following morning. Skylark rolled out of bed and lifted the handset. "Skye," he croaked.

"Commander Skye, this is Major Thom. You and your team are required in auditorium 7 ASAP."

"We'll be there." Skylark hung up and turned on the lights in his room. He dressed in his USC fatigues and woke the others. By 0230, they were in the elevator heading down to the main tower of the base. At precisely 0243, Team 6 was sitting in the auditorium. Not one of them had spoken. Binky looked across at Skylark.

"What's going on?" he asked.

"I haven't a clue."

"There's been another attack," someone from Team 56 said. She turned to face them from the next row. "A mining station, this time."

"How do you know that?" Binky demanded.

"I overheard the report to the admiral."

"Well," Binky said, leaning back. "Fuck."

"More bugs?" Doorman asked.

"Looks like," the woman replied.

At 0315, the admiral walked onto the stage. The auditorium fell silent.

"Good morning, USC Strategic," he said sardonically. "I'm not really one for speeches, so I'll just get to the point. We received a distress signal from a Fraggle relief transport team shortly after they docked on one of their asteroid mines past the Outerworlds.

"Attempts to contact the station by both Fraggle Resources and the USC have been ineffective. It might be a simple equipment malfunction, or solar interference. We're assuming the worst—ragnar."

Someone on Team 56, a tall Swede, leant over to a teammate. "The world is ending, my friend. The ragnar? On a rock? Ragnarok."

"You are an idiot," his teammate replied.

"—teams to investigate," the admiral continued. "The rest of the teams are required in orbit. Two destroyers and a research vessel will be deployed under command of Commodore Gergiev. All teams not aboard the *Magellan* or her sister ships are to be in space should there be a direct threat to Earth. We have not been able to locate any ragnar hives to date, and we need to be vigilant. They could be anywhere.

"Teams, when I call your number you are to prepare for immediate departure upon the commodore's destroyers. Team 6."

"Of course," Doorman muttered. "Who else?"

"Suck it up, princess," Skylark said, standing. "Let's move."

"Team 87," the admiral continued. Skylark caught Wheeler's eye and they nodded to each other. They met outside of the auditorium.

"Us again, huh?" Wheeler said.

"Wouldn't want anyone else with me," Skylark said.

"Did you catch the other teams?"

Skylark shook his head and grimaced.

"Teams 89, 94 and 98," the tahorah said.

"How do you know that?" Binky demanded.

"The majan told me."

"The majan aren't here," Skylark said, with a frown.

"It's true," Butan said. "I heard them."

"The fuck?" Spike demanded.

"Telepaths," Skylark said. He grunted. "Of course," he muttered. He glanced sidelong at the tahorah. She smiled.

"Do not worry, Commander," she said. "We cannot read thoughts unless you permit us."

"Oh good," he murmured.

"Much to hide, Commander?" Jack asked.

"Hush."

Jack laughed.

Commodore Gergiev watched the screen. They were three days into their journey. Commander Skye and his team behaved much like the last time. He had them up and physical early in the morning. They continued their persistent jibes and generally undisciplined behaviour during the training, and almost everywhere they went. However, Gergiev was the first to note that when Skylark became serious, so did they. Unlike the other teams, with perhaps the exception of Team 87, Team 6 had fully integrated their daemon member.

Of Team 6, the tahorah was the most professional, remaining relatively distant from the rest of the team, though as the days wore by, that became less and less an issue. More and more she had started giving input. No doubt she was encouraged by Skylark's respect for her opinions, the same respect he showed for everyone in his team.

Teams 87 and 6, both most experienced in dealing with the ragnar, were treated with some deference by most of the crew aboard the *Magellan*. The other teams, too, understood that Commanders Skye and Wheeler were leads in this mission. That was not to say they liked it.

The stress of coping with the new alien members had frayed at the nerves of the commanders of teams 89, 94, and 96, due in large part to their own team members' reaction to the hulking warriors from space. The commodore hoped that Teams 87 and 6 would serve as an example of how it could be done, and done well.

The USC sciences division aboard the *Magellan*, once primarily mechanical and electrical engineers, were almost exclusively biologists, with the British Army and Canadian Air Force providing the majority of electrical and mechanical engineers. As the daemon had been granted full access to the USC, several on the team of biologists were daemon. The daemon called them scholars. Commodore Gergiev had found that so amusing it had entertained him for an entire evening. Granted, he had little other entertainment that night save for a glass of brandy.

The scientists had very few problems getting used to their daemon colleagues. Enquiring minds paid little heed to physical differences and the exchange in knowledge and information happened at an astonishing rate. In the mess, the scholars and the scientists sat together, often deep in discussion as their curious minds soaked up new information like sponges.

It was something that Skylark noticed as well. He watched them at dinner sometimes, a small smile on his face. What it meant was anyone's guess, but the commodore like to think the sight did something to restore the commander's faith in people, if such a thing were possible.

Three more days of travel, and the fleet of ships left the slipstream just shy of the Aborgini Asteroid Belt. The commanders had gathered at the commodore's request on the bridge.

"We're too big for in there," Gergiev noted, nodding his head towards the asteroid belt. "The *Magellan* would get chewed up in a matter of minutes."

"The long-haul fighters should fit," Skylark said. "If they're as agile as Christie says."

"They are," the commodore said. "This will be their first real test."

"We have the location of the station?"

"The station is no longer broadcasting, but the last known location has been noted. The pilots know where to start looking."

"Let's get on with it, then."

USC Strategic *One* hummed gently as Team 6 boarded.

"We've gotta come up with a better name for this ship," Binky told his commander.

"And what would you suggest?" Skylark asked.

"I don't know. Something better than *One*."

"Welcome aboard, Team 6," a Scottish-accented voice said over the comm. link.

"Oh no," Binky said. He turned to Skylark.

"I'd like to thank the commander for his recommendation. Warmed the very cockles of my heart, it did."

"You requested him?" Binky demanded.

"I like him," Skylark said with a grin.

"We're gonna die."

"For the record, this bird may appear to be a little big, but I guarantee you, she's as spry as a twelve-year-old gymnast."

Binky glared at Skylark and received the barest of shrugs in return.

"I hate you, man," Binky muttered.

"Pussy," Jack said, throwing a punch at Binky's armoured shoulder.

"We are a-go, Team 6. Strap yourselves in. This is going to be fun!"

"I really hate you," Binky said to Skylark.

The team gathered in the common room and sat, their armour making it difficult to find room. Only the tahorah seemed comfortable. The special requirements of daemon warriors, namely a channel for their retractable electro-magnetic blades, made it impossible for them to wear USC regulation armour. Their armour, though they matched the USC armour in function, proved less bulky and far more flexible.

The tahorah remained silent as she listened to the team tease Binky. Skylark noticed.

"Nervous?" he asked.

She nodded.

Skylark patted her shoulder. "We've got your back," he said. She smiled at him and returned to her private thoughts.

The five teams, each in their own long-haul fighter, moved steadily through the asteroid field, keeping in close contact with one another.

After two hours, Christie called Skylark to the cockpit. "I think we're coming up on it, sir."

"Cutting it a bit close, aren't we?" Skylark asked when he arrived only to see the edge of an asteroid brush past the fighter's nose.

"Don't worry," Christie said with a grin. "I've got it."

"Is that it?"

An asteroid drifted up to reveal a large hunk of rock, almost the size of Earth's moon though nowhere near as regular in shape.

"I think so. It's this one or the tiny fella behind it."

The comms crackled to life. "Strategic *One*, this is Strategic *Two*, over."

"We're here," Skylark said into his comm. "What do you see?"

"We're on the sunny side of the street, sir. It's definitely bugs."

"You see the station?"

"Yes, sir. At least, it used to be. It's covered in brown stuff, sir."

"All right, Strategic *Two*. We're on our way. Can you do a fly by and see if anything is moving down there?"

"Yes, sir."

Skylark pressed the comm. link in the panel at the door of the cockpit. "All right, Team 6, it's go time. Teams 87 and 94 will meet us on the ground. Teams 89 and 98 will be providing aerial cover. Binky, you're transport today. Start the shuttle. Everyone, suit up." He turned to Christie. "Take us around, Christie."

"Yes, sir."

Strategic *One* banked, taking the ship to the side of the asteroid lit by the red-gold glow of the sun the asteroid belt circumnavigated.

"I see it, sir," Christie said.

Skylark squinted at the screen. A tall outcropping stood at the edge of a crater. Were it not for the shade of dark brown, which contrasted with the charcoal of the asteroid surface, and for the fact that it was not a slender, bizarrely pointed spire common on the asteroid made the station stand out. Had it been on Earth, it might have easily been overlooked as a nothing more than a tall outcropping of rock.

"Strategic *Two*, this is Skye, do you read?"

"Yes, sir."

"Something's moving on the station surface. I advise you to pull up."

"Yes—son of a bitch!"

Something reached up at the USC Strategic *Two* fighter, latching onto one of the guns. The Strategic *Two* banked hard, but the many-legged thing wouldn't let go.

"Christie!" Skylark barked.

"Got it!" Christie said. He fired a shot between Strategic *Two* and the station. The bug let go of Strategic *Two* and retreated.

"Jesus fucking Christ!" the pilot of Strategic *Two* breathed into the comm.

"You all right, *Two*?"

"Yes sir. There appears to be no damage."

"Did you get a look?"

"Something like a giant soldier ant, sir. Only with teeth."

Skylark swore. He pressed the comm. link in his chest plate. "Commodore Gergiev?"

"We read you, Commander."

"Did you get any of that?"

"Yes, Commander."

"I'd appreciate a couple of fly boys, sir."

"Already on their way. ETA fifty-six minutes."

"Thank you, sir." Skylark turned to Christie. "You keep close enough to save our asses," he said. "But stay well clear of that station."

"Not a problem, sir."

"I'll call you in when we need you."

"Yes, sir."

Skylark turned and headed down to the flight deck. "Heads up all teams," Skylark said into his comm. "Last time we hit an abandoned nest. Looks like these space bugs are still around in this one. I'm going to be honest. I have no idea what to expect. As far as I know, we're considered food, so shoot first and ask questions later. If we're lucky, we might just find survivors. Don't shoot them."

Binky scoffed. "Noted, sir," he said as Skylark climbed into the transport shuttle.

Skylark grinned at him, tapped him on the shoulder and shut the transport door. "We're good to go, Binky."

"Binky, this is your favourite pilot," Christie said over the comm. "You are cleared for departure. Flight deck doors are open."

"Thank you, Christie," Binky said. "Lifting off now." Binky guided the transport carefully past the single-person fighters and out of the doors. "Christie, we're clear."

"Thank you, I can see that. Deck doors closing. Call me if you need anything!"

"Thank you, Christie," Skylark said.

"Cocky bastard," Binky muttered.

"He's a pilot, Binky." Skylark reminded him.

"Ben?" John Wheeler's voice said over the comm. link.

"I'm here, Wheeler. What can I do for you?"

"Tell me that the station isn't crawling all over with bugs right now."

Skylark looked past Binky in the cockpit to the station. The brown skin that covered it had suddenly become darker and it moved as hundreds of ragnar swarmed the surface.

"Fuck," he said.

"Not what I was looking for."

"All right, Binky, bank left. Put us down behind that range." Skylark spoke into his comm. "John? Follow us, we're touching down behind cover."

"Yes, sir!"

"Helmets on, Team 6."

In silence, the team attached and secured their helmets. They touched down gently on the uneven surface of the asteroid. Binky shut the door of the cockpit. "See you soon, Skylark," he said. "Don't do anything stupid."

"Yes, Mom," Skylark said, grinning.

He and the remainder of Team 6 exited the shuttle and waited for Team 87 to land. Team 94 landed a few feet back, behind another ridge. The three teams gathered.

"All right," Skylark said. "The station has one entrance, a hatch on the sun side. We know there are bugs in there. We don't know if there are any survivors. Team 94, you and Team 87 will draw fire. We have some fly boys on their way, but for now, we have two teams in space to provide support. Team 6, we're going in. If it isn't human, it dies. If there are survivors, we get them out. If there are none, we blow this whole thing to hell and hope there aren't more bugs hiding out there somewhere. Everyone clear?"

"Yes, sir," everyone answered.

"All right, after you 87 and 94."

The teams moved out. They walked as quickly as they could in their magnetized boots.

"Holy mother of God," Wheeler said as he peered around the curve of a spire.

Skylark chanced a look as well.

The entire station, as well as a good portion of the ground around it, was covered in the undulating bodies of creatures that looked something like the unholy, giant lovechildren of ants and scorpions... with teeth. They formed a defensive circle around their new nest, their many-eyed heads ever watchful.

Skylark pulled his head back. "Getting through is going to be tough."

"Commander Skye, this is Flight Commander Rwigamba. We have you on visual."

"Nice to know, Rwigamba. Feel like squishing a few bugs for us?"

"Yes, sir! Inbound now."

Skylark looked up and waved as the squadron of single person fighters approached. They opened fire on the insects, clearing a path to the station. The path closed immediately as more insects poured out of the station and some that had been shot struggled back to their feet.

One, clinging to the side of the station, leapt as a fighter flew too close. It took the ship to the ground, its pincers slicing through the metal with ease.

The teams joined in the fight, taking cover to load and reload their weapons.

"Ready, Team 6?" Skylark said. He looked directly at the tahorah. She nodded once and her eyes lit up with purple light. The commander grinned at her.

"On my mark. Three... two... mark!"

And they were off, running full tilt down the passage that Teams 87 and 94 as well as the now beleaguered flight squadrons created and kept open for them. They did not pause, except to take down the ragnar that crossed their path, their longest fight happening just outside of the hatch. The ladder had remained lowered and the hatch itself was wide open. One particularly large ragnar hovered at the mouth of the hatch. Skylark opened fire, striking it twice in the eye. It scurried backwards, allowing him to climb the ladder.

He had thought the creature dead. He had been foolish. No sooner had he climbed halfway into the hatch than strong pincers closed around his waist and lifted him out of sight.

"Fuck!" Spike yelled, readying his weapon.

"No!" the tahorah said. "You'll hit him!"

"Well, what the fuck—" but Spike didn't finish. The tahorah scurried up the ladder. A purple glow from the chamber above told everyone that she had drawn her blades.

Skylark pulled a knife from his boot. Almost the length of his forearm, it would more correctly be called a dagger. He slashed furiously at the ragnar's head. Though the knife cut, it didn't do much damage. The ragnar arched its vicious tail. Skylark stopped struggling and stared as the end of the tail lengthened into a sharp javelin-like point, dripping with pale venom. The spike drew back, then plunged forward.

A purple flash and the javelin fell to the ground, severed from the ragnar in a single stroke. The creature spasmed, dropped Skylark and turned. Skylark rolled onto his side to see the tahorah standing near the hatch, long purple electric blades sizzling, extending from her forearms. Her eyes glowed fiercely.

The ragnar turned, clicked its pincers and scuttled forward. The tahorah was both elegant and fierce. She turned and ducked, reaching back behind her to slice off the foremost leg. Seizing the brief moment when the ragnar lost sight of her, she ducked beneath it and forward to where the neck met the thorax. The barely visible joint split cleanly as she thrust her blades into it, tearing the ragnar's head from its body. The ragnar stumbled backwards, shuddered, then collapsed. The tahorah ran to Skylark.

"Commander!" she said.

"I'm good." Skylark struggled to rise to his feet. He managed, with the tahorah's help. "I'm good." He retrieved his gun from the ground and peeked over the hatch. "You guys coming up or what?"

"Good to see you, sir," Doorman said. He holstered his gun and climbed, Spike and Jack fast on his heels. They shut the hatch and sealed it.

"Pressurizing," the mechanical voice said. They waited for the console light to turn green before opening the door to the station proper. The halls were deserted, but filled with the sounds of scuttling and clicking, picked up by the armour's external microphones.

"You know the drill," Skylark said.

"You better hurry, Ben," Wheeler said over the comm. "We're not doing so well out here."

"You betchya, John. We'll be out soon."

A blood-curdling scream turned Skylark's head. He led the way down the corridor towards the sound. The team walked carefully up two flights of stairs before signs of ragnar occupation began to show. Masticated skin lined the walls and floor. Ragnar, of a different variety, scurried along the surfaces, depositing, packing, and shaping pink lumps to extend the lining.

There were three. Skylark dispatched the first two and Jack the other. The translucent white bugs exploded when fired on. Team 6 walked forward. Someone was blubbering loudly, praying in what Skylark recognized as Arabic. The team moved forward until they came to the largest room in the station.

They had guessed that, like the way station, this is where the ragnar preferred to nest. They were not wrong. The lounge and recreational room had been transformed into a smaller version of the nursery Team 6 had encountered on the way station. The room did not have any doors, so the ragnar had stretched the skin of two flayed people across the opening.

As of yet, the team remained unnoticed. Skylark chanced a glance into the room. Three hundred or so skeletons hung by their feet on mucus threads from the ceiling. One man remained, hanging upside down and naked, facing a massive ragnar with a swollen belly. She was laying, the large white eggs carefully gathered by smaller, white, more ant-like creatures and placed in hexagonal piles around the room.

Another kind of ragnar, one with blade-like extensions on its forelegs, scurried down the chain. The man's blubbering grew louder, changing to a scream as the scuttling insect cut into him. In a matter of seconds, the ragnar had made a series of cuts and then, in a single move, ripped the meat right off the man's bones.

Skylark turned back as the meat fell in a pile on the ground, where it was swarmed over by workers.

"There are no survivors," he choked into the comm. "Setting the explosives."

Two high-grade explosives were attached by the door. Skylark sent Team 6 back out. He took one of the small, round grenades Strategic had dubbed "Rovers" and armed it. He set it on the ground in front of the door. It sprouted six mechanical legs.

"Good boy, Rover," Skylark said, patting it affectionately. He turned and ran, following his team back to the fight outside.

The fight on the ground continued as Team 6 dropped through the hatch. After a brief assessment, Skylark led his team to Team 87's position.

"Where's John?" he demanded to Hank. Lieutenant Hank looked around, then froze.

"Ben!" Wheeler yelled over the comm.

Skylark turned. Commander Wheeler had been separated from his team, and three ragnar now circled him, their venomous tails raised and ready to strike.

"John!" Without thinking, Skylark leapt forward. He shot as he ran, but most of his bullets bounced off the thick armour of the ragnar.

"I can't shoot them," Commander Wheeler said, trying nonetheless. "Their armour is too thick!"

"Shoot at the narrow section between their head and body," Skylark barked. He slid into the circle, tackling Wheeler out of the way of a ragnar strike. Three more strikes shot out in rapid succession.

Wheeler screamed as the spike went through his armour, piercing his shoulder.

"John!" Skylark yelled as Wheeler was lifted off his feet.

Another spike shot forward. It did not land. The tahorah leapt from the back of one of the ragnar, slicing through the tail of the attacking insect with her glowing blades. Wheeler slid off his spike and landed on the ground, his armour losing pressure quickly. Skylark ran to him as Team 6 arrived, driving back the ragnar. He pulled out a small gun, pressed it into the hole in the armour and pulled the trigger, sealing the armour.

"Binky!" Skylark barked into his comm.

"Coming."

Inside the station, the Rover scuttled into the nursery, drawing the curious attention of the ragnar busy within it. They gathered in a clicking, chirping circle. The Rover exploded. The effects of the explosion on the ragnar defending the nest were immediate and obvious. They became suddenly confused. They stopped their defence, some attacking one another. Others simply crumpled, dying on the spot. Most fled, scurrying back towards the nest as the circling fighters continued to pick them off.

"Ben," Wheeler said.

"Hold still, John. We'll get you out of here soon."

No sooner had he spoken than Binky landed the shuttle and the door opened. "Doorman!" Skylark barked.

Doorman holstered his gun on his back and ran forward. He helped Skylark lift Wheeler. Team 6 retreated into the shuttle. The door closed and Binky took off, followed by the shuttles for Teams 87 and 94. The other explosives in the station caught and the whole thing exploded in a silent flare of bright orange.

Skylark lowered his friend to the floor and took his helmet off. Commander Wheeler's eyes had rolled back into his skull, and his head lolled as he teetered dangerously close to the edge of consciousness.

"Stay with me, John," Skylark said. "You're going to be all right." He slapped Wheeler's face lightly. "Come on. Wake up."

Wheeler tried. His eyes snapped forward. "Ben?" he whispered.

Skylark took off his helmet. "I'm here."

"Fuck. It hurts."

"No shit," Skylark said with a smile. He started to remove Commander Wheeler's armour.

"What are you doing?"

"We have to stop the bleeding, or you'll drown in your own armour."

"Charming." He coughed, wincing in agony as he did.

"Can you sit up?"

Wheeler nodded. "I'll need help."

"Got it," Jack said, leaving her seat. She knelt on the far side of Wheeler and she and Skylark lifted him into a sitting position. Wheeler groaned.

"Sorry," Skylark murmured. He removed the pauldron to reveal an enormous hole in Wheeler's shoulder.

"Oh man," Spike said.

"That bad, huh?" Wheeler asked. He was fading again.

"Don't you dare," Skylark said, slapping his face again. "You're staying with me."

"Ben..."

"No excuses, John."

The commander of Team 87 smiled slightly and a small trickle of blood escaped the corner of his mouth. Skylark noticed, but said nothing. He pressed his lips into a thin line and pushed a sterile pad onto Wheeler's shoulder.

"Hey," Skylark said. "You'll get a nice scar out of this. Scars are sexy, right?"

"I don't know, are they?"

"Franz had one. Right across his forehead. You didn't seem to mind."

"He was a good kisser," Wheeler said, wheezing a small laugh.

Skylark grinned. "I'm sure."

Wheeler grunted. "I miss him."

"I know. You guys met in flight school, right?"

Wheeler shook his head. "Infiltration. The bastard wasn't even in my division."

"Yeah? So how did you two become an item?"

"I know what you're trying to do, Ben."

"You're staying with me, you hear? Now talk me through it."

Wheeler blacked out and returned in close succession. Skylark pressed his comm. link. "Christie!"

"I'm almost at your location, sir," came the response. "We'll have you on board in no time."

Skylark turned back to Commander Wheeler. "How did you meet?" he asked again.

Wheeler grunted, trying hard to focus. "It was like those books you read. Across a crowded room. Boy sees girl. Girl sees boy. Only, I guess, there was no girl." Wheeler fainted.

"Shit," Skylark said. He ripped his gauntlet off and checked for a pulse. "Wheeler," he said. "I know you're not dead. I can feel your pulse. Now wake the fuck up. Wheeler! John!"

Commander Wheeler stopped breathing. Skylark pulled him down so he lay on the floor of the transport and breathed into his open mouth while Doorman fetched the pump. Skylark pushed air into Wheeler's lungs pausing briefly to check for a pulse.

"We're on board, sir," Binky said, unbuckling himself from the pilot's seat and popping open the transport door.

"Christie," Skylark said. "Get us to Gergiev."

"Yes, sir."

Jack and Spike leapt from the transport, running to Medical to retrieve a gurney. They returned quickly and hauled Wheeler onto it, Skylark still pumping his lungs. They entered Medical. Wheeler coughed up a thick globule of blood, and began to breathe on his own. Skylark tossed the pump aside and took Wheeler's hand.

"Wake up, you bastard," he growled.

As if he had taken the command to heart, Wheeler's eyes opened. "Ben?" he croaked.

"I'm here."

"Fucking ow."

Despite himself, Skylark laughed.

"Commander, coming up on the *Magellan* now."

"Alert Medical."

"Already done, sir."

"It's all right, John. We'll get you patched up as good as new."

"I have no doubt, Commander Skye," Wheeler said. He smiled faintly. "You're bleeding."

Skylark touched his bloodied cheek. "That's yours," he said.

"Oh."

"We're on board, Commander." Christie made the announcement just as the medical team of the *Magellan* appeared in the doorway of the infirmary aboard the Strategic One. Skylark followed the gurney out of the long-haul fighter. He followed it as far as the flight deck door, where a medical officer stopped him.

"We've got this, Commander," he said gently. Ignoring him, Skylark stepped forward, only to be restrained by Team 94. Skylark pushed them off, but didn't follow Wheeler's gurney as it was rushed from the deck.

Team 6 and 87 gathered around him.

"He'll be okay, right?" Jack asked.

"Yeah," Spike said without conviction. "He'll be fine."

Commander Skye went to Medical the minute debriefing concluded. He did not care for food at the moment and skipped dinner. He stood at the window of John Wheeler's room, watching the medics work on his friend.

The following morning, Team 6 gathered in the gym to find Skylark absent again. They waited a half hour before returning to their quarters to amuse themselves. Skylark, in the meantime, stood at the window of Wheeler's room.

"It's safe to go in," a medic said, when she noticed he hadn't moved since well before breakfast. "There's nothing contagious that we've found. Quarantine is over."

"Has he woken?"

"Not yet, Commander, but there's no infection. He should be back with us soon."

Skylark nodded. He thanked the medic and entered the room. Pulling up a chair, Skylark sat by Wheeler's bed until lights out.

When he returned the following morning, he was told that

Wheeler had awoken in the night and was asking after him. Skylark entered the room.

"It's a sauna in here," he said. The medic looked up at him and nodded. He indicated Wheeler asleep on the bed, covered in blankets and shivering.

Skylark approached. He sat in his usual spot.

Feeling the pressure on the bed from Skylark's resting elbows, Wheeler opened his eyes and turned his head. He smiled. "Ben."

Skylark stood. He took Commander Wheeler's hand and frowned down at it. "You're freezing!"

"I can't seem to get warm," Wheeler said. His teeth chattered, but he struggled to a sitting position. Skylark helped, then arranged the blankets around him.

"You look like hell, Commander," Wheeler noted. "You haven't been eating, have you?"

A small smile touched Skylark's lips. "You know me too well."

"You should eat."

"I've been worried."

"About me? I'm flattered."

"You should be."

Wheeler grinned. Laying back on his pillows, he closed his eyes. "I was in love with you, you know. In flight school. You with your... your smarts and looks and your damned cheekbones."

"Yeah," Skylark said, smiling softly. "I know."

"Of course you do, you cocky bastard. Then you had to go and be straight." Wheeler laughed quietly. "I've never forgiven you." He glanced sidelong at Commander Skye, who looked down at his hands.

"I'm not so special," Skylark said quietly.

Wheeler shuddered. "Can you ask them to turn up the heat? It's freezing in here."

Skylark frowned. He pressed his hand to Wheeler's forehead. "You're burning up," he said.

"I'm cold," Wheeler said. "Hey, you know what made me get over you?"

"Franz?"

"You know it. Sometimes I regret following you to infiltration.

But if I hadn't, I'd have never met him. It was the most amazing six years of my life. I can't regret that." Wheeler faded quickly.

"John? Stay with me John." Skylark pressed the buzzer on the bed. He watched in alarm as the colour drained from Wheeler's face.

"Ben?" Wheeler whispered.

"I'm here."

"Why is it so cold?"

At a loss for words, Skylark wrapped Commander Wheeler in as much blanket as he could and pulled him close. Wheeler rested his head on Skylark's shoulder.

"You've been a good friend," Wheeler said. "Thank you."

Skylark pressed the buzzer frantically. "John?"

But Commander Wheeler did not respond. His eyes stared blankly and his jaw fell slack.

"John!" Skylark barked as Commander Wheeler slumped in his arms.

The medics arrived and wordlessly took over. They pushed Skylark out of the room. He stood at the window and watched, chewing on his thumb. After fifteen minutes of frantic activity, the medics stepped away from the bed. One glanced up at Skylark and sadly shook his head.

18

News of Commander Wheeler's death shook the personnel of USC Research Vessel *Magellan*. Announced sombrely over dinner, which Skylark did not attend, the crew and infiltration teams sat in shocked silence. Team 87 excused themselves shortly after the announcement, retiring to their quarters to grieve in private.

Team 6 retired to their quarters moments after. Skylark was not there, so the team collapsed into their bunks in silence. Shortly after lights out, the tahorah rose, put on her boots and went in search of her commander.

Skylark sat in the darkened gym. The heavy bag still swung, moved by the force of his blows. His mind had left him, leaving him in a shell of silence that left his ears ringing.

He was dimly aware of the gym door opening and shutting, but his mind was too distant to comprehend it fully. He sat on his legs and stared at the swinging bag in the dark.

Two small, warm hands touched him, the palms pressing against his shoulder blades. He straightened under the touch. A warm pulse moved through his tense muscles and, despite himself, he felt his body relax. His pulse calmed and the oppressive weight that had squeezed at his chest slowly melted away. He closed his eyes and let the warmth wash over him.

The hands left his back, taking their gently pulsing warmth with them and Skylark opened his eyes.

"You should be in bed, Tahorah," he said softly. He stood slowly and turned to face her.

She cocked her head at him. "He was dear to you. I am sorry."

Skylark turned away again. He looked down at his hand wraps. Though not bloody, the knuckles beneath throbbed viciously. "It was my command," he said quietly. He felt her hands touch his shoulders again, and turned around, catching them in his own. They were impossibly close now. She did not step away. Skylark stepped closer. Still, she did not step back. Instead she tilted her head up to meet his gaze.

"You should probably go," Skylark murmured, still clutching her hands. "Bad things could happen."

"Bad things?" she asked.

"Wrong things."

The tahorah frowned. "I do not understand. What wrong things?"

"This," Skylark whispered. He pulled her close and kissed her. She did not resist. The kissed lasted a long while. When Skylark pulled back, he half expected to get slapped. Instead, the tahorah stepped forward and kissed him again, with urgency.

Skylark bent down, wrapped an arm beneath her bottom and lifted her from the ground. Her legs wrapped around his waist, and his mind went blank. The dim awareness that he was the tahorah's commander, that relations of this sort were punishable by expulsion from the USC, that relations between a human and an alien so early in the alliance could spell disaster if others caught wind of it, and all the other reasons why he should push the tahorah away vanished into a pool of desire, a need to be held, and an unending, pounding ache in his heart.

He could feel her pulse pound against his flesh, every gasping breath she drew resonated in his own lungs. He was lost in the taste of her lips, the smell of her skin, the strength of her body. He buried himself in her, taking refuge from the pain of loss that had driven him into the dark and for some time, at least, it worked.

Skylark awoke to find himself naked, his arms wrapped around the tahorah, who was awake and stroking his head, which rested on her shoulder. She glowed faintly, a soft purple light just bright enough to register in the commander's eyes. He did not want to move. Moving would mean he had to leave the comfort of the tahorah's warm embrace. Moving would mean he was forced to face her and tell her that what had happened could never happen again. Knowledge of this drove a spike of ice into Skylark's chest.

"Hush," the tahorah said softly, sensing his distress and pulling him in close. "Hush."

Skylark closed his eyes and rested his head on her shoulder for a moment longer before pulling away. He sat up. He looked down at her glowing, naked form and swallowed. He had never seen anything more beautiful. He leant forward and kissed her.

"You're beautiful," he murmured.

"You are troubled," the tahorah replied. She searched his eyes for answers and Skylark looked away.

"Yes," he said. He sat up again looking around for his trousers.

"Why?"

"You should dress."

The tahorah pulled herself up onto her elbows and watched the commander dress with a cocked head. Skylark noticed. He smiled slightly, went to her and held out his hands.

"Come on," he said. "Up."

The tahorah took Skylark's offered help and he hauled her easily to her feet. He gently stroked her cheek as he drank in the sight of her. He wanted to remember her, exactly as she was now; her serene beauty. He knew he could never see it again. He pulled away.

"Dress," he said. He kissed her gently on her forehead then turned and left. He paused a moment after the door to the gym closed behind him. Caught between a desire to run back to her, and the knowledge of the dangerous position everyone was in, he stood in the hall unable to move one way or another.

At length, he walked on, retiring to his bed where he promptly fell to sleep.

The tahorah returned almost half an hour later, sliding carefully into her bunk. In the bunk above, Jack turned over, her eyes on Commander Skye. She frowned slightly, then fell back asleep.

No one moved when the lights came up that morning. Skylark lifted his pillow and placed it firmly over his head. He did not want to face the day just yet. The tahorah spent several minutes staring up at the bunk above her, then she rolled out of bed and showered. She was out of the room before anyone else moved.

Jack clambered down from her bunk and sat on Skylark's bed. Skylark peeked at her from under his pillow.

"You doing okay?" Jack asked.

Skylark grunted and tossed his pillow aside. He sat up. "John was a friend."

Jack nodded. She knew what friendship meant to her commander, if only by virtue of the fact that he referred to so few people as friends. She reached out and clutched Skylark's shoulder briefly before leaning over and kissing his cheek. Skylark smiled sadly at her as she rose and hit the showers. He noticed the tahorah's empty bunk and frowned.

Slowly, achingly, Team 6 began their day. They were late to breakfast. Team 87 was not there at all. Neither was the tahorah.

Skylark leant over to Jack. "Where is she?" he asked.

"The tahorah?" Jack asked in return. She shrugged. "I don't know. She might be with Team 87."

Nodding, Skylark returned to his meal and found it thoroughly unappetizing.

"Eat," Binky said when he noticed Skylark toying with the eggs.

Skylark sighed and tried. He couldn't take more than two mouthfuls before he gave up and pushed his plate away. He stood.

"Skye," Binky said, about to begin a lecture.

"Not now," Skylark said quietly. He finished his coffee and left the mess.

Binky put down his fork in disgust.

Not really knowing where he was headed, Skylark began to walk. He headed first to the gym, and found it full of personnel. Deciding that being in such a crowd was probably not the best option at the moment, Skylark turned and headed elsewhere. He stumbled upon the tahorah quite by accident.

She sat in a maintenance hall. Butan sat with her. They were not speaking, simply sitting with their arms around each other's shoulders, their foreheads touching. Tears slid silently down Butan's cheeks.

Knowing he was intruding, Skylark turned and walked back the way he had come.

"Commander," Butan called softly from the hall. Skylark paused, then turned.

Butan stood at the entrance to the maintenance hall, his hand extended. Skylark took it.

"I am sorry," Butan said. "I know you and he were close."

"He was a good friend," Skylark said.

Butan watched him closely. "And a good commander," he said.

Skylark nodded. "That too."

"Will you join us?" Butan indicated the hall and Skylark frowned. "I—"

"It is nothing sinister, Commander," Butan said with a smile. "We are sharing."

"Sharing what?"

"Comfort. Come, I will show you."

Curious, Skylark followed the daemon back into the maintenance hall. The tahorah looked questioningly at Skylark, then Butan.

"I invited," Butan said with a shrug.

The tahorah nodded and adjusted her position. Butan knelt by her and indicated for Skylark to do the same, forming a small circle.

"You must trust," Butan said with a small smile. Skylark looked at him, frowning.

Butan placed one hand on the back of Skylark's head. The tahorah placed her own over the top of Butan's, then placed her other hand on the back of Butan's head. Understanding, Skylark covered her hand with his own, and placed his other hand on the back of the tahorah's head. Butan completed the circle by covering Skylark's hand with his own. They leant forward and touched foreheads.

Following the example set by the tahorah and Butan, Skylark closed his eyes.

He felt the warmth first, the soft, tingling sensation that was, after last night, familiar. It started in his head and moved through his entire body along the complex network of his nervous system.

Then his mind slipped away from the strangeness of his current experience, into the easy dark of nothingness. After a brief moment, memories began their stately march across his mind, as if seeing them for the first time. Skylark recalled the first time he met Commander Wheeler. So much younger then, and more carefree, Wheeler had seen him enter the nightclub at the USC base in Johannesburg alone.

Skylark had only one friend in the world, Binky. Binky was involved with a woman and left Skylark on his own. Belligerently, perhaps, Skylark refused to let that keep him from anything fun. John Wheeler had taken pity on Skylark that night and invited him over to sit with him and his friends.

Their friendship began, one that John Wheeler had stuck with despite Skylark's temper and propensity for vicious sarcasm. Though John kept to his gang of friends, Skylark was never excluded from anything, save what he chose. Several times at flight school, John's quiet encouragement kept Skylark from quitting.

Does that matter? the memory of Wheeler said when the memory of Skylark told him that he was just some orphan from the ghetto. *I mean, it sure explains why you're so angry. But what has that got to do with the kind of person you are?*

That had been a turning point for Skylark, the one question that pulled him short and made him take responsibility for his own fate.

Skylark had known from the beginning that Wheeler was gay. It had never bothered him. What did bother him was that Wheeler couldn't bring himself to tell Skylark. The memories marched on.

Images of Christmas parties, of difficult days in training, of the enormous celebration that happened when everyone found out they had been accepted into the infiltration program, each joyous occasion in turn filled Skylark's mind. They were mixed with Butan's memories of the commander. John's smile flashed at him, and suddenly Skylark understood just how much that smile meant to Butan. It was a smile that assured him that Butan was safe, that the commander had judged Butan worthy and had accepted him into his little clan. Butan's pride at that filled Skylark.

On and on, the three shared their happiest memories of John Wheeler. Then, slowly, the images faded, leaving behind the fire of the joy that had accompanied them. Skylark's eyes opened slowly. Despite himself and his grief, a small smile played across his lips.

"He was good," Butan whispered quietly.

Skylark pulled himself upright, blinking rapidly. "Do you...? What was that?"

"Mihir," Butan said. "Soul sharing."

"It is how the daemon grieve," the tahorah said.

Nodding, Skylark sat back, revelling a moment in the feeling of joy that lingered. "It's beautiful," he said.

"There you are," Sub-Lieutenant Rast said, appearing suddenly in the hall. "What are you doing?"

Skylark could not find a brief way to explain, so he simply asked, "Why are you here?"

"Hank sent me. He wanted me to tell you that the funeral is about to start."

Skylark nodded. He stood. "Lead the way, Sub-Lieutenant."

"Yes, sir," Rast said. She cast an enquiring look into the corridor, then turned and left. Skylark followed her, with the tahorah and Butan following him.

The majority of personnel held vigil in the mess. Team 6, however, had been invited into the crematorium by Team 87. Skylark entered. Lieutenant Commander Hank greeted him with a drawn smile and a firm handshake.

"Thank you for coming," Hank said. "I know it would have meant a lot to him."

"To me as well, Hank," Skylark said. "Thank you for inviting us."

Hank smiled again, then took to the podium that stood beside Commander Wheeler's coffin. Skylark went to his team. Jack greeted him with a hug. Binky simply clasped Skylark's shoulder. The tahorah was also subjected to Jack's affection, which she accepted graciously. Butan left her side to stand with the rest of Team 87.

"Words," Hank said after everyone had settled, "seem so hollow. How can you adequately express grief at the passing of a man like Commander John Wheeler? How can you express how deeply you are affected by the death of the man to whom you owe your life? Simply saying that Commander John Wheeler was a good man does not do his goodness justice. Telling the world that he was a capable commander does nothing to indicate the lengths he went through to ensure that his team came out of every scrap intact. It does not speak to his ability to bind even the most unlikely of us into a family. Nothing I can say, standing here, will ever shed light on just what kind of a man Commander John Wheeler was, and how much humanity has lost in his passing. Nothing I can say will ever tell just how much better we are for having known him."

Hank paused a moment. "He was a rare example of the kind of person we all have the potential to become. It was an honour to have served under him. It was a greater honour still to have been able to call him friend. Please join me in a prayer as we send our commander home at long last."

Everyone present bowed their heads as the coffin made its slow way into the cremation chamber. The door shut and locked and the dark room lit orange as the casket with Commander Wheeler was torched.

Jack sobbed quietly, comforted by the tahorah, who held her close. Skylark lifted his gaze to watch the little window in the cremation chamber. He could see nothing but orange flame. He struggled to hold onto the warmth that the Mihir had inspired, and found he could not. Oppressive cold settled in his chest, and he silently vowed vengeance against the ragnar.

A meeting had been called the day following the funeral. One of the chief biologists on the *Magellan*, Doctor Tang, had requested that all teams be present. Her presentation would also be broadcasted to the Admiralty of the USC as well as the United Council.

"Thank you for attending," she said as the small hall fell silent. "Um. I know this is a sombre day so I'll try and be as brief as possible, but it is imperative that everyone knows what we're up against."

"The ragnar," someone piped up from the back.

"Bravo," the biologist answered. "Yes. The ragnar. A great place to start. Analysis of several of the specimens brought back from various missions indicate that these are, in fact, insects, or as close to insects as we have the capacity to identify. Like many insect species, there are several different types of ragnar, each with a specific task. Much like ants, termites and bees, the ragnar display a social hierarchy with the queen at the top.

"What makes the ragnar stand out against other insect species that we are more familiar with, however, is the extraordinarily different phenotypic expressions of each kind of ragnar."

"What?" someone else interrupted.

"They all look very different despite being the same species," Skylark said, not bothering to turn around.

"Yes," the biologist said. "Thank you. That's it exactly. So far, we've been able to identify three different phenotypes. There are those who build the nests and care for the eggs and larvae. They are usually soft-shelled and generally harmless. Their best defence is an acid they squirt from their abdomens. It is strong, but it would take an hour to eat through your armour. Given their structure, it is unlikely that they can survive any length of time in space. The ragnar that you encountered out in space protecting the nests are essentially soldiers. Like soldier ants, their sole function is to protect the nest and queen. They are uniquely evolved to deal with space, consisting of two exoskeletons. The one underneath is soft, like the workers. The one that covers them is thick armour that, I'm sure you've noticed, your bullets have difficultly penetrating. In between the two is a space that can be expanded or contracted depending on their immediate surrounds."

"So, what you're saying is that these bugs have naturally occurring pressurized space armour?" Skylark asked.

"Precisely! Yes."

"Brilliant," Binky muttered darkly.

"There is some good news, thanks largely to the tahorah," the biologist said, offering the tahorah a brief smile. "The under section of the armour where the head meets the thorax is a weak spot. If that is punctured, the suit, as it is, loses pressure and the bug inside dies. If you have blades, you can sever the head completely."

"What about the venom?" Skylark asked.

"It's actually not a venom," the biologist said. "For the longest time we couldn't figure it out, until a scholar recalled an old children's rhyme. With that as her clue, we've been able to figure out that the venom is actually an injection of a virus, of a sort."

"A virus?"

"Yes. The virus acts as an agent for biological change, a consumption of the host, if you like, changing his makeup at a molecular level."

"Wait," Binky said. He turned to Skylark. "You understand any of this shit?"

"The virus changes the DNA?" Skylark asked, ignoring the lieutenant commander.

"Yes," the biologist confirmed. "In fact, it destroys sections of DNA and inserts parts of itself in the empty slot."

"And that's what killed Wheeler?"

"Ah, no. It was Wheeler's own autoimmune response. It destroyed the replaced viral sections of DNA in his own cells, causing a complete cellular breakdown."

"Christ," Skylark whispered.

"We think," the biologist said, "that the queen is responsible for the suppression of any host's immune system, thereby facilitating the change without killing the host. We believe this is achieved psychically, rather than through pheromones as one might expect. Conduction of pheromones through the vacuum of space is, well, problematic. If the queen is killed, the host's immune system leaps back to life and kills the virus. And the host."

"What does the host change into?" Skylark asked.

"We don't know," Doctor Tang said with a shrug. "According to the daemon rhyme, the host essentially becomes a mindless drone and is put to work by the queen in the nest."

"Sounds like nothing more than a fairytale," Commander Speedman, leader of Team I, said.

"Yes," Doctor Tang agreed. "However, given the fact that Wheeler was, in fact, changing at a molecular level, I'm going with a fairytale steeped in a good helping of truth."

"So, moral of the story is don't get stung," Speedman said.

"It's kill the queen," Skylark answered.

"Yes," the biologist agreed. "If we are correct, and their society is something akin to ants or bees, then the queen ensures the working of the nest and everything in it. If the queen is killed, the ragnar become confused and disorientated, and, eventually, we think, die."

"So, you actually mean to tell us we've accidentally been doing it right?" Binky asked.

"Yes. Essentially. That and knowing everything you can about your opponent will help you out in a fight."

"Yeah, 'cause what I needed to know is that the stinger is a giant virus-filled syringe."

"She's right, Binky," Skylark said. "It's good to know what we can."

"I concur," Commodore Gergiev said. "Thank you, Doctor Tang."

"You're welcome," the biologist said. She stepped back and turned off the projector, then left the small stage to the commodore.

"Councillor," the commodore asked of the holographic projection standing on the platform at the back of the room. "Is there anything else you wish to ask?"

"No," Councillor Brand said. "Everything looks in order."

"Well, then. I think it goes without saying, teams, but on your next encounter, aim for the neck. Dismissed."

Out of deference for Commander Wheeler, Commodore Gergiev kept his three ships floating in space for three days, circling around the way station but never engaging it. It was an honour usually reserved for flag officers, but Gergiev had insisted. For three days, for the same reason, Skylark left Team 6 to their devices. Ordinarily, he would have joined them in their time away from training, but he was, in truth, trying to avoid the tahorah and shirk his responsibility as commander. He did not want to tell her what had to be said, and so for three days he kept to Team 6's quarters while they went out to expend their grief in whatever way they saw fit.

At the end of the three days, Skylark sent for the tahorah. He stared out into space, not turning when he heard the door open and shut.

"You sent for me, Commander?" the tahorah asked softly.

"Yes," Skylark said, without turning. He watched the white wall of the slipstream a moment longer before turning. "How is Butan?"

"He is still sad. He liked the commander a great deal." She stepped forward. "How are you?"

Skylark responded with the barest of smiles before turning to his bedside table, where a bottle of scotch and two glasses stood. He poured a helping of scotch into each glass and handed one to the tahorah. Their fingers accidentally brushed as the tahorah accepted the glass. Skylark pulled away from the burn of their connection. The tahorah frowned.

"Have I offended you, Commander?" she asked.

Skylark took a deep drink of scotch. "No," he said finally. "No, you haven't."

"And still you've been avoiding me."

"Yes," Skylark admitted. "I have."

"Why?"

"Because I have to tell you something I don't particularly want to say." He glanced at the tahorah, who cocked her head. "About us," Skylark said. "About what happened that night that... after John died."

The tahorah stood in silence, her head cocked and frowning. Skylark could not look at her without wanting to kiss her, so he turned away.

"It was wrong. It should never have happened."

It never occurred to Skylark that silences could change their mood. But the tahorah's silence did. The room seemed to darken slightly and the confused silence became angry.

"I do not understand," she said at last.

Skylark looked down at his scotch. "I take full responsibility," he said. "I should have put a stop to it before anything untoward happened. But I didn't."

"Why?"

Taken by surprise at the tahorah's question, Skylark turned to face her. "Why didn't I?"

"No. Why is it wrong?"

Skylark sighed. He didn't want to answer this question. "You mean besides breaking several strict USC behavioural guidelines?"

The tahorah watched him expectantly.

"We just can't, Tahorah," Skylark said quietly. "This alliance is hanging by a thread at best. The war between our peoples just ended forty years ago, and there are still people nursing hurts. All they need is one excuse. We can't afford to give them that."

"How would we be doing so?"

"The daemon are still very much the other, Tahorah. If we were caught, if people found out, the backlash could very well destroy the USC and the alliance."

Scowling, the tahorah placed her glass of scotch on the table and turned to leave. Skylark impulsively reached out and grabbed her arm.

"Please understand," he said softly.

But the tahorah did not understand. It was clear in her expression and the hurt that clouded her eyes. She pulled away from Skylark's grasp and wordlessly left the quarters.

Knowing he could not follow her, Skylark sank onto his bed and stared blankly out into space.

The six-day journey back to Earth was uncomfortable at best. The tahorah remained distant and cool when dealing with Skylark, though her warmth towards Jack had not faded. The sudden difference had been noted by the rest of the team.

"What's her problem?" Binky asked Skylark as he watched Jack and the tahorah leave the mess together, giggling.

Skylark shrugged. "Women," he said, as if that explained anything at all.

It appeared to satisfy Binky, who grinned and returned to his meal. Skylark had lost his appetite, however. He excused himself and went to expel his frustration on the heavy bag in the gym.

19

The return to USC Headquarters, Vancouver, did nothing to ease the tension between Skylark and the tahorah. They ignored one another as best they could, considering they lived together. But Skylark struggled with it. He could not forget that night as easily as he had nights with other women. Worse, he craved it. Other women seemed to have lost their shine. He barely even noticed their smiles anymore.

"Are you sick?" Binky asked when Skylark ignored the advances of a waitress in the restaurant they frequented for breakfast.

"Sorry?"

"Seriously, Skylark. Are you feeling all right? 'Cause you haven't taken anyone home in a while, and you just brushed off that incredibly gorgeous waitress."

Skylark blinked stupidly.

Binky shook his head. "Never mind," he muttered. "Eat your breakfast."

"Yes, sir," Skylark said with a lopsided grin.

"Is it just me, or could you cut the tension with a knife?" Doorman asked Jack later that night as he watched the tahorah and Skylark set the table. Jack looked up from her magazine at Doorman.

"What's it to you?" she asked archly.

"Come on. You can't have missed it!" Doorman shook his head. "Skye's been pining after her since she came on board. I've never seen him like this."

"Yeah, well," Jack said returning to her magazine. She didn't elaborate.

Doorman narrowed his eyes at her. "What do you know?" he demanded.

"Nothing," Jack answered, not looking at him.

"Jack."

"Drop it, Doorman," Jack said.

"Drop what?" Spike asked as he walked past.

"Nothing," Doorman and Jack said in unison. They exchanged a look of annoyance. Spike shrugged and returned to the kitchen where he hummed happily as he grilled portabella mushrooms and eggplants.

"Hey," Binky said as he entered the common living space. "You guys want to go clubbing tonight? We're only a couple of days away from heading up again."

Jack brightened. "I think Sarah is bartending tonight!"

Skylark laughed softly. "You still keen on her, Jack?"

"Oh come on, like you wouldn't be if you knew you had a shot!"

Skylark shrugged. He looked between Binky and Jack, both of whom wore a hopeful expression. "Fine," he said. "We'll go."

"Yes!" Jack said, jumping up. "I have to find my shirt!" She dashed from the room and into her bedroom.

The tahorah smiled to herself and finished setting the table.

Before very long, the members of Team 6 found themselves downstairs in Untied sharing a drink over the pounding music. Jack bought the first round, using it as an excuse to flirt with the very pretty bartender, Sarah.

"Hey," Spike said to the tahorah. "Come up and dance."

Smiling, the tahorah nodded and she and Spike hit the dance

floor. Doorman watched Skylark watch the tahorah. He had to bury his grin in his drink.

"So," Jack said to Binky. "Whatever happened to that girl you were seeing last time?"

"What, Liz?"

"Yeah."

Binky shrugged. "I got bored."

Jack rolled her eyes. The night continued on in much the same fashion. On occasion, the tahorah would return to the team's table, breathless and laughing. She danced with everyone, save Skylark, who did not dance.

When his turn came around, Skylark instead offered a round of drinks, to which everyone agreed was a fine compromise. He grinned and made his way to the bar to order.

"Commander," Miranda Rast said as she stood at the bar, turning to him.

"Lieutenant," Skylark said. "Congratulations on the promotion."

"Thanks," Rast said grinning. She crossed her long legs, the motion drawing Skylark's eyes. "You gonna buy me a drink to celebrate?" she asked.

"It seems only fair," Skylark answered. He ordered two shots and handed one to Rast. "Congratulations," he said, raising his glass. They drank them down.

"Come dance," Rast said, resting her hand on Skylark's arm.

"Thanks," Skylark said. "But I owe my table a round."

"Come on, Skylark," Rast said. She leant forward and wrapped an arm around his neck. "You owe me at least one dance."

Skylark gently unwound her arm. "Not this time," he said. He leant over to Sarah and placed his order.

"No worries, handsome," Sarah said, flashing a bright smile. "I'll have them brought out."

"Thank you." Skylark turned to leave, but Rast's extended leg blocked his path. He ground his teeth and looked at her.

She smiled. "I've heard a rumour about you."

"And what's that?"

"I heard you haven't slept with anyone in *ages*. Is that true?"

"What's this—?"

Lieutenant Rast slid off her barstool, standing close enough to Skylark that her chest brushed his with every breath.

"If it's true," she said, "you must be pretty stressed out."

"Rast," Skylark said coldly. "Step back."

"Some people are saying it's because you're gay, but I know for a fact you're not. Other people are talking about you and your daemon. But that can't be right, right? I mean, you're not sleeping with her, are you?"

Skylark took Lieutenant Rast by the shoulders and pushed her back a step. "You're drunk, Lieutenant," he said. "You should go home." He started to walk away.

"You are, aren't you?" Rast demanded loudly. "You're sleeping with that alien bitch!"

Skylark stopped walking, standing still as stone, his muscles coiled like springs. After a pause, he slowly turned. Rast shrank away from his barely contained rage.

"You are drunk," he repeated. "Go home."

"You're not denying it," Rast spat.

"He doesn't need to," Jack said, walking to Skylark's side. "You're being an idiot and should know better. Now stop acting like a spoiled brat because you got rejected."

"Fuck you, Jack."

"If you insist," Jack said, smiling. She folded her arms and glared at Lieutenant Rast. Rast rolled her eyes, finished her drink, then stormed from the club.

"Thank you," Skylark murmured to Jack, who shrugged.

"No worries. Our drinks are here."

Jack led Skylark back to the table. Binky raised his glass. "Bitches be crazy," he declared loudly. Everyone cheered and drank.

The USC had kept to the asteroid belt in the Outerworlds, reasoning that if one nest was to be found there, then there were likely others. Bio scanners confirmed their assessment. Abandoned mining stations now had new occupants.

USC Strategic teams were sent there on cyclical tours, five teams for three months at a time. Some teams, depending on their performance, were kept for double tours. Their mission was simple:

search and destroy. They had become affectionately known in the way station closest to the asteroid belt as fumigators.

Team 6 had been up twice since John Wheeler had died. Each time, Skylark's mood darkened. His singular focus on the mission was much admired by the people who did not know him. Those who knew him best watched on in concern.

"Dude needs to get laid," Binky declared loudly as Skylark showered after training.

"Not so loud!" Jack hissed.

"Oh," Binky said. "He knows. I'm starting to think he's fallen in love with the damned heavy bags."

"It keeps him calm," Doorman said. "Don't knock it."

"You know what else keeps him calm? Sex. And he hasn't had any in almost a year."

Doorman shrugged.

"It's not natural," Binky grumbled.

The tahorah remained silent through the argument. She sat on her bunk and pretended to read, but her mind was on the commander. Jack's head popped into view from the bunk above. "Can I?" she asked.

The tahorah nodded and Jack jumped down from her bunk. She took up the tahorah's hairbrush and sat behind her. "It's really very pretty," Jack said as she ran the brush through the tahorah's raven black hair. "It changes colour a bit in the light."

The tahorah smiled. "Thank you," she said. Then, "Why did you shave yours?"

"It's easier to take care of," Jack said. When the tahorah giggled, she said, "Seriously. I hated fussing around with the regulation hairstyles. And the amount of fucking hairspray I went through just trying to get it to stay. Christ!"

The shower stopped and Skylark entered the room in just a towel. He searched around the drawer under his bed briefly. He frowned as he did so, noting everyone had stopped what they were doing to watch him.

"What?" he demanded before returning to the bathroom.

"I know I'm gay," Jack said, "but that was pretty damned sexy."

Binky rolled his eyes and climbed into his bed. The lights dimmed before Skylark finished in the bathroom. He slid into bed just as they went out.

Sleep did not come for the commander that night.

It had been another frustrating day. The scanners that flew ahead of the five long-haul fighters had not picked up any signs of ragnar in three days. Team 6 returned to the flight deck of the *Magellan* annoyed and tense. Skylark's bad mood had worsened significantly and it infected the rest of the team. Of late, there had been only one thing that seemed to put him in a better mood—killing ragnar. It had been one week since the last nest was destroyed, and Team 1 took the honours there.

To make matters worse, vicious rumours had been spreading about Commander Skye. The suspicion that he shared his bed with the daemon member of his team had been replaced with one where he had sworn allegiance to the daemon and was actively working against humanity. Though the rumours had not reached Skylark's ears, he was acutely aware of the manner in which many of the USC personnel looked at him. As a child of the ghetto, he had become accustomed to disdain, but this was entirely different. It was malicious.

Shrewd as ever, Commander Skye guessed that the personnel took exception to the tahorah, but he was not aware just how deeply the undercurrent of resentment ran until one engineer made the mistake of calling the commander out.

"Fuckin' traitor," the engineer said, as Skylark disembarked the USC Strategic *One* loudly enough to be heard by most everyone in the vicinity.

Skylark stopped walking and turned to him. "I beg your pardon?" he demanded of the engineer.

Emboldened by arrogance and self-righteousness, and the suddenly tense audience, the engineer stepped forward. "I said, you're a traitor. You and your alien bitch both."

Skylark lashed out. He grasped the engineer by the throat, lifted him from the ground and then drove him down hard onto his back, knocking the wind out of his lungs.

"Have you any idea how much we owe her and her people?" Skylark growled down at him. Only the greatest exertion of self-control stopped Skylark from crushing the man's windpipe. "Or are you too ignorant to notice that they're fighting our damned war? You want to talk about traitors, start with the people who are threatening this alliance! We can't win this alone. Do you understand?"

"What the devil is going on here?" Commodore Gergiev demanded. "Let him up!"

It took Skylark a moment to release the engineer. He stood back at attention. The engineer rose slowly to his feet, his hand at his bruised throat as he struggled to draw breath. Commodore Gergiev took a moment to collect himself, looking between Skylark and the engineer, his jaw clenching and unclenching rapidly.

"Now someone tell me what is going on."

"He attacked me, sir," the engineer said.

"Did you?" Gergiev asked Skylark.

"Yes, sir," Skylark answered.

"For fuck's sake, Commander." Gergiev rubbed his forehead.

"Forgive me, Commodore," the tahorah said, stepping forward. "The commander was explaining the delicate nature of our alliance, which seems to have escaped this man's understanding."

Gergiev raised his brows. "Commander, Private, my study. Now." He turned and marched away from the flight deck. Skylark followed, as did the engineer, who paused long enough to throw a poisonous glare at the tahorah.

Binky and Doorman walked forward to flank her protectively.

"Fucking asshole," Jack muttered. Sighing, she took the tahorah's hand. "Come on. Skye's going to be in a really bad mood after this meeting. Let's find him some scotch or something."

Team 6 left the flight deck, the personnel giving them a wide berth.

Commodore Gergiev shut the door behind Skylark and Private Kusnesov and moved to his desk. He did not sit, so neither did the two men.

"Now tell me exactly what happened," Gergiev said.

No one spoke.

"I do not like to be kept waiting."

"The commander's a traitor, sir," Kusnesov said suddenly.

The commodore raised his brows at him. "That's a heavy accusation, Private. I take it you've carefully compiled evidence to support it."

"Everyone knows he's screwing the daemon whore."

Gergiev looked at Skylark. He stood, his face impassive and stared at the wall behind Gergiev's desk. Though he appeared outwardly calm, one look at his hard blue eyes and Gergiev felt certain that Commander Skye could, at any moment, fly into a homicidal rage.

"The tahorah," Gergiev said slowly, "and her people have proven very valuable members of the USC, Private. I trust you understand that she ultimately decides the fate of this alliance and that any misstep on our part will cause us to lose a fighting force we really cannot do without?"

Private Kusnesov remained silent.

"Or is that more or less what Commander Skye was explaining to you when I arrived?"

Still, Private Kusnesov did not speak.

"Now, if you have any evidence to prove your accusation against Commander Skye's conduct, I want to see it. Do you have such evidence?"

"No, sir."

"So, what you're telling me is that you've accused Commander Skye, in front of USC personnel, of something of which you have absolutely no proof. Are you drunk, Private?"

"No, sir."

"Then there is no excuse for this. If we are very lucky, Commander Skye and the tahorah have enough trust between them that he can smooth over the damage you've done. His efforts will in no way spare you, however. You are to report to Petty Officer Davis in the brig. And you will stay there until I can decide what to do with you. Dismissed."

Private Kusnesov saluted and left and Gergiev turned his attention to Skylark, who had not relaxed.

"Are you sleeping with her, Skye?" the commodore asked.

The barest flicker of ire crossed Skylark's face. "No, sir," he said coldly.

Gergiev sighed and sat slowly down. "Things had been going so well," he said wearily. "I had thought that most personnel had adjusted quite well to the presence of the daemon in our ranks. It seems I was mistaken. There is an undercurrent of resentment that threatens to tear all this apart. More than a year of hard work undone. I trust you realize that?"

"Yes, sir."

"Then tread carefully, Commander. You and your team have become the shining example of what can be achieved if we work together. I'd hate to see it come to nothing."

"Yes, sir."

"Good. Dismissed, Commander."

Commander Skye left, leaving barely contained anger in his wake. Gergiev sighed and sat slowly down. The next few days would be telling.

The lights dimmed on Skylark as he pounded the heavy bag in the gym with everything he had. He looked up at the lights, then down at his hand wraps. He sighed. He had bought them only a month ago and now they were soaked in blood.

Giving up on training, he returned to his quarters after lights out only to find them empty. Team 6 was not where it ought to be. Skylark smiled slightly. He was glad. He didn't feel like dealing with them right now. He knew they knew that.

He walked to the bathroom and turned the light on.

The door to the quarters opened and Skylark turned back. The tahorah stood in the doorway, her petite frame outlined in the lights of the hall.

"Permission to enter, Commander," she said softly.

"These are your quarters as well, Tahorah," Skylark said. He exited the bathroom and leant one shoulder against the doorframe, watching her. "Where is the rest of the team?"

"Taking refuge with Team 87, Commander," the tahorah answered. She hesitated, then stepped into the room. The door slid shut behind her. "I've come to apologize," she said.

Skylark frowned. "Apologize?"

"Yes…" The tahorah trailed off when she noticed Skylark's bloody wraps. She moved swiftly to him and took one of his hands. Sighing, she dragged him over to the small table past the bunks and left to fetch some water. She returned a short while later with a dish of warm water and first aid supplies.

"I'm fine," Skylark protested.

Pressing her lips into a thin line, the tahorah pushed firmly on Skylark's shoulder. He sat and she unwound his wraps. She examined his hands after she had cleaned them.

"There are old scars. This is not the first time?" She looked up at Skylark, who shook his head. Frowning, she returned to caring for the self-inflicted wounds.

"It helps," Skylark said, feeling as if he owed the tahorah an explanation.

"How?"

"I don't know. It just does."

The tahorah shook her head. She did not speak again until she had finished wrapping Skylark's wounds.

"I did not understand," she said at length. "When you said it endangered the alliance. I could not comprehend how it could be so."

Skylark watched her, but she did not meet his gaze.

"I have spent so much time with you and the others, I forgot that not all are so good. I was angry. I am sorry. I understand now."

"Do you?" Skylark asked. "Because I don't." He stood and walked to his bed, turning his attention out to the window where the stars floated slowly past. "Our first mission together, you saved my life. Thank you for that, by the way. Every mission since, you have risked so much to ensure we get it done. Every nest we destroy means a safer future for all of us. I don't understand how they can't see that."

Sensing Skylark's growing agitation, the tahorah moved behind him and placed her hands against his shoulder blades. His muscles relaxed immediately under the spreading warmth. Skylark closed his eyes briefly.

"How do you do that?" he asked.

"Terrible daemon magic," the tahorah replied, smiling.

Skylark turned around, taking her hands in his own. "I have given the USC my entire life," he said. "And they call me a traitor for having the audacity to love you."

The tahorah twitched, her eyes widening. She opened her mouth to speak, but Skylark pressed his fingers against her lips.

"Don't," he said. "Don't say anything. I shouldn't have said it. Things are complicated enough as it is. I'm sorry. Tahorah—"

The tahorah took Skylark's fingers away from her lips. Her fingers played along his until they clasped hands.

"Naschari," the tahorah said. "My name is Naschari."

Skylark stepped closer and kissed her.

"We'll find a way," he whispered. "We'll make this work."

Unable to argue, the tahorah returned his kisses and they fell together onto Skylark's bed.

The difference in Skylark the following morning was palpable. He ate breakfast with his team, as always. But he was more relaxed and smiled more often. He remained so for the rest of their tour. No one on Team 6 questioned it. They were simply glad to be relieved of their concern. Team 87, now led by Commander Hank, often joined them at meal times, making the collection of twelve USC Strategic personnel one of the loudest groups in the mess.

Only Jack knew the cause of Skylark's change in temper, and she smiled quietly to herself. Though they were both careful not to publically show their affection, there had been times when the team had been walking down a hall together, but when Jack turned to her commander, she found that both Skylark and the tahorah had disappeared. Jack wondered if she was the only one on the team who noticed.

Butan, from his seat with Team 87, noticed something Jack could not see. The respective lights of Skylark and the tahorah would bend towards one another, stretching out to touch even if they sat at opposite ends of the table. Even if he had been blind to the lightening of Skylark's mood, or the manner in which Skylark looked at the tahorah, their lights alone told Butan all he needed to know.

The daemon majan smiled secretly to himself. His eyes met Jack's and the lieutenant grinned at him. Without a single exchange of words, it became Jack and Butan's shared secret and the two would often giggle about it together without even speaking to one another.

"You're humming," Binky said to Skylark as Team 6 sat in the transport that would take them down to USC Headquarters, Vancouver.

Skylark stopped humming and looked surprised. "Was I?"

Everyone stared at him.

"What? You've never heard a man hum before?"

"We've never heard you hum before," Spike said.

Skylark shrugged. He noticed Jack trying very hard not to burst out laughing and narrowed his eyes at her. She grinned broadly at him and turned away. Her shoulders shook.

"I'm missing something," Binky said.

"I think we all are," Doorman replied. He closed his eyes and leant his head back. "I can't wait to hit the sauna."

"Not a bad idea," Skylark agreed.

"I never have bad ideas."

"Shirley," Spike said. "She was a bad idea."

"Fuck off," Doorman replied. "Like her sister was any better."

"Lucy was a goddess."

"Sure," Doorman said with a shrug. "Just like Kali."

"Screw you."

The banter continued until Team 6 arrived at their apartment. Everyone happily entered their rooms and the place fell silent for a time.

"I'm heading down to the sauna," Doorman yelled as he left a few hours later. "Who's coming?"

"I'll come," Binky said. "Give me a moment."

"Me too," Spike said. "Coming, Commander?"

"Maybe later," Skylark replied.

Spike shrugged. "Jack?"

"Not right now," Jack said.

"Tahorah?"

"She's in bed asleep," Jack said. "I'll let her know she's invited if she wakes up."

"All-right-y," Doorman said. "We're good to go."

"Have fun," Jack said as the three men left the apartment. A few minutes after they had left, Jack jumped up from the couch.

"Where are you going?" Skylark asked.

"Shopping," Jack said with a smile. "It's Sarah's birthday soon, and I want to get her something special."

Skylark grunted.

"Have fun," Jack said cheekily just before she closed the door to the apartment. Skylark raised his brows at her. He put down his magazine and went to the tahorah's room. She was indeed asleep on her bed. Skylark smiled, shut the door and retired to his own room. He lay on his bed and stared up at the ceiling for a while before he dozed. The sun had set when he stirred to find the tahorah asleep beside him, glowing softly. He smiled, pulled her in close and settled down to a deeper, more peaceful sleep.

USC Strategic Team 6 had precious little down time before the bio scanners picked up an enormous amount of activity in the Aborgini Asteroid Belt. Half the teams, including Team 6, were sent into space to deal with the issue. Boarded on the USC Research Vessel *Magellan*, as always, Team 6 settled in quickly.

Teams 1, 17, 98, and 99 accompanied them. The two other ships, Space Frigates both, under Commodore Gergiev's command flanked the *Magellan* as she sped along the artificially generated wormhole en route to the belt.

Team 6 were enjoying their lunch when Sarcen entered the mess looking like a thundercloud. He went immediately to the tahorah and whispered something in her ear. She looked up at him in surprise.

"Excuse me," she said to her team. She followed the majan to a spare table and there stood, having a discussion that looked heated. After a short while, she returned to her team as if in a daze.

"Everything all right?" Skylark asked.

"They're changing the teams," the tahorah replied, as if not quite believing it. "The daemon are being reassigned."

"What?" Skylark stood. "That's idiocy. Are you sure?"

"I was told this morning, Commander," Sarcen said. "I have come from a lengthy argument with Commander Speedman."

Commander Speedman, Team 1's leader, was not well known to Skylark. In the class ahead of Skylark in both flight school and infiltrator training, he had remained distant and aloof. Even on their missions together, Team 1 had retained an air of disdain for everyone around them. Skylark had dismissed it as tribalism, something which all the teams displayed to one degree or another.

"I was not so informed," Skylark said.

"You were about to be, Commander," Gergiev said, having just arrived. "Though I hoped to call you to my office to do so."

Skylark looked him over. The man looked tired. "You cannot be serious, Commodore," Skylark said. "It's insane to mess with team dynamics like that."

Gergiev sighed. "My office, Skylark. We'll discuss this in private."

Wanting to say more, but knowing it would be unwise, Skylark gave a curt nod. Leaving behind his half-finished plate, he followed the commodore to his private study in silence.

"I don't like this any more than you do," he said, shutting the door. "But it's out of my hands, Skye."

"We're about to hit the biggest cluster of nests we've ever seen, and they decide to do this now?"

Commodore Gergiev shrugged. "The argument is that the teams should get to know the other daemon as well as possible to facilitate greater integration."

Skylark stared at the commodore incredulously.

"I know. I spent almost all of last night arguing against it, but Vice Admiral Hunt was adamant."

"Hunt is behind this?"

"Not as far as I know. There is a chain of command, Commander."

"No," Skylark said. "No one is tearing apart my team!"

"There's nothing that can be done."

"I want to speak to Brooke."

"I tried. The official line from the admiralty is that Admiral Brooke is unavailable for comment."

"Then I want Councillor Fisher."

"I tried that too. Look, Skye. This is a shitty turn of events. And I disagree with it as much as you do. But it's out of our hands, Commander. You will just have to adjust to your new daemon, that is all."

"That is not the issue!" Skylark barked. He rubbed his forehead.

The commodore raised his brows. "What is the issue, Skye?"

"The tahorah is my team, sir. My tribe. I look out for her. I don't trust anyone else to do the same."

Gergiev observed Skylark in silence a moment. "I am aware of how you feel about your team, Commander. It is remarkably primitive. And yet I think it is something of the secret to your success and, if I'm honest, I find it admirable. But that doesn't change anything. These are our orders. We have no choice but to obey."

"There is always a choice," Skylark growled. He turned and stormed from the room. Gergiev let it slide. Chasing after him would do nothing but earn him a few missing teeth, he suspected.

Skylark stood at the heavy bag, too angry to even move.

"It's true, then," Jack asked from behind him.

Skylark turned to find Team 6 standing behind him, their eyes watching him expectantly.

"Yes," he said at length.

"This is bullshit!" Jack said. "They can't do that!"

"Hey," Skylark said, dragging Jack into a hug. "I know." He reached out his hand to the tahorah, who took it. He pulled her in close as well, resting his forehead on hers. The rest of the team closed in, huddling into one another in silence.

Someone cleared their throat. "Uh, Commander Skye." It was Commander Speedman who spoke. Skylark looked up at him and scowled. Sarcen, Team 1's daemon team member stood glowering behind Speedman.

"No offence, sir, but Team 1 has been given their marching orders. The tahorah should suit up."

Skylark set his jaw. "You're taking her?"

"Those were our orders."

It must have been obvious that Skylark was preparing for a fight. The tahorah touched his forearm, squeezing it gently before stepping forward.

"I will be ready soon," she said.

"Good. Meet us on the flight deck."

"Team 1 is the only team going?" Skylark asked with a frown.

"No, Commander. As I understand it twelve teams are going, four from each vessel. One team is to remain behind in case the ship is attacked directly."

Skylark tensed again. "I guess we're that team," he muttered.

"I guess so, Commander." Speedman turned to the tahorah. "Hurry up, soldier," he said.

The tahorah nodded. She left the protective circle of her former team and immediately went to collect her belongings and suit up.

"This is Saracen," Speedman said, indicating the daemon majan behind him.

"Yes," Skylark said. "We've met." He offered the majan his hand. "Welcome to Team 6, Saracen."

Sarcen took Skylark's hand and shook it firmly but did not speak.

Commander Speedman turned to leave.

"Commander," Skylark said. Speedman turned. "Bring her back." The words were softly spoken but tenderness did not make them so. Buried in the softness lay hidden a threat. Bring her back, *or I'll kill you.*

Commander Speedman offered the barest of smiles, an answer to Skylark's threat. *Try it.* Wordlessly, he turned and left.

"I do not like him," Sarcen growled.

"No," Skylark agreed. "Neither do I. I don't like any of this. Something's off."

"Commander?" Doorman asked.

Skylark could not explain, so he simply shook his head.

"This is Commodore Gergiev," the intercom announced. "We are approaching our destination. Teams 1, 17, 98, and 99 are to report to their fighters immediately."

"Let's go," Skylark said.

The shuffle of daemon amongst the teams left a sour taste in almost everyone's mouth. The daemon scholars did not understand the move, and the human friends they had made in their divisions shared their concern. Those teams that had become used to and, even if they would not readily admit it, liked their newest members were left reeling, trying to form a bond with another daemon who had an entirely different personality from the daemon they had replaced.

USC personnel, feeling uneasy, had gathered on the flight deck to watch the teams board their long-haul fighters. Skylark pushed his way through the crowd in time to intercept the tahorah, who walked behind Team 1. He caught her at her elbow.

For a brief moment, no one else existed. Then, she gently squeezed his arm, offered him a small smile and resumed her march. She entered USC Strategic *Three*, followed by Commander Speedman. Speedman's smug expression met Skylark's concerned gaze.

Jack moved to Skylark's side and wrapped her arms around him. Together they retreated behind the glass divider and watched the long-haul fighter lift off the flight deck and disappear into space.

Sarcen placed one large, heavy hand on Commander Skye's shoulder. Skylark found it comforting.

"Commander Skye?" a young docking administrator said. Skylark turned.

"Commodore Gergiev has invited you to the bridge, sir."

"Thank you," Skylark said absently. "I will be there presently."

"Yes, sir."

Jack released the commander from her hug. "It'll be all right," she said. "You'll see."

Skylark grunted but declined to comment. He turned and made his way to the bridge.

"Welcome up, Commander," Gergiev said. "At ease. If that's possible for you."

"Thank you for the invitation, sir," Skylark said.

Gergiev scoffed. "You would be pacing mercilessly in your quarters otherwise."

"By which you mean to say you'd like to keep an eye on me."

Gergiev smiled and turned his attention back to the screen that now served to monitor the progress of the twelve long-haul fighters. Skylark watched them intently.

"She's going to be fine, Commander," Gergiev said quietly. "Speedman might be a pompous ass, but he's a very capable commander."

Skylark simply grunted in response.

It took two and a half hours for the fighters to reach their target. During that time, Skylark stood at the railing of the top tier of the bridge, watching the screens, and did not move.

"Approaching target," said the pilot of USC Strategic *Three*. The monitors changed to show the view of the belt from the cockpit of the three fighters.

"Christ," Skylark murmured.

An entire mining settlement had been attacked and subsumed.

Each of the seven domed residences had been covered over in the brownish skins favoured by the ragnar. The processing plant at the centre of the settlement now looked like nothing more than a giant, glossy anthill.

The comm. crackled once more. "You seeing this, Commodore?"

"I see it," Gergiev answered. "Be careful out there."

"Yes, sir. Preparing to land."

The monitors split to display the individual team members' cameras.

"You see this every mission, sir?" Skylark asked.

"I do. I must say, your first mission as a team of six had us all holding our breaths."

Skylark smiled slightly. "Thank God for the tahorah," he said.

Gergiev glanced at him but said nothing.

The teams advanced, carefully moving between twisted spires and jagged ranges as they proceeded to the nest.

"I don't see any bugs," someone said through the comm.

"Keep your eyes peeled," Speedman said.

A few minutes later, all hell broke loose.

"Contact! Contact!"

Someone cried out. The monitors displayed brilliant flashes of light as the teams on the asteroid fired on the images of leaping ragnar which filled the displays. Neither the gunfire nor the clicks and hisses of the ragnar being fired upon could be heard, so the bridge filled with the sounds of heavy breathing, and a great deal of swearing.

Skylark searched the monitors frantically for signs of the tahorah. Every so often, brilliant purple would flash into view as the tahorah abandoned her gun in favour of her blades.

Someone started screaming.

"Russian!" Someone yelled over the comm. link.

On the third square, Skylark spotted a man being dragged into a press of ragnar by his foot. The tahorah's blades flashed into view, then her armoured frame as she gave chase.

Skylark leant forward, wrapping his hands around the railing. He stared at monitor three as the purple blades that danced through the press of ragnar bodies.

"Get him out of there!" Speedman screamed.

The teams opened fire, creating a passage through the ragnar. Skylark could more plainly see the tahorah. The man they called Russian lay on the ground, a hand wrapped tightly around the stump at the end of his leg where his foot used to be. The tahorah danced and whirled, her glowing blades slicing through armour that USC bullets could not breech.

Three men broke formation, running to the Russian and pulling him free. The tahorah skipped and danced, avoiding the javelin-like tails of the ragnar with grace and speed. She began her retreat.

"Fire!" Speedman yelled once the retrieval team was clear and the ragnar pressed in again, closing the tahorah off from view.

Skylark's grip tightened on the rails as he watched the purple glow dance through the back.

"Sir, we can't get through," Speedman said over the comm. "There's too many of them."

"Acknowledged, Commander. Pull back," Gergiev said. Skylark spun.

"Not without the tahorah!" he barked.

Gergiev simply nodded at the monitors, which revealed the teams firing into the lines of ragnar. Enough of a channel was created to view the tahorah again. She was still alive, and still fighting.

Skylark could not relax as he watched, his hands wrapped now so tightly around the railing his knuckles turned white. He watched as she danced aside, narrowly missing a venomous strike. Then, unexpectedly, her knee gave out. She fell to the ground, followed by a ragnar tail. It pierced her hip.

Skylark's breath caught.

She grasped the tail with one hand and sliced through it with the blade on her other hand.

Another tail lashed out, striking her back. She arched back and was lost to sight as the ragnar closed in again.

"Pull back!" Speedman yelled. "Pull back! Get the fuck out of here!"

The teams fled to their transports and were away from the asteroid in a matter of minutes. After a long pause, Commander Speedman pressed the comm. link in his chest plate.

"We lost one," he announced.

Commodore Gergiev bowed his head momentarily. He turned to speak to Skylark, but Skylark was no longer on the bridge.

The return of the four fighters to the flight deck was sombre. The nest had been destroyed, the asteroid upon which it sat blown into space dust. But it did not feel like a victory. While the personnel ran to their posts once the door had been sealed and the room pressurized, a crowd had gathered.

Team 1 disembarked. No sooner had they removed their helmets than Skylark appeared. He threw a hard right hook, hitting Speedman flush on the cheek. The rest of the team swarmed Skylark. He fought back, white rage and infiltration training making him difficult to subdue.

Team 6 arrived on the scene at a sprint. They grabbed for their commander in an effort to break up the fight, but it was not until Butan and Sarcen stormed onto the flight deck that Skylark was successfully restrained.

"You didn't even try!" Skylark hissed, when Butan, succeeding where three men could not, grabbed him by both his elbows and dragged him off Commander Speedman. He struggled hard against Butan's firm grasp. "You didn't even try to save her!"

"Fuck you, Skye," Commander Speedman said, struggling to his feet. He lunged forward to strike Skylark now that he was defenceless, but Sarcen stepped between them. His eyes glowed fiercely and his blades were extended. He snarled a deep, guttural curse at Speedman. The commander stumbled backwards.

"Did Hunt put you up to this?" Skylark demanded.

"What the fuck?" Commodore Gergiev roared as he stormed on deck. Skylark did not hear him.

"Did he?" he demanded of Speedman. "Did Hunt put you up to it?!"

Commander Speedman set his jaw and refused to answer.

"Get him out of here," Gergiev told Team 6.

"Sir," Binky said affirmatively. He looked back at Commander Speedman, his eyes narrowing before he turned and helped Butan and Sarcen drag their still struggling commander to their quarters.

Skylark did not stop struggling until Sarcen threw him onto his bed. Even then, he attempted to get up and the massive daemon had to hold him down.

"Calm yourself!" Sarcen growled.

"He shot her!" Skylark barked. "He shot her leg. Christ! Let me up! God damn it! Let me up!"

The majan growled something in his own language. He pressed his palm against Skylark's forehead and the commander fell slack.

"The fuck did you do?" Binky demanded.

"He is grief-sick," Sarcen growled. "He needed to be calmed."

"So you knock him out?"

"It was easier than holding him down. He is strong, for something so small."

Binky's jaw fell slack, but he was not given the chance to retort. Commodore Gergiev arrived and the team snapped to attention.

"At ease," the commodore growled. He looked past Sarcen and Butan at the unconscious Skylark on the bed. "What happened here?"

"Saracen knocked him out, sir," Binky replied.

"Good," Gergiev replied. He beckoned to three burly medics. They nodded and together lifted Skylark and placed him on a gurney just outside the door.

"What—" Binky started to demand.

"Team 6 is hereby suspended from active duty pending a full psychological evaluation of your commander," Gergiev said.

Everyone began to protest.

"Enough!" Gergiev barked. The room fell silent. Gergiev's posture softened. "I'm sorry. I truly am. But space dementia is a real threat and Commander Skye was never the most stable of men."

"He doesn't have space dementia, sir," Binky said.

"That remains to be seen."

"She was our tribe, sir," Jack said softly. "Skylark felt personally responsible to all of us. And, sir, to her especially. The alliance depended on her."

Gergiev nodded. "I know," he said gently. "But I cannot take any risks, Lieutenant. As you were."

The commodore left the room, leaving Team 6 in shocked silence.

"Mission complete, sir."

"You are certain, Commander?"

"They got her. Twice, sir. That I could see. And the asteroid was blown to shit. Even if she manages to survive that, there's no way for her to get back. She's as good as gone."

"Good."

Commander Speedman hesitated. "Commander Skye knows, sir. I don't know how. He figured it out, I guess."

"That is not important, Commander. I can deal with him easily enough. You did well."

"Thank you, sir."

"Dismissed."

"Yes, sir."

The holographic image of Vice Admiral Hunt faded and Speedman sank onto his bed and pondered.

Skylark awoke in Medical, in his own private room, strapped to the bed with thick leather bindings.

"The fuck is this?" he demanded of the medic by his bed, making her jump.

"It's for your own protection, sir," she said meekly.

"Bullshit," Skylark muttered, but he could do nothing, so he lay back in his bed and stared up at the ceiling.

The medic scurried off to inform the commodore that Skylark had awakened. Before long, a physician examined Skylark as a psychiatrist asked him questions. Commodore Gergiev looked on from beyond the door.

"What is your name?"

"Commander Bennejin Skye," Skylark answered. "United Space Corps, Strategic Division, Team 6."

"You mind telling me why you attacked Commander Speedman?"

"The bastard deserved it," Skylark growled. He jerked his head away from the penlight that unexpectedly shone in his eyes.

"Responses are all normal, sir," the physician reported.

"Why did he deserve it, Commander?" the psychiatrist asked, looking up from his tablet with arched brows.

Skylark ground his teeth. He could not explain without sounding completely insane. He could not tell the psychiatrist that he knew that Hunt had ordered Speedman to ensure that the tahorah never returned from their mission. He could not explain that he knew that Vice Admiral Hunt and Councillor Brand were working together to undo the alliance. He could not explain because he wasn't quite sure how he knew. But he knew.

"Commander? Why did he deserve it?"

"I want to speak to Saracen."

"Why?"

"I want to speak to Saracen."

"Commander—"

Skylark levelled the psychiatrist with a vicious glare. The psychiatrist sighed and made notes. "I will come back tomorrow."

Skylark rolled his eyes but did not speak further.

The psychiatrist shook his head at the commodore. Gergiev followed him some distance to confer.

"It's not space dementia," the psychologist said.

Gergiev waited, but the psychiatrist did not elaborate. "So? What is it, then?"

"To be honest, anger."

"Say again?"

"He's angry, Commodore. Honestly, it seems he's skipped denial altogether, and has headed straight for anger."

"What?"

"The five stages of grief. First, it's denial, then anger, followed by bargaining, depression, and then acceptance. The first stage, denial, if it ever occurred passed swiftly."

"Denial isn't really an option. He saw it happen."

"I see. Well, I haven't read his file yet, but I would assume he's dealt with a fair amount of loss in his life."

"He's an infiltrator, Doctor. Of course he has."

"A cheap guess, I'll admit. Is he depressed, Commodore?"

"I'm sorry, what?"

"Depressed. Depression often manifests as anger. He might also be prone to self-harm."

"That has not been an issue to my knowledge, Doctor."

"Hm. Since that is the case, keeping him bound may not be

necessary. Still, I would like to clear him before the bonds are removed. Perhaps you could convince him to talk to me tomorrow."

"I will try, but I cannot guarantee anything. He's always been difficult."

The psychiatrist raised his brows. "How did he make it this far in the USC in that case?"

"He's damned good at what he does."

"Ah. Do try."

"I will."

The psychiatrist nodded and went on his way. Commodore Gergiev returned to Skylark's room.

"He's not talking," a medic said as she exited the room. "Good luck, sir."

Pausing a moment to try and figure out how to approach the grieving commander, Gergiev entered the room.

"Commander Skye," he greeted.

Skylark glanced at him, then returned his attention to the ceiling.

"Team 6 has been withdrawn from active status pending your psychological review."

Still saying nothing, Skylark continued to stare at the ceiling.

"You really need to cooperate this time, Skye."

"What would you have me say?"

"The truth would be a good idea."

"You want the truth, Commodore? Ask Hunt why Admiral Brooke is unavailable. Ask him why Councillor Brand is the only councillor to be seen or heard from in months. Tell me why I saw a muzzle flash and blood spray seconds before the tahorah's leg gave out."

"You cannot be serious!"

Skylark turned his head and met the commodore's eye. "Then I have nothing to say," he said. He turned back and stared up at the ceiling.

Knowing full well that he would get no more from the commander, Gergiev sighed and left Medical.

Skylark closed his eyes.

"Commodore?" a young US Army mechanic said from Gergiev's study door.

"Yes, Private?"

"You need to see this, sir. The daemon. They're doing... things."

"People tend to," Gergiev said.

"No, I mean on the flight deck, sir."

"What? Speak sense boy."

"Please, sir."

Sighing, Gergiev stood. He followed the mechanic to the balcony that overlooked the flight deck. Gathered below, the entirety of the USC Research Vessel *Magellan* daemon crewmembers huddled close together, their heads bowed, their hands linking them all in a remarkably complex lattice of hand to head connections.

Gergiev stared through the thick glass walls of the balcony. "What are they doing?" he asked his guide.

"I don't know, sir," the mechanic said. "But we were hoping you might be able to get them to move. We can't get our work done and they've been there for an hour already."

"They're mourning," Jack said quietly from behind the commodore.

Gergiev turned to her. "Lieutenant? You know what this is?"

"I forget the daemon word, but it basically translates to 'sharing.'"

"Sharing what?"

Jack shrugged. "Their grief, their anger, their memories of the one they lost. The tahorah told me about it. The daemon are much more communal than we are, sir."

"How long does this kind of ceremony last?"

Jack shrugged. "I don't know, sir. She never told me that."

Gergiev looked Lieutenant Green over. She had been crying, he could plainly see. Her eyes were rimmed with red and still filled with tears as yet unshed. She refused to meet his eye and stared glumly down at the daemon gathering.

"I am sorry for your loss, Lieutenant," the commodore said gently.

"She was our team, sir. One of us," Jack replied.

It was clear that she expected the commodore to understand just how profound that loss was and Gergiev chided himself on the fact that he did not know. He could guess, but he had not been part of any USC Strategic team. He could not fathom how closely knit each unit was and, he was ashamed to admit to himself, he had never come close to accepting the daemon as "one of us."

Gergiev turned to the mechanic. "Let them be," he said.

"But sir—"

"It can wait, Private. Let them mourn."

The mechanic nodded. "Yes, sir." He saluted and ran off to relay the news. Jack remained. She turned to the commodore.

"Sir, about—"

"If you're asking after your commander, Lieutenant, I have nothing to say other than I cannot discuss it with you at the moment."

Jack opened her mouth.

"No," Gergiev said before she had the opportunity to ask. "You may not. We don't know the state of his mind and, it has to be said, the state of yours. No one is to see him until he has been cleared."

Anger flashed across Lieutenant Green's face. She clamped her mouth shut and nodded.

"Good. Dismissed."

"Yes, *sir*," Jack said. She didn't bother to salute before turning around and stalking away.

A pale hand with dark nails pressed against the soft, fleshy material. Pulsing echoed in the air, a heartbeat slow and irregular. Pain. Excruciating pain, throbbing through the mind, and down the back. Breathing was laboured and burned the throat and lungs.

The hand balled into a fist as the pain shot through, narrowing the vision, as if staring down a tunnel.

Suddenly there was more than one consciousness.

Ben.

Skylark's eyes snapped open.

"What the hell is going on?" Commodore Gergiev demanded as the medics scrambled in and out of Skylark's room.

"He won't calm down. He's been fighting his bonds. Not a word, just struggling."

Gergiev scowled and moved into the room. Skylark struggled against the thick leather straps which bound his wrists to the bed.

"Get sedative!" a medic yelled.

"Let me go," Skylark growled.

"Commander!" Gergiev snapped. Skylark barely glanced at him.

"Saracen," he barked. "I need to talk to Saracen!"

"You need to calm down, Commander."

"Saracen!"

"Sedating!" a medic yelled, pushing past the commodore with a large syringe.

"No!" Skylark said, straining hard. He had no choice, however. The syringe slipped into his vein with ease. He did not stop struggling as the medic pushed the sedative into his bloodstream.

The medics waited expectantly. It appeared to have no effect.

"Get me Saracen!" Skylark growled straining against the bonds.

"Get me more sedative," the medic holding the now empty syringe said.

"Infiltration training," Gergiev muttered. "This is what it looks like when it goes wrong."

Handed a second syringe, the medic placed her hand around Skylark's elbow. An enormous, dark hand wrapped around the hand that held the syringe. The medic looked up in surprise as a daemon pushed her gently aside.

"Commander," Sarcen said softly.

Skylark looked over at him and immediately stopped struggling. "Saracen," he breathed. "She's alive."

The leader of the majan blinked in surprise. He looked into Skylark's eyes a moment, as if searching for something. Satisfied with what he saw, Sarcen started undoing the leather straps.

"What the hell are you doing?" a medic demanded. She moved over to stop him. Sarcen grabbed her hands and growled. The medic slowly moved back. Sarcen helped Skylark into a sitting position.

"Show me," he said. He placed one palm over Skylark's temple and leant forward. Skylark did the same and together, their foreheads touching, they closed their eyes.

To Skylark, it felt as if he was falling. Thousands of images floated past, whirling around in no particular order as he fell. He landed in that body concealed behind the strange fabric, stretching a pale, dark-nailed hand towards it, hoping to break free of it. The unsteady heartbeat filled the tiny space, and pain wracked throughout. Then the word, a name—the only name remembered from time spent in this living hell.

Ben.

It was her voice. Naschari's voice.

Tahorah, another voice whispered. Saracen.

Skylark felt him pull away. *Wait!* he implored. *There is more.*

He struggled through an increasingly groggy mind, trying to find the images that told the daemon majan all he knew. It took several attempts before he struck upon the correct train of thoughts and images.

Skylark showed Sarcen all he had guessed about Vice Admiral Hunt and Councillor Brand. He showed the daemon what he had seen on the bridge, how the tahorah had fought and how she had been betrayed. Recalling it now showed the event in greater detail. There had been blood when Naschari's leg collapsed from under her; a small spray of crimson escaping her thigh near the knee. It had not been caused by a ragnar tail.

Control failed Skylark. The sedatives finally began their work. He felt his mind slipping. More images raced past and Skylark began to fall again. Sarcen's presence left as all conscious thought ceased.

The medics and Commodore Gergiev watched on as Skylark and Sarcen held their private communion.

"What the fuck are they doing?" Gergiev asked. The nearest medic shrugged.

"I have no idea, sir."

Skylark slumped, his weight caught by the daemon standing at the bed. Gently, the daemon set him down. He pressed one palm to Skylark's forehead briefly and Skylark shuddered, then relaxed.

The daemon looked up.

Everyone in the room took a step backwards. Sarcen's eyes glowed blue, blazing with naked fury. Gergiev felt his knees go weak as those flaming eyes fell upon him.

"What do you know?" the daemon growled at him.

Gergiev scowled. "What are you talking about?"

The daemon looked him over. He muttered something in his own language, then left Medical, his eyes still burning.

"Will someone tell me what the fuck is going on?" Commodore Gergiev demanded.

20

Doctor LeBruin had been trained primarily as a biologist, taking a second degree in medicine when it became clear employment in biology was not a well-paying field. On the *Magellan*, she played both roles, being on call with Medical while she worked in the biology labs aboard the ship.

At the moment, she was examining the behaviour of the DNA altering virus that had killed Commander Wheeler under various environmental conditions. Working opposite her was a daemon scholar. He had proven a very curious and capable scientist, easy with jokes and smiles, who had a propensity for humming as he worked. LeBruin found she rather liked him.

At the bench behind him stood another scholar. She worked on separating blood samples.

The humming stopped abruptly. LeBruin looked up to find both daemon frozen in place, their eyes glowing electric blue. She almost dropped her slide.

"What is it?" she asked.

Neither answered. They exchanged a glance, dropped everything and left the lab. LeBruin stared incredulously after them.

Team 6 looked up as the door to their quarters slid open. Binky slid off his bed when he saw Butan, in full daemon armour, standing at the door. The daemon majan offered a sad smile.

"I have come to say goodbye," he said.

"Wait, what?" Spike asked, standing up.

"What do you mean goodbye?" Binky asked.

"I have been summoned by the chtakah. We all have. The alliance has been—" Butan cocked his head. "Revoked."

"What?" Jack demanded. "Why?"

Butan shrugged. "The chtakah has not said. You are under no threat from us," he said smiling sadly again. "But we will no longer be helping you in this fight. I am sorry. It was good to have met you."

Butan turned away.

"Buddha, wait," Jack said. She ran forward and embraced the daemon, who gladly returned it. "Look after yourself," Jack whispered.

"You as well," Butan replied.

Sarcen arrived, taking his fellow majan at the elbow. He said something in his own language. Butan released Jack and waved at the rest of Team 6 before turning away. He and Sarcen walked down the hall together. Sarcen stopped suddenly, turned and jogged back to Team 6. He looked Binky square in the eye.

"I have seen your commander's mind," he said. "He means to go after her."

"Go after who?" Binky asked. "The tahorah?"

"Yes," Sarcen said. "Soon. Do not let him go alone or he will die."

Binky nodded. He extended his hand. "Thank you," he said. Sarcen took his hand.

"You are good, Lieutenant Commander," Sarcen said. "I should have liked to have known you better."

"Maybe one day."

"Perhaps." Sarcen nodded, turned and disappeared back down the hall.

Commodore Gergiev stood on the balcony of the flight deck and watched the daemon gather. Majan, scholars and warriors alike wore near-identical armour and, with their helmets on, it was impossible to tell who was who. They stood, awaiting the arrival of their own ship, which had left Earth moments ago.

"You're just going to let them go, sir?" Commander Speedman asked.

Gergiev looked sidelong at the commander. A purple bruise had already formed on his jaw, and the split above his brow had three stitches.

"I am just a commodore, Commander," Gergiev said. "And in the terms of this alliance, the chtakah is of equal rank to the admiral. I can't exactly refuse, can I?"

"Vice Admiral Hunt –"

"The chtakah outranks him," Commodore Gergiev reminded Speedman. He watched Speedman as the commander clenched and unclenched his jaw rapidly.

The arrival of Team 6 to the balcony drew the commodore's attention. They stood in their now diminished group at the railing, joined a few moments later by Lieutenant-Commander Hank and Team 87.

Gergiev walked to them.

"Sir," Hank greeted, saluting.

"As you were," Gergiev muttered. He turned back to watch the daemon. "Any ideas as to why they're leaving?"

"No, sir," Hank said. "But Buddha was good to have around. I'll sure as hell miss him."

Gergiev grunted. "There are few who share your sentiment, I'm afraid."

"I wouldn't say that," Doctor LeBruin said, walking to the commodore. "Two of the best friends I ever made are down there, awaiting their mother ship. More to the point, they were an incredible font of information and extremely able researchers. We'll be poorer for their absence, it has to be said."

"Any word on the commander, Doctor?" Hank asked.

"Skye, you mean? I wouldn't know. I haven't been called to Medical in a while. Word is that he stares up at the ceiling and does nothing else."

"Sounds like him," Binky muttered.

All talk ceased as the flight deck doors flashed their red warning light. Those not dressed for space retreated hastily behind the thick glass wall which then sealed itself. The light above the doors turned green and then the doors parted. One by one, the daemon allowed themselves to be sucked out into the vacuum of space.

Beyond the door, the large twisting form of the daemon ship hovered a short distance away, surrounded by riderless machines looking not unlike a skidoo that zipped into action to meet its rider as they floated out of the *Magellan*. The daemon mounted the machines and rode them into the open doors of the daemon ship. When the last daemon had returned to their ships, the ships vanished, leaving nothing of its presence or direction save a small thin line of grey smoke that trailed off into nothingness.

The flight deck doors closed.

"That's it then," Commodore Gergiev said. "We're on our own."

The brandy was smooth and warming, a mouthful of liquid fire that hit the stomach and spread warmth throughout the whole body. Of course, this being the first glass of Commodore Gergiev's second bottle for the evening, he felt none of it.

He stared down at the amber-coloured liquid. A small point of blue light appeared in the glass. He frowned and stared down at it.

"Brandy isn't supposed to glow," he muttered to himself. He squeezed his eyes shut and shook his head. He opened his eyes again. The point of light was larger, the glow stronger.

"The fuck?" He held the glass up and peered through it. It took him longer than a minute to realize that the source of the light reflecting in his drink was actually standing beside the door. He lowered his glass and stared at the glowing blue figure at the door.

"Who the fuck are you?" he demanded, his words slurring.

The blue man cocked his head. "Are you drunk, Commodore?"

"Yeah. What's it to you?"

The figure smiled slightly. Commodore Gergiev narrowed his eyes at it.

"I'm hallucinating, aren't I? Did I accidentally drink Absinthe?"

"You are not hallucinating, Commodore. We have met but briefly. I am the chtakah."

Gergiev leant forward, squinting. "Bullshit," he said. "He doesn't glow."

"I do if I am projecting myself from my physical form."

"What?"

"I am—what do you call it? Having an out of body experience? Deliberately. So I may speak with you. Privately."

Gergiev stared. "All right. Let's assume I haven't had Absinthe and am not suffering from space dementia and this is actually possible, why in the known universe would you seek me out?"

"You are the commander's commander."

"I am many commanders' commander. Which particular commander do you happen to mean?"

"You have him kept prisoner at the moment."

"Ah. *That* commander. That brings me to my next question. So what?"

"One of the majan told me he trusted you."

"Did he?"

The projected image of the chtakah cocked its head. "Yes to both."

"Both what?"

"Both implications of your question."

"What?"

"Yes, he told me and yes, he trusted you."

"Oh." Gergiev looked down at his brandy. He carefully set the glass down and attempted to stand. Twice. Then he gave up.

"Commodore, I have sought you out because I felt I should explain our sudden departure."

"Actually, I would very much appreciate that."

"On several occasions I had made efforts to reach Admiral Brooke, even resorting to searching for him as you find me now. But I could not find him. Nor could I find any of the Council, not even our own grebar. I did, however, find Vice Admiral Hunt and Councillor Brand."

"So you're saying?"

"I fear that they are all that remains of the Council and USC Command. I fear that they have done great evil, perhaps in a misguided attempt to be rid of the daemon. I cannot guess as to their motives, for every option seems too foolish to consider. But I can guess as to their actions. I feared that all the daemon were in danger and so I took them back and fled to safety."

"That's very noble of you."

The chtakah's image smiled slightly. "I also want you to know that I am not prepared to abandon our alliance altogether. Nor are most of my warriors. Many have grown fond of your warriors. Find Admiral Brooke and the councillors. When I speak with them and am assured all is well, I shall rejoin the USC."

"Wait. You want me to work for you? Smacks a bit of treason, don't you think?"

"I want you to work for the admiral. Perhaps he is in grave danger."

Gergiev opened his mouth then shut it again. "I'll need to think about this."

"Do not take too long, Commodore."

The glowing form of the chtakah disappeared. For a time, Commodore Gergiev sat in stunned silence. Then he shifted his weight and said, "I've gone mad."

Skylark moved quickly, padding barefooted through the quiet halls of the *Magellan*. Most of them were deserted, lit now only with the red night-lights. The night crew made their rounds infrequently and were so loud that Skylark could find a place to hide well in advance of them rounding a corner.

Caution kept him moving undetected. He reached Team 6's quarters in a little under half an hour, sparing no thought for the young medic he had strapped to the bed in his place. Escape from his bonds came at the cost of a broken little finger, hardly a crippling injury. He would look after it when he returned. If he returned.

The quarters, he discovered, were empty. He didn't stop to ponder his good fortune. Bringing his team along on what was, essentially, a suicide mission or at least a certain court-martial was never an option. Team 6 would brave it, he knew. But he could not let them. This was his mission, and his alone. Binky would take command of Team 6, and he would be exceptional.

Skylark hurriedly dressed in his armour. Sneaking around in it would be remarkably difficult, but he felt certain he could manage. Armoured and armed, he made his careful way to the flight deck. Infiltrator training proved invaluable in getting him aboard the USC Strategic *One* without being detected. He watched, crouched in the shadow of a personal fighter as the ramp closed.

Safe at last, he stood and made his way up to the cockpit.

"Don't even think about touching the controls," a Scottish-accented voice said as Skylark entered the cockpit. Skylark froze in place.

The pilot's chair swivelled around, revealing Christie sitting in full formal Scottish regalia.

"You'll crash her before you've even cleared the flight deck."

Skylark slowly reached for his weapon.

"Besides, we've all been grounded and you'll need someone who can hack into the control."

Skylark blinked. "I beg your pardon?"

"Thinking of leaving without us?" Binky asked from behind Skylark. Skylark spun and stared incredulously at his lieutenant commander. Binky grinned at him.

"What the fuck are you doing here?" Skylark demanded.

"We're saving your arse" Jack said reaching the top step. "You're not going to be able to pull off this rescue without us, and you know it."

"No," Skylark said. "Absolutely not. Take off your armour and get off this boat."

"No," Binky said, crossing his arms.

"You will all be court-martialled!"

"Good," Jack said. "Because they're going to break up Team 6, and I'm not going to fight for any other commander, sir."

"We're not going anywhere," Doorman called from his seat in the common room of the fighter.

"The fuck?" Skylark muttered. He walked to the railing and looked down. Spike and Doorman looked up from their card game and waved.

"Is it true, Skye?" Jack asked. "Is she alive?"

Skylark turned back to her and nodded. "Yes."

"Ben, they blew that asteroid to smithereens. Nothing could have survived," Binky said.

"She's alive, Binky. I know it!"

"How?"

Skylark paused a moment. "I just know," he said quietly, shrugging.

"Good enough for me," Christie said. "You know where to go?"

"Not exactly, but I know where to start."

"Well, that's a start. Hmm. Redundant. Let's get going, shall we?" Christie spun back to the controls and fiddled with the interactive holograms. The ship sprang to life.

"And just getting into control... there we go!"

Skylark looked out of the cockpit to the doors of the flight deck. They slid open smoothly.

"USC Strategic *One*, what the fuck are you doing?" someone from control said over the intercom. "No one is cleared for flight."

"I'm – chhhhhhhhh – th – chhhhhhh," Christie replied, mimicking the sounds of interference as he flicked the comm. link on and off.

"USC Strategic *One*, power down. Do you hear? Power down immediately."

Christie grinned and the long-haul fighter lifted up from the deck.

"See you later, tossers," he said before pushing hard on the thrusters, sending the fighter into space.

"Christie? Christie is that you? You are so dead, you Scots bastard."

"Oops. Forgot the comm. was on." Christie flipped the switch, cutting off communication with the *Magellan*. He turned the fighter and jumped the stream that passed the Aborgini Asteroid Belt.

"They'll probably send fighters after us," Christie said. "But by the time they scramble, we'll be well and truly lost in the belt."

Skylark said nothing. He looked down at the floor, deep in thought. When he realized everyone was watching him, he lifted his head. He gave a small smile. "Thank you."

"She's our tribe, too," Binky said. He clapped Skylark's armoured shoulder. "Come on, let's join the twins."

It took Private Hodgins of the Australian Air Force some effort to wake Commodore Gergiev. The commodore snored through most of the shouting and the shaking, only waking when ice water was poured over his head.

"The fuck?" he demanded loudly. He regretted it. He pressed his palm against his left eye in an effort to quell the pounding in his head.

"Sorry, sir," Hodgins said. "We have a situation, sir."

"What situation, Private?" Gergiev demanded.

"Commander Skye and Team 6 have hijacked USC Strategic *One*, sir."

Gergiev blinked. "What?"

"Commander—"

"No, never mind. I heard." The commodore stood abruptly. "How? The commander was strapped to a damned cot in Medical!"

"He escaped somehow and put the medic on duty in the bed."

The commodore let loose a string of curses that would have shamed even the most ardent blasphemer. He marched down to the flight deck to find the place in total chaos. Mechanics stood staring slack-jawed at the spot where USC Strategic *One* ought to have been.

A flight coordinator leant on the rails of the balcony overlooking the deck, his head in his hands.

"Lieutenant," Gergiev snapped. "What the fuck happened?"

"I—don't—" The flight coordinator sighed. "It was Christie, sir. He's piloting Strategic *One*. He hacked the controls, unlocked the wheel jacks and opened the flight deck doors."

"Christie. The Scotsman?"

"Yes, sir. Smart little fuck who spent his time before military school hacking databases for fun." The lieutenant slammed his palm against the rail. "I couldn't close the doors in time to prevent them, sir. I'm sorry, sir."

"They took us by surprise, Lieutenant. I'm certain Skye planned this carefully. I'll need a full report."

"Yes, sir. Right away, sir."

"Private?"

"Yes, sir?"

"Get me a comm. link with the good Commander Skye, please."

"Yes, sir!"

Skylark sat quietly on the sofa in Strategic *One's* lounge.

"I like that name," Jack said.

"What?" Spike asked. "*Fuck 'Em All*?"

"Yeah. It's an appropriate name for a pirate vessel. What do you think, Commander?"

"I prefer *Raid*."

"It sounds like bug spray!"

"That's the point, doofus," Doorman said. "And it has more than one meaning. Besides, what do pirates do if not raid?"

"No," Jack said. "It needs something else. Something with some, I don't know, panache!"

Skylark smiled slightly.

"Well, Commander, you might want to get up here," Christie said over the comm.

The conversation went dead as Skylark stood and made his way to the cockpit. After a brief hesitation, Binky followed.

"What is it?" Skylark asked when he reached Christie.

"We're here," Christie said, nodding towards his viewscreen. Skylark looked. Nothing remained of the infested asteroid where the tahorah had been taken. A gaping hole that once contained one of the largest asteroids in the Aborgini Asteroid Belt now held nothing but dust and the occasional tiny lump of grey stone.

Skylark said nothing for a long time.

"What now, sir?" Christie asked.

"There," Skylark said, pointing. A small passage between the large rocks drifting through space led to nothing.

"You sure?" Christie asked.

"Yes."

"I don't see anything."

"Not yet," Skylark replied.

"All right," Christie answered doubtfully as he carefully navigated his way through the asteroids, along the roughly diagonal channel until the USC Strategic *One* entered a pocket of empty space surrounded by rocks.

"Now what?"

But Skylark had not heard the pilot's question. His eyes were distant and he pulled himself away from his body, searching space for her warmth, scanning the boulders for her purple glow.

"Turn forty-five right," Skylark said. Christie did.

"No, sorry. It's the other way."

Christie raised his brows but turned the nose of the fighter around ninety degrees.

"There," Skylark said. "Go to the sun side of that one there."

"The one that looks like a ball sack?"

Skylark smiled slightly. "Yes. That one."

Christie whistled. "Not without a sense of humour, these bugs."

Nevertheless, Christie carefully guided the fighter to the bright side of the asteroid, only to discover the spacecraft now sat in the centre of a large colony of ragnar occupying several asteroids.

"Christ all mighty!" he breathed. He looked up at Skylark. "How the fuck did you know?"

Skylark shrugged. "The same way I know she's alive."

"Well, I'm going to sink us a little. I get the distinct impression that bugs could jump on us from any angle and I'm not keen on having their pincers cut through my baby's shapely body."

"Good idea." Skylark turned to Binky. "I'm going in alone."

"What? Like hell!"

"Binky, five people will make too much noise. We'll be too easily discovered. And I need you and the team to create enough of a distraction for me to get into that nest undetected."

"Still no."

"This is not a request. It's an order."

"If anything happens to you—"

"If anything happens to me, you get out, you tell Commodore Gergiev about the giant nest you found, and then you come back and blow this place to hell."

"Sir—"

"Someone has to make it out and warn the rest of the USC, Binky."

"Why's it gotta be me?"

"Because, Binky, I would rather die than come out of that nest without her. This is it for me."

Binky stared at Skylark. "Holy shit," he said.

"What?"

"You're in love with her!"

Skylark smiled slightly. "You seem surprised."

"I, well, I, It's just, you. In love. That's new for me."

"Yeah, well, it's new for me too."

Nodding, Binky held out his hand, which Skylark took. "We'll get you that distraction," he said.

"Thank you." Skylark pressed his comm. "Suit up. We're here."

Spike nodded to his commander as he manoeuvred the transport for touchdown behind a ridge. He did not appear happy, but then no one on the team was happy when the plan was announced. Skylark appreciated Binky's endorsement and Jack's threat more.

"If you die in there, I'm going to kill you."

Skylark smiled at the mere memory of her angry words.

"You're good to go, sir," Spike said. He opened the transport door.

"Thank you, Spike."

"Sir?"

"Yes?"

"Come back. Or else."

Skylark smiled back at his corporal. "Take care, Spike." He unholstered his gun and jumped down from the transport.

"Right," Spike mumbled. He shut the door and took off.

Skylark watched him go, then made his way towards the nest.

"I'm in position," Skylark said into his comm. He hid behind a long ridge that opened near an entrance to the nest. "It looks like a pirate mining settlement."

Though not terribly common, the USC had been deployed before the ragnar threat to deal with pirate miners who had set up shop illegally. Still, the lure of the fortune that could be made in the rare minerals from space ensured that, no matter how many mine collapses and explosions there were, pirates were always willing to risk life and limb to make their fortune.

"Alrighty, Skylark," Binky said over the comm. "Creating your diversion."

"Technically, it's your diversion."

"Potato, potahto."

Skylark grinned. A bright light flashed on his right and the asteroid shuddered. The two ragnar guards at the entrance of the mine turned towards the light. After a hesitation, they both scuttled towards the activity. Skylark stepped forward, then ducked back as several more ragnar soldiers scuttled past his hiding spot.

Commander Skye checked carefully around the corner before sprinting for the entrance.

The covered tunnel of the pirate mining settlement had been extended a little by the ragnar, creating an odd sort of concealed porch in front of the air lock door. Skylark did not pause to wonder at it. He opened his pouch and attached a square box over the keypad at the door.

"All right, Christie. Do your thing."

"Thing is doing," Christie answered. "Give me a moment."

Skylark crouched and spun as a shadow fell briefly over him. He saw only the tail of a ragnar soldier as it scuttled towards yet more flashes of light.

"You should be good now, Commander."

Turning back, Skylark removed the hacking device and pressed the glowing green button on the keypad. The door slid open and Skylark stepped in. He waited in the airlock until the door closed and the room pressurized. The door into the settlement opened automatically. He peered around the corner and found the flesh-covered hall empty. He entered.

"I'm in," he said.

"You watch yourself," Binky demanded.

"Always," Skylark answered.

"Bullshit."

Pausing only briefly to find his bearing, Skylark turned right and made his way into the nest. The diversion appeared to be working. The workers had left their regular duties to repair the damage that Team 6 had inflicted on the outside of the nest and the soldiers had flooded towards the scene in an effort to thwart their attackers. The tunnels of the settlements were empty.

Skylark paused at a crossroad, turning inwards to his gut to help him find his way. The external microphone picked up a click and a chirp. Skylark turned.

"Shit!"

A ragnar soldier stood behind him, its tail raised high over its back. It flashed down. Skylark jumped back, narrowly escaping the strike. He opened fire, shooting the ragnar in the face and taking out most of its eyes. The creature squealed and stumbled. Two more ragnar appeared.

The fight was vicious and Skylark had emptied his clip before the ragnar lay in pools of their own gloopy, clear blood. He looked down at his supply. Nine more clips. Sighing, he ejected his empty clip and inserted another. Instinct turned his head.

A sharp tail shot out of the dim light. Skylark dove forward and twisted, rolling to his feet. He shouldered his gun and fired at the newly arrived ragnar.

"Fucking bastard!" he muttered.

The ragnar lifted its claws up to protect its eyes as Skylark sprayed bullets at it. Skylark launched himself forward. Blinded by its own claws, the ragnar soldier did not notice Skylark run beneath it. He lifted his gun and shot half his clip into the weak joint in the ragnar's armour. The ragnar shuddered, then the head slowly detached. Skylark barely made it out before the body of the alien crashed down.

A claw struck down, knocking Skylark's gun from his grip. Skylark turned and leapt backwards as another ragnar scuttled into the centre of the crossroad. His elbow struck the claw of another soldier as he landed. He rolled forward to avoid the tail strike, then jumped to the side to avoid the next one.

Three ragnar in total crowded the space, sending Skylark dancing in an effort to avoid their infecting tails. He spied his gun beneath the front foot of one of them and unsheathed his long knife. Careful to aim at the joints, Skylark struck back, spinning between two ragnar as his knife flashed.

They dodged around as much as their bulk permitted them to, freeing Skylark's gun. He dived for it, but the ragnar had moved first. It kicked Skylark's gun out of reach and closed its claw around his waist. Twisting in its grasp as the ragnar lifted him from the ground, he brought his knife down into the joint at the base of the claw. The creature spasmed in pain and its grip loosened. Skylark squirmed free and dropped. His feet never hit the ground. Another ragnar grabbed first one wrist, then the other, holding him high above its head. Skylark struggled hard.

Another ragnar, after several attempts, grabbed both his ankles. They pulled, stretching Skylark until he thought his limbs would come free of their sockets.

Skylark watched as the ragnar holding his ankles raised its tail and the dripping stinger extended. The tail flashed forward. Skylark twisted, narrowly missing the imminent impaling.

The ragnar raised its tail again and struck forward. This time, the stinger was caught in the grasp of a fourth ragnar, which had arrived on the scene moments ago. Skylark noticed that the armour on this new ragnar sported a jagged crest on the creature's massive, many-eyed head.

Those eyes regarded Skylark a moment before the creature began clicking and chirping. It turned and scuttled away. The two ragnar holding Skylark followed, the one gripping his ankles moving backwards. Despite knowing it was futile, Skylark struggled.

The journey took the better part of half an hour. The dizzying number of twists and turns left Skylark thoroughly lost. He felt certain of one thing, however. Naschari was getting closer with every step. He stopped struggling, earning a querying series of clicks from the ragnar holding his wrists. The one holding his ankles chirped in return.

"Son of a bitch," Skylark whispered to himself. "They're talking."

The tunnels eventually opened out into a massive cavern. At the angle Skylark was held, all he could see were the skeletons hanging by their feet from the ceiling. They reached so high that darkness swallowed the uppermost ones. Settlements like this often held as many as a million people—the miners, the engineers, the farmers and, of course, all their families.

Skylark swallowed hard.

A sudden drop and Skylark found himself on his back. He struggled to sit up. Faced with the ragnar queen, he stopped short of making it upright. His jaw fell.

The queen was massive. An enormous engorged abdomen filled with pearly white eggs made up most of her bulk. By comparison, the thorax was miniature, though still longer than Skylark was tall. Long forelegs, not unlike those of a praying mantis, folded in close to her body. At her back, ludicrously small, translucent wings twitched and shifted.

A triangular, multi-eyed head cocked this way and that, her many eyes observing him as her labium moved, revealing sharp, needle-like teeth.

"Sir?" Binky said. "Any luck, sir?"

Skylark moved slowly. He pressed his comm. link. "Define luck, Binky."

"What?"

"The good news is, I'm alive. The bad news is, I'm probably not going to be for long."

"Sir?" It was Jack this time.

"I've been captured."

"What?!" The entire team spoke in unison.

"I've been captured. I'm in the hatchery in front of the queen. All exits are covered. I've lost both my weapons."

Silence answered him.

"Go," he said. "Get to the *Magellan*."

"No, sir." Doorman said. "Not until Christie tells us your vitals have ceased."

Skylark smiled slightly. "I don't think I'll be getting out of this one."

"Yeah, well, you better find a way, or I'm coming in!" Jack said hotly.

"Negative, Jack. The others need to know that the biggest mother-fucking bug I've ever seen is laying eggs in the millions. Now go. All of you. That's…"

Skylark trailed off. The queen extended one of her long forelegs. Skylark followed the line she made and saw Naschari walk slowly in. She wore her armour still, the two holes the ragnar had punctured in it covered with the same brown substance that covered the outside of the settlement. Her helmet swung loosely in her right hand, barely even noticed. Skylark's heart almost stopped as she stopped in front of the queen and turned to face him.

Muscles twitched into action before Commander Skye had time to think. They did not take him anywhere. As soon as he moved, ragnar pincers grabbed his wrists again. Once again he was hauled into the air and his ankles were grabbed. Pulled into a starfish, struggling became painful.

The queen moved, lowering herself down and forward so that her largest eyes looked squarely at him. A pale ragnar, roughly the size of Skylark's head, scuttled over the queen's head and onto Skylark. It chirped and clicked as it worked the locks on Skylark's helm. Unable to struggle, Skylark remained still as the helmet came off and tumbled to the ground. The tiny ragnar returned the way it came.

The queen placed both her forelegs on Skylark's shoulders and continued to look at him with her unblinking, glassy eyes.

"You have something that doesn't belong to you," Skylark said. "Give her back."

The queen clicked and, a short while later, withdrew. She sunk yet lower, placing her forelegs on Naschari's shoulders. She brought her mouth to the tahorah's ear and clicked.

The tahorah's eyes lit, glowing purple. She dropped her helm and her blades extended. Skylark was dropped to the ground again and the gathered ragnar shuffled around, creating a circle. Skylark pushed himself to his feet and faced the tahorah.

"Naschar—"

Before he could finish, the tahorah leapt forward, her blades flashing. Skylark ducked and rolled away from her. She attacked again. This time, Skylark stepped forward, blocked her striking arm and spun her around. Trapping her arms at the elbow, he pulled her close.

"Naschari," he barked. "Snap out of it!"

The tahorah swung her leg out, catching Skylark's knee. It collapsed under him and he lost his lock on her arms. She spun free and whipped her blades around. Only the last minute dip of Skylark's head saved him from an unpleasant lobotomy. He launched forward again, tackling her to the ground. Catching her wrists, he pinned her down with his weight.

"Damn it, Naschari! It's me! Wake up!"

She bucked him off and they rolled across the ground a while before she managed to kick him away from her. Standing again, Skylark defended himself as best he could, but an unexpected kick to his cheek sent him tumbling to the ground, seeing lights. The tahorah pulled him up by his collar. The edge of one of her glowing purple blades pressed against his gullet.

"Naschari," Skylark whispered when his vision returned. His eyes met hers and she frowned. Her hand trembled, the electric blade vibrating at his throat.

Skylark brought his arms up, knocking away the bladed arm and delivering a powerful backhand across her face in a single movement. The tahorah spun around and Skylark caught her, wrapping his arms firmly around her, pinning her arms at her side.

"Naschari, stop! It's me. Please." His voice dropped to a whisper. "Please remember."

The tahorah shuddered and Skylark pulled her in tighter. He rested his cheek against the side of her jaw and continued his whispered pleas.

"You have to remember. Naschari. Please."

"Ben?" the tahorah asked weakly.

Skylark smiled. "I'm here. It's me. I'm here."

"Let me go." Sensing Skylark's hesitation she said, "Ben, please. Let me go."

Slowly, Skylark released his grip on the tahorah. She spun and kicked him hard in the chest. He rolled onto his side and prepared another defence, but the tahorah did not chase him down. Instead, she leapt over him and, using a ragnar soldier as a launch, leapt into the air. She swung her blade in a graceful arc as she descended.

"No!" Skylark screamed, but too late.

The queen's head fell, rolling to a stop moments before the tahorah landed. She fell to her hands and knees, pressing her palm against her temple.

"Naschari!" Skylark ran to her. She cried out in pain as he helped her to her feet. She blinked up at him.

"Ben!"

"Come on."

Skylark ran to retrieve their helmets, no easy feat amidst the convulsing ragnar. He returned to her, put on his helm and, once she had done the same, grabbed her arm and ran.

"No," she said, pulling back. "This way."

They ran hand in hand through the labyrinthine tunnels of the pirate mining settlement, dodging the suddenly crazed ragnar until they found themselves out and on the surface of the asteroid.

"Spike!"

"Christ on a stick! I see you! I can't land there. It's too hot. Can you get past them all?"

"Heading out," Skylark answered. He reached back and took the tahorah's hand again. They sprinted out.

It was a mad dash involving spinning jumps, retreating, ducking, sliding and rolling. How long or short the run was, or how tired and winded he felt never registered with Skylark. He ran until he saw the transport and did not stop until he and the tahorah were inside it.

Only once he sat in the seat, with his arms wrapped protectively around the tahorah did he realize just how much his legs ached and his lungs burned. Only once the transport lifted away did the enormity of everything that had transpired hit him. He struggled for breath as grief squeezed on his heart with a crushing pressure.

The tahorah trembled against him so violently he could feel it through both their suits of armour. He swallowed back his angry questions and pulled her close. They sat in silence for the few minutes it took Christie to swoop down and get them boarded.

21

Skylark and the tahorah were greeted by the stunned members of Team 6 as they exited the transport holding hands. The tahorah was roughly embraced by everyone on the team the moment she took her helm off, momentarily pushing Skylark away. Skylark pushed his way back to her.

He grabbed her by the elbow and dragged her away from the team. She yanked herself from his grasp.

"What the hell were you thinking?" he demanded. He grabbed her armoured shoulders and shook her angrily. "Have you any idea what you've done?"

"Skye!" Doorman snapped.

Skylark did not even look at him. "Do you?"

"It was the only way," Naschari whispered. "We were surrounded. You would have never gotten out."

"I wouldn't have wanted to!" Skylark yelled. His voice dropped to a whisper when he said, "Not without you."

The tahorah's eyes filled with tears. "You are needed."

"No—"

"The alliance needs you. Your *team* needs you."

"*I* need *you.*" Skylark pulled her roughly in and wrapped his arms around her. "I can't be without you. I can't."

The tahorah closed her eyes and returned his embrace, fighting back tears.

"What the hell is going on?" Spike asked his brother.

"She killed the queen," Jack whispered, her eyes fixed on her commander and the woman he loved.

"But that would mean… oh."

"Fuck," Binky spat. He turned abruptly and stormed from the flight deck.

"It was all for nothing," Spike said.

"Maybe," Doorman said. He put his hands on Jack's sagged shoulders. "Come on. The commander and his woman need some privacy."

"I need to bathe," Naschari whispered after the long embrace ended.

Skylark nodded. "You can use my quarters. Come on." He took her hand and they walked slowly away from the flight deck.

The ship felt deserted. Not a single member of Team 6 showed their faces as Skylark and Naschari made their way to Skylark's quarters. Once there, Skylark noticed the tahorah's gown and robe hanging over one of the chairs at his table. On the table, still softly glowing, sat Naschari's bioluminescent orchid.

"Jack," he said, answering Naschari's unasked question. "Most likely. No one else is that thoughtful." He shut the door. "Come on. I'll help you get your armour off."

Naschari accepted Skylark's help. The clothing beneath her armour clung to her, plastered to her frame by a cement of dried blood and sweat. Skylark took a sharp breath in when he saw the extent of the blood on her clothes.

"Come on," he said. He guided her to the bathroom only to find he could not fit through the door clad in his armour. He grunted as his pauldrons hit the doorframe on either side and he bounced backwards slightly.

Naschari giggled. "Here," she said. She removed his pauldrons and smiling, took his hand. They walked in together.

It took some work to remove Naschari's clothes. The two wounds created when she had been infected had not yet healed over properly, and the cloth of her undershirt had become embedded in the scar tissue. She winced as Skylark carefully dislodged the shirt from the wound in her back. Blood and fluid trickled down from the re-opened lesion.

"I'm sorry," Skylark said, wincing.

"I'm all right." Naschari worked at the wound at her hip. It took some time and she had to tear off a considerable amount of scabbing in order to remove her shirt from the wound. Skylark, in the meantime, observed her back.

"It doesn't look infected, at least. See me after your shower and I'll patch these up for you."

Naschari nodded. She smiled slightly at Skylark, who moved past her to start the shower.

"Take as long as you need," he said once the warm water started pouring from the showerhead. "I'll be outside if you need anything."

Naschari nodded. Skylark bent and kissed her brow. He smoothed her hair, then left, giving her the privacy she needed.

The sounds of the shower working as Naschari bathed felt oddly comforting to Skylark. That she was in the shower, upright, and functioning helped him keep his head. Though he knew that it would not be long before her suppressed immune system would start attacking her own body, he was never more certain that everything would work out.

They would find a way.

Sighing, Skylark removed the rest of his armour and his undershirt. He searched through the small bag he had brought aboard for a change of clothes. Not expecting help, and not expecting to be successful, Skylark nevertheless prepared for every eventuality. He had thought to pack a casual uniform.

He had unpacked the uniform and laid it out on the bed before he noticed Naschari standing in the doorway to the bathroom. The shower still ran. She stood, watching him with a soft smile, completely naked and dripping.

Skylark smiled, reminded of the first time he had ever met her. She had been the enemy then; strikingly beautiful, yes, but the enemy.

Naschari reached one arm out, extending her hand to Skylark. Commander Skye dropped the shirt he was holding and walked forward, taking her hand. He opened his mouth to ask if everything was all right. Naschari silenced him with a finger pressed against his lips.

"I need you," she whispered.

Skylark did not hesitate. He pulled her close and kissed her deeply. She guided him back into the bathroom and, though he still wore his trousers, into the shower.

Jack found her commander and the woman he loved an hour later, both naked as the day they were born, asleep in each other's arms in the commander's bed. She almost burst into tears at the sight. Neither she, nor anyone else on Team 6 shared their commander's optimism regarding the tahorah's fate.

"Commander," Jack said softly, touching Skylark's shoulder. "Sir?"

Skylark stirred and groaned quietly. "Jack."

"We'll be back at the *Magellan* soon."

Sighing, Skylark nodded. Jack retreated from his quarters and he turned to wake Naschari. Frowning at her flushed face, he pressed his palm against her forehead. Fever.

Naschari stirred. She smiled up at Skylark.

"We're almost there," Skylark said quietly. "We should get dressed."

"Yes," Naschari replied, but her eyes closed again.

Skylark bent over and kissed her cheek before sliding out from between the covers. He dressed himself before attempting to wake Naschari again. This time, she slipped from the warmth of the blankets and walked to the chair over which her clothes hung.

"Wait," Skylark said. He pulled a small first aid kit from its place on the wall and walked forward. Naschari smiled a little and stood patiently as Skylark opened the kit and pulled out anti-bacterial gel and two sterile pads.

"You just want me naked for as long as possible," she teased.

Skylark flashed a smile. "Guilty."

Naschari laughed softly, but the laugh turned into a cough. Skylark looked up sharply. Naschari smiled sadly.

"Ben—"

"No," Skylark said. "It's not going to happen. Not to you."

Naschari sighed. There was no point in arguing. Skylark had made up his mind, and he would not be proven wrong until he had been proven wrong. Skylark dressed the wounds and helped Naschari dress. She shivered.

Skylark pulled her in, feeling the heat from her fever acutely. "You're burning up," he whispered.

"I'm cold."

"Come on. We'll get you something warm to drink." He took her hand and they walked to the kitchen.

Team 6 sat in the lounge of the long-haul fighter in glum silence. Spike spied Commander Skye and the tahorah first. He stood, faking his best smile as Skylark led the tahorah to the sofa.

"You look lovely, Tahorah," Spike said.

The tahorah smiled at him. "Thank you," she said. She reached up and kissed his cheek. "Liar."

Spike grinned, suddenly relaxed.

"We were about to start a game of craekers," Binky said. "Would you like to join?"

"Yes. That would be fun."

Doorman pulled a deck of cards from one of the various compartments built into his armour. Skylark smiled.

"You carry your cards in your armour?"

Doorman grinned. "Never leave home without 'em."

Skylark shrugged and went to the kitchen. "Anyone else want tea?" he called back.

"Yes please," Doorman said.

"Yeah, I'll take one too," Binky said.

"Not for me," Spike replied, pulling a face.

"I'll help," Jack said, jumping up.

"What? You're not playing?" Binky demanded.

Jack shook her head and dashed to the kitchen.

"How is she?" Jack asked when she arrived. She pulled three mugs from a cupboard.

"Sick," Skylark said. "A fever." He turned off the tap and placed the kettle on its stand.

"You know, for a spaceship, this place is decidedly low-tech." Jack grinned at her commander.

Skylark laughed softly. He leant against the counter and folded his arms across his chest. The typical loud argument announced the commencement of the game played in the lounge.

"What are you going to do?" Jack asked. "When we get back?"

Skylark shrugged.

Jack sighed. "We're in for a court-martial, I'm sure."

"That I don't doubt."

"I always wondered what I would be doing if I wasn't in the USC. Fix up bikes, I suppose. What about you? What would you do?"

"I actually haven't thought much about it. I always figured I'd be dead before I left the USC. Now I don't know. Perhaps I'll try and find the daemon, take her home."

"Skye—"

Skylark scowled at Jack's tone. "She'll pull through," he said. "She will."

Jack closed her eyes briefly. "The queen is dead, sir."

"That doesn't mean anything."

"Sir—"

"Jack!" Skylark barked.

Jack jumped. Skylark had never yelled at her, nor anyone on his team, for that matter. It simply wasn't his style. She stared at him briefly before turning and fleeing the kitchen.

The game of craekers stopped. Everyone in the lounge watched as Jack escaped the kitchen, fleeing to the now dark flight deck. The tahorah reached out and touched Spike's wrist.

"Yeah," he muttered. He put down his cards and went after Jack. The tahorah moved to the kitchen.

Skylark stood with his hands on the edge of the sink, leaning his weight against it as if trying to push it somewhere. He felt two small hands press against his shoulders and immediately turned.

"No," he said gently. "You need to conserve your energy."

"Ben," Naschari whispered. "I am dying."

"No." He pulled her close and wrapped his arms around her. "You're not. You're just a bit sick. You'll pull through. You have to."

Naschari said nothing. She sobbed quietly against Ben.

"Hey," Skye said gently, pulling away slightly. He wiped the tears from her cheeks with his thumb. "It's going to be all right. We'll find a way." He leant forward and kissed her gently. "I love you."

They fell into a close embrace again and there they remained.

Spike found Jack sitting in the transport, sobbing.

"Piss off!" she snapped when he clambered in.

Not easily intimidated, Spike simply wrapped his arms around her. She struggled briefly before collapsing against him and bawling.

"She's dying," Jack said between wracking sobs. "And he, he—"

"Is in denial," Spike whispered. "Yeah. I know."

Jack pulled away. "It's going to kill him."

Spike pulled her back into a tight hug. "I know." He held Jack until the lieutenant cried herself out. He wiped the tears from her face.

"We probably don't have that much time left as a team," Spike said. "Let's make these last moments good memories, huh?"

Jack smiled slightly and nodded, though fresh tears fell.

"Look at you," Spike said. "You great big softie."

Jack laughed and punched his shoulder. "Fuck you."

"If you insist. Now come on. There's hot tea and a game of craekers to be had."

The tahorah saw Jack returning, Spike walking behind her like a bodyguard. She slipped from Skylark's embrace and went to her. Jack smiled sadly and the tahorah threw herself around the lieutenant.

"Promise me you will look after him," the tahorah whispered in Jack's ear.

"I promise," Jack whispered back.

The tahorah pulled away and smiled at Jack. The lieutenant smiled back and stroked the tahorah's raven black hair. "May I?" she asked.

"Of course," the tahorah answered. She took Jack's hand and led her back to the lounge.

"Kettle's boiling," Spike said to Skylark before joining the others in the lounge.

Skylark raised his brows at him, then silently turned back to make the tea. When he arrived at the lounge with a tray of steaming mugs of tea, the game of craekers was in full swing. The tahorah sat on the edge of the sofa frowning down at her cards, the throw from the back of the sofa now hanging over her shoulders.

Jack sat behind her, combing her dark hair. Spike and Doorman started arguing.

The scene looked completely normal, but the thick haze of melancholy that touched every word, every movement and every breath weighed heavily on Skylark's shoulders. He said nothing of it as he handed out the tea.

Binky made room for him on the sofa, but the commander was not given a chance to sit down.

"Uh, Commander," Christie said via the comm. "You're needed up top."

Sighing, Skylark straightened and headed for the cockpit. Everyone in the lounge exchanged a glance, then abandoned their game and followed him.

"What is it, Christie?" Skylark asked when he arrived.

"Well, we're here," Christie answered. "Only that USC ship there isn't the *Magellan*."

Skylark frowned out at the space destroyer that hovered where the *Magellan* ought to have been. "Who is she, then?"

"Let's see, USC Destroyer *Starborn*."

Skylark straightened, drawing himself in with surprise.

"Hey," Binky said, the first of the team to arrive at the cockpit. "Isn't that Vice Admiral Hunt's ship?"

"Shit," Spike muttered.

Skylark turned back to the balcony where his team waited. They looked at him expectantly. His eyes were drawn to the far end of the balcony where the tahorah stood. She leant heavily against the railing, one hand holding the throw tightly against her, shivering. He went to her.

"Hey," he said.

She looked up and smiled. "Hey."

Skylark touched her cheek and frowned. The fever had worsened. He turned back.

"Hail her, Christie."

"Okay. USC Destroyer *Starborn*, this is USC Strategic *One*. Do you copy?"

"Copy you, Strategic *One*. We were just about to send a search party."

"We're flattered. We're carrying precious cargo. Permission to dock is requested."

"What cargo?"

The tahorah reached out and touched Commander Skye's arm. "Ben," she whispered before her legs gave out and she collapsed.

Skylark turned and caught her seconds before her head hit the metal floor. "Naschari," he said. He shook her. "Hey! Wake up."

The tahorah's eyes fluttered open.

"There you go," Skylark said, smiling. "Here you are."

"Ben—"

"Hush now. It's all right. We're almost home. We'll get you fixed up like new. Just hold on for me, all right?"

The tahorah nodded weakly.

"Did you read, USC Strategic *One*? What cargo?"

"Give me the comm.," Skylark growled. He stood, cradling the tahorah in his arms. She rested against him, her eyes closed and her arms wrapped around his neck.

"All yours, Commander."

"USC Destroyer *Starborn*, this is Commander Bennejin Skye, USC Strategic, Team 6. We have the tahorah. We request permission to dock and a medical team. Now."

"The tahorah? She's dead, Commander."

"The fuck she is," Skylark barked back. "But she will be if she doesn't get medical attention. Now, are we allowed on the damn ship or not?"

"Hold on, Commander."

"Jesus fucking Christ. Just open the fucking doors!"

The comm. remained silent for too long. Skylark was about to speak again when it crackled to life.

"Permission granted, Commander Skye. Medical is on stand by. Welcome aboard the *Starborn*."

"My ass," Skylark muttered to himself. "Thank you," he said into the comm. He looked at his team. "You best keep your armour on and your guns close."

"Sir?" Jack asked.

"Hunt is still USC so I'm hoping you won't need them. But I don't like him and I don't trust him."

"You sure you want to board, then, sir?" Doorman asked.

Skylark looked down at the woman in his arms. "We don't really have a choice. We'll be in the brig either way, what does it matter which brig?"

"Fair enough," Binky said. He unholstered his gun. "Let's go."

The team turned and made their way to the flight deck of the Strategic long-haul fighter *One* to await the opening of the ramp.

Christie joined them a few minutes later. "That's touch down," he said. "It was nice knowing you all." He flipped the switch and the ramp slowly lowered.

"Here goes," Binky murmured.

Team 6 flanked Commander Skye and the tahorah in a protective semi-circle as they moved down the ramp. The flight deck was full. Everyone, it seemed, had arrived to witness whether or not Skylark had spoken the truth when he claimed to have rescued the tahorah. A soft murmur rippled through the gathering when they spied the woman in Skylark's arms.

Two teams waited for Team 6, their guns drawn. Skylark looked both commanders in the eye as he slowly descended the ramp. Neither of them looked pleased to be pointing their guns at him. Looking up, Skylark saw Vice Admiral Hunt standing on the balcony that overlooked the flight deck.

"Arrest them," Hunt said.

The movement was sudden, but Team 6 had been prepared and so the struggle lasted longer and was bloodier than might have been otherwise. Even Christie joined the fight, fists flying from his kilted frame.

In the madness, the tahorah was ripped from Skylark's arms. He lost her in the press soon after, but he could hear her crying out as she struggled against her captors.

She screamed—a high-pitched, ear-shattering scream—and suddenly everyone flew off the ground, pushed backward by a psychic pulse so powerful, it even moved the fighters on the deck. Freed of her captors, the tahorah fell to the ground and did not move.

Skylark was the first on his feet. He ran through the stirring forms of the crew of the USC Destroyer *Starborn* to the tahorah's position. Her pulse had cleared the space around her by some ten feet.

Commander Skye dropped to his knees beside her and lifted her up, turning her over so she rested in his arms.

"No," he whispered, when she did not respond to his touch. "No, no, no. Come on." He lifted her more, bending his head down to rest his ear on her chest. Her heart beat a frantic, irregular rhythm.

"Naschari," he said. "Come on. Wake up. You can't die. You can't. Open your eyes. Gods, please. Naschari."

The tahorah's eyes fluttered open. Their purple gaze was unfocussed and filled with pain

"Ben," she whispered.

"I'm here," Skylark said. "I'm here." He pulled her close. She returned his embrace weakly, then pushed against him.

"Ben, please—"

"You're not going to die," Skylark whispered, his voice trembling. "I'm going to save you."

The tahorah smiled. "You already have," she said. "Remember?"

"You can't die."

Still smiling, the tahorah raised her hand and placed it on the back of Skylark's head. She pulled his head down until their foreheads touched.

"I need to show you something," she said. She closed her eyes and Skylark followed suit.

The first sensation was warmth. It flooded Commander Skye, enveloping him and filling him. Love in its purest form buoyed him in the free fall into the tahorah's mind.

Then the images started. Everything the tahorah had learnt of the ragnar whilst under their sway she now showed to Skylark. She showed him their sentience, and their regard for other life forms. She told him their history and revealed the name and location of the first queen, the one who had first contracted the virus and passed it on through her offspring, and how the virus altered to each individual queen so that she might create her own mindless armies loyal to her. The ragnar first queen was the one who started the ragnar's never ending quest for food. And the key to victory.

Destroy her, the tahorah said. *And they will lose their way. Destroy her, and you will win.*

Naschari, Ben answered. But he found he had nothing to say.

The warmth started to fade.

No. No, no, no, no! Naschari!

The connection broke and Skylark's eyes opened. He looked into the serene violet eyes of the woman he loved as she gazed up at him.

Her hand moved from the back of his head to his cheek. "I love you," she whispered. "Commander Bennejin Skye."

Skylark trembled uncontrollably as her eyes slowly closed. Her hand slipped from his cheek and fell, lifeless, to the floor.

"No! No, you can't be dead! I did not drag you out of hell for you to just die! Naschari."

Skylark kissed her as tears fell unheeded down his cheeks. "Come back," he whispered to her. "Come back to me."

He waited, as if expecting her to awaken. But her light had gone from him, leaving a gaping void numbed by the sudden cold vacuum of her absence.

Skylark screamed. He pulled her close and buried his face in her hair, weeping uncontrollably.

He did not notice that the crew of the flight deck had gotten to their feet some time ago. He didn't feel his team as they formed a protective circle around him, their guns raised. For a time, he was aware of nothing but blinding pain that drew sobs from him, wracking his body like a stoning.

Exhaustion saved him from the sobs. He stopped, not because the pain had ebbed, but because he did not have the strength for more tears. Still, he remained kneeling on the ground, his face buried in the tahorah's hair, until he heard the words,

"Take the specimen."

Skylark's head snapped up, making the approaching science officer freeze on the spot.

"Touch her," Skylark growled, "and I will kill you."

The science officer looked across at Vice Admiral Hunt, who had descended to the flight deck.

Pulling the tahorah's lifeless body close, Skylark stood.

"You will stand down," Vice Admiral Hunt snapped. Skylark looked at him for a long, unsettling minute.

"Fuck you," he said.

"Shoot them," Vice Admiral Hunt told the teams who still had their guns trained on Team 6. Skylark turned to face Commander Cortez, leader of Team 12. Slowly, Cortez lowered her gun.

"No, sir," she said quietly.

Binky blinked in surprise, then smirked as Team 12 lowered their guns.

"Shoulder your weapon, Cortez," Hunt yelled.

Cortez turned to him. "No," she repeated. She turned back to Skylark. "Where are you going, Skye?"

"Crematorium," Skylark said quietly.

"You can't!" the science officer exclaimed. "You'll destroy the specimen."

"She's a fucking woman, you pointy-headed bastard!" Doorman growled. "And she's Team 6. She's getting her fucking funeral!"

Vice Admiral Hunt stormed forward. Binky met him halfway, elbowing him in the face, then pulling him up and pointing his gun at the vice admiral's head.

"You all are going to clear us a path," he said loudly. "And my boy Skye here and the rest of us are going to give the tahorah the funeral she deserves. What's not going to happen is anyone taking her to some lab to be dissected for some soulless asshole's science project. Am I clear?"

"You're a dead man!" Hunt snarled. "You're all dead."

"Shut the fuck up," Binky said, pressing the barrel of his gun against the vice admiral's temple for emphasis.

"Lead the way, ma'am," Binky said to Cortez.

Commander Cortez nodded. She and her team led Skylark and Team 6 to the ship's crematorium. Binky led Team 6, the struggling vice admiral still firmly pinned to him.

"I'm putting you all against the firing squad," Hunt spat as Commander Skye gently laid the tahorah on the cremation slab once the mutinous group arrived at the crematorium. Skylark ignored him.

"I want you to know," Skylark said quietly in the tahorah's ear, "that no matter what happens now, it was all worth it. You were worth it." He looked down at her face a moment, tracing the gentle lines with his fingers, committing them to memory. He bent down again and kissed her on her brow. "I love you."

He pushed the slab into the cremation chamber and locked it. He raised his hand to turn on the machine.

"Don't you fucking dare, Skye," Hunt snapped. "Press that button and nothing will save you, do you hear me? Nothing! You're finished!"

Skylark did not turn around. He smiled slightly. "I resign." He pressed the button and flames lit the chamber orange.

Hunt took advantage of the sudden flare. He jumped and swung his head back, hitting Binky's nose. Binky grunted and stumbled back, dropping his gun. Hunt spun and kicked him hard in the head. In the same spin, he dived for the gun, took it up, and shot Cortez in the head. The commander's head snapped back and she dropped like a stone.

"Team 77!" Hunt screamed.

Team 77 entered the room, quickly disarming Cortez's team. With Binky unconscious on the floor, Team 6 had few options before them.

"Guns down," Skylark said softly to his team. He raised his hands.

"Sir?" Spike said.

"It's all right, Spike," Skylark answered. "There's no need to get yourselves killed. Guns down."

Slowly Doorman, Spike, and Jack lowered their guns only to have them snatched away by members of Team 77.

"Sorry," one corporal muttered to Doorman as he took his gun.

Skylark remained standing in front of the cremation machine, his hands raised. Hunt circled around to face him. "You interfering bastard!" he said, striking Skylark's cheek on the word "bastard." Skylark fell on his forearms.

Vice Admiral Hunt swung his leg to kick Skylark in the face. Skylark blocked the kick and, having caught the leg, yanked hard, sending Hunt onto his back. The gun flew from Hunt's hands and skittered across the floor. Both men rose to their feet at the same time.

Team 77 raised their guns.

"No," Hunt said. "I want to break his pretty face myself."

In this regard, Vice Admiral Hunt proved more courageous than clever. Though of roughly equal size, Skylark's infiltration training and field experience put him at a distinct advantage, when it became clear that Hunt could not win this fight, Commander Rikker of Team 77 raised his gun. He took careful aim.

"No!" Jack said, leaping forward and pushing the barrel down just as Commander Rikker pulled the trigger. He missed Skylark's head but struck his leg. It collapsed from under Commander Skye. Using the momentum of the fall, he threw Hunt away from him.

The vice admiral rolled, coming to a stop beside his lost gun. He grabbed it and, as he rolled to his feet, fired thrice.

The bullets ripped through Skylark's chest, sending the commander tumbling backwards.

"No!" Jack screamed. She ran forward but was restrained by Commander Rikker.

"You son of a bitch!" Jack yelled at Rikker. "You fucking coward!"

Gritting his teeth, he struck Jack across the jaw, knocking her out.

The orange light of the cremation fire ceased suddenly.

"No," the medical officer said, running in from beyond the door of the crematorium. "No, no, no! Ruined! The specimen is ruined!"

From the ground, Skylark laughed, spraying blood from his mouth. Hunt looked down at him. Grabbing him by the throat he lifted Skylark from the ground and slammed him hard against the door of the cremation machine.

"You think this is funny, Skye? Do you know how much data you destroyed in your misguided affection for a fucking alien bitch?"

Skylark turned his head to look Hunt in the eye. "Fuck. You."

Hunt snarled, he pulled Skylark's shoulders down and kneed him hard in the chest. Skylark spat blood as he tumbled unceremoniously to the ground. He did not move.

"Take these clowns to the brig," Hunt snapped at Commander Rikker.

"Yes, sir," Rikker said. He motioned to his men and Teams 6 and 12 were rounded up and marched smartly away, the unconscious forms of Lieutenant Commander Binks and Lieutenant Green dragged behind the group.

"And someone get this worthless bag of meat out of here," Hunt said kicking Commander Skye's body before storming off.

22

News of Skye's mutiny and subsequent death whipped through the USC like fire through kindling. Team 6 were court-martialled and dishonourably discharged. Team 12 were given similar treatment, though were gaoled for a short time before being reintegrated into the USC as cleaning staff.

When Gergiev, grounded as punishment for letting Skye and his team escape, received the news, he sat in his study at the USC Headquarters, Vancouver and stared at nothing for the entire day.

At dinner, he downed a bottle of brandy and fell asleep in his chair. In the morning, through a blinding headache, he reached into his desk drawer and withdrew a much-folded and refolded sheet of paper.

Major Frank Hallow had little enough to give the friends he left behind after his death. All Gergiev received was two scraps of paper. One of them was nothing more than a list of names with all but one crossed off. The other was a simple note.

"Look after him."

Gergiev scrunched that note up and tossed it into his empty fireplace. He took up his pen and, placing it beside Commander Skye's name, drew a line in a single, firm stroke.

"Fuck you both," he slurred, before dropping his head onto the table. He cried for perhaps two seconds before slipping back into sleep.

"Hello, Commander Skye!" the man greeted in a cheery voice.

Tied to a flimsy metal chair in front of a sturdy metal table in a cement room with a single hanging lamp, Commander Skye watched the man. He had been brought here roughly two weeks after he recovered from his coma.

"We weren't sure you were going to make it, you know. I, for one, am really glad you did, hmm?"

Skye's eyes narrowed, but he did not speak. The man wore a thick leather apron with a deep pocket at the front. The pocket bulged.

"I'm sure you've guessed what my function is. Am I right, hmm?"

Skylark had, but he did not articulate it. He continued to stare at the man, who bent down and peered into Skylark's eyes.

"You know, you have eyes of a remarkable shade of blue. I've seen it only once before." He straightened, reached into his apron pocket and pulled out two objects. They gleamed a dull gold. It took Skylark a moment to recognize them. He twitched involuntarily when the realization hit him.

"Ah," the man said. "Your mind is lamentably slow, Commander. When I was told about you, I thought I would be facing a challenge worthy of a man of my skill. I fear I will be disappointed now, hmm? Now him," the man pointed at the two halves of the daemon crown. "He was a challenge! Did you know that their pain tolerance is remarkably high, hmm? It took me a month of innovation to get him to scream. Of course, by then I was so frustrated all I wanted were screams. He never did tell us what we wanted to know. Still, he lasted a year."

Skylark glared at the man.

"What about you, Commander Skye?" He pulled out a long, jagged knife from his apron pocket. "Will you prove an equal challenge, hmm?"

The man caressed Skylark's cheek with the point of the blade. Skylark gritted his teeth but did not flinch.

"Ah! Brave! Good. It's always more fun breaking the brave ones. Shall we get started? Let's start with the questions you know you're allowed to answer, hmm? Rank and name?"

Skylark turned his attention to the far wall. Infiltration training involved torture simulations, yet his training had not prepared him for their reality. His pulse raced and he could feel a slick sheen of sweat glossing his skin.

"Commander Bennejin Sk—" His surname turned to a scream as

the man brought the knife down in his lower thigh, sliding perfectly between his knee cap and thigh bone.

"Oh, come now, hmm?" the man said. "That was barely anything! Do try again. Rank and name, hmm?"

Before Skylark could even begin to speak, the man twisted the knife slightly, raising the kneecap away from its proper place. Skylark swallowed back another scream.

"Commander Bennejin Skye," he grated through the pain. "United Space Corps, Strategic Division, Team 6."

"Good!" the man withdrew the knife and clapped his hands together. Skylark's own blood splattered across his chest.

"Very well done! Let's try another one, hmm? Oh, and before I forget, you should know that everyone save for myself and about five others think you're dead. There will be no rescue. So it's probably better you cooperate, hmm?"

"Fuck you," Skylark spat.

"I was rather hoping you would say that." The man walked behind Skylark and pressed the point of the blade on the edge of his shoulder blade.

"Now, rank and name?"

For hours, the man walked around Skylark with his knife, always speaking softly, almost lovingly, and never asking for anything but Skylark's name and rank. For hours, Skylark repeated his answer over and over again.

"Commander Bennejin Skye, United Space Corps, Strategic Division, Team 6."

Then the pain stopped and Skylark, unable to walk, was dragged bleeding and barely conscious into the medical bay, a depressing series of cement boxes with mostly empty beds. There he stayed until he was healed enough to be dragged back into the torture room.

It went on for months. Sometimes, no questions were asked. It was just a series of experiments set to determine Skylark's pain tolerance. Sometimes questions were fired at him so fast he could not make out their meaning. It mattered little. All he ever said in response to any question was, "Commander Bennejin Skye, United Space Corps, Strategic Division. Team 6."

The methods of torture varied greatly. Occasionally, Skylark was water boarded. Twice he very nearly drowned, only to be resuscitated by the soft-spoken man in the leather apron. Once, he was hung from the ceiling by two large meat hooks beneath his scapula. No questions were asked that day. He was simply hung and left there, the man in the apron leaving to tend to someone else, if the screams Skylark heard were any measure.

He was taken down moments before his own body weight tore his shoulder blades from his skeleton. He was only in Medical a week before it happened again, this time, hung from a single meat hook embedded in his hip.

Sometimes, the man in the apron would be joined by two holograms. Who they were, Skylark could not tell. He had the vague impression that he knew them somehow but could not remember where or when. Three months in, he could not even remember his own name.

He recited the same thing over and over. But the words lost all meaning. They were simply sounds, uttered in a particular rhythm with no weight or significance. He was nothing but a bag of meat meant for the titillation of the man in the apron.

Often driven to the point of unconsciousness, he spent days, sometimes weeks, and on one occasion a month, in the medical centre. Sedated and fed through intravenous fluids, he lost all sense of time and self.

Now, hanging by his wrists, naked, with the holograms watching on, Skylark stared slack-jawed at the far wall. The man wore a smirk and the woman looked thoroughly bored.

"So," the man in the apron said, holding a red-hot poker. "Are we having fun yet, hmm?"

"Commander Bennejin Skye, United Space Corps Strategic Division, Team 6."

The man in the apron chuckled. He brought the poker close to Skylark's skin. Skylark sucked air into his lungs and twisted to avoid the heat that bubbled his flesh.

"Hold still now," the man in the apron said. "We don't want to slip and kill you, hmm?"

He did not wait for Skylark to answer. He pressed the poker against Skylark's hip. Skylark refused to scream. It had become a game to him. Some deep, dark spark gloried in his ability to withstand his physical agonies, revelling in the power to frustrate his tormentor.

It also usually ensured that he ended up unconscious very shortly thereafter. Unconscious was his favourite way to be. The pain, though now a constant, was dull and far away, no longer mattering. In his time away from consciousness, he found himself surrounded and supported by a soft purple light. Warm and loving, the light came from the dark-haired woman who waited for him in his deepest subconscious. There, floating in the loving safety of that light, they embraced. No words were exchanged. No words were needed.

All that mattered was that she loved him, and he loved her; his own personal goddess.

One day, the man in the apron would go too far and he would be with her forever.

For hours the man worked with his various instruments, using exposure to either extreme heat or extreme cold to weaken his target. Skylark lost strength. His responses grew slower, quieter until, at last, they ceased.

He stopped speaking, stopped struggling, stopped comprehending. He stared blankly at the back wall.

"Hello? Are you there?" the man in the apron asked. He waved his hot poker in front of Skylark's face and received no reaction. Just to make sure, he prodded Skylark's shoulder with the glowing end. The skin sizzled and smoked, but Skylark barely twitched.

The man in the apron turned to the holograms. "You see?" he said, smiling. "Everyone has their breaking point, hmm? Even the infamous Bennejin Skye. Now, the programming?"

"Exactly the same as we discussed," Vice Admiral Hunt said.

Dimly aware of the exchange of words happening, no words caused alarm to the man hanging naked by his wrists in the torture chamber. His mind had other business. It ran through his memories, showing them in no particular order.

He saw the death of the raven-haired woman he had loved like none other. She looked up at him with large, violet eyes.

"I love you, Commander Bennejin Skye," she whispered.

Then she died. The pain of her death struck him full in the chest but before he could scream, the images changed.

He was a cadet in flight school. The next step after basic training for those interested in becoming a USC infiltrator, Skylark had only signed up because it gave him the broadest range of options. Not certain where he ought to be yet, it was the smartest choice he could make.

John Wheeler and his close group of friends spied him as he entered the club alone.

"Hey!" John called across the room. "Skye! Over here!"

The scene changed.

Eight years old and starving, Skylark sat glumly by himself in the living room. His mother entertained yet another John in her bedroom. They came and went in a disturbing parade. Some days she entertained as many as twelve men. She needed the money. Stardust, a highly addictive narcotic, had claimed her as a victim. Her pimp was also her dealer. She needed the money just to pay her debt to him. Often, there was no money left over for food, and certainly none for schooling. Skylark's fondest wish was to attend school.

Tired of the hunger, he went to the kitchen and snuck into his mother's purse. He stole some money and left to find a seller. All he wanted was a carton of eggs and some milk. He could survive a week on eggs and milk.

As he walked the grimy streets of the ghetto at the fence, he thought of his mother. He loved her more than words could say. But that love was a pain so terrible it left him breathless at night. It was a continual oppressive weight on his chest.

Every so often, just as he resolved to run away, his mother would come out of her drug-induced haze. She would swear to him that she would get better. She would improve. After that, she would clean the house and go grocery shopping. They would eat dinner together and she would even read him a bedtime story.

It never lasted.

Once she went a whole week without using. It had been the happiest week of his life. When she started using again, the beatings resumed; beatings like the one that almost claimed his life when he returned home with eggs and milk. She had been furious with him, calling him a sneak thief, telling him he had destroyed her life and just how much she hated him. She screamed insults and profanities as her fists flew in a drug-induced rage.

She beat him into unconsciousness. He woke up the following morning. The carton of eggs lay open beside him, the eggs smashed to pieces. The milk had been left out and had spoiled.

Down the hall, he could hear his mother entertaining. He rose to his feet and left the house. He never looked back.

That was the exact memory he recalled during infiltration training, on the first day of their torture simulations. Death had not worried him, not because he was certain they wouldn't kill him, but because life had never been something he would mind leaving behind. Every time his instructor's fist hit his face, he saw only his mother. Anger and pity, love and hate rolled together as the blood poured from the various lesions in his face that day, but he did not give in.

No one had passed that section of training quite so well as Skylark.

The scene changed.

He was eight again and hiding. He, and five other hopefuls who knew survival on the streets would not happen unless they had friends to rely on, had jumped the fence and disappeared into mutant territory. Skylark had been the first to note that these shambling creatures couldn't really climb very well. Their best chance of survival was to get to the roofs of the eerie dead city.

Two children followed his lead. Two did not. He never saw those two again. The mutants had, eventually, found their way to the roof. Skylark slid under a vent, a young girl hiding behind him. Her name was Martha. Another boy, whose name Skylark could not recall, had hidden in a similar vent across the roof.

But he was too afraid. He could not stay still. They found him. Skylark clapped his hands over his mouth to stop his own screams as the mutants dragged the boy out of the vent. They ate him, killing him in little mouthfuls. The sound of the boy's screams and the popping of joints as the mutants fought over him haunted Skylark for the rest of his life.

The scene changed.

"Do you know why you repeat this when faced with torture?" the instructor demanded.

Skylark looked up, pulled back into the lecture hall from his memories by the instructor's irritating voice.

"You all right, man?" Binky whispered to him. "You've gone green."

"Fine."

"Lieutenant Binks," the instructor snapped. "Answer the question."

"To provide a focal point, sir?" Binky replied.

"That's one reason, I suppose."

"So you don't forget," someone else called out. "So you remember who you are."

The scene changed.

The sound of the medical machine beeping in the dark roused the eight-year-old boy from slumber. He didn't want to open his eyes. Ever since returning from mutant territory, he had been curled into himself, his eyes squeezed tightly shut, praying for death.

Now, he slept on his back, an IV drip feeding him nutrients, in the medical centre of Gate Compound 19. He wasn't sure how he got there. He just woke up there.

"Any change?" a voice asked. Hallow. Major Frank Hallow. Only he was not a Major, just an MP, hauling kids off the street in the ghetto.

"Some. His heart sounds better, and his breathing has improved. He's getting stronger. Didn't think he would, poor little guy. Maybe he's meant for something big."

A grunt. "Can he hear me?"

"I don't think so but tell him anyway. It'll make you feel better."

A warm, calloused hand grabbed Skye's skinny arm. For a time nothing was said, then Hallow took a deep breath.

"I pull kids off the street all the time, did you know that? Not many of them make it. I'm sick of putting tiny coffins in the ground, so you're going to wake up. Whatever it is that's keeping you sick, you've got to fight it. Fight. Do you understand? Fight!"

Skylark's head snapped up, his eyes locking with those belonging to the man in the apron. His blue gaze was clear for the first time in many months. He remembered. He knew how he came to be here and what they were hoping to achieve. He knew who he was.

In a swift move, he wrapped his legs around the man-in-the-apron's neck. Twisting savagely, he flipped the man over, bending him backwards into an uncomfortable position. The man flailed.

"Commander Bennejin Skye," he growled. "United Space Corps, Strategic Division, Team 6."

He squeezed and twitched his legs. The man in the apron's neck snapped. Skylark released him and he slumped to the ground. Skylark looked at the hologram of the man, which was frantically pressing an unseen button.

"You're next, Hunt," he hissed.

Two massive guards entered the room. Commander Skye did not struggle as they sent him once again into blissful unconsciousness.

Mars. Doctor LeBruin hated the planet. Everything here was brown. Brown plains as far as the eye could see, punctuated by brown mountains, brown valleys and brown craters. She walked through the brown halls of the brown prison medical centre gritting her teeth. If she never saw the colour brown again, it would be too damned soon.

The building, built of Mars soil brick, was one of five prisons that had been constructed on Mars early on in humanity's quest to conquer space. They had also constructed a weapons testing facility, built a long way away from the prisons.

This particular prison had been built to house Earth's most dangerous criminals. As a result, the medical centre took roughly a quarter of the structure and was almost always full.

LeBruin had found herself stationed here shortly after the USC Research Vessel *Magellan* had been grounded, pending an inquiry into Commander Skye's escape. She never did hear what happened to the vessel, or to its commanding officer. She genuinely hoped that Gergiev had not been punished. There was nothing anyone could do to stop Skylark, short of killing him.

Perhaps they ought to have. He ended up dead anyway, shot by the vice admiral. The official line was that he had gone insane and turned violent. LeBruin did not doubt that Commander Skye had turned violent. The man had been trained from childhood to kill. That he had gone insane, however, was another matter entirely.

The unofficial version, whispered between sympathetics in the halls when their superiors were not listening, was that Skylark and his team embarked on a suicide rescue mission to bring home the tahorah, with whom he had been secretly in love.

She died on the flight deck.

According to these rumours, Vice Admiral Hunt had tried to take the tahorah's body for dissection, as if she were some new animal instead of a valuable member of the USC.

LeBruin decided that she could more easily believe the unofficial version, if only because it appealed to her well-concealed romantic nature. Vice Admiral Hunt, she therefore decided, was a colossal asshole.

It did not help that he had reassigned her to Mars to stitch up prisoners after their frequent riots.

Sighing, Doctor LeBruin entered the locker room and pulled on her white robe. She tidied her hair in the mirror and began to apply her lipstick. She stopped.

"Why are you bothering?" she whispered to herself. "Fuck it," she said. She wiped the lipstick off with a cloth and left the locker room.

Work that day went the same as it usually did. The inmates all threatened to rape her the moment they got free. She rolled her eyes at them, projecting an air of confidence that she did not feel. The worst of the worst were sent to this facility. If ever they did manage to take over the prison, she would be in more trouble than she could deal with.

She would do anything to get off this miserable rock.

On her way back to the locker room, she spied Doctors Montpellier and Francis entering the classified section of the medical centre. She did not have the clearance necessary to work there, but she often wondered what went on behind the heavy steel door. On impulse, she seized her chance and ducked inside the door before it closed.

The halls here were grey; cement from Earth. They were also deserted. The curses and threats from the inmates in the medical centre could not be heard here. LeBruin found it refreshing. She walked quietly down the hall. Peeking around a corner, she noticed the two doctors retire into a room. She decided to skip past that hall and continue on. She encountered no one as she stole down the halls, getting lost, until she found herself in a small ward.

All of the rooms she walked past were empty. All, save one.

Her curiosity now in control, she entered the room and slipped behind the grey curtain that surrounded the occupied bed. Air caught in her lungs in an unexpressed gasp when she looked at the face of the man in the bed.

Though a clear oxygen mask covered his mouth and nose, there was no mistaking who lay there.

"Skye?" LeBruin whispered. She pressed her hand against his forehead. A slight fever, but the machines indicated that his vitals were otherwise strong. A little too slow, perhaps, but strong.

Skylark's chest rose and fell as he breathed, but his eyes remained firmly shut. One of them showed signs of an old bruise. The other was most definitely bruised, swollen so large that it seemed unlikely he would be able to open it even if he were conscious.

A scar on his neck prompted LeBruin to lift the blanket from him. It travelled all the way down his torso, ending at a particularly large, circular scar at his hip. LeBruin almost choked on bile when she saw the lattice of scars, some very fresh, that littered his body. Burns and bruises accompanied scars that were clearly created by a sharp tool.

Taking up her stethoscope, LeBruin listened to Skylark's heart, then his lungs. The presence of a deep rattle signalled significant lung damage.

There could be no mistaking it. They were torturing him.

"Son of a bitch," LeBruin muttered. "Sick bastards!" She searched the cupboard beside Skylark's bed briefly before finding what she was looking for. She prepped the syringe quickly and drew a small amount of blood from Skylark's arm. She capped the needle and dropped it into her pocket.

"Hang in there, Skye," she whispered, placing her hand on his shoulder. "We'll get you out of here."

Her heart racing, LeBruin turned and left the ward as quickly as possible.

"What are you doing in here?" Doctor Montpellier demanded in his thick French accent.

Almost at the door and out of the cement rat maze, Doctor LeBruin bit her tongue to keep from yelping. She turned around and smiled.

"I really don't know. I was on my way to the locker room. I was daydreaming and when I looked up I was here."

"How did you get in?" the doctor demanded.

LeBruin shrugged. "The door was open."

Montpellier narrowed his eyes at her.

"How else could I have?" LeBruin demanded. "I don't have a code, do I?"

"No," Montpellier replied.

"Right. Anyway, I realized I was in the wrong place, so I turned smartly around and was just about to leave when you rounded the corner." Hoping that her racing heart could not be as loud to Montpellier as it was to her, LeBruin raised her brows at him expectantly.

"What?" Montpellier said with a frown.

"May I leave?" LeBruin asked.

"Yes," Montpellier said. "And don't ever come back here again!"

"Oh, I won't. Trust me. I want nothing to do with whatever it is you lot have going on back here."

Doctor Montpellier grunted. LeBruin turned and marched away, slipping out past the heavy door and trying very hard not to appear guilty. She shut the door tightly behind her and walked away until she got to the locker room. Then she ran into a toilet stall and knelt over the toilet bowl, fighting her stomach as it tried to empty itself. When the threat of vomiting passed, Doctor LeBruin rose slowly and sat down on the toilet. She struggled to control her ragged and strained breath. She stayed there until her breathing calmed and her trembling ceased. Then she changed, slipping the sample of Skylark's blood into her make-up bag, and returned to her quarters.

Commodore Gergiev grumbled to himself as he shuffled to and fro in front of his desk in the study at USC Headquarters, Vancouver. It had been a little over a year since Skylark had been killed, and he had received his first flight order since the inquiry began. It was nothing much, really, just a short probe beyond Way Station S8-09. The station, now up and functioning again, was once again preparing for a long-distance wormhole past the edges of the galaxy.

The USC Research Division was overjoyed. Gergiev was not. Who knew what lay beyond the galaxy, and why the hell had the USC abandoned the search for the ragnar? More to the point, Gergiev did not believe a word of the press conference he had just witnessed on his television.

Admiral Brooke, taking full responsibility for the media-dubbed "Skye Scandal," had resigned. Only, it had not been Brooke who made the announcement. It was Vice Admiral, now Admiral, Hunt. It was Hunt's press conference from the start. He issued the media invitations. He spoke. And he answered the questions.

It should have been Brooke, but no one had heard from him in a year and a half. Skylark's insane accusations did not seem quite so insane now.

Still, he was lucky to be going up into space again, and rocking the boat now seemed inadvisable. Yet it plagued Gergiev and he fully intended to get to the bottom of it. He thought briefly of his hallucination the night he heard Skylark had been shot.

"You're right," he whispered. "I'll find out what's going on."

Thank you. I know.

Gergiev jumped and spun, looking for the glowing blue figure of the chtakah. It had been his voice he had heard. No such image appeared.

"Chtakah?"

Yes?

"Just checking. Wait? Are you in my head all the time now?"

No. But you called me, and so I came.

Gergiev shook his head. "I'm losing my mind," he muttered.

No, Commodore. You are not.

"Shut up."

As you wish.

Gergiev scowled.

A knock on the door turned him again. "Enter."

A young private entered, carrying a small parcel and a number of envelopes. He saluted. "Mail for you, sir."

"Thank you, Private...?"

"Pierce, sir. Scott Pierce."

The commodore frowned. "Pierce. Why is that name familiar?" He brightened. "Oh yes! The runaway cadet! Graduated now, I see."

"Yes, sir."

"Well, good. Glad to see you weren't expelled."

"Yes, sir."

"Dismissed."

"Yes, sir. See you aboard the *Magellan*, sir." Private Pierce saluted and vanished from the office leaving behind the small pile of mail. Gergiev sorted through them.

"Bill. Bill. Bill. Hmm." He stared down at the parcel. He raised it up to his ear and shook it. Nothing rattled. Shrugging, he opened the box. A small, folded piece of paper covered the contents. Gergiev lifted it out and stared dumbly down at the interior of the box. A syringe filled with a small sample of blood rested snuggly in a foam cushion.

Gergiev checked the box for a return address. There was none. He picked up the paper he had cast aside and opened it.

They are killing him!

PMs-04-FS 40°44'N 9°28'W/40.74°N 9.46°W

Gergiev stared down at the paper, shaking. "Brooke," he whispered.

He shut the box up and sealed it again before reaching for his personal computer. Signing in, he looked up the file on Private Scott Pierce.

"You called for me, sir?" Private Pierce said at the door. He looked uneasy.

"I did," Commodore Gergiev replied. "Come in."

Private Pierce did so, closing the door gently.

"Sit."

Pierce sat down opposite Commodore Gergiev, feeling very small under the commodore's intense gaze.

"I understand that you have been assigned to the *Magellan* on this particular mission, is that right?"

"Yes, sir. My first tour."

"I had a look at your file. You were almost expelled for your exit thesis, I understand. An extensive paper on treason in the USC and why, precisely, Commander Skye was innocent of the charge."

Pierce looked down at his lap. "Yes, sir," he whispered.

"Based, as far as I can tell, on conjecture and hearsay."

Pierce did not reply, but the defiant set of his young jaw made Commodore Gergiev smile.

"I take it Commander Skye was a hero of yours?"

Pierce did not look the commodore in the eye, but nodded. "He was a good man, sir."

"And you know this based on what? Rumour?"

"I met him," Pierce said angrily.

"Briefly."

"Long enough."

Gergiev laughed softly. "Son, you need to understand that heroes simply do not exist. And Commander Skye was impulsive, rash, unreasonable, and undisciplined. He was most certainly not a hero."

For a brief moment, it looked as though Private Pierce was preparing to argue the point. At length, he simply slumped into silence.

"Despite this," Gergiev said, "I am willing to give you a chance to prove your case."

Pierce looked up sharply. "Sir?"

"Take this to Doctor Liang in Medical. You'll find him in ward 2B. Tell him I want it cross-referenced with the USC database immediately. Do not leave until he hands you the file. Do not look inside the box. Do not look in the file. You will return the file to me immediately. Do this, do it well, and I'll make you my personal assistant on the *Magellan*. Understood?"

"Yes, sir."

"I want men around me I can trust, Pierce. Do you understand that?"

"Yes, sir."

"Good. Hurry up. I expect that file on my desk before dinner."

"Yes, sir." Pierce jumped to his feet, grinning wildly.

"Dismissed."

Gergiev paced impatiently around his office waiting for the private to return. At 1805, a knock on the door made the commodore jump.

"Enter," he croaked.

Private Pierce entered, carrying an old-fashioned manila folder. "Here, sir," he said, handing the file over.

"Thank you. Dismissed, Private. I'll see you back here immediately following dinner, do you hear?"

"Yes, sir."

No sooner had Private Pierce shut the study door than Gergiev opened the file. His body stiffened in shock as he stared down at the image of Commander Skye, complete with his entire medical history. Stamped across the sheet, in bold lettering, was the word "Terminated."

"Son of a bitch," Gergiev whispered. He turned to his fireplace and threw in the file before heading to the phone. He called Medical.

"This is Commodore Gergiev. I need to speak to Medical Officer Liang, please. Liang, you old dog! How are you? I'm just calling to see if you were going to make good on that drink you owe me… no? Are you certain? I see. Maybe another time, then. Thanks. Bye."

Gergiev hung up the phone and sat for a time, grateful Liang was clever enough to know he was being questioned on the test results, and shook. He reached into his drawer and pulled out the paper he had drunkenly scribbled on the night he received the news that Commander Skye had been shot dead.

The line he had drawn was straight as a pin, but diagonal. He had succeeded in crossing off only the "B" of Commander Skye's first name. He carefully folded the paper and slipped it into his breast pocket.

Not long after, Pierce reappeared. "Reporting for duty, sir," he said with a smart salute. He noticed the remnants of the manila folder in the fire and raised his eyebrows. Wisely, he did not question it.

"Thank you, Private. Please sit." Pierce did.

Gergiev took out a stylus and an electronic pad. He scribbled something on it as he spoke.

"I'm putting you in charge of the administration of the supplies for this mission." Gergiev held up the pad, which read, *Find Team 6*.

"It might seem like an annoying exercise in patience and logistics—"

Get them on board before mission commencement.

"—but it is actually to teach you forethought and planning."

Start with Lieutenant Commander Binks.

"As my personal assistant, I need to be sure you can handle the responsibility. Do you understand?"

Private Pierce stared incredulously at the commodore. "Yes, sir," he said slowly.

"Good. You have a week. Get it done, Private."

A slow smile spread across the young private's face. "Yes, sir!" he said smartly. "I won't let you down, sir!"

"Dismissed."

If a march could have been a dance, it would be what Private Scott Pierce managed to do as he left Gergiev's study. Gergiev closed his eyes and took a deep breath.

"Chtakah?"

I am here, Commodore.

The doorbell rang.

"Ma," Binky called from the deck as he grilled steaks on a large barbeque. "The door!"

"Get it your damn self," came his mother's response from inside the house.

"You're inside!"

"I'm busy!"

"So am I!"

The doorbell rang again. Swearing, Binky put down the tongs and, hoping the steak wouldn't burn, headed inside to answer the door.

"Why you couldn't be a doctor like your brother Bobby," his mother muttered for the thousandth time as Binky passed. Binky rolled his eyes. He had been home for over a year now and had not managed to keep a steady job. He lived with his parents, receiving a small allowance in exchange for his work around the home, perpetually branded the one that failed. Suffice it to say, he was in a bad mood when he opened the door.

"Good afternoon, sir!" a chirpy young private in full USC dress uniform said. He held up a box of chocolate cookies. "Help us raise funds for a new way station?"

"Piss off," Binky said, slamming the door shut.

The boy placed his foot in the door. Binky growled and opened it again. "Is there something wrong with your ears, boy? I don't give a fuck about no USC bullshit way station."

"You really want one of these cookies, Lieutenant Commander," the boy said. His cheerfulness vanished almost as quickly as the Vancouver sun.

"Why?" Binky asked slowly.

"Because they're delicious, sir," the boy replied, suddenly chirpy again. "The choco-mint ones are a favourite of Commodore Gergiev's."

Binky twitched slightly, he narrowed his eyes at the boy, who indulged in a wide, self-satisfied smile.

"Yeah, all right. How much?"

"Fifteen credits, sir."

"Fifteen? I ain't paying no fifteen credits for no damned cookies!"

The private shrugged but looked up expectantly at Binky.

"Fine. Wait here." Binky closed the door. "Yo, Mum! I'm borrowing money, okay?"

"You earn your own damn money!" his mother yelled back at him.

Binky rolled his eyes and dug around her purse regardless. He pulled out fifteen credits and returned to the private.

"Here," he said, handing over the money.

The private took it, removed a cookie and a slip of paper. "Your cookie, sir, and your receipt. Thank you for supporting the USC!"

"Yeah, whatever. Now beat it."

"Yes, sir!" Binky shut the door, watching the young man walk down the path and across to the next street. He grunted, opened his packet and took a large bite of the choco-mint cookie. He looked down at his receipt.

The bird is a phoenix. I require 6. Gifts for friend.

Deliver to Private before 0500 5th May.

Binky blinked. "Bird is a phoenix?" he asked himself. "The fuck does that mean?" His gaze fell to the tattoo of a skylark he and the rest of Team 6 had done in the drunken haze that followed their dishonourable discharge.

"Fuck off. Mom!"

"What?"

"I'm going out!"

"The hell you are! Who's going to cook the steaks?"

"Get Bobby to do it."

"Bobby?"

"He's a doctor. He can figure out how to cook a damned steak! I have to go!" Binky grabbed his jacket and left the house, heading to a certain diner where he knew the waitresses well.

"Hey, big boy," Jascinda said as Binky rushed inside The Food Stop, an ancient diner in one of the seedier parts of Vancouver.

"Hey beautiful," Binky replied, kissing the matronly woman on the cheek.

"You lookin' for Jackie, sugar?"

"You know it."

"Take a seat, honey. I'll have her out in a bit."

Binky smiled and sat at the bar.

"Hey! Jackie!" Jascinda screamed into the kitchen. "Get out here and do your job."

"Coming, Momma," Jack called back, using the Jamaican woman's preferred address. She rushed out into the diner and stopped dead.

"Hey!" she greeted Binky, throwing her arms out wide and hugging him.

"Hey good-lookin'," Binky replied. He played with her ponytail. "Still not used to you having hair."

"Yeah, well, it gets me better tips. Get over it. What can I do for you?"

"You still serving that roadhouse steak?"

"Yes, sir. Hungry?"

"Starving."

"It'll be up in a minute. Want something to drink?"

"Water."

"Just water, huh?"

"Yeah."

"Alrighty. One roadhouse steak coming up." Jack turned to leave. Binky bent down and picked something up from the ground.

"Here. You dropped this."

"No, I didn't."

"Yeah," Binky said pointedly. "You did."

Frowning, Jack took the piece of paper and headed into the kitchen, reading it as she went. To her credit, she paused only briefly at the door to the kitchen before folding the paper and putting it in her apron.

Binky smiled to himself and waited, arms on the table, for his meal. Jack made sure the order took its time getting out to him, and then stayed behind the bar and chatted with him as he ate. She couldn't help but smile as he cut small chunks of beef and ate them slowly.

"What?" Binky demanded.

"You've been hanging with your parents too long, Binks," she teased. "Look at you, all delicate-like."

"Shut up."

Jack laughed.

Binky stayed until closing and Jack leant over the bar. "Hey, wanna go dancing tonight? I know this hot club where we can get in VIP."

"Yeah?"

"Yeah."

Binky shrugged. "You know what sounds like fun. I haven't been out in an age."

"Come upstairs while I get ready."

"You hitting on me, girl?"

Jack rolled her eyes. "Hey, Momma?"

"Go on with you, girl. Get your groove on. I can finish up here."

Jack pranced up to her and placed a firm kiss on the woman's ample cheek. "You are the best, Momma."

"Go on, now."

"Bye!"

"Bye, beautiful," Binky said with a wink. Jascinda giggled and waved them out of the diner.

Jack did not have to walk far. Her apartment sat atop the diner, and the entrance stood right beside it. She unlocked the door and led Binky upstairs.

"Yo, how come you never invited me to your house before?" Binky asked.

"Because it's a fucking hole, rich boy," Jack said.

She had not been wrong in her description. "I like it," Binky said before sitting down. "Feels homey you know."

"Idiot," Jack said affectionately before disappearing into the bathroom.

Binky sat on a ratty old couch that rested but a few feet from the end of her bed and waited patiently as Jack showered and changed.

Ready in record time, she and Binky were gone from her apartment in under half an hour, heading towards the club district on foot.

"So, how exactly do you get in VIP when you're poor and me, being rich and all, can't."

Jack grinned and indicated a club with her chin. Binky looked at the door of the White Noise club and groaned.

"Of course," he muttered.

Spike noticed Jack and Binky first. "Hey, hey!" he greeted cheerfully. "Look at you two!"

"Spike!" Jack said, bouncing girlishly into his arms. She pecked him on the cheek before doing the same to his twin brother.

"Hey, man!" Spike greeted Binky, clasping his hand. "Haven't seen you around much."

"When did you guys start working here?" Binky asked.

"'Bout six months ago," Doorman replied. "I'm guessing you don't get out much anymore?"

"Not really," Binky admitted.

"Hey boys, mind letting Binky and me in?" Jack said, holding out her hand with Binky's paper in it. Spike shook her hand, palming the paper.

"Sure thing, lovely," he said. "Go right ahead."

Jack smiled and grabbed Binky's hand, dragging him into the club. The person in the front of the velvet-corded line complained. Jack blew him a kiss, then gave him the finger.

"There's the Jack I remember," Binky said with a laugh.

They partied well into the night and into the next morning. Jack's low-cut blouse ensured she received many free drinks, and her willingness to kiss various drunk women earned her yet more.

At closing, Spike and Doorman appeared, helping various partiers out, sometimes forcefully. Then, for the first time in over a year, all of Team 6 sat together at the same table.

"So," Spike asked quietly, putting the paper on the table. "The fuck is this supposed to mean?"

"He's not talking about...?" Doorman started. Everyone stared at him and he looked pointedly down at the tattoo on his forearm.

"Not possible," Jack said firmly. "He's dead. You saw it yourself!"

"Yeah, but," Binky said, "what else could it mean?"

"So, what now?" Spike asked.

"We make the delivery," Doorman said. "If there's even a chance that this means what we think it does, we fucking deliver."

"It's a long shot, man," Spike said.

"He'd have done the same for us," Binky said softly. He straightened and looked around. "Look lively, Team 6. We're up in a month."

Sleep did not come easily for Doctor LeBruin. Her mind constantly fretted about Commander Skye, tortured and unconscious now in a top-secret medical facility in the building in which she lived and worked. The possibility that Commodore Gergiev did not get the package she sent him, or, worse, he ignored it or didn't know what to do with it constantly worried her. Then there was the anxiety that the parcel had been intercepted. She would be arrested at any moment, then tortured.

For a month, she fretted and fussed, sleeping poorly and barely eating. No one noticed. Most of the female staff in Medical were stressed. Dealing with the constant threat of violence was not an easy task.

On the thirty-third day since her parcel ought to have been received, a deep boom followed by what felt like an earthquake rocked through the prison. LeBruin froze in place, certain she'd been discovered as the lights flickered and the alarm began to ring. The patients in the medical centre began to hoot and holler as a second boom shook the building.

"Warning," the tinny voice of the automatic Tannoy system blared. "Wall breech. Losing pressure. Please stay calm and put on your pressure suits. Warning. Wall breech. Losing pressure. Please stay calm and put on your pressure suits."

Doctor LeBruin did not do calm. She dropped everything and sprinted to the emergency cupboards where the pressure suits were located. She hurriedly dressed before sprinting down the hall to the designated bunkers. She was not the only one. Wardens had sealed the prisons, ensuring the cells did not lose their atmosphere, then ran to the bunkers. The wall in front of LeBruin collapsed in a hail of dust, making her scream.

Five daemon strode through, their blades extended and their eyes glowing brightly through the visors of their helmets. One spied her and advanced menacingly.

"Wait! Wait!" LeBruin screamed holding her hands out and backing up. "You're looking for Skye, right? Commander Skye?"

The daemon cocked her head.

Yes, the daemon said, her voice in LeBruin's head.

"I know where he is. Follow me!"

The daemon signalled to her companions and the five of them followed LeBruin through the chaotic halls, easily dispatching anyone with heroic intentions.

Doctor Montpellier exited the classified medical centre just as LeBruin and the daemon arrived.

"What the—?" he demanded.

Running on adrenaline, LeBruin did not let him finish. She grabbed him by his collar and hair and slammed his head against the wall, knocking him out cold.

"You deserved that," she said to him as she ran through the open door. The daemon behind LeBruin grinned behind her visor.

Doctor LeBruin led them through the maze-like concrete tunnels of the medical centre to Skylark's room. She noted with relief that he was still there, still unconscious, but very much alive.

"You can't move him without the equipment," she said. "Here," she pressed a button and the gurney on which he lay covered over, trapping Skylark and his equipment into a clear tunnel of pressurized, sterile air. The legs of the gurney detached, and it hovered.

"It'll go anywhere you push it," she said.

You sent the warning, the daemon said.

"Yes," LeBruin answered.

Come. The daemon cocked her head indicating an exit. *You come, too.*

There was nowhere else for her to go, so Doctor LeBruin nodded. They left at a sprint, barely fighting back now as they headed to the gaping hole they had blasted through the wall of the prison. The air was thick with daemon fighter ships, drawing fire for the escaping rescue team.

In a blur, LeBruin found herself on the floor of a daemon transport, Skylark's gurney hovering beside her. The door slid shut and the transport took off. Just as suddenly as they had arrived, the daemon fighters banked away, heading towards the daemon mother ship that hovered out of firing range of the prison's guns. They were gone before the USC space frigates arrived to lend aid.

The attack lasted less than half an hour.

23

Gergiev smiled as he stepped onto the bridge of the *Magellan*. He took a deep breath in.

"I'm home, my love," he said, quietly stroking the railings near the commanding officer's seat.

"Sir," one of the pilots said, turning. "We're about ready for launch. Way Station S1-01 has cleared us for travel.

"Let's get to it, then."

"Yes, sir."

"Comm. is yours, sir," a young communications officer said.

Gergiev nodded. "Ladies and gentlemen," he said into the microphone at his seat. "This is Commodore Gergiev. Welcome aboard the USC Research Vessel *Magellan*. We have been given the go, so we are off into space at long last."

The sounds of cheering erupted from the comm. Gergiev grinned.

"It will take us a week to arrive at Way Station S8-09. Please enjoy that time responsibly. I promise this will be a mission you won't forget." Gergiev looked at the screen in front of him. "All right, pilots," he said. "Let's get going."

"Yes, sir," they replied in unison.

The engines powered up and the ship rocked slightly as they entered the slipstream. One pilot turned back and grinned wickedly at Gergiev. To his credit, the commodore only twitched his lips in return.

"Oh, we live to see such interesting days," he whispered to himself.

The week wore on with unusual monotony. The crew aboard the *Magellan* were almost delirious with joy at being up in space again. The working crew, engineers, technicians, and medical staff were all former crewmates. They knew the ship, they knew her commanding officer, and they loved them both.

Combined, they would not be enough to overcome the meagre three USC Strategic teams that had been assigned to the *Magellan*, but Officer Christie had hacked into the system and made certain that the teams assigned were the most likely to be sympathetic to the commodore's new direction. Team 87, the team most likely to join the cause, had been deployed to prison guard duty on PTS1YX67. Gergiev had chaffed at that, but there was nothing for it. The teams they had were good enough.

Hopefully.

"Greetings, Commodore Gergiev!" the man on the comm. said a week later. "This is Way Station S8-09, ready to deploy. Please upload your coordinates."

Gergiev looked down at Flight Officer Christie, sitting in the far seat on the team of pilots.

"Good evening, Station S8-09!" Christie said cheerily. "Downloading coordinates now."

"Thank you. Coordinates received and entered. Wormhole generation in three… two… one! You are go. I repeat, you are go."

"Smashing," Christie said, his gleeful laugh sounding not a little like a comic-book villain. The five pilots manoeuvred the ship into the slipstream and she vanished.

Navigation Officer Sunti of Way Station S8-09 looked through the viewscreen and scowled.

"Hey, Biggs?"

"Yes?" Navigation Officer Biggs replied, spinning around in his chair.

"Where did you send them?"

Biggs frowned. He looked down at his control panel. "Here," he said, pointing to the coordinates that flashed on his screen.

"No you didn't."

"Yes, I bloody did. Those were the coordinates they downloaded. Those were the coordinates I entered."

Sunti shook his head. "No, you didn't, you dumbass. The wormhole should have fired in that direction." He pointed. "It went that way." Sunti pointed ninety degrees to the right.

"No, it—" Biggs dropped the pen he was holding. "Oh shit. Oh shit, oh shit, oh shit!"

"Well done, Christie," Gergiev said with a smile.

"She's all yours, Commodore," Christie said, grinning back.

The crew looked at each other nervously. Most of them had been selected for this mission precisely because Gergiev knew he could rely on them. They had flown with him before, and he knew that, even were they not loyal to him, they were fiercely loyal to the USC mandate. "The comm. is yours, Commodore," a communications officer said.

Gergiev nodded. "Ladies and gentlemen," he said into his microphone. He paused. "We were scheduled to arrive at our destination in two hours. There has been a change in plans." He stopped again and considered his words carefully. "Admiral Hunt has lied to you. I believe that he, along with Councillor Brand, have staged a silent coup and taken control of both the United Council and her military arm. Admiral Brooke has not been heard from in over a year, and neither have any of the councillors, save Brand. For this reason, I am declaring them traitors.

"Unfortunately, they are also the top of the command chain. But, I believe in justice. And I believe in the USC mandate. The daemon are not our enemy. The ragnar are not their puppets. And Earth is in very real danger. In order to apprehend the traitors, and continue the mission to save our species, I have been given no choice but to go rogue.

"Team 6, you may come out of hiding now. Welcome, everybody, aboard the pirate ship *Magellan*."

Gergiev waited a moment for his speech to sink in. Then the comms. erupted with noise, some of it cheering.

Sitting in the living room of USC Strategic long-haul fighter *One*, Team 6 had been playing a fierce game of craekers when the comm.

announced the smooth transition from research vessel to pirate ship.

"Yarrrrr!" Spike said outrageously when Gergiev's speech ended.

Binky grinned. "All right! Let's find our quarters, yes?"

The team stood and made their way out of the long-haul fighter. The deck crew grinned at them.

"Sir," Private Pierce said, saluting. "I was just on my way to find you."

"Not difficult when you know where we were hiding," Binky replied.

"No, sir," Pierce answered. "I'm here to show you to your quarters."

"Lead on, then, Private."

"Yes, sir."

No sooner had Binky and his team settled into their quarters on the pirate ship *Magellan* than a meeting was called. Binky, the commanders of the other teams, and all the heads of staff were called to Gergiev's study. It was a tight squeeze.

"I'm hoping to hell you have proof of this, Commodore," Commander Koch said, his light German accent lending sobriety to his words.

"Does it matter?" Commander Bauer, also German, demanded. "This is mutiny!"

"Yes," the commodore said. "This is mutiny. Against Hunt. Not against Admiral Brooke, the United Space Corps or the United Council. This is me taking responsibility for my own actions and doing everything I can to save our planet. We're following the USC mandate to the letter."

"I need evidence," Koch repeated.

The other commanders looked on. Gergiev sighed. "You believe everything Hunt has said to date? Commander Skye went insane, became violent and was shot dead. The daemon created the ragnar threat to try and take over Earth. Admiral Brooke, who no one has seen nor heard from in over a year, has resigned."

"I have no reason not to."

"Oh really? Well, I can say for certain that Commander Skye is alive."

Binky's head snapped up.

Gergiev smiled sadly at him. "He was held hostage in a prison compound on Mars, in a top-secret section of the medical centre of the max security prison. I don't know how long they had him, but during his stay he was tortured. Just over a fortnight ago, he was rescued and has remained in a coma ever since."

"Where is he?" Binky demanded.

"With the daemon," Gergiev replied.

"Bullshit," Bauer spat.

"Not quite," Koch said slowly. "A prison facility on Mars was attacked two weeks or so ago. My team were part of the reinforcements, but we arrived too late. The wardens swore up and down that it was daemon."

Gergiev nodded. "I received a tip from an insider in the facility. They sent me a small syringe with a sample of blood and a note that read 'They're killing him' as well as the coordinates of both the planet and the prison. I had thought it was Admiral Brooke at first, but analysis of the sample returned with Commander Skye's name all over it. It has since been confirmed that it was indeed Skye."

"I need to see," Koch said.

"We're on our way to rendezvous with the daemon mother ship now. We will reach them in just under three hours. Commander Skye and the doctor who sent the tip are aboard."

Koch narrowed his eyes. "And Admiral Brooke?"

"Since when has a vice admiral ever held a press conference to speak about the resignation of his superior? Why didn't Brooke do it himself? Why has no one heard from Brooke in over a year? Why does every single command slip have Hunt's signature on it? Hunt lied about Skye. He broke the United Council declaration 478Ib, condemning torture and its use. In case you missed my point, he broke USC accords against the use of torture. Tell me my concerns about Brooke are unreasonable and unfounded, Commander."

"Anyone know where the admiral is?" Binky asked.

"No," Gergiev answered. "At least not yet. I have eyes looking for me, both on board and at home. I tell you this, though, I have had confirmation that the admiral's office and quarters at the Vancouver headquarters have stood empty for precisely one year and eight months."

The commanders exchanged glances. "I can't believe Hunt would do something like this," Koch said quietly.

"The thing with actions like these," Gergiev said, "is that the ones perpetrating them honestly believe they are doing the right thing. Hunt hates the daemon with everything he has. He probably truly believes that they created the ragnar somehow in an effort to subjugate humanity. What he fails to see, probably because he doesn't want to, is that the daemon could have easily destroyed us in the war. Sure, it would have cost them. But we were the ones who sued for peace. And we did it on a hope and a prayer that they did not want that fight. We're damned lucky they didn't. They don't need to invent any human-devouring monsters."

Silence settled over the gathering.

"I'm in," Binky said.

"Of course *you* are," Bauer shot back.

"What's that supposed to mean?" Binky demanded.

"Stoppen!" Koch barked.

"And we're just supposed to what?" Bauer shouted. "Go along with *mutiny*? Do you know the punishment for mutinous insurrection?"

Koch levelled his countryman with an even glare. "Do you know how much suffering in human history could have been avoided if men stood up and did what was right instead of what they were ordered to do?"

Bauer fell silent, frowning. Koch turned to Commodore Gergiev. "I am in," he said. "On one condition. Should this prove to be all some fabrication of yours, Commodore, you submit to the fullest extent of USC law."

Gergiev smiled. "I was about to offer the same. If it is proven that I am wrong, then on my oath as a commodore of the USC and as a man, I swear to surrender and go quietly to justice."

Koch nodded.

"You already know where we sit," the chief of staff, engineering said, folding his arms.

Gergiev nodded. "Thank you, Lamarr."

"Medical, too."

"Thank you, Delindt."

Commander Ling smiled slightly. "I've probably read too much *Hornblower* as a kid, but damned if you haven't convinced me, sir. Team 46 is in."

Everyone turned to Bauer.

"Not much choice now, is there," he grumbled.

"Certainly is. You can sit this fight out. You will be removed from active duty and kept to your quarters. Command of Team 5 will be given to your lieutenant commander, unless he feels the same as you." Gergiev folded his arms and smiled at Bauer. "And I swear. If I'm wrong, you can put the cuffs on me yourself."

"All right. Fine. Team 5 is in. For now."

"Good. Now everyone about your business."

The study emptied, except for Binky who looked the commodore over. "He's alive?" he asked. "Actually alive, not shot dead like everyone in the team saw?"

"He's alive, Lieutenant Commander; unconscious, but alive. I'm given to understand that he is in a bad way. The physical trauma is extensive. As to the state of his mind, I have no idea. If he wakes up, you can be sure he won't be the same man you saw killed a year ago."

"It's enough that he wakes up," Binky said quietly.

Gergiev offered a sad smile. "I'll keep you informed. I promise."

"Thank you, sir."

"Dismissed."

"Yes, sir."

Three hours later, Commander Gergiev and the team commanders stood on the bridge as Christie gently guided the ship out of the collapsing wormhole. Deep, uncharted space greeted them as the rushing white of the slipstream wall vanished. Gergiev held his breath.

We're here, Chtakah, he thought fiercely. *Now where the hell are you?*

As if on command, a section of space vibrated, then melted away, revealing the daemon mother ship.

"Oh thank the gods," Gergiev muttered in a single rush of breath. He had conducted his side of the plan with confidence, though he was never certain that it was, in fact, the chtakah communicating with him, and not his own broken mind.

"We are being hailed, Commodore," the communications officer said.

"Go ahead," Commodore Gergiev said.

"Commodore Gergiev," the chtakah said over the comm. link. "Can you hear me?"

"Indeed I can. It is good to hear your voice."

A deep chuckled informed the commodore that the chtakah was cognizant of his doubts before now.

"Any news on Skye?"

"The commander's condition is unchanged. Your healer believes that moving him at the moment would not be optimal. She has suggested he stay until he awakens."

Binky trembled. "I need to see him," he said.

"Lieutenant Commander," the chtakah greeted. "It pleases me to see you well. How is the rest of your team?"

"Anxious to get our commander back, sir," Binky answered.

"Understandable. I will consult with your healer. Perhaps a visit can be arranged."

"I would very much appreciate that."

"Chtakah," Commodore Gergiev said. "I'm fairly certain that the folks on the way station have realized the error by now. I would appreciate a quick disappearance."

"Of course. Initiating docking now."

"Steady as she goes, Christie," Gergiev said as a large, claw-like extension made its way from the base of the daemon mother ship. "Take us around 49 degrees and slide us in nice and slow."

"Aye, aye, Commodore," Christie said. He giggled at his own personal joke.

With help from the five pilots, the ship moved so that her docking extension would line up perfectly with the daemon hatch found at the centre of the claw. The ship shook slightly as the claw enclosed it, securing it firmly.

"Deploying tunnel," Christie said. "Annnnnd... we have a lock. Hmm."

"What?" Gergiev demanded.

"Nothing, it's just... what a coincidence they fit."

"Hardly. The daemon have been busy with modifications ever since the alliance first formed."

"Ah."

"We are preparing a jump, Commodore," the chtakah informed

Gergiev. "You may feel slightly nauseous. It will pass in roughly half an hour. We will wait until then before attempting a second jump."

"All right. Give me a moment to warn the crew?"

"Let me know when you are ready."

"Will do." Gergiev pressed the comm. link in his chair. "Ladies and gentlemen, we have re-established the alliance and are now preparing to 'jump.' This is new daemon technology and I have been informed that some of us may feel a little nauseous after the jump. It should be short lived. Brace yourselves."

"Ready?" the chtakah asked.

"As we'll ever be."

The ship lurched and Gergiev flew backwards, tumbling across the ground as the daemon mother ship leapt through space. The travel was instantaneous, sending them deeper into space.

"Is everyone all right?" the chtakah asked.

Gergiev stood, finding that his stomach rolled. "Ugh," he muttered. He pressed the internal comm. link. "All sections report."

"This is Medical, all good here, sir. But, uh, Delindt is ill.

"That will pass," the chtakah noted, unprompted.

"Engineering all good. Man! That sent my heart against the back wall!"

One by one, the crew reported the status of their divisions to the commodore.

"Brace yourselves, people. We jump again in half an hour." Commodore Gergiev took his own advice, settling into his chair and gripping the armrests tightly. To the chtakah, he said, "We're all good. Some of us are sick. We can jump again when you're ready."

In half an hour, they did just that. This time, several people on the bridge had to excuse themselves, rushing to the washrooms on the level to empty their stomachs.

"Man," Binky groaned. "Tell me we aren't going to do this again."

"We are not," the chtakah said over the comm. "I believe our flight has been undetected and we should be safe. Lieutenant Commander of Team 6, the doctor wishes you and your team aboard after your evening meal and rest. Commodore Gergiev, you are also very welcome aboard."

"Thank you, Chtakah," Gergiev said, swallowing past the thick lump in his throat. "We will be there tomorrow."

"I shall see you then. Rest well, Commodore."

"And you, Chtakah." Gergiev looked around at the people languishing on the bridge, clutching their stomachs and doubled over.

"I suppose everyone is dismissed," he said.

Binky groaned.

Team 6 and Commodore Gergiev walked steadily through the tunnel that connected the pirate ship *Magellan* with the daemon mother ship. Team 6 had dressed in their casual uniforms: navy blue T-shirts, black trousers, and standard boots. Gergiev had elected to dress in his formal uniform, a white jacket trimmed in gold with navy blue trousers and polished black shoes.

They were warmly greeted in the enormous, cave-like room that the daemon favoured for meetings. The chtakah stood beside a roughly hewn stone table, Sarcen standing behind him.

"Commodore," the chtakah said, reaching his hand out. "I am very pleased to see you."

"The feeling is mutual," Gergiev said with a smile. The chtakah turned his attention to Binky.

"Lieutenant Commander. I am happy you are here."

"Yeah," Binky said, smiling. "Me too. Mostly."

"I will not keep you waiting. Come." The chtakah turned and led the way up the stairs to a concealed elevator. He stepped inside, as did his guests and Sarcen.

"The majan has volunteered to assess the state of the commander's mind," the chtakah said. "I wish you present, so you will know nothing untoward is happening."

"And how is he going to do that?" Gergiev asked.

"Mihir," Sarcen said simply. "Sharing. If I can."

"If you can?" Binky asked.

"If there is still a mind left to share," Sarcen said.

"Christ," Jack muttered. Spike took her hand.

"Is it really that bad?" Binky asked.

"We do not know," the chtakah said. "But if the extent of his physical trauma is any indication—"

"Then yes," Sarcen finished.

"He's surprised us before," Gergiev said, as if trying to convince himself as much as the people in the elevator. "He was shot three times and is still alive, after all. He's a tough bastard."

Sarcen and the chtakah exchanged a glance but did nothing to contradict the commodore.

The elevator stopped, spinning around to expose an opening partly concealed by hanging vines. They stepped through, revealing a wide corridor. A thick strip split the corridor in half with blue and purple leafed shrubs, grass and glowing flowers. Six-winged butterflies flitted lazily through the branches. The walls were covered in fern-like plants and various flowering creepers, some of them obscuring the doors found at regular intervals along the vegetated walls.

"Wow," Doorman said. He slowed down as they walked, touching the velvety soft leaves of one bush as he passed.

"Plants are natural circulators of air, water purifiers, and providers of food," the chtakah said. "We have as many of them on every level as we can as well as extensive food gardens on every third floor."

"Fucking brilliant," Spike said. He took a deep breath in. "Can you smell that? I feel like I'm on a hike with Skye."

"It must be very complex," Gergiev said to the chtakah, who shrugged.

"And how complicated are your systems, Commodore?"

"Good point," Gergiev conceded. "And ours are probably a damned sight more expensive to boot."

The chtakah smiled. He stopped walking and knocked on a door twice. It opened and he led them through.

"Chtakah," Doctor LeBruin said, smiling. Her smiled brightened when she saw Commodore Gergiev stride through the door. "Commodore!"

"LeBruin? It was you who sent the message?"

"Yes, sir. I'm so glad it got to you!"

"Me too. Though, we might yet regret where it has led us."

"I don't think I will. Not after all this."

"How is he?" the chtakah asked.

"The same. His vitals are improving, albeit slowly. His lungs, especially. But there is still a long way to go. You know, I think the plants are helping."

"We had long ago known this," Sarcen growled.

"Known what?" Gergiev asked.

"Plants willingly share their light, Commodore," the chtakah explained. "Helping heal the ill and wounded more quickly than could be achieved without them. And they sing."

"I'm sorry?" the commodore asked, blinking. "They what?"

"I don't hear anything," Spike murmured to his brother.

"They sing," the chtakah replied, perfectly serious. "And though our ears cannot detect it in a way our consciousness can comprehend, the songs are nevertheless healing."

"Right. Perhaps your plants are different," Gergiev said.

The chtakah cocked his head and smiled slightly. "It is sometimes easy to forget how young you are, and how little of your own world you know."

"We know plenty, thank you," Spike said defensively. The chtakah smiled graciously and inclined his head slightly.

"Can we see him?" Binky asked the doctor.

LeBruin smiled. "There is room for two people at a time. Don't stay long. Don't touch him. We don't know precisely what's been done to him. We don't know how sensitive his skin is, or what his state of mind is like. If you feel compelled to speak, speak softly and slowly."

"Will he be able to hear?" Jack asked.

LeBruin shrugged. "Conventional wisdom says not. But, there is plenty of anecdotal evidence to suggest otherwise. If it helps you, talk to him. It might help him as well."

"We'll go first," Spike said, indicating his brother.

"Through that arch," LeBruin said, indicating a dark room where the soft glow of bioluminescent plants outlined the frame of the arch. "Not too long."

"Five minutes," Doorman said, following his brother.

"There is an observation window around the side," LeBruin told the others. "It is simulated night in the room at the moment, so we won't be able to see much, but it's better than staring at a bunch of vines." She led the group around to the side of the room. They stood and watched as the dim figures of Spike and Doorman stood beside an occupied bed.

It took some time for the twins' eyes to adjust to the low lighting of the room. They blinked in surprise as they looked down on Skylark's unconscious form.

"Son of a bitch, it's true," Doorman said.

Spike had nothing to add. He stared numbly down at his commander, noting every scar, every bruise on Skylark's face.

"Sir," he said quietly. "It's me. It's Spike. I don't know if you can hear me, but, man, shit has hit the fan. We need you back. So you need to wake up, all right?"

Doorman placed a comforting hand on his brother's shoulder, and found it was trembling. Spike stepped back from the bed, furiously wiping unbidden tears from his cheeks.

"Well, look at you," Doorman said. He smiled slightly. "You look like shit." He sighed. "I don't know if you can hear me, but we're all here, Skye. Our whole little tribe. And we've got your back." A motion at the observation window turned Doorman's head. LeBruin stood at the window and pointed to her wrist. Doorman nodded.

"I'll see you when you're up and about," he said down at his commander. He paused, almost hoping that Skylark would magically open his eyes. Nothing happened. Doorman sighed. He turned, took his brother by the shoulders, and guided him from the room. Binky and Jack passed them.

Jack reached out and squeezed Spike's hand briefly. Spike managed a shaky smile, but could not stop the tears that streamed down his cheeks.

Like the twins, the reality of Skylark alive proved overwhelming for Jack and Binky. Though they had believed the commodore, there was something gravely cementing about seeing it for themselves.

"Hey kitten," Jack whispered before bursting into tears and, now unable to speak, retreating from the bed.

"Look at what you've done," Binky said to his commander. "You've gone and made Jack cry. It's worse than when you punched her gut. Remember that? Man, we were so pissed at you. Now it's just funny."

"Fuck you," Jack murmured through barely controlled sobs.

Binky grinned back at her. "Until you were shot, I didn't think Jack knew how to cry. Did you know she could? Bet you did. You know all of us, don't you? Always have. Man, since you were shot, I've had a lot of time to think about you. You played the game so well.

You got us to do exactly what you wanted, sometimes against our will, because you knew precisely how we would react to any given situation. I didn't really appreciate that about you until after you were gone. I'm kinda thinking that you got yourself shot just to teach us one of your subtle lessons about ourselves. You know what I learned? I ain't no soldier of the USC. I am your soldier. And I'm fucking useless without you, so wake the fuck up. Okay?"

LeBruin tapped on the glass. Binky nodded.

"I have to go now. But I'll be back. I'll see you soon."

Binky turned to leave and Jack, finally in control of her weeping, stepped forward again.

"You're going to get better, you bastard," she said. "'Cause if you don't, I'm going to kill you, you hear?" She took a long, shaky breath in. "We need you, Skye."

Binky took her by the shoulders and guided her back to the observation window.

"Aren't you going?" Doorman asked Gergiev.

The commodore shook his head. "I have nothing to say."

"Is it just me or is the room lightening?" Doorman asked.

"Yes," LeBruin said. "Simulation sunrise. They do this all the time. It's beneficial for the plants, but I cannot tell you how incredibly good it's been for me too. It keeps the sleep cycle regulated, and, I am beginning to believe, the body responds to the presence of light and dark beyond merely the sleep cycle. I intend to make a study of it when this stupid war is over."

"It is time," Sarcen said.

LeBruin nodded. "You do what you need to. We'll stay and watch."

"Commodore," Sarcen said. "Please come."

"Me? Why?"

"To observe," the chtakah said.

"I can't observe from here?"

"Not effectively."

The commodore barely contained a sigh. He nodded slowly and then followed Sarcen around the corner and into the room that slowly filled with grey light.

Gergiev paused once inside. It could not have been a secret that he did not feel he had the stomach to see Commander Skye brutalized and unconscious. His reaction to the sight was mixed, and unexpected. His heart thrilled to see Skylark's chest rise and fall in steady rhythm. The bruises and scars had largely healed, so his stomach did not perform any of the expected summersaults.

Yet tears struck his eyes the moment it hit him that it was Commander Skye in that bed, that everything he had suspected was likely true and that he was now the figurehead of a rebellion that could only end in civil war.

"In order to initiate the sharing," Sarcen said, "I will have to wrap one hand behind his head and touch his forehead with mine."

"Okay," Gergiev said slowly.

"I tell you so you'll understand what I'm doing."

Gergiev nodded and moved to the end of the bed. Sarcen stood beside the bed and did precisely what he said he would. After a brief pause, he closed his eyes.

24

Sarcen found himself in a square room. Dull grey cement walls enclosed the space, which contained neither doors nor windows of any kind. From the ceiling hung a single, rusted iron lamp providing a weak yellow light. Directly beneath the light, bound to a flimsy, rusted metal chair, sat Commander Skye, naked and bloody from the waist up. His head had fallen forward onto his chest.

In front of him sat an old metal table, rust showing through the grey paint. Upon that table, in a small dish, sat a heart, beating a steady rhythm.

Sarcen swallowed and looked back to Commander Skye. A gaping hole in his chest where that beating heart ought to have been revealed his innards. Lungs expanded and contracted as he breathed, pushing broken ribs in and out of the hole.

Walking slowly, Sarcen took small steps forward. He reached out to Skylark. When he stood but a hand span away from him, the commander's head snapped up, revealing empty eye sockets that streamed blood down his cheeks. The commander lunged forward with a snarl.

Sarcen leapt backwards, and out of the Mihir.

Commodore Gergiev jumped with fright when Sarcen yelped and leapt backwards from the bed. Not yet fully returned from the Mihir, Sarcen blinked stupidly as he stumbled, then fell. He scrambled to his feet and fled the room, leaving Gergiev bewildered at the foot of the bed.

Everyone standing at the observation window shared the same

wide-eyed expression of surprise. The chtakah leapt into action immediately, moving swiftly after the majan.

"That can't be a good sign," Spike murmured.

"Majan!" the chtakah barked as he ran towards Sarcen, who crouched in the bright hall, his hands pressed firmly on his temples. The chtakah placed a hand on Sarcen's shoulders and knelt down to look him in the eye.

"Majan, what happened? What did you see?"

Unable to find words, Sarcen reached up and pulled the chtakah's head to his own. He shared what he had discovered in Commander Skye's mind. It was a brief Mihir, but disturbing. Afterwards, the chtakah had to pause to collect himself. He nodded.

"Go," he said. "Find rest. I will explain."

Sarcen nodded. He allowed the chtakah to help him to his feet, then turned and moved slowly in the direction of the gardens. The chtakah sighed and returned to the waiting humans.

"What the fuck was that?" Binky demanded the moment the chtakah reappeared.

"Your tongue," Gergiev snapped at him.

The chtakah raised a hand. "No offence taken," he said gently. He looked at the expectant faces before him and sighed. "Your commander is clever," he said at last. Then he shook his head.

"Do go on," Spike drawled.

The chtakah smiled slightly. "When we are first learning about sharing, we are also taught how to prevent someone stealing your memories. Sharing, as a rule, is voluntary. To force someone to give you their thoughts and memories is a terrible crime to us. It is unusual for it to happen, but in case it does, we are taught to build barriers in our minds."

"Okay," Gergiev said.

"Most build walls too high to be scaled. Some fabricate monsters. None of these methods are entirely effective. There is always a risk that a stronger mind will scale the wall, or slay the monster, leaving your mind and memories vulnerable to them. The commander has done none of these things."

The chtakah explained what Sarcen had seen when he entered Skylark's mind.

"I don't understand," Gergiev said.

"My God," LeBruin said. "He's the monster." Everyone turned to her.

"Yes," the chtakah said. "He made himself the monster. In order to get to his mind, you must first slay him. Of course, if you do—"

"Then he dies," Doorman finished softly.

The chtakah nodded, "And his mind along with him. The attacking mind would achieve nothing. It is likely that those responsible for his current condition received no information from him."

"So, that means what? In order to wake him up, you'd have to kill him first?" Binky asked.

"Yes. It is a—" The chtakah cocked his head as he tried to think of the correct word. "Difficulty."

"That is an understatement," Doorman observed.

"He was always too clever for his own good," Gergiev growled.

"What now?" Binky asked.

"Now," the chtakah said quietly. "It is up to him. There is reason to hope. If he created a monster of himself to protect his mind, then there is still a mind there to protect."

Team 6 concealed nothing of Skylark's condition when questioned directly, but they did not volunteer any extraneous information either. Rumours flew thick and fast aboard the *Magellan*, but the insinuation that the commodore's claims of Skye being alive was a lie was no longer part of the rumour mill.

A mass conference was held with Doctor LeBruin, who was now officially recognized as Skylark's personal caretaker, in which role she explained, in unnecessary detail, that the commander's wounds were the product of torture. She also stressed that he was unconscious, and though improving, would likely not be the man most remembered him to be if he ever woke.

She went through protocol for dealing with someone in Skye's position.

Team 6 found it all thoroughly depressing, and retired to their quarters immediately after, refusing to return to the mess for dinner. They were not seen again until breakfast the following day.

A fortnight went by with little incident. Team 6, under Binky's command until Skylark returned, resumed their tradition of waking early to train. They found the routine comforting and necessary for putting their minds at ease. LeBruin spent most of her time with Commander Skye, and most of that time was spent writing in her journal.

"I don't know where you are, Skye," she said quietly as she checked the readings on the equipment at the head of the bed. "But we're dead in the water until you come around."

She looked down to find Skylark's blue eyes open. She gasped and leapt backwards.

"Jesus Christ!" she whispered. "You scared the ghost out of me!"

Skylark frowned at her. LeBruin could tell he was struggling to stay awake. His vitals scattered, showing an elevated heart rate. His breathing also increased and became irregular. Had he the strength, he probably would have been thrashing on the cot.

"Hush," she said, placing her hand on his shoulder. "It's all right, Skye. You're on the daemon mother ship. You're safe. Sleep now. You're safe."

Despite his best efforts, Commander Skye's eyes closed. LeBruin waited for ten minutes, watching as his heart rate and breathing settled again, before she turned and sprinted down the halls to the elevator.

"Team 6," Gergiev's voice said over the intercom. "Report to the commodore's study."

Binky looked up from his cards, then over at his teammates. They dropped their cards on the table and scrambled from the mess like children expecting presents at Christmas.

They tumbled into the commodore's study in a breathless heap. Gergiev raised his brows at them.

"Sir," Binky said, standing to attention and saluting.

"Sit," Gergiev said, waving his hands vaguely.

With only two chairs available, Jack and Spike sat. Doorman and Binky stood behind them respectively.

"Is this about Skye, sir?" Binky asked.

"Yes. It is."

"Good or bad, sir?"

"Good. I think. He opened his eyes this morning."

Binky relaxed and his face split into a wide smile.

"But," Gergiev said. "He was in pain and disorientated. LeBruin is certain he did not recognize her, when he clearly should have."

"Sir?" Jack asked.

"It's none of your business," Gergiev said primly.

Jack grinned. "Oh, so *she* was the doctor he was screwing on our first tour with you!"

Gergiev stared at her.

"What?" she demanded. "Girls talk, all right?"

The commodore shook his head. "In any case, it is unwise to be admitting visitors at the moment. Too much too soon will cause problems. The chtakah and I have decided that, with the exception of LeBruin, Skylark will meet only with daemon. He will recognize them as allies and will not be mistaking them for his jailers and torturers."

"Makes sense," Doorman said. "When will we get to see him?"

"When he is ready. It might not be for a while yet. The chtakah will have to brief him on everything that has happened after he was shot, including who his new allies are and what we plan to do about the situation we find ourselves in. Then he and I are going to meet for a briefing. When he feels up to the task, then you'll get your reunion. It is imperative that we get him healed and fit for duty as quickly as possible. So, we are following the doctor's orders to the letter. No sneaking in to see him."

The shoulders of every member of the team slumped slightly. Gergiev concealed his smile behind his hand as he pretended to yawn.

"Yes, sir," Binky said, not bothering to conceal his disappointment.

"Good. You are dismissed."

Recovery proved slow at first. Skylark slept a full week before opening his eyes again. When he did, the chtakah was standing at the end of the bed. It took Skylark a moment to realize who was there. His brows rose, then knitted together in a frown.

"Good afternoon, Commander," the chtakah said quietly, offering a slight smile. "I am pleased to see you again."

Skylark tried to speak and found himself unable. He reached up and tried to remove the oxygen mask from his face. The chtakah moved around and stopped him.

"You have extensive damage to your lungs, Commander. You should wear this."

Skylark shook his head and tried to pull the mask off again. He spoke, the words muffled. The chtakah frowned and Skylark became agitated. He pulled the mask away from his face, though the effort drained him.

"They killed the tehoros," he croaked.

The chtakah blinked. "What?"

"They killed him. They had his crown." Away from the medicated oxygen and made to work too hard, Skylark's lungs revolted and he started coughing. The chtakah helped him into an upright position. He placed his hand on Skylark's back and concentrated. Skylark's coughing slowed as the spreading warmth soothed his spasming muscles, then stopped. The daemon leader laid the exhausted Skylark back down and replaced the oxygen mask. He pressed his forehead against Skylark's brow and closed his eyes.

It was a very brief Mihir. The chtakah did not want to drag Skylark's mind back to that place, but he needed to see what the commander had seen. He broke contact the moment the evidence was presented.

Exhausted, Skylark fell asleep again. The chtakah left the room in a rage.

"They did what?" Commodore Gergiev said, his jaw dropping slightly as the chtakah paced in an effort to stem his overflowing rage as he explained to the commodore what Skylark had said, and what he himself saw.

"Jesus," Binky breathed. As the commanding officer of Team 6, and privileged because of his connection to Commander Skye, he had been permitted into the otherwise private meeting.

"You are certain?" Gergiev said, standing slowly.

"Yes," the chtakah growled. "There was no mistake. What the commander said, and what he saw... your people abducted the tehoros and then, in torture, killed him." The daemon snarled, his eyes lighting up electric blue despite his efforts at self-control.

"I cannot speak for Brand, but the Council would not have allowed that!" Gergiev said. "Torture is, it's just not done!"

"Clearly," the chtakah snarled, "it is."

"Wait. Was this before or after the alliance?" Binky asked.

"Does that matter?" Gergiev asked in return.

"It explains why the capture was done. I mean, if they were looking to reclaim Canada, of course they'd go for the leader of their enemy, right?"

"And what excuse would you give for the torture and murder of their prisoner of war?"

"Maybe the Council just didn't know?"

"At least one would have," the chtakah said. "She was present often when the commander was made to suffer."

"You saw that, too?" Gergiev asked.

The chtakah nodded. "The commander was weak and in pain. He could not control his thoughts as well as he might have done otherwise. She was there. In... what do you call it? Holographic form."

Gergiev rubbed his forehead. "Fucking sons of bitches," he muttered.

Binky looked at him in surprise, then smiled slightly, nodding his agreement.

The commodore sighed. "I am so sorry, Chtakah. I did not know about this. Not the torture. Not the capture. Even if I had known of the capture, the moment the alliance went into effect, he should have been released."

"Did your admiral know?" the chtakah asked. "Would he have known?"

Gergiev shrugged. "There's no telling anymore. Hunt has been operating on his own agenda for a while before anyone began to suspect that something was off. I suppose it's possible that the command came from the admiral. It could also be that Hunt had issued the command himself, keeping his operations hidden from everyone."

"I hope it is the latter," the chtakah said quietly, dangerously. He sighed and the glow that had struck his eyes flickered, faded and then vanished. "I liked the admiral. He seemed good."

"We'll get to the bottom of this, Chtakah," Commodore Gergiev promised. "I swear it."

The chtakah studied the commodore, his head cocked as he thought. "I believe you, Commodore. In the meantime, we must get the commander strong again. What he has seen... he is integral to our success."

"He is the face of the rebellion," Commodore Gergiev agreed. "When the teams realize they have been lied to, when the world knows what Hunt has been up to, we'll have a much easier time of it. But they will need proof. He's it."

"Then we wait," the chtakah said.

"I hate waiting," Binky muttered.

Two weeks later, Gergiev received a call. He had been in a meeting with the commanders of the teams and the heads of the various divisions, explaining what Skylark had discovered during his time in the prison on Mars. Even Bauer's usual protests fell silent when Gergiev finished his story.

He stared down at the flashing light on his desktop comm. device with a frown. He pressed the speaker function button.

"I'm a little busy," he said.

"Good morning to you, too," a feminine voice answered, sounding amused.

"Doctor LeBruin. Can this not wait?"

"Uh, not really, sir. He's getting out of hand."

"Who? Skye?"

"Who else? He is demanding to see his team, sir."

Binky straightened.

"It's a bit soon, no?" Gergiev asked.

"I've tried to tell him, sir. He can barely stand without fainting. But he's getting insistent."

Gergiev glanced over at Binky who looked hopeful. The commodore smiled. "Tell him that he'll see them this afternoon, if he behaves himself."

"Yes, sir."

"All right, fine," Gergiev said to Binky. "Dismissed. Team 6 is to be presentable immediately following lunch. You will meet Doctor LeBruin at 1300 at the docking tunnel airlock. You will obey her to the letter, is that understood?"

"Yes, sir!" Binky said.

"Go on, then. Get out. All of you."

Binky sprinted.

At 1245, most of Team 6 arrived at the airlock. Jack appeared a short time later.

"You shaved your hair again," Spike said.

"You sound disappointed," Jack teased. Then she shrugged. "It was getting on my nerves. Besides, Skylark hasn't seen me with hair. Ever. I wanted to make this easier on him."

Spike shook his head. "You should have left it. It was pretty."

Jack grinned but said nothing.

The docking hatch opened and Doctor LeBruin stepped through. She blinked. "You're early."

"So are you," Doorman noted.

LeBruin smiled. "I shouldn't have expected you to be otherwise. You are probably just as anxious for this as he is."

"You have no idea," Spike said.

"There are rules. He is still very weak. He's out of bed now and will meet you in the Great Hall. But," LeBruin paused to emphasize the word, "no loud noises. No sudden movements. You will keep your distance unless otherwise invited. You will not keep him up long. It's taken two weeks of intensive work just to get him on his feet. I will not have you undoing it all. Am I clear?"

"Yes, ma'am," Team 6 replied in unison.

LeBruin narrowed her eyes at them. "All right. Come along then."

The walk across the docking tunnel was brief, but to the members of Team 6, it felt long and surreal. Time had slowed. The details of the tunnel, every chip of paint, every bolt holding the sections together jumped out at them in unnatural contrasts.

At the end of the tunnel at the bottom of the ramp, Team 6 paused.

Taking a collective breath in, they entered the Great Hall of the daemon mother ship.

Commander Skye leant heavily against the stone table near the far end of the hall, staring up at the luminous blob that made its achingly slow way across the top of the wall. The chtakah stood at the other end of the table and the majans Sarcen and Butan stood protectively behind Skylark. When Doctor LeBruin and Team 6 arrived, Sarcen reached out and clasped Skylark's shoulder, whispering in his ear.

Skylark turned his head, saw his team huddled close to one another at the entrance to the hall, and stood, turning to face them. They paused, uncertain now that they were faced with Skylark awake. Their gazes fell to the scar that cut a diagonal line across Skylark's lips for a brief moment.

Skylark had never felt so awkward.

The team walked forward slowly until Jack, unable to contain herself, broke from the group and ran forward.

"Jack!" Spike hissed, trying to grab her. He missed and Jack sprinted forward.

Commander Skye smiled and opened his arms as Jack flew into them. He pulled her close, wincing as she wrapped him in her own strong embrace.

"Jack," he whispered, still smiling.

Jack sobbed.

"Fuck this," Binky said. He strode forward and wrapped Jack and Skylark in a hug. Doorman and Spike looked at each other, then ran forward. LeBruin opened her mouth to chastise the team, but they would not have heard her no matter how loud she yelled. Team 6, at last reunited, formed their own bubble of affection, immune to anything on the outside. They remained in their group embrace for a few minutes before moving silently apart to give their commander room to breathe.

"You bastard," Jack said, wiping the tears from her eyes. Skylark grinned and she giggled.

"It's good to see you," Binky said.

"You too," Skylark rasped. He cleared his throat, the action causing his lungs to spasm. He started coughing. LeBruin rushed forward with an oxygen tank and mask. Skylark pushed them away, shaking his head.

"No," he said. Speaking only made it worse.

Too weak to support his weight any longer, Skylark's legs gave out. Sarcen stepped forward and caught the commander moments before he hit the floor. Still coughing, he tried to push away LeBruin's second attempt to put his mask on. Too feeble to be effective, Skylark's resistance failed and LeBruin managed to fit the straps over Skylark's head. The mask fogged up as the medicated oxygen filled it. For five more minutes, Skylark coughed, fighting unconsciousness, cradled in Sarcen's arms.

"Come on," LeBruin said quietly. "Let's get him back to the bed."

"No," Skylark said through the mask, trying to twist out of Sarcen's arms as the massive daemon rose to his feet.

"Stop it, you stubborn old goat," LeBruin snapped.

"I can walk," Skylark insisted, his words muffled but discernible.

"No, you can't."

"I can fucking walk!" The agitation made him cough again. The coughing didn't stop him from attempting to struggle. Sarcen grunted as Skylark slipped in his arms a little.

"Oh, for fuck's sake," LeBruin snapped. "Put him down."

Sarcen, smiling slightly, set Skylark on his feet.

The commander closed his eyes and took a moment to dispel the sudden bout of dizziness. He took a step forward and collapsed again, held up by Sarcen. Sarcen steadied him again.

"I told you!" LeBruin said.

Binky ran to Skylark's other side and wrapped one arm around his shoulders. "The man said he can walk, so he's walking," Binky snapped.

"Fine," LeBruin said "But the mask stays on."

"Yes, ma'am," Binky said.

Together, Binky and Sarcen shuffled forward as Skylark made his painfully slow way to the grand stairs that lead up towards the gallery and elevator. Butan, carrying the oxygen tank, and the rest of Team 6 trailed behind. The stairs proved especially difficult, and Skylark's breath became laboured by the third step. Still, he refused to be carried and so, after an hour, he slid quietly into bed, the oxygen mask still attached.

Exhausted and in agony, he slipped quickly into sleep with the aid of a strong sedative. LeBruin fussed with the equipment a moment.

"You shouldn't have encouraged him," she chided.

Binky shrugged. "I know him, Doc. He'd have crawled if he had to."

"His pride will kill him," LeBruin muttered.

"It's all he's got left," Binky said quietly. Then he grinned. "It must have frustrated the hell out of Hunt."

LeBruin shook her head. "All right, everyone out. He needs his rest."

"We'll be back tomorrow," Binky said. LeBruin opened her mouth to argue, then pressed her lips in a thin line.

"Fine," she said. "But no more gainsaying the doctor, got it?"

"Yes, ma'am."

True to their word, Team 6 came visiting the next day, bringing with them cards to play with their commander. They would take turns helping LeBruin with Skylark's rehabilitation. He pushed harder in their presence and, though it worried LeBruin to see him work himself to the point of dropping, Skylark began to improve rapidly. After a week, he could walk unassisted. By the end of the month, he was running short distances without medicated oxygen. And the end of two months, his cough all but disappeared, appearing only under extreme strain. LeBruin suspected he would never truly be rid of it.

To her amazement, at the end of three months, he passed the rigorous entrance physical and was reinstalled as Commander of Team 6. He moved out of the daemon mother ship and into the team's quarters. This achievement was celebrated well, the team heading out to the nightclub in the civilian sector of the *Magellan*. The team spent the following day in bed, recovering.

Team 6 was once again whole. The return of their commander set them back on the top, and they were riding high on the wave. It felt an age since they had laughed so much, drank so much, played and trained so hard. The unit gelled as if Skylark had never been away. In every regard, they had returned to normal.

Everyone except Skylark.

In his dreams, he spent the nights in Naschari's embrace, hearing her heartbeat, feeling her warmth, suspended in the warm glow of her purple light. Every morning he awoke hours before his alarm, his chest aching with her absence. He would rise, swing his legs over the side of his bed and bury his face in his hands to weep. Though he tried to fight back the tears and was perpetually unsuccessful, he did at least manage to control them so that they were quiet enough that no one else was disturbed.

For hours he fought his sorrow until it was time to rise. Then he disappeared into the bathroom to shower and prepare his poker face. During the day, he would eat, play, train and joke with his team, all the while wracked with sorrow and a deep, unfathomable guilt. Part of him resented his good health. He had been close to death, close to leaving it all behind, close to being with her forever before he was rescued. He almost had everything he wanted.

Guilt and anger chased each other around his body, pressing in on his chest and stripping his stomach of the desire for food. He felt guilty that he looked forward to the night, when he could leave his team behind and rejoin the woman he loved; guilty that given half the chance, he would abandon them if it meant reclaiming her; guilty that he could not share their joy in his return; guilty that he lied to them every second of every day. He hated them for it. And he hated himself for it. He could barely stand to look at his own reflection; he hated it so much.

The strain of his grief and guilt began to take its toll. Though Skylark's troubles had largely gone unnoticed, or, more correctly, wilfully ignored by his team, Gergiev saw straight through Skylark's efforts at normalcy. One afternoon, three weeks after reuniting with his team as their commander, Skylark found himself in Gergiev's office, sitting before the commodore and Doctor LeBruin.

"How are you?" Commodore Gergiev began in a breezy, conversational tone.

"Good," Skylark lied. "I ache sometimes still. But good."

Gergiev crossed his arms and gave Skylark a pointed look. Skylark set his jaw and kept his gaze irritatingly mild.

"Skye," Gergiev said patiently. "Your recovery has been remarkable."

"Thank you, sir."

"But no one is expecting a miracle."

"Sir?"

"The human body is an astonishing thing. It can be dragged through hell and still find a way to fix itself so that it can function. The mind, on the other hand –"

"There is nothing wrong with my mind," Skylark said.

"I have been briefed on your legendary stubborn pride by the good doctor here," Gergiev said with a slight smile. "And you're not fooling anyone. Not even your own team."

Skylark frowned and shifted in his seat.

"They know something is wrong, but they're too damned afraid of the consequences of staging an intervention. And that's part of the problem. A commander should be respected, but feared?"

Skylark remained silent.

Gergiev pulled out a card from his desk drawer. "This is the name of my personal psychiatrist."

Skylark looked at the commodore in surprise.

"You're not the only one who's ever hurt, Skye."

Commander Skye did not reach for the card.

"For fuck's sake, Skylark! Your mind is a bomb waiting to go off. It's only a matter of time, and when you do finally snap, chances are you're going to end up hurting someone you love, and there will be more grief for you to deal with."

Still, Skylark did not reach for the card. Gergiev tried a different tactic.

"We're going after the bastards that killed her, Skye. We need you in this fight. But I can't let you out there unless I know you're not going to snap and do something stupid and dangerous to our cause. Do you understand?"

Very slowly, Skylark reached across the desk and took the card.

"You will see him twice a week. Your first appointment has been booked for tomorrow during lunch. Your inclusion in the fight is contingent upon his approval. You will not get the satisfaction of putting a bullet in Hunt's brain unless he clears you to hold a gun. Am I clear?"

Skylark gritted his teeth and nodded.

"It's not weakness to ask for help, Skye," Gergiev said, softening his tone. "You haven't failed anything."

"May I be dismissed?" Skylark grated.

"You may."

Skylark stood abruptly and left. Gergiev looked across at Doctor LeBruin, who grimaced and shook her head.

"Well, at least he didn't snap here," Gergiev said with a sigh. "Let's get a drink. I'm buying."

25

Skylark sat in Doctor Takahashi's consultation room. The doctor had it painted a cheery yellow, with turquoise picture frames filled with photographs of flowers. The contrast actually looked good, but the joviality of the room grated on Skylark's nerves.

"Sorry I'm late," the psychiatrist said as he rushed into the room. A tiny man of Japanese descent, he spoke with a surprising Parisian accent.

Skylark shrugged. He sat on the comfortable sofa feeling very uncomfortable. The doctor looked at him over the top of his gold-rimmed glasses and smiled.

"Relax, Commander," he said. "We're only going to talk."

Skylark did not relax.

Sighing, the doctor sat down in the armchair opposite Skylark, an electronic pad on his lap, the stylus at the ready.

"I've read your file," Takahashi said.

"A lot of people have," Skylark noted. He let his fingers run over the micro suede of the sofa cushion.

"Not all of them are psychiatrists."

"Are you going to ask me about my mother?" Skylark asked, his lips twisting up in a mirthless smile.

"Well, no. I wasn't. But since you clearly want to talk about it, why don't you tell me about her?"

Skylark narrowed his eyes and crossed his arms. Doctor Takahashi smiled slightly.

"Let me tell you something about yourself that you may be unconscious of," he said.

Skylark raised his brows and remained silent.

"Right now, you are displaying a mix of typical threatening and defensive behaviours. Your arms are crossed, creating a barrier between you and I. You've pulled your lips back, ready to snarl. And you've sat upright and squared your shoulders, making yourself look as large as possible. Right now you're telling me, without any words whatsoever, that you dislike this situation, you want nothing to do with me, and you are perfectly capable of beating me to a bloody pulp. Were I an easily intimidated man, I'd be fleeing this very second."

Skylark did not budge and he did not talk.

"Now, just looking at your file," Doctor Takahashi tapped his electronic pad with the stylus as he spoke. "You were found on the street suffering from severe PTSD at the age of eight and were taken into the USC Military School in Vancouver where, after a rocky first two years, you became one of their brightest students. You then went on to distinguish yourself in every field of training you've ever engaged in, rising to the rank of commander faster than most. You have been variously described by your instructors as arrogant, brilliant, disciplined, undisciplined, aggressive, focussed, and my personal favourite, deeply repressed."

Skylark stared at the coffee table sitting a little to the side of the rug on which both the sofa and armchair rested.

"You've had a very distinguished career, earning some interesting praise from your commanding officers, as well as a list of complaints as long as my arm. And then, one day, according to this, you snapped. You became violent and had to be, and I quote, 'put down like a rabid dog.'"

"Hunt wrote that I bet," Skylark said.

"Good guess. Hardly difficult, though. Looking at all this, at first glance, you're a mess."

Skylark resumed his silent sulk.

Doctor Takahashi smiled. "Except that clearly you're not."

The commander scowled.

"You are evidently a master of your own emotions. Despite never actually being cleared of PTSD, you forged ahead and became one of the most valuable members of the USC. Your team adores you to the point of worship and you have managed to garner considerable respect from creatures twice your mass and thrice your strength. This is highly commendable."

"Then why am I here?"

"Because, Commander Skye, something has changed. Whatever coping mechanisms you had in place that held you together for so long aren't working anymore. Just looking at you I can tell that you aren't sleeping. Sooner or later that incredibly powerful dam you've built to contain and control the storm of emotions that you have learned to live with is going to crumble, and it won't be pretty."

Skylark rolled his eyes. "Why don't you just shoot me now, then, and get it over with?"

"Because that is the easy way out," Takahashi said. He tapped his pad. "And, according to this, you're better than that."

"I'm really not," Skylark whispered.

Takahashi leant forward. "You want to die, Commander?"

Feeling his defences suddenly crumble away, Skylark clamped his mouth shut. He stood abruptly and left the room. Knowing trying to stop him would be a futile exercise at best, Takahashi leant back in his chair and pondered.

Despite Skylark's general lack of cooperation with his new obligation, Doctor Takahashi cleared him for combat. Takahashi had thought it best to keep Skylark busy for now. Work had, after all, saved his own life when his wife was killed during the first ragnar attack on Way Station S8-09, and the rebellion needed its figurehead.

To that end, Skylark sat with Team 6 in a meeting room, waiting for the commodore. The other teams sat in their groups, staring at him.

"The fuck is their problem?" Spike muttered.

Skylark smirked and looked up briefly from his electronic pad where he and Binky had been playing a game of noughts and crosses. "It's not every day a man comes back from the dead," he told the corporal.

Spike grunted.

Skylark handed the pad across to Binky, who scowled. "Fuck," he spat. "Again?"

Skylark grinned and the commodore walked in, followed by the chtakah and the majans Sarcen and Butan.

Everyone stood.

"As you were," the commodore said. He waited for the rustling to stop before he opened his mouth to speak. "We've found him," he said.

"Who?" Bauer asked.

"Admiral Brooke."

Skylark raised his brows.

"He's alive, or he was when the intelligence was sent through."

"Where?" Skylark asked.

"GBS P107-005," Gergiev answered.

"Descriptive," Binky whispered. Skylark smiled.

"It's a prison planet, unsurprisingly," Gergiev continued, ignoring Binky. "Located in the Gerber System just on the inside of the Outerworlds. It is one and a half times the size of Earth, most of it gas. Luckily enough, the atmosphere is less dense than Earth's meaning that the pressure on the surface is roughly equivalent. However, it is toxic. This stuff will melt your lungs in under three seconds."

"We're going in, I take it?" Koch asked.

"Yes, you are. Specifically, Team 6 is going in. You and Bauer's team will be providing aerial support."

"Do you think that's wise?" Bauer asked. "No offence, Skye, but you're still limping a bit. And we don't know where your head is."

"Now you listen—" Binky started, rising from his chair slightly. Skylark's firm grip on his shoulder prevented him from flying across the table at Bauer.

"It's all right, Binky," Skylark murmured. He turned to Gergiev. "Are you certain?" he asked.

The commodore smiled. "I discussed this extensively with both doctors. I'm certain."

Skylark shrugged. "Good enough. What time do we head out?"

"We're on our way immediately following the briefing. It will take four jumps."

"Crap," Jack said. "I hate jumping."

"We all do," Spike said.

"That's not all," Commander Gergiev said. "We're using this

rescue as a statement. We're letting the USC and the world know that Councillor Brand and Admiral Hunt are criminals. And we're going to do that by proving them liars. Specifically, Commander Skye is going to prove it."

"Me, sir?"

"Yes, you. Christie has assured me that he can hack into the networks, broadcasting your voice over every single station in every single corner of the world, and in every off-Earth settlement there is."

"What do you want me to say, sir?"

"The truth."

Skylark thought a moment, then nodded. "I have something."

"All right. Good. Everyone suit up. We're jumping soon. Dismissed."

Upon their return to their quarters, Team 6 noted new armour waiting for them. Engineers had integrated daemon technologies into the suits, making them far more flexible. Skylark inspected his with interest.

"Permission to enter, sir?" Private Pierce said from the door.

"Granted," Skylark said, barely looking up.

"The majan sent me, sir. He said he would come himself but is busy in negotiations with the commodore."

"Which one?"

"Sir?"

"Which majan?"

"Oh, the tall one that never smiles."

Skylark grinned. "Call sign Saracen, then. Any idea what they're negotiating?"

"Not officially."

"Unofficially, then."

"From what I overheard, he wanted to be included on your team, sir."

Skylark blinked in surprise. "Is that so?"

"It seems so, sir."

Nodding Skylark changed the subject. "Why did he send you?"

"To explain the new functions of your armour, sir."

"Go ahead then."

"Well, you probably know most of it already. It is a modified version of the old USC Strategic armour. The fabrics have been changed, making them more conducive to movement, particularly twisting motions. Also, there is what the daemon called a second skin coating the armour. It bleeds, so to speak. The liquid hardens almost instantly, healing any breech of the armour in under a second."

"Oh, I like that," Binky said.

"For that reason, the sealing guns have been removed and replaced with pistols."

"I like that too." Binky grinned.

"Most everything else is the same. You still have the compartment for your gun on your back, first aid pouches, and second long knife. Also, and the majan was especially proud of this, retractable blades in your vambraces. You activate them by closing your hand into a fist and curling it towards your forearm."

Jack, already dressed in her armour, tried it. A twenty-inch blade shot from her left arm.

"Nice!" she said.

Skylark smiled. "How long did it take the engineers to fix this up?"

"Quite a while, sir. They had been puzzling it out long before the commodore went rogue. I suspect he had been planning this for a long time."

"It wouldn't surprise me. Thank you, Private."

"A pleasure, sir."

"Could you do me a favour?"

"Yes, sir. Of course."

"Could you tell Commodore Gergiev that I respectfully request that the majan Saracen accompany my team and I in this fight?"

Private Pierce grinned. "Certainly, sir. Right away." He saluted and exited the quarters.

"I think you have a fan," Doorman said, clapping Skylark on his shoulder.

Skylark grunted.

"These are pretty badass," Binky said as he waited on the flight deck with Team 6. Skylark smiled to himself as the team continually checked each other out. He stood straighter as Commodore Gergiev approached with the chtakah.

"Commodore. Chtakah," he greeted.

"Commander," the chtakah said, inclining his head slightly. "Do you like your new armour?"

"Are you kidding?" Jack said. "It's completely boss!"

The chtakah frowned slightly and turned to the commodore for translation.

"That means 'yes,'" Gergiev said, a smile tugging at the edges of his lips.

"Ah. Good. I am glad." The chtakah smiled. "Commander, the majan will be along shortly. You will be ferried—is that the word? By his companion majan. I understand that several teams guard the skies around this prison. The entire daemon fleet will provide aerial support. We will try not to kill these teams, but I cannot guarantee that doing so will not prove necessary."

Skylark nodded. "I understand."

"I am sorry. Many are good men."

The commander nodded. "Yes. But we have to get this done. If the admiral is alive, we need to get him out."

The chtakah nodded.

"Christie is on the bridge," Gergiev said. "We'll give you the go ahead once he's hacked into the system. Admiral Brooke's life will likely be in danger the moment you finish. The end of your speech is the signal to attack. Your new armour has all the old equipment. You still have a camera and comm. links as per your old armour. We'll be able to see everything. You have the schematics of the building?"

"Committed to memory, sir."

"Good. You should be in and out in half an hour. Try not to dawdle."

Skylark grinned. "Yes, sir."

"All right then. Good luck."

"Thank you, sir."

The chtakah and Commander Gergiev retreated behind the protective glass barrier. Sarcen arrived in his armour. Skylark grinned and extended a hand in greeting.

"Welcome to Team 6, Majan. Again."

"Thank you, Commander," Sarcen said gravely. Then he flashed a grin. "Your armour becomes you."

"It's not as good as yours," Spike noted.

The majan smiled. "The spikes are just for show." He waved vaguely at the row of three curved spikes on his pauldrons, matched by those on his vambraces and the sides of his greaves.

"They're damned intimidating," Spike said.

"That's the point," Skylark said. "Are we ready?"

"Yes, sir," Team 6 answered in unison.

"Let's go."

Skylark led the way to the waiting daemon transport. He greeted Butan, who sat in his spiked armour in the pilot's seat. The majan grinned at the commander before closing the door.

"Prepare for jump," Commodore Gergiev's voice said through the comm. "Jumping in three... two... one."

The ship lurched and Skylark's stomach rolled. He curled over in his seat and placed his head in his hands.

"Ugh!" Jack grumbled. "This fucking sucks."

"You will get used to it, Lieutenant," Sarcen said, smiling.

"Right," Jack murmured.

"We're here. Team 6, you have fifteen minutes."

"How do you do that?" Doorman asked suddenly. "Jump, I mean."

"It is not dissimilar to your wormhole technology," the majan said with a shrug. "From what I understand."

"From what you understand?"

"I am not a scholar," Sarcen said. "It is not my function to understand."

"Oh. Makes sense, I suppose."

Skylark straightened. "Everyone good?" he asked.

"You still look green," Binky noted, grinning.

"Shut up," Skylark said. He pressed the comm. link on his breastplate. "We're good to go, Commodore."

"Good to know, Commander. We're still hacking in."

"It won't be long," Christie's voice said, sounding flustered. Skylark grinned and leant back, closing his eyes.

"All right, Majan," Commodore Gergiev said. "You are cleared for take-off."

"Thank you, Commodore," Butan said. The transport came to life, noted only by the strengthening of light in the hold. After a moment,

Butan said, "We are clear of the craft. Arrival at destination one in three minutes."

"Acknowledged."

Silence filled the transport, broken only by the sounds of armour creaking as Team 6 shifted in their seats.

"All right," Christie said. "We're in. Show time, Commander."

Skylark sighed. He stood and walked over to the comm. link at the door. He paused briefly before depressing the button.

"This is Commander Bennejin Skye, United Space Corps, Strategic Division, Team 6." Reciting his name and rank caused memories of his torture to flood back and Skye had to step away from the comm. momentarily. Sarcen stood and placed a comforting hand on Skylark's shoulder. Taking a shaky breath, Skylark depressed the button again.

"You may have been told I was shot dead following a violent episode of space dementia. You've been lied to. I was shot. Then I spent the next year in a prison facility on Mars, under interrogation that was a blatant violation of the United Council resolution on the treatment of prisoners of war.

"Make no mistake. We are at war. Just over two years ago, Admiral Hunt and Councillor Brand staged a coup, removing Admiral Brooke and the United Council. They convinced you that the ragnar threat was an attempt by the daemon to subjugate humanity and claim Earth for themselves.

"I'm here to tell you that it is not true. The daemon are not our enemy. The ragnar are real, and they're not just coming, they're here. My team, and those still loyal to Admiral Brooke and the USC mandate, along with our daemon allies intend to stop them. Anyone who gets in our way will be summarily executed for treason.

"That means you, Hunt."

Skylark paused.

"Admiral Brooke, if you can hear me, sir, hang in there. We're coming for you. Commander Skye out."

"Beautifully said," Spike said, wiping non-existent tears from his cheeks.

"Shut up," Skylark replied.

"All are go," Gregiev announced to all teams. "I repeat, all are go."

"Sit tight," Butan said from the cockpit. "Did I say that correctly?"

Binky grinned. "Yes. Yes, you did."

"Good."

Team 6 unholstered their weapons as the transport dived towards the surface of GBS P107-005, surrounded on all sides by daemon fighters, which appeared out of thin air, their cloaking devices deactivated.

Brooke stared up at the small speaker in the far corner of the room. He grinned, a spray of blood escaping his mouth as his lips stretched over his teeth. The hologram of Admiral Hunt stood as if frozen by a communications malfunction.

"I told you, you bastard," Brooke slurred.

The hologram turned slowly around to face Admiral Brooke.

"Kill him," the hologram of Admiral Hunt instructed Admiral Brooke's interrogators. "Kill him now!"

Shrugging, one of the men wearing a thick hide apron lifted a large knife from the table. He raised it high. Admiral Brooke stared at him defiantly through swollen, bleeding eyes.

The door of the interrogation room flew open, kicked in by the majan, Sarcen. Through the concrete dust, glowing blue blades flashed out, cutting the interrogator with the knife into three pieces before he could slash down on the admiral's neck. Sarcen quickly dispatched the other interrogator as Skylark and Binky ran in to free the admiral.

"Skye?" Admiral Brooke croaked. "Is that really you?"

Skylark pressed a button in his helmet. The visor slid open. "It's really me, Admiral," he said. He and Binky helped Brooke to his feet. "Now let's get you out of here."

"Jesus God," Admiral Brooke breathed before Jack covered his head with a helmet of his own. He felt the skin at his neck pull as the helmet sealed itself and pressurized.

"We're good," Skylark said. "Let's go."

Doorman and Spike took point, fighting their way back out of the compound. Knowing that the wardens would move to the areas they had already been through, a different escape route had been devised. Skylark pressed a large red button as they moved through the control room, releasing those locked in their cells. Escape would be easier if the wardens had to face down angry inmates.

The ruse worked. Team 6 encountered little resistance as they moved through the building to their designated exit. In under twenty minutes from the beginning of the mission, they were outside, running for the transport that sat waiting for them behind a ridge.

Jack took over from Skylark when the commander began to tire. Skylark fell behind with Sarcen, guarding Team 6's back. Team 6 had managed to drag the admiral aboard the transport when Team I appeared from across the rocky field.

"Shit," Spike said, firing shots as Sarcen clambered aboard.

"Commander!" Jack yelled. "Let's go."

Skylark, who had been drawing fire, stood and ran. A bullet ripped through his knee. He stumbled, then fell, rolling on the ground.

"Skye!" Jack screamed. Bullets began striking the inside of the transport.

"We have to go," Butan said.

"No!" Jack yelled, preparing to jump out. Spike held her back.

"Go!" Skylark barked over the comm. "Get Brooke to safety. I'll hold down as long as I can. Get me aerial cover and a ride." He crawled behind a large boulder.

"Sir," Jack said over the comm., sounding like she intended to argue. There was little she could do, however. The transport had already pulled away.

"Jack, I'll be fine."

Jack looked up at the transport ceiling, fighting back angry tears. "Yes, sir."

"That's my girl."

Skylark coughed. Though the suit's second skin had done its job, sealing the armour breach in under a second, enough of the toxic atmosphere had made it into the suit to create problems for his already weak lungs. He struggled into a kneeling position and readied his weapon. Team I moved forward cautiously.

Skylark had no time for that caution. He dived over the boulder, fired two shots and vanished behind another rock, narrowly missing the volley of bullets that flew at him.

"Stand down, Team 1," he said into his comm. using the open frequency.

"Fuck you," Commander Speedman answered.

"Buy me dinner first."

He played cat and mouse with Team 1, using the rocky terrain well. But his bleeding leg and troubled lungs quickly wore him down. He found himself pinned, the three remaining members of Team 1 flanking him on three sides, leaving a large swath of nothing but sand between him and the nearest rock. He could never run that distance and escape a bullet.

"Inbound on your location," Commander Koch said over the comm.

"I'm in rough shape," Skylark answered, ducking to avoid a fresh volley of bullets. "Out of ammo. Can't breathe." As if to prove his point, he started coughing.

Koch answered by leading his team in their individual fighters in a low flyby, firing on Team 1.

Skylark peeked around the boulder to find the barrel of Commander Speedman's gun in his face. He dived to the left, releasing his vambrace blades as Speedman fired. Rolling to his feet, Skylark lunged forward, kicking Speedman's gun from him. He bit back a scream as his wounded knee protested the effort. He threw a series of five punches, all of which Speedman ducked or blocked.

"Getting slow, Skye," Speedman said as he kicked the commander to the ground.

Skylark could only cough in reply. His body had given up. Though his mind screamed at his limbs to move, all he could manage was to roll on his side and crawl slowly away.

Speedman bent down and grabbed Skylark by his breastplate and lifted him. "I'm going to enjoy this," he hissed.

In a last desperate flail, Skylark swung his right arm. Speedman dodged, avoiding his head being lopped off by Skylark's blade. But the blade shattered Speedman's visor.

Seeing his chance, Skylark rolled up, delivering a powerful knee to Speedman's stomach. Air rushed out of Speedman's lungs and before he could stop himself, he breathed sharply in.

The toxic atmosphere worked on Speedman's lungs immediately. Speedman spasmed in pain, falling to the ground and scratching at his own throat. Skylark limped backward, watching as pink foam flowed through Speedman's mouth and nose. He unholstered his pistol and aimed it at Speedman, but he did not fire. He holstered his weapon again, denying the commander of Team 1 any mercy. He watched as Speedman convulsed until, unable to breathe himself, Skylark fell to his hands and knees in a coughing fit.

He felt strong arms lift him up. Looking up sharply, he saw USC armour and struggled.

"Easy, Commander," a familiar voice said. Skylark couldn't place it. "Don't make this harder than it has to be."

Coughing harder for his struggles, Skylark nevertheless fought as fiercely as he could.

"Christ, he just doesn't give up!" someone else said over the comm.

"That's why he's famous. All right, in you get."

Skylark was unceremoniously dumped on the floor of a USC transport. The team that captured him kept their helmets on as a guard against the toxins that were released when they removed Skylark's helm. They covered his face and nose with an oxygen mask, which Skylark tried to pull away from his face.

"Stop it, you idiot," one of the team barked at him.

Skylark did not. In the end, it was his own weakening body that betrayed him. He struggled until he could no longer move. His eyes rolled as he grudgingly surrendered to unconsciousness.

Commodore Gergiev scowled. "Say again?"

"He's not here sir," Koch said over the comm. "Just a very dead Commander Speedman."

"You're certain that's the location?"

"They were fighting hand-to-hand, Commodore," Koch said, annoyed. "Of course I'm sure."

"All right, all right," Gergiev said.

"Commodore?" Christie said. "We're being hailed."

"Keep looking, Koch. We're not leaving without him."

"Aye, aye, sir."

"Patch them through, Christie."

"Commodore Gergiev, this is Commander Hank, USC Strategic, Team 87. We have Commander Skye."

Gergiev closed his eyes briefly. He switched channels. "Koch, return to the ship."

"Sir?"

"Skye's been captured. Return."

"On our way."

The commodore switched channels again. "State your terms, Commander."

"First, sir, I want to know is Buddha with you?"

Sarcen and Butan had joined the chtakah and commodore on the bridge upon their return. Butan stepped forward.

"I am here, Commander," he said hesitantly.

"Good to hear your voice," Commander Hank said. "Glad you made it out okay when the shit hit the fan."

Butan smiled slightly. "As am I."

"All right, these are my terms, Commodore. Skye's in bad shape. We think he breathed some of the not-so-friendly air. We want Medical on the flight deck, a place on your ship, and Buddha back on our team."

Butan turned back to the chtakah, looking surprised and hopeful. The chtakah nodded at the commodore.

"Welcome aboard the *Magellan*," Gergiev said.

"Thank you, sir."

Grinning like a madman, Butan ran from the bridge, eager to greet his old teammates the minute they landed.

"Like a baby Goutabad," Sarcen growled. The chtakah rumbled a soft laugh.

26

All of Commander Hank's demands were swiftly met. Skylark, who had lost his battle with unconsciousness, was whisked quickly away to Medical. Butan greeted Commander Hank with a broad grin and firm handshake, then roughly embraced him.

"I have missed you, Commander," he said.

"And you," Hank replied, though plainly embarrassed.

Team 6 also arrived to greet Team 87.

"Man are we glad you are here!" Binky said. "Thank you for bringing him back."

Hank shrugged. "We thought he was dead," he said. "Hearing his voice again... Christ. We fucked up royally."

"Hardly your fault, Commander," Binky said.

"Still. I knew something was off. It's been off since Wheeler died."

"We're going to make it better," Binky said. "Come on. I'll show you to your quarters."

Skylark's recovery was uncertain. His left lung was far too damaged to save and had to be removed. A machine helped him breathe while a new lung grew in the cavity. His knee fared little better. The bullet shattered the joint and had torn his ligaments. The whole structure had to be entirely replaced. Eight hours in surgery had strained his body's defences and he developed a fever.

For a week, LeBruin remained at his side, obsessing over his readings. His heart stopped twice but began again before LeBruin intervened. Team 6 took turns in the room, keeping their commander company in pairs. Sarcen took the majority of the shifts, refusing to budge and watching Skylark carefully.

"What is it you see when you look at him?" Jack asked Sarcen one day as she idly shuffled a deck of cards.

Sarcen's gaze flickered to her briefly before settling back on Commander Skye.

"His light changes," he said.

Jack frowned.

"When he is asleep or unconscious, his light becomes fuller, stronger, familiar. But when he wakes..." Sarcen shrugged.

"What? What happens when he wakes?"

"The light shatters, splinters into thousands of fragments, none touching the other."

Jack looked over at Commander Skye, his chest rising and falling as the machine regulated his breathing. "What does that mean?"

"I cannot be sure. But I think, in his sleep, he is with *her*. And her presence heals him."

"Her? You mean the tahorah?"

Sarcen shrugged. "His light takes on her tone. I would know it anywhere. It could only be her."

"Is that even possible? Is she, I mean...?"

"Does that mean that death is not the end? I cannot tell. Human minds are stronger than you know and do much without your conscious comprehending. It may be that the mere memory of her recalls some of her essence, and it is his own mind that heals him."

Jack looked at Sarcen.

"Or," Sarcen said, a small smile touching his lips. "It could mean that on some plane, the tahorah is safe and whole, and she stands guard over the commander's sleeping mind."

Jack smiled sadly. "I hope it's the latter," she whispered.

"As do I," Sarcen admitted.

It took three weeks before Skylark opened his eyes. Consciousness brought with it a violent cough.

"Hush," LeBruin said, touching Skylark's shoulder. "It's all right. You're back on the *Magellan* now. You're safe."

"How?" Skylark croaked through his oxygen mask.

"Commander Hank," LeBruin said with a smile. "Team 87 are our first converts. Your knee was blown and had to be replaced. The robotic integration went very smoothly. Your lungs, on the other hand..." She sighed. "Your left lung had practically melted away and had to be removed. You have a new one growing, but until it is fully mature, you are not permitted out of Medical."

"Brooke?" Skylark croaked again.

"In better condition than you. But he's not as young either. He's in the room next door. You can visit each other when you both can move."

Skylark nodded and let himself fall back to sleep. LeBruin sighed, checked the equipment and left Skylark to rest.

"Stubborn bastard," Admiral Brooke said when Skylark's eyes next opened. The admiral sat in a wheelchair, the bruises now nothing more than vaguely green patches on his skin. An ugly red scar crossed his face from his left eyebrow to his right ear.

Skylark smiled and raised his hand in a weak salute.

"Stop it," Admiral Brooke snapped. He sighed. "I owe you everything, Commander Skye. I was a dead man when you and your team came knocking."

"Gergiev," Skylark said, struggling against his machinery to speak. "Contacted the chtakah. Saved me."

"Yes. I know the story. Gergiev also noted that he would not have done anything had you not planted the thought of Hunt's treason in his head. How did you know?"

Skylark shrugged. "I just did."

"Hm. In any case, thank you. I'm about ready to make an announcement to the world. I want you at my side when I do, so get better quickly, soldier."

"Yes, sir."

"We'll make those bastards pay."

"Ragnar," Skylark said, shaking his head.

"I know. The majan told us about what he saw when you showed him what the tahorah had learnt. We know there is a single queen controlling the rest, and we know she is sentient and has a particularly nasty plan for us; like cattle to the slaughter. We're not going to let Hunt distract us from that. But I want that bastard's head on a plate."

Brooke looked up to find Skylark asleep. "Later then, Commander." He waved his hand to signal Private Pierce, who rushed forward and wheeled him back to his room.

A combination of stem-cell growth-accelerating drugs and Skylark's own extraordinary will power had the commander out of bed the following week. Forced to use a cane as his bionic knee programmed itself to respond to his commands, Skylark hobbled around his room, wearing his oxygen mask and scowling like an angry old man.

"Aren't you supposed to be resting?" Commander Hank said from the door, smirking at Skylark.

Commander Skye looked up in surprise, then smiled, though it could be barely seen through the fog of his mask. "Hank!"

Hank strode forward and the commanders roughly embraced. "I can't believe you're alive," Hank said. "I should have expected it. What are five bullets to the chest for Commander Skye?"

"Three," Skylark corrected.

"Your colour is better," Hank remarked, finding a seat.

Skylark grunted and resumed pacing.

"You going to do that all day?"

"It's better than nothing."

Hank grinned. "I think you have undiagnosed ADHD."

Skylark smiled again and paused to cough.

"Sounds nasty."

"Not as bad as it was," LeBruin said from the door. "You, sir," she told Commander Skye, "are supposed to be in bed. Get. Go on."

Skylark scowled, but didn't argue. He hobbled back to the bed and laid down. LeBruin checked his readings, waited 15 minutes, then removed his mask.

"We're going to start weaning you off this now," she said. "We'll start with half an hour a day and see how it goes. You will feel discomfort, and possibly some dizziness. Try not to talk. No moving from this bed. Understand?"

Skylark nodded.

"All right then." LeBruin checked her watch and left.

Hank walked over to the bed.

"Why?" Skylark asked.

"Why what? Why did we switch sides quicker than a spring breeze?"

Commander Skye nodded. Hank shrugged.

"I thought you were dead. We were told you went insane and had to be shot; that you had died and your team were on trial for treason for following your madness. Christ. I couldn't believe my ears. Then I started hearing rumours amongst the various crews about what had gone down. They said the tahorah was shot by Commander Speedman, and that you went after her on a suicide rescue mission. I had a ship mechanic swear up and down that he saw you disembark USC Strategic *One* with the tahorah in your arms, and that she died on the flight deck."

Hank glanced over at Skylark. His eyes were closed, and tears could be seen dancing along his lashes, seeking an escape.

"It's true then? You went after her?"

Skylark nodded.

Hank shook his head. "That is insane." When Skylark did not respond, he continued. "That same mechanic talked about Hunt wanting to dissect her, but you fought him off and cremated her. And was shot dead for it."

Skylark nodded.

"Hunt's a bastard," Hank spat suddenly. "Fuck. It hit all of us hard to hear you were dead. When I found out that there was an unofficial version of the truth, I started to dig. When I couldn't reach the admiral, or any of the Council except Brand, I started thinking that maybe Hunt was up to something. Then I heard your voice over the comm. And you just happened to attack the prison we had been sent to guard. I didn't even have to ask. The whole team just stood up together and that was it."

Skylark smiled slightly. "Thank you."

"Yeah, well. Turns out we were guarding the prison where Hunt had thrown the admiral. That just pisses me off. I hear that the space bugs we're fighting have a plan for us?"

Skylark nodded. "Breeding program. For food."

"Wow. That's... wow."

Commander Skye shrugged. "We don't do any different."

Hank shuddered. "That's it, I'm going vegetarian."

Skylark scoffed, then coughed.

"Easy now," Hank said. "You've talked too much. My fault. I'll come back later."

With the careful attention of Doctor LeBruin, Skylark once again passed the rigorous physical required of a USC infiltrator. Doctor Takahashi, however, was reticent about clearing him for combat. He watched with concern as Skylark's dark humour deepened, how he often lost focus during important conversations, and the return of the nightmares that kept him awake through most of the night. Only when exhaustion had depleted his reserves did he make it past the dream stage of sleep.

Takahashi suspected that Speedman's gruesome death plagued Skylark more heavily than the commander would admit, even to himself. It was justice, Skylark had said during one of their twice-weekly sessions. The tahorah had died in a similar fashion because of Speedman.

Yet knowing the incredible pain that came from having one's lungs dissolving in one's chest and the panic of being unable to draw breath, Skylark could not dismiss Speedman's death just as he could not forget the tahorah's. Rather than the former relieving the pain of the latter, it compounded it.

In short, Skylark was spiralling dangerously and given his personality profile, Doctor Takahashi was worried about what damage Skylark's impending meltdown would do.

Slowly integrating back into their former roles in the alliance, the daemon had returned to the *Magellan*. Scholars and healers had rejoined the scientists and medics and the teams welcomed back a daemon member.

Team 6, whose daemon member had been killed, accepted Sarcen into its ranks. He was vastly different to the tahorah. Frighteningly intense, the team had difficulty relaxing around him. Similarly, Sarcen did not seem intent on integrating with his team, choosing instead to remain on the outside, observing. He was never disrespectful, always prompt, but disturbingly quiet.

Team 6 and 87 sat together often in the mess. Their antics did not distract Skylark from noticing the looks that were often cast his way. They were often unfriendly. At dinner, shortly after his return from Medical, Skylark could bear it no longer. He cast his fork down onto his plate in disgust and left the mess, taking his team and Team 87 by surprise.

"I will go," Sarcen said quietly, clapping Binky on the shoulder. "It will be easier coming from me."

"Nuh-uh," Binky said. "Don't you dare talk about it."

"The longer it remains unsaid, the more damage it will do," Sarcen replied.

Binky, muscular though he was, could not hope to overpower the daemon majan, and so simply watched him leave the mess, chasing after Commander Skye.

"This about Speedman?" Hank asked Binky quietly. Binky nodded slowly.

"Well," Spike said, cheerfully. "Best get ready for a shit storm."

Sarcen found Commander Skye in the relative darkness of a maintenance tunnel. His forehead rested on the cold metal of the tunnel wall.

"Commander," Sarcen greeted.

"Go away," Skylark grumbled.

"It is not good to hide in darkness."

Commander Skye looked up with a frown. As always with the majan, his words could be interpreted in any number of ways.

"It serves me just fine," Skylark replied, returning to his previous position.

"It will kill you, in the end."

"Good," Skylark whispered.

Sarcen cocked his head and stepped into the tunnel. He leant with his back to the wall.

"The crew. It will pass. They are just afraid."

"Of what?"

"Of you, Commander."

Skylark scoffed but did not look up.

"What you did to the Commander of Team I... it was not good."

Again, Skylark scoffed. He stood and looked at Sarcen, not bothering to disguise his anger.

"Do you know how she died, Majan?" Skylark asked quietly. "Her own body turned traitor, started attacking itself. She drowned in her own lungs." Skylark began to tremble. "Damn your 'good' to hell. He got what he deserved."

Skylark turned and left the tunnel.

Sarcen scowled after him but knew better than to chase him now. The commander's light had all but vanished, swallowed by an unrelenting, fathomless dark.

Skylark stumbled down the halls, not quite certain where he was going. Rage, grief and guilt worked against him. Sarcen had been right. Evil though Speedman's actions had been, Skylark's own were no better. Speedman's death had been cruel, and the image of his dying throes, his pleading eyes and panicked expression as blood-flecked foam escaped his lungs plagued Skylark now.

The walls closed in around him, pushing against his chest so he could not breathe. His vision blurred as he fought back the weight of the entire ship. Shapes moved, some made unintelligible sounds, and the walls pushed ever in. Skylark broke into a run. He needed to get out. He needed air.

"No luck?" Commodore Gergiev asked the chtakah. He had called a meeting with the daemon war-leader and the head of the majan shortly after dinner in an effort to locate Hunt. They were hoping for a quick infiltration and capture before embarking on the journey to the ragnar queen's location as revealed to them by Skylark.

The daemon war-leader shook his head. "I cannot sense him."

"So, what, then? Dead?"

"Not necessarily," Sarcen said. "It might be that—" The majan stopped abruptly, his eyes lighting up.

Gergiev raised his brows. "Majan?"

Sarcen growled something in his native tongue and left the

commodore's study. Gergiev turned to the chtakah, demanding an explanation. The chtakah shrugged. Together, they chased Sarcen out of the study and down the halls.

They encountered a large crowd near one of the maintenance airlocks. Some sort of altercation was happening at the centre of the gathering.

Sarcen pushed through the crowd, followed closely by the chtakah and the commodore. Shock made the commodore's body rigid the moment he arrived at the scene.

"No!" Skylark shouted as he struggled against five men who hauled him away from the airlock. Bruised and bloodied, the commander's face twisted with rage. He coughed violently as the struggle worked to undo all of Doctor LeBruin's efforts. Blood and vomit choked his words. "Let me go! Let me go!"

"What the fuck?" Gergiev murmured.

Sarcen strode forward. He wrapped his muscular arms around Commander Skye and relieved the five men, who were having difficulty containing the incensed commander. Sarcen spoke quickly and quietly in soothing tones as Skylark mindlessly struggled against his captor, trying to reach the airlock.

Out of patience, Sarcen wrapped his palm around Skylark's forehead and the commander slumped. LeBruin arrived on the scene.

"What the hell happened?" she demanded as she ran forward to treat the man in Sarcen's arms. Sarcen said nothing, cradling Skylark as he would a child.

"You took the words out of my mouth," Gergiev said. "What the hell happened?"

"We don't know, sir," one of the mechanics said, nursing a bruise on his jaw. "He just came running up out of nowhere all bloody like that and tried to open the airlock."

"I need to get him to Medical," LeBruin said.

"I'll carry," Sarcen said.

LeBruin nodded. She stood and led Sarcen down the halls at a run.

"Clean up this mess," Gergiev said. He turned and marched down the hall to Team 6's quarters. He entered and stopped dead.

The quarters were a disaster. Skylark's bed had all but been destroyed, the metal frame bent and twisted, the sheets torn and down from the pillows still floated lazily down from the ceiling. The door to the washroom had been kicked in and it whirred and clicked as it continually tried to slide open, only to be thwarted by its own bent surface.

Team 6 was present, though in shock. Binky knelt on the floor, holding Jack close. She sobbed into his chest. Spike sat a little way off, staring at them both with a blank expression. Only Doorman seemed in any way lucid. He stood and leant his back against the wall, deep in thought. He spied the commodore and the chtakah standing in the doorway and walked over.

"Is he all right?" Doorman asked quietly, the words sounding odd spoken through his bloodied lips. "Skye? Is he okay?"

"Commander Skye is unconscious," Gergiev said. "And back in Medical. He'll be restrained on his bed. What happened, Corporal?"

"Skye happened, sir. He just strode through the door in a rage and started destroying everything. I don't think he even saw us in here, until Jack tried to stop him. Then it was a four on one fight. The four lost. He put us all down, then vanished again."

"He tried to go out an airlock," Gergiev said. Doorman blinked in surprise, then shook his head.

"It was like he wasn't even present, you know? Was it...? Could it have been his programming?"

"From the torture, you mean?" Gergiev asked. He shrugged when Doorman nodded. "There's no telling."

"We're not a team without him, sir."

"Whether or not he ever commands again is not up to me, Corporal. It's up to him. Now get everyone down to Medical. I'll have a repair crew in here, but you should all be prepared to move to new quarters."

"Yes, sir." Doorman hesitated.

"We'll do everything we can for him, Corporal," Gergiev said. "I'm not giving up on Skye just yet."

"Thank you, sir."

Gergiev nodded. He and the chtakah left the quarters.

27

Skylark opened his eyes and frowned. He lay in bed, his mouth and nose covered by an oxygen mask. His body ached like he had taken a beating. He tried to sit up and found himself bound to the bed. A sudden panic struck him. Disorientated and confused, he thought himself back in the prison on Mars. He struggled.

"Hush," Doctor LeBruin said as she appeared at his bedside. She placed her hand on his shoulder. "Hush, now. It's all right. You're safe."

Skylark frowned at her but stopped struggling.

"You've caused quite a stir, you know," Doctor LeBruin said, smiling gently down at him. "Drama queen."

Skylark tried to ask where he was and what had happened, but all the effort achieved was a coughing fit. Each cough burned like fire in his chest.

"Hey, hey," LeBruin said. "It's all right. Your lungs are still in bad shape, and you pushed a little too hard yesterday. Just breathe, Skye. Close your eyes and breathe."

Following LeBruin's advice and with her counting, Skylark closed his eyes and fought to breathe in, taking in as much of the foggy medicine from the mask as possible. His coughing slowed, then stopped, and he went to sleep once more. When next he woke, he found himself looking at a gently smiling Doctor Takahashi.

"Good afternoon," Takahashi said in his unexpected Parisian accent.

Skylark scowled.

"You gave us all a good scare."

"What happened?" the commander croaked.

"You don't remember?"

Skylark shook his head.

"Ah. Well, not unexpected I suppose. You, Commander, suffered a violent psychotic episode. Well, I say psychotic. What probably happened was that you had a panic attack and, given your training and your personality profile, it had a violent expression. It is not unusual for people suffering such episodes to blank out."

Forcing himself to think back, obscure images and strange memories flashed through Skylark's mind. He twitched.

"Jack...?"

"She is fine, Commander. Well, by which I mean she is alive and functioning. She's very upset, though. It will take some time before she can look at you without wanting to hurt you, I imagine."

Commander Skye closed his eyes. The image of him flinging her across a room and against a wall replayed in his mind. He had left her unconscious.

"The rest of your team is a little less distraught. They've been preparing for an outbreak for a while. I would say they're actually relieved. It could have gone a lot worse."

"Pierce?" Skylark asked. He remembered encountering the young private in a corridor, though where and when exactly were unknown. He did know that he had struck the boy.

"Ah, now he's an interesting case. He is fine. A bit heartbroken, though. You were his idol, I understand. We had a lengthy chat about post-traumatic stress disorder and, while he's still angry with you and upset to the point of tears, he'll come around nicely."

Skylark swallowed. "I want to speak with them. Jack and Pierce."

"Later. Emotions are high on both sides. Your team is right, though. It could have been a lot worse. One or more of them might have ended up dead."

Skylark looked at the doctor.

"Can you deny it?" Takahashi asked.

Commander Skye could not. He had not been in control of himself. He had recognized no one in his rage and barely even remembered his own actions now that he had calmed.

"Are you prepared to speak with me now? Or did you want to wait until after the next episode?"

Unable to answer without tears, Skylark closed his eyes and gritted his teeth in an effort to control his emotions.

"In order for me to help you, you have to talk to me. I am an impressive psychiatrist, it is true, but I am not a miracle worker. I need you to help me help you. Now, we'll start with the biggest question. What is bothering you, Commander?"

"I was tortured," Skylark grated.

"Ah. Yes. You were. But I do not think that is the source of your anger."

Skylark opened his eyes and frowned at the doctor.

"You see, you are an infiltrator and a talented one at that. You have been in the military since you were eight years old. Every single day of your life has been lived with the threat of violence and death. You have, from some of your earliest moments, developed a plethora of methods for coping with pain. Needles and knives do not scare you, Commander. Why would they? Cuts and bruises heal. No, the source of your problem goes much deeper.

"Let's see. You are in your thirties and unmarried. A serial womanizer, you've had a string of very short-lived relationships. In every relationship, you were the one who decided when to cut it off. You were always in control."

"What of it?"

"Well, I suspect that you were never serious about anyone because you were deliberately trying to protect your only weakness—your heart. I think you had, before coming to the military, opened your heart to someone, only to have them stab it. Metaphorically, of course. Perhaps your mother? You decided that nothing was worth that pain, and so you, whether consciously or not, did everything in your power to avoid it.

"And then you met her. And you fell in love. You didn't want to, and I'm sure you fought it for as long as you could. But love is a curiously powerful thing. It's impossible to ignore. And you caved and plummeted, out of control, into territory you knew nothing about."

Takahashi watched Skylark carefully. The commander kept his eyes tightly closed, frowning as he tried to fight whatever welled inside him.

"At first it was wonderful, as love so often is. And being out of control, although terrifying, was exhilarating. Every time you saw her, you tripped over yourself. But it was never an issue. Not for a while.

"Then something happened. Something out of your hands. Even though you knew you could do nothing, you tried anyway. You tried with everything you had, and still..."

A tear escaped Skylark's closed eyes and slid silently down his cheek.

"And now she is gone and you, who have never had your heart broken before, don't know how to cope with this loss, this kind of pain; a wound that does not bleed. Am I close?"

"Stop," Skylark whispered. He did not open his eyes. "Stop it."

Struggling to regain his composure, Commander Skye took a deep, shaky breath in. He opened his eyes and looked directly at Doctor Takahashi. He couldn't continue. He closed his eyes again and struggled against his tears, the effort making his breathing ragged and irregular. His whole body trembled.

"I dream of her," he said, tears streaming down his cheeks from beneath his closed lids. "Every night I'm with her again."

"And these dreams upset you?"

"No," Skylark said, so quietly that Takahashi was forced to lean forward to hear. "Waking up does. She died in my arms. It wasn't supposed to happen that way. I was going to save her. But she—" The commander shook his head. "And now, every morning, it's like she dies again. Over and over. I can't keep saying goodbye. I can't."

"And throwing yourself out of an airlock would solve that problem?"

Skylark bowed his head. "I couldn't breathe," he said. "I just needed to breathe."

"In outer space?"

"I—" Skylark scowled. "I don't know."

"You said to me before that you didn't want to live. Do you think that you'll be with her when you die? That your souls will meet again in some vague paradise?"

Commander Skye shrugged. He looked at Doctor Takahashi. "I hope," he said. "And if it isn't true, if there truly is nothing, then it wouldn't matter. I'd be dead."

"And the pain would stop," Takahashi finished for him.

They sat in silence for a while. Skylark struggled to get control of himself and Doctor Takahashi observed. He reached out and grasped Skylark's arm.

"Let it out, Commander. Sometimes you have to let the water flow to avoid destroying the dam."

Skylark shook his head and continued to fight.

Doctor Takahashi sighed.

"Make it stop," Skylark said between short, sharp breaths. "I can't do this anymore. Make it stop."

"That is up to you, Commander. You have to let it out."

"I can't. Please." The begging broke him. Skylark cried out as the dam finally burst. Doctor Takahashi removed the thick leather that bound Skylark's arms to the bed, allowing the commander to roll on his side. Pulling a pillow in tight, Skylark curled into a foetal position and wept.

Doctor LeBruin, alerted by the various machinery attached to Commander Skye of an arrhythmic heartbeat and difficulty breathing, rushed in. Doctor Takahashi held her back.

"Don't," he whispered. "He needs to do this."

LeBruin stopped and straightened, looking down on Skylark as he fought for breath, coughing and sucking air in when he wasn't sobbing hysterically.

"You might want to bring a bucket, though," Takahashi said.

He had not been wrong.

The wracking sobs and the struggle for air set Skylark's stomach rolling. He vomited, though he had nothing in his stomach. His paroxysm of grief lasted for almost half an hour when, too exhausted to continue, Skylark collapsed into his cot and unconsciousness.

LeBruin collected the bucket while Doctor Takahashi fixed the blankets around the commander.

"There you go, Commander," he said gently. "You will feel better in the morning. I promise."

28

Jack was sitting on Skylark's bed when he opened his eyes. Surprised at her presence, he took in a sharp breath, drawing her attention.

"Hey," she said softly. "How are you feeling?"

"I'm sorry," Skylark said automatically, not bothering the check the tears that came unbidden to his eyes at the sight of her. A large bruise on her cheek and several more on her forearm were all that could be seen of their violent altercation the night before.

Jack nodded. "Yeah. I know." She sighed. "You know, I had this huge speech prepared. I was going to give you a piece of my mind. But looking at you now... Christ, Skylark. You're a mess."

Skylark closed his eyes, opening them again when he felt Jack take his hand. She slid over on the bed, lay down beside him, and wrapped his arm around herself. She smiled sadly at Skylark.

"We were all so happy to have you back," Jack whispered. "We weren't ready to face the fact that you were dragged through hell. It was tough for us all. I can't imagine how difficult it must have been for you. We wanted everything to be the same, but the truth is, everything has changed. Everything. We tried to ignore it and it blew up in our faces."

Feeling her commander tremble, she wrapped an arm around his head and he leant into her.

"I'm so sorry," Skylark whispered.

"It's all right. We'll work through this. We're still your team, Commander," Jack said. "We will always be your team."

"Thank you."

"You miss her a lot, don't you?"

Skylark closed his eyes and nodded. "I dream of her," he murmured. "Every night. And every morning is a painful goodbye."

"You're lucky. I'd give anything to see her again."

Smiling, Skylark pulled her close.

"Look at you," Jack said, smiling. "You great big kitten."

Despite his misery, Skylark laughed and she giggled. They lay together in silence until Skylark fell asleep, resting against his lieutenant. Jack remained still, moving only when LeBruin arrived to give Skylark his lunch.

At dinner, Skylark opened his eyes to find Private Pierce standing sullenly at the end of his bed.

"You called for me, sir?" Pierce asked.

"Yes. I did. Sit down, Scott."

Surprised that the commander remembered his first name, Private Pierce pulled over the nearby chair and sat.

"I want to apologize," Skye said carefully.

"You don't have to, sir. Doctor Takahashi explained about what PTSD does to people. You've been through a lot. It's a good reason."

"It might be a reason, but it is not an excuse."

The private blinked and frowned. "Really, sir. It's all right."

"No. It's not. I should never have struck you. I should never have lost control." Skylark paused to try and collect his thoughts. He looked squarely at Pierce. "I'm not a hero, Scott," he said gently. "There is no such thing as heroes. You will have to learn that sooner or later."

Pierce looked surprised, then shook his head. "That's not true. You went after the tahorah. You knew she was the key to the alliance. You fought for her. You brought her back. Then you fought Hunt. You were the only one to call him out. The only one!"

Skylark shook his head. "I went after her expecting to fail, expecting to die. It was foolish and reckless and I could never have gotten the tahorah out if I didn't have my team behind me. Not that any of it matters. She died anyway. I couldn't have fought Hunt if my team, if Cortez and her team didn't back me up. Everyone celebrates the man who lifts the flag," he said. "But that flag pole stands on a mountain of bodies; the corpses of brave men and women who gave their lives so that one man could raise the flag. They remember the name of the flag bearer, but never the thousands of dead who helped him get to where he needed to be. Do you understand? Heroes are nothing but myth."

Private Pierce observed Skylark for a moment before smiling. "I accept your apology," he said. He stood and walked to Skylark's side to shake his hand. "But not your thesis. You are the best of us, Commander. What you've managed to achieve, sir, no one else could have. You are a hero." Pierce grinned. "You will never be able to convince me otherwise."

The following day, Skylark was released from Medical. He arrived at Team 6's new quarters, standing nervously at the door, unnoticed, as the team argued over the rules of craekers. Sarcen noticed him first and immediately stood.

The argument ended abruptly and Team 6 stood to attention. The room was tense until Binky grinned. "Welcome back, sir," he said, walking forward and embracing his commander.

"Thank you," Skylark said. Team 6 flooded forward and enveloped Skylark in a group hug, except Sarcen who watched with a small smile. When the team disengaged, Sarcen walked forward and took Skylark's hand in a firm shake.

"You look better," he said.

"I'm feeling better," Skylark replied.

"Let's get you settled," Doorman said. He grabbed Skylark's overnight bag and tossed it onto Skylark's bed.

"Nice," Jack said, rolling her eyes.

"Hey," Spike demanded from the table. "Are we playing or what?"

"So, Commander Skye, back on your feet, I see," Doctor Takahashi said, looking over the thin, golden frames of his glasses at the commander sitting on his couch.

"Yes," Skylark answered.

"How are you feeling?"

"The same as before. Calmer, though."

"A good cry will do that."

Skylark looked away.

"You still dream of the tahorah?"

"Yes."

Doctor Takahashi sighed. He put down the electronic file and stylus he had been holding and folded his hands over his crossed legs. "I can stop those dreams, Commander," he said quietly.

Skylark looked sharply at him.

"There is a pill you can take that stops the sleep cycle going into the dreaming stage and beyond."

"I'll take it," Skylark said.

Doctor Takahashi put up one hand. "Let me finish," he said gently. "The thing is, the dream stage of the cycle is incredibly important. Prolonged disruption of the sleep cycle as it naturally occurs can do a great deal of damage, in the long run. You must weigh this against your pain."

Skylark nodded.

"And there is something else to consider," Doctor Takahashi said.

Commander Skye raised his brows at the psychiatrist.

"In your dreams, you are with the woman you love. At the end of the day, you get to return to her. You must be certain that you truly never want to see her again, because that is what this medication will do for you. Is the pain of saying goodbye each morning, knowing you will see her again, greater than saying goodbye forever?"

Blinking, Commander Skye scowled. He sat back on the sofa, lost in thought.

Doctor Takahashi tossed him a small bottle of pills. "Those are them. If you decide you cannot bear to see her, take one every evening a half hour before bed."

Skylark stared down at the bottle.

"All right, you may go."

"Are we in?" Admiral Brooke asked Christie as he stood in front of the viewscreen.

"Almost," Christie answered curtly.

Commander Skye hid a smile at Christie's impatience with the admiral. With the viewscreen dark, Admiral Brooke saw it all in the reflection. He raised his eyebrows at Skylark, which served only to broaden the commander's grin. His mood of late had improved greatly.

After much thought, Skylark had refused Doctor Takahashi's offer of a drug to stop him from dreaming. However painful the goodbyes were each morning, Skylark would rather suffer a few tears than be rid of the tahorah altogether. Though he still wept every morning, he did not regret his decision, and the degree of control he had over that decision helped him to cope with the heartache. Smiling came easier, and each one was more genuine than the last.

"Well, hurry up," the admiral grumbled. He remained dependent on his wheelchair while the stem cells responsible for reconnecting his severed spinal chord grew. An occasional tingling in his toes told him that, however impatient he was to be walking again, he was healing. Still, being stuck in the chair irritated him no end.

"All right," Christie said. "We're in. The comm. is yours, Admiral."

"Thank you." Admiral Brooke cleared his throat and looked at the small green light that blinked from its place above the camera in the screen. "Good afternoon. I am Admiral Gregory Brooke, United Space Corps aboard USC Research Vessel *Magellan*. You have been told that I had retired. I had not. I *was* retired. Forcibly. By Admiral Hunt. During a raid on prison planet GBS P107-005 in the Outerworlds, I was rescued by USC Strategic Team 6 under Commander Skye with the aid of the daemon. Under United Council treaty 809, section A, subsection 2c, as Admiral of the USC fleet, I am declaring martial law. Hunt and his accomplice Councillor Brand are to be apprehended and incarcerated pending trial for treason. In the meantime, all USC personnel are required to return to their respective USC Headquarters. Intelligence suggests that the ragnar have a plan for a hostile take-over of Earth, and the enslavement of her inhabitants. We all need to be briefed on what the fuck is going on. This is not a drill. This is not a joke. Admiral Brooke out."

"Good enough," Christie said.

"Well, then," Admiral Brooke said, turning to the chtakah. "Get me home."

Two hours and five jumps later, the personnel of the USC *Magellan* looked upon the heartening sight of Earth. They cheered.

"Are you certain?" Admiral Brooke asked. He had been back in his proper position for barely a month before worrying intelligence came through that several enormous ragnar nests had been discovered inside the solar system.

"Yes, sir," Commander Koch answered. "I saw them myself."

"All right. Get USC Strategic together. We've got to move now."

"Yes, sir."

In a matter of minutes, the teams that made up USC Strategic's combat arm were sitting in the enormous auditorium in the USC Headquarters, Vancouver. The admiral and the chtakah stood on stage.

"Good morning," Brooke said. "I apologize for taking you away from breakfast. We've had some troubling reports of several ragnar nests close by. Reports are that they are massing for an attack. We're moving now. Home teams, it is your duty to ensure that Earth holds out as long as possible. Away teams, Commodore Gergiev is ready with the fleet. You should reach the location of the ragnar queen we've dubbed Lilith, if the intelligence proves correct, in a week. It is expected that Earth will come under attack in that time. As you all know, she is the source of our current troubles. You are to destroy her. I am certain that I do not need to tell you just how imperative your mission is. You all know your assignments. Report immediately. Get it done. Dismissed."

Working at speed, in under an hour, the USC had split in two. Commodore Gergiev with half the fleet and three quarters of the sizeable daemon fighting force headed into deep space. The rest remained behind to defend Earth.

Each militia of the countries on Earth had been warned and coordinated their activities closely through the temporary USC Council, made up of five former USC ambassadors and three daemon delegates.

Two days after Commander Koch raised the alarm, Earth was attacked.

"They are fighting now," Sarcen said quietly. He looked stolidly at the back wall of the quarters he shared with his team. Skylark clasped his shoulder briefly.

"They'll hold," he said.

Sarcen nodded. "They'll hold." He did not sound certain.

Fifty teams sat aboard the *Magellan*, with another four following in their long-haul fighters. They were four days out from their destination, riding the long-distance slipstream provided by S8-09, the first of its kind.

"We're here," Christie said.

The *Magellan* and the larger transports of the fleet had exited the slipstream a safe distance away from the target planet, an unchartered giant in the Byzantium System. The long-haul fighters in the fleet made the daylong journey to the planet in a tight formation.

Skylark peered through the screen of the USC Strategic long-haul fighter *One*. "It looks like paradise from here," he said quietly. It was true. Green and gold continents set in glittering sapphire oceans provided an idyllic backdrop to layers of fluffy, white clouds.

"So does Earth," Christie answered. "From space. Hit the ground and you feel like you've landed in hell."

Skylark smirked. "You have the coordinates of the nest?"

"Aye. Let's hope your lady love was right and killing Lilith will solve all our problems."

"All right." Skylark pressed the comm. link on the wall of the cockpit. "This is Commander Skye. We're here. It's go time."

The comm. crackled to life as each fighter reported their readiness.

"All right, Christie. Take us in."

"Yes, boss."

Skylark clapped Christie on the shoulder then headed to the Strategic *One*'s flight deck. He smiled up at Binky, who flashed him a thumbs-up from the cockpit of his personal fighter, before climbing into his own.

"We're all strapped in and good to go," Binky reported.

"Good," Skylark replied as the hatch of the cockpit closed over him. He put on his helmet and looked across at Sarcen. The daemon grinned from the cockpit of his fighter, a bizarre-looking plane with an impressive arsenal of guns and two long, curved blades extending from the underside of the fuselage.

"I'm curious to see that thing in action," Skylark said.

"You will not be disappointed, Commander," Sarcen replied via the comm., grinning.

"Nest in sight," Christie said over the comm. "Opening up."

"Power up," Skylark told his team.

The fighters whined as the team prepared for deployment. One by one, the doors beneath the fighters opened. They dropped and were away. Christie kept the Strategic *One* behind the V-shape formation as the fleet approached the nest.

"This is Commodore Gergiev. You all know the drill. The queen's chamber is underground. Concentrate your fire. Protect the drill. We need a direct line. Skye?"

"Bombing drone strapped on and ready, sir."

"All right. Good luck, gentlemen."

"Fuck you," Jack said over the comm.

"And Jack," the commodore added.

Skylark laughed to himself.

Movement at the top of the mountainous nest caught the commander's eye.

"Heads up," he said. "We've been spotted."

The brown earthen nest turned black as the soldier ragnar poured from the opening at the top like living lava.

"Ground teams are in position," Commander Bauer said through the comm.

"All teams, engage." Skylark pressed his joystick down and his fighter shot forward. He opened fire.

Commander Gergiev stood on the bridge, his eyes glued to the viewscreen as multiple digital screens displayed the battlefield. Private Pierce stood behind him, his jaw slack at the sheer volume of ragnar soldiers.

"Christ!" Commander Koch yelped as a black body buzzed past his fighter. "They can fly! The fuckers can fly!"

"Son of a bitch!" someone else yelled.

Mayhem broke out as the soldier ragnar spread thick gossamer wings and took to the air.

"Teams 19 and 55, pull up!" Skye barked. Too late. Five screens blacked out as ragnar took the planes to the ground.

"Jesus! Gregg!"

"All fighters, evasive manoeuvres. Christie, we need your guns!" Skylark ordered.

"On my way."

"All teams, clear a path."

Tactics changed. Formations broke as the fighters rolled and dodged to avoid the airborne ragnar. Two teams broke off to guard the long-haul fighters as they followed the Strategic *One* into the fight. The communications continued to sound in a confusing cacophony.

"Ground teams are stuck. Setting rovers."

"Acknowledged."

"Get it off! Get it off!"

Private Pierce could not keep up with the frantic chatter that filled the bridge. He kept his eyes fixed on the screens displaying Team 6.

"Flies like a damned hummingbird, doesn't he?" Gergiev said, nodding towards Skylark's screen as the image rolled, dipped, reversed and flipped. "He was one of the top students in flight school in his time."

"I know," Pierce said quietly. "I didn't even know PF 90s could do that."

"Neither did we," Gergiev said with a smile. "Until Commanders Skye and Wheeler."

"Skylark! Look out!"

Skylark dived as a flying soldier appeared from nowhere. The fighter shook as the beast narrowly missed getting a grip on it. No one saw the second soldier.

"Skye!" Jack screamed.

The warning came too late. Skylark grunted as the javelin-like tail of the soldier plunged through his screen, piercing his chest. Sarcen had bolted forward, flipping his fighter over Skylark's, the sharp scythes cutting the soldier's tail cleanly off a split second after it landed. Binky came from the other side, firing with precision. The ragnar spasmed and fell away from the fighter.

"Skye? Skye, can you hear me? Do you read?" Gergiev demanded, leaning against the railing on the bridge. The commander's screen went wild as Skylark's fighter spun out of control.

"Heart rate elevated," an officer reported. "He's going into arrest."

"Skye!"

Pierce bit his tongue as he watched.

"What the?" the officer tracking Skylark said. "Heart rate slowing."

"Skye, God damn it! Report."

"I'm here," Skylark whispered over the comm. "Left lung pierced. Damn it. It was new." Skylark's short laugh turned into a liquid cough. The screen steadied as Skylark regained control of his fighter. He coughed again, the sound thick with blood. "Automatic controls offline. Bomb, drone, offline. I can't launch." He coughed again.

"Get back to the *Magellan*, Skye," Binky said. "Get patched up."

"All right, Skye. We'll find an alternate bomber. Return to the fleet," Gergiev said.

"Sir," Koch said. "Drill has been launched. On course. We'll reach the queen in fifteen minutes."

Skylark closed his eyes briefly as he hovered just out of the range of the fight. He thought of home. The last report to come through proved dire. Desperately outnumbered, it would take nothing short of a miracle to fight off the attacking ragnar. It was destroy Lilith or accept defeat. Opening his eyes, he watched as the USC fighters dodged and rolled their way. Grabbing the tail, Skylark ripped it out of his chest. His armour released its special liquid, sealing the breech and repressurizing.

"All right, Skye. We'll find an alternate bomber. Return to the fleet."

Breathing sent burning pain through his whole chest and every breath released air behind his ribs, increasing pressure on his lungs. He would not live through the next half hour, let alone the daylong trip back to the *Magellan*. Even if he could have made it, his own body would begin to destroy itself the moment Lilith was killed – and if Earth was to survive as a free planet, she had to be destroyed.

Fighting the pain, Skylark pressed the comm. link.

"Negative, sir."

"Skye…"

Skylark blacked out briefly before clawing his way back to consciousness.

"Get back to the fleet, Skye," Jack said over the comm.

Skylark smiled slightly. "I'm a dead man either way, Jack."

"No. You're not. They're going to patch you up."

"And do they have a miracle cure for this virus, yet?"

No one answered and Skylark coughed again. Blood splattered his visor. "Sir, I can still arm the bomb. I'm not going to hell if I can't drag that bitch with me."

Skylark looked through his screen to find Sarcen hovering a few feet away from him, peering into his fighter. He felt the majan's familiar presence reach his mind. The presence left and Sarcen moved his fighter around to flank Skylark.

"It is true, Commodore," Sarcen said. "The commander will not reach you in time."

"No," Jack said weakly.

"It's okay. I'm all right, Jack."

After a brief, sombre silence, Binky spoke. "Commodore Gergiev, requesting Team 6 escort Commander Skye on his last flight."

Gergiev closed his eyes. His mind searched frantically for a way around their situation. He opened his eyes and nodded once.

"Permission granted, Lieutenant Commander."

"No!" Pierce cried. "You can't let him!"

"Stand down, Private!" Gergiev barked. "There is no other option."

"Hey Pierce?"

"Commander?"

"Do you remember what I told you about heroes?"

"Yes, sir."

"I'm the flag-bearer. That's all. I'm just the guy with the flag."

"No, sir," Pierce said fiercely.

Koch's voice crackled over the comm. "The drill is through. I repeat; the drill is through."

"Commander Skye, you are cleared. Dive 67 degrees on my command."

"Yes, sir."

"All units, Commander Skye is the bomb. Clear the skies for him. This is our only shot."

Skylark grimaced. "Let's go," he told his escort.

They pushed back into the fray. Every jostle of the fighter ripped through Skylark's pierced chest. He coughed up blood even as he fought against the building air in his chest that pressed against his lungs, making it difficult to draw breath. Consciousness became increasingly fluid.

All he could see before him was a sea of black thoraxes and gossamer wings as he pressed forward, the ragnar falling away from him as his escort shot them out of the sky.

"Now, Commander! Dive!"

Gritting through the agony, Skylark pushed on the joystick, and the fighter plunged down. His escort followed, sometimes physically tackling the ragnar from his path. The enormous hole created by the drill flashed in Skylark's swimming vision, and then darkness swallowed everything. It took a moment for his eyes to adjust to the sudden dark of the tunnel.

Worker ragnar were everywhere, frantically trying to repair the damage to the nest created by the drill. Skylark ground his teeth as he fought to remain lucid enough to not crash his fighter into a wall. Sparks flew as the side of his fighter scraped the walls and ceiling of the tunnel.

29

"Impact in twenty seconds," an officer announced.

"We're losing him," another said.

Commodore Gergiev's eyes flickered to the enlarged image of Skylark's vitals that flanked the screen displaying Skylark's plane. No one could be conscious with a heartbeat that irregular.

"Come on, Skye," Gergiev whispered. "Hold on. You're almost there."

"Fifteen seconds to impact."

Sweat trickled from Skylark in small rivulets as he fought to remain awake.

"Ten seconds to impact," his comm. informed him.

He could no longer draw breath. Too much air had filled his chest cavity, crushing his lungs. Bright spots obscured his vision and his limbs were heavy and unresponsive.

"Five seconds to impact."

"Skye, if you can still hear me," Jack said softly. "It was an honour, sir."

Skylark managed a small smile.

"Three seconds."

The tunnel opened out suddenly, revealing a large cavern. The ragnar All-Queen raised her enormous head in alarm as Skylark's fighter fell through the opening. Skylark saw her a brief moment.

"Two seconds."

Two warm hands pressed gently against Skylark's shoulder

blades, flooding him with soothing warmth. The cavern faded from sight, replaced by a steady, soothing purple glow.

Commander Bennejin Skye smiled, relaxing into the familiar embrace.

"Naschari," he whispered.

"Naschari."

The whispered word cut through the mayhem of the comms from the battle on the bridge. The barely pulsing image of Commander Skye's vitals fell dark. The screen broadcasting images from Skylark's fighter flared brightly and then went blank.

"Impact."

"Pull up! Pull up!" Binky screamed into his comm. All teams responded, turning their thrusters to the ragnar soldiers.

"Jack! Pull up, God damn it!"

"Say hello to her for me," Jack whispered to her commander before turning her fighter.

The nest exploded outward, spewing rock, dust and fire.

Gergiev stood on the bridge of the *Magellan* and watched the view screen carefully. Of the fighters that attacked, less than half made it out and the majority of those were severely damaged.

"They're veering off!" Koch said. "We got her!"

"Commodore," a daemon communications technician said, standing. She grinned. "The chtakah reports the ragnar have ceased their attack on Earth."

Commodore Gergiev relaxed as the bridge erupted into boisterous celebration. The officers cheered and hugged. Some danced.

Pierce did not. He stared dumbly at the blank screen where once Commander Skye's progress was marked, unaware of the tear that made its tentative way down his cheek. Gergiev reached over and squeezed the boy's shoulder, eliciting only a vague response. The commodore's sad smile was barely returned before Pierce reverted his attention to the screen.

"You are right," Gergiev said quietly. "He is a hero."

"Yes," Pierce replied. "He is."

30

"This is Commander Binks. We request a slipstream to the coordinates uploaded."

"G'day, Commander. This is Private Hudson aboard Way Station S7-03. Going after Hunt?"

"You bet your ass."

"Excellent. Kick his head in for me. Initializing wormhole."

"Will do and thank you." Binky patted Christie on the shoulder before leaving the cockpit. "Yo, Lieutenant Commander!"

"Call me that again," Jack yelled from the kitchen, "and I'll knock your head off!"

"Which one?" Corporal Pierce asked with a scoff, handing her the plate of onion he had just chopped. Jack grinned viciously as she checked the pot of pho simmering on the stove.

"Smells good," Binky said as he walked past to join the twin lieutenants in the lounge.

"Commander Skye's recipe," Jack quipped. She brushed off the sudden ache in her chest and reached for a packet of cinnamon.

Pierce hugged her unexpectedly.

"Yeah," Jack said, returning the embrace. "I miss him too."

"I beg your pardon, Lieutenant Commander," Sarcen said from the dining room. "But the lieutenant is stealing your hand."

"Put those down!" Jack roared at Spike when she peeked around the corner.

Spike threw the cards down in disgust and glared at Sarcen. "Snitch."

Sarcen grinned. He leant against the wall as he watched another fight break out over a game of craekers.

SKYLARK

The newly christened USC Long-Haul Fighter *Skylark* entered the slipstream.

EPILOGUE

It took Team 6 eight long years to track and apprehend former United Space Corps Admiral Hunt. The man still held the loyalties of a number of former USC personnel who felt threatened by the new alliance. The number of accomplices he had mustered astounded the world.

Despite many leads and reported sightings, Councillor Brand was never found.

In that time, the newly formed Allied Space Corps settled into a routine. The daemon relinquished Canada back to the Canadians. One of their massive ships remained grounded, serving as an embassy for the daemon race, in Saskatchewan. The expansive stretch of land surrounding it became recognized daemon territory and is kept by them as a protected reserve. The remaining three ships retreated to orbit as the search for a habitable planet began anew. As of the writing of this, the search continues.

Commander Bennejin Skye remains a controversial character in this chapter of our history. Depending on who you ask, he is variously a dangerous renegade or the most noble of men. However, while it remains true he could have accomplished none of what he achieved without his team, it is Skye's name that has become synonymous with the creation of a new era in human history, tumultuous as it is.

As far as I am concerned, Commander Skye remains one of the best men to have ever lived. His selfless devotion to his team, his cause, and the woman he loved, and the brave sacrifices he made to ensure humanity and daemon-kind alike live on has cemented him as the greatest hero of our age, however much he would have protested this label.

My own insignificant role in this time is something I carry with a profound sense of accomplishment. But nothing fills me with a greater sense of pride than my memories of Commander Skye. Slated for failure from the start of his life, he stood tall, stayed true, and proved everyone wrong.

For my part, I am honoured to have known him.

- *Parting Words.* **Renegade: The Formation of the First Intergalactic Alliance. Admiral Scott Pierce, ASC. Penny Whistle Publishing. 2452.**

Acknowledgements

I need to thank so many people, all of whom were absolutely crucial in bringing this book to life. First, and perhaps oddly, I'd like to thank Judith de los Santos, who goes by the moniker Malukah. We don't know each other at all, but I wrote this entire novel listening exclusively to her music. I'm not saying her voice is magic, but it was one of the easiest writes I've ever had.

To my beta readers, Rosa Christian, April Laramey, and Robert Carrière, who whipped my manuscript into shape, thank you. Your insightful work was outstanding.

Thank you must also go to the vivacious Cait Gordon, whose pre-submission editing was both exceptional and joyous.

And lastly, I need to thank the afore-mentioned April and Cait, as well as Pierre-Yves, whose enthusiastic support of this manuscript restored my faith in it, and assured me it was a worthy read. Without you, I might have never dared have it published. A thousand thank-yous for your support. You will never know how much it means to me.

Shine on, you beautiful people!

ABOUT
RENAISSANCE PRESS

At Renaissance, we treat our authors like family. We are all authors and artists ourselves, and know that their books are their babies. With Renaissance, the authors are involved in every step of the process and their input is highly valued, though devoted committees take on the difficult tasks of copy editing, designing and marketing to achieve professional results. The authors are asked to do a minimal part of the marketing (for example, sharing our social media posts, inviting their circles to the launch, participating in blog tours) and will receive guidance and help every step of the way.

At Renaissance, we do things differently. We are passionate about books, and we care as much about our authors enjoying the publishing process as we do about our readers enjoying a great, professional quality and affordable product on the platform they prefer.

renaissancebookpress.com
info@renaissancebookpress.com.

Daughters of Britain
By S. M. Carrière

Historical

6 8 ad. The Roman Empire has swallowed most of Europe. There are pockets of resistance but nowhere, no one, is safe.

Refugee. Slave. Queen.

Mederei, eldest daughter of the fallen war-queen, Boudicca, fled north with her sister to continue the fight for British freedom.

But nowhere is safe from Rome.

Now she must fight for her life for the amusement of her enemy.

Soldier. Hostage. Prince.

Adalbern, a proud Batavian, serving in the Roman auxiliary, lived by their rules.

But no one is safe from Rome.

His people scattered and his nephew held hostage in Rome itself, he is now nothing more than a glorified prisoner.

https://renaissancebookpress.com/daughters-of-britain/